When the Turaco Calls

Gisela Hoyle

Published by Fledgling Press 2012
www.fledglingpress.co.uk
Printed and bound by:
Martins The Printers, Berwick-upon-Tweed, TD15 1RS
ISBN: 9781905916498

Cover illustration by Camilla Botterell.

Acknowledgements

I am much indebted to the following books for a better understanding of the Knysna forest, its geography and its elephants - particular the last elephant hunt: Dan Wylie's *Elephant* (Reaktion Books: London, 2008); Margo Mackay's *The Knysna Elephants and their Forest Home* (Wildlife and Environment Society of South Africa: Knysna, 1996) and John Manning's *Field Guide to Fynbos* (Struik Publishers: Cape Town, 2008).

For the extracts from Racine's *Berenice* I am indebted to the Penguin Classics translation by John Cairncross of Jean Racine's *Andromache and other Plays* (Penguin Books: London, 1967). The translations from German are my own.

Thanks also to Mike Strizic and Clare from Fledgling Press.

For my parents

PART I

ONE

Thinking about who you were and how it would be if you *weren't* you was fun, was a way of making yourself dizzy without spinning, which damaged the brain and so was forbidden. The first time Marta realized that she was Marta and no one else, was the day she met Ishmael.

She had learnt her date of birth –24 April 1967 – because she did not want to be like the orphans of Mother's war, who were lost for not remembering their names and birthdates and hometowns. But she did not think being born was a real beginning, not of her; of her body perhaps and for her parents, but not for her. The day Marta properly began was 25 August 1972, because Ishmael, who had been fearless in the forest, had been scared of the open lawn of her garden.

Marta stood perplexed and half-frightened herself of her daily world, as she looked at the cowering form of her friend. This friend, who was so quick in the forest, who knew everything in the forest and was scared of nothing in the forest, was cowering now, covering his eyes – his whole face from the brightness of the sun.

'What is it?' Marta asked, trying to pull the thin brown arm away from his face and his shivering body up at the same time. Ishmael whispered something through his snuffling. Marta had to bend down to hear, finally squatting to wait, as she had seen Narina do when she coaxed orphaned chicks to start eating:

'What is it?' she asked again, growing impatient.

'It is so bright,' Ishmael said, 'so bright, there are no trees.'

'Yes, there are,' Marta contradicted him. She pulled his arm as she stood up to point at the apple trees in the orchard.

But he did not look up and hissed, 'Hide your shadow,' tugging her back down.

'Why?'

'So the ancestors don't see it.'

'Who? Why?'

'The ancestors must never see your whole shadow.'

'Why not?'

'They will take you away – to the land where there are only shadows.'

'Why?'

'To punish you – for your wickedness, for your bad blood.'

'I don't have bad blood.'

'I do.'

'How do you know?'

'My grandparents told me – that's why I am wicked and they must beat me – and then hide me, in the forest, amongst the half-shadows, when the police come.'

Marta felt the twist of that word in her stomach. Distracted, she missed the moment he had turned, crouching to run back into the forest. She heard the rustling, saw the flash of movement, and followed. When they finally stopped and lay panting next to each other on the dark floor, she looked curiously at the scratches on their arms and the blood trickling from them.

'Look Ishmael, our blood is the same.'

They examined the scratches. Marta caught his blood on her fingertips and held it up to the light to see if she could see the wickedness.

'Can you see it?' she asked.

'Perhaps you need to look in the dark,' he moved her hand into the shade.

'Now can you see it?' he asked.

'No.'

'Well, perhaps you don't know how wickedness looks.'

'I do, too.'

'How does it look, then?'

'It's fierce and angry – like the Roman soldiers in the Bible.'

'That's different.'

'Why?'

'Because mine is blood-wickedness.'

'Jesus could take it away for you.'

'No.'

'Yes, he could, too. My father says …'

But Ishmael was gone, before she could tell him what her father said about Jesus and wickedness.

Marta found him, lying in the orchard at the edge of the lawn, looking into the bright light. He had not liked being afraid.

'I don't think your ancestors will come into my father's garden.'

'Why not?'

'Because it's my father's. He does not believe in ancestors, only in God.'

Gradually Ishmael ventured onto the lawn. He stretched his arm out and wiggled his fingers in the light. They stayed whole.

Then he crawled onto the grass, shifted to his heels, and gradually stood up. He stared down at his shadow – green and whole.

'That's me,' he whispered.

'Yes, and here's me.' She stood next to him.

'Bet yours can't catch mine.'

'Bet it can.'

But he ran almost too fast for his own shadow to catch him – so Marta knew he was still afraid.

When they were tired of running in the sun, Marta showed Ishmael how to make a butterfly shape with his hands against the light. And a wolf. They played shadow games, disguising their dark, flat selves as bloubokkies and wild pigs by climbing on each others' backs and using their arms as tusks and horns.

'Now no ancestor can find me,' Ishmael was glad at last.

But try as they might, even between them, in the late afternoon when shadows were long, they could not make an elephant shape.

They stood together, panting, waiting for their shadows to reach the trees. And as they watched them grow, Marta knew that she was Marta; shapes might change in changing light, but she was Marta and next to her stood Ishmael, for whom this lawn was not home. Yet now he sat in the shade with her, drinking the Oros Mother had brought out to them.

Mother was not entirely happy with this addition to Marta's days. Marta heard her talking in the evenings when she had gone to the kitchen to get some water.

'Johannes,' she had said to Father, 'All we know about Ishmael is that he is a handful; too much for Solomon and Ellie and that Narina can barely bring herself to acknowledge his existence.'

'Anita,' her father's voice was stern, 'that is not the child's fault.'

'No, but maybe there's a reason. Maybe we should not let Marta play with him every day.'

'The reason is what happened seven years ago.' He stopped and his voice was suddenly louder: 'Marta, go to bed.'

Marta went to bed and thought about the day. It had

4

begun like any other day. Jacob, Ruth and Simon had gone off to school, which left her to play with baby Ben. She pushed his small cart about the lawn and he crowed happily, gurgling 'Mada' now and again. She had sung him the song of the little hunchback imp: full of mischief all day, but in the evening asking to be remembered in a child's prayers. It was Ben's favorite and Marta tried to imitate Simon's actions to make him laugh, and though she knew it was not the same, Ben did not mind. Ben did not see any reason to begin speaking – everyone understood him anyway.

That morning she had taken him to the edge of the dam, after they had fed the rabbits. She knew they were not to go up on the wall, but the willow branches were hanging low and the catkins were just, just coming out.

'Look Ben, look, the catkins are out. It will be Christmas soon.' And Ben had stroked the small grey furry catkins delicately and with shining eyes.

Then her father had come back unexpectedly from his rounds of the farm and parish. He walked quickly into the house, called first her mother and then Narina. Then he had come, calling urgently to where she was playing with Ben.

'Marta,' he said, 'I need you to come with me.' And she was so proud though Ben had cried to see her go.

Father stopped the car where the road came to an end, the forest too tangled and the road too steep for the car to go on. Dimly, between the vast trees, she could make out a lonely, small house. They both got out and Marta swung on her father's arm, when she could, as they walked towards it. Her father explained that the people who lived here, so deep in the forest, were Narina's parents and that her child lived with them.

'Why are we visiting them?'

'Narina's mother is very ill.'

Suddenly the dappled bright morning with her father

beneath the trees had dark fingers reaching out to them. They walked on quietly, saving their breath and keeping their eyes only on the treacherous ground.

Her father knocked gently on the door and then they waited – and waited –for it to open. Marta thought she heard a rustle and a snort of laughter in the leaves at the side of the house and with a brief glance for her father's permission, she went off to investigate. She glimpsed the strangest child she had ever seen: his skin was neither dark nor pale but somewhere in-between and on his head was a shock of curly hair, hanging down to his shoulders. His eyes were shimmery green, like the forest on a cloudless day.

'Hey,' she called, 'hallo, I'm Marta.'

But he had thrown a stone at her and then run away. Marta followed immediately, anger at her stinging arm overcoming the fear of never having been so deep into the dark forest before. He would allow her just another glimpse of his yellow T-shirt before he darted off again – like an animal, quick and easy over the forest floor, without making a sound. Yet if she looked like she might give up, he would stop longer, allow her to catch up and point silently to a bird or a flower – or even the bright orange mushrooms that grew on the fallen trees. When she opened her mouth to speak to him, he laid his finger on his lips and sprang away again.

They played this cat-and-mouse game for a long time until she sat down and cried with exhaustion and bewilderment; for the forest here was darker than any she had been in before, and she suddenly had lost all sense of the markers of her world – Father, Mother, Narina, Ben – and she was afraid.

'Crybaby,' he mocked, 'listen, the loerie is warning the forest that a crybaby has come into the forest. All the birds are laughing at you.'

That stopped her crying. 'What?'

But he was no longer interested in her tears. 'Listen.'

So Marta listened and heard the deep hoarse caw, caw, caw and the bubbling that followed.

'Where, where is the loerie?' She asked eagerly, for she could not see the bird. But when she had dried her tears, she saw the young trees just beginning to come up through the forest floor; the mushrooms, banded and bright orange on the side of the ironwoods. As she walked on with him he no longer ran from her.

Instead he had suddenly grabbed her shoulders and pushed her forward, to where the forest floor dropped away. He held her for a moment, just above the glistening of winking gold on the floor of the river and she had screamed and he had laughed and pulled her back. She was furious and slapped him, but he caught her arms and told her he was playing.

'Playing? Playing? That was dangerous.' She spoke primly, the way her mother spoke when they had been too rough with Ben.

Just then they had heard her father call in the distance. Ishmael, whose name she had not yet known, placed his finger on his lips and motioned to her to hunker down in the undergrowth and then crawled deeper into the forest. But she had pulled him back. He slapped her hands away, anger distorting his face.

'Your grandmother is ill,' Marta said, 'we must not worry them.' She got up, left him there in the undergrowth alone and headed back towards her father's voice. He had sulked with her and thrown a few stones but then followed, secretly impressed with her, though he would not look at her.

She in turn found him fascinating; and she stored away his refusal of an adult's command to think about later. No one she knew would ever have done that so brazenly. She found it a little frightening, and very, very interesting. Marta watched him walk in the trees and only then had she thought to ask his name.

'Ishmael,' he said, 'my name is Ishmael.'

She stared at him: 'Ishmael? Like in the Bible?'

'I don't know anything about that,' he had answered rudely and she thought he might throw a stone again.

So she smiled at him. 'It is a beautiful name,' she said.

He smiled back – for the first time – and his eyes were alight as he darted swiftly towards her and kissed her cheek, before ducking back into the forest. She wanted to follow him but her father's voice was louder now.

'Come on, Marta. Did you find Ishmael?'

'Yes.'

Inside the small dark house which was cramped and smelt of illness, Narina's old father, who could barely move for arthritis at the cold end of winter, laboriously made tea for Marta and her father. There was even a Marie biscuit for her on a white enamel plate with roses on. The tea was thick and sweet and relaxing but Father was concerned.

'Solomon,' he was saying patiently, 'you and Ellie cannot possibly look after the boy now that he has become so difficult.'

'Umfundisi, what must we do?' the old man replied, clearly not expecting an answer. 'Narina cannot have him; she is busy,' he went on, 'and the child is wicked and harder to hide now. She cannot live with that sin every day staring at her.'

'Well, she may have to. He is her child and she cannot forever hide him from the world, or from herself.' Her father sounded firm and like he meant something more than was said. Marta had been shocked at Solomon's words – she had never seen her father accept that a child be called wicked before. But his warning on her arm kept her quiet too. So she asked no questions, but resolved to love Ishmael always.

8

'It is hard, Umfundisi Johannes,' the old man said quietly.

'I know,' he said, more gently now, 'I know – but she cannot leave him here as your problem. He is hers. You and Ellie are too old for such a lively child. And a firmer, younger hand will be good for him.'

'I will help,' Marta said loudly, wanting them to realize that she was there and listening. 'I will play with him.'

They had turned to look at her and her father had nodded at the old man.

'It might be good for him to be around other children.'

Just then a groan came from the other room and a querulous voice called words Marta did not understand.

Solomon sighed. 'I will go and pack his things.'

'Good,' her father said, while Marta began to sidle out, wanting to tell Ishmael.

'But Umfundisi,' the old man paused anxiously.

'Yes, what is it, Solomon?'

'Do not blame Ellie and me for his wickedness – it is his blood.'

'Solomon, don't say that.' Now the father she knew was back, 'He is God's child, no matter how he came into the world. He loves Ishmael as he loves all His children.'

'Well,' Solomon said, 'you have not met this one. He is a punishment from the ancestors. I only hope you have a strong whip.'

Marta had opened her mouth to ask why, but again her father had laid a warning hand on her arm and shaken his head.

'Not now,' he said softly as the old man shuffled away into the darkness of the next room where Marta could hear labored breathing. She looked questioningly at her father.

'It is pneumonia,' he said, 'her lungs are struggling

and we must take her to the hospital. Ishmael must come and stay with us for a while – with his mother.' There was more, Marta felt it, but she did not know how to ask and guessed she would not get answers now. Her father and Solomon carried the old woman to the back seat of the car where they bedded her down. She smiled and cried all at once, deeply embarrassed by the fuss she was creating. Marta was asked to find Ishmael. She called at first and then went to walk around the untidily cleared patch of garden surrounding the house. She called again.

'I-i-i-shma-a-a-el,' she cried. When she was ready to give up, he sauntered out of the forest just where she had been calling and walked casually to the car.

His grandfather had been relieved to see him but her father looked sternly at him: she could tell by the lines around his mouth that he was angry. 'Young man,' he said, placing a firm hand on Ishmael's shoulder. 'You know your grandmother is sick?'

Ishmael's eyes flickered as he tried to twist out of her father's grasp. But her father turned him round to face him. 'Do you?'

'Yes.' The eyes were insolent as they looked up at her father.

'Well, you should not have kept us waiting – she needs to go to hospital.' Marta had never seen her father's anger evaporate so fast.

The boy looked briefly contrite but was distracted almost instantly by the car and sitting in front near the steering wheel and cubby hole and the windows which slid up and down when he pressed the buttons Marta never dared to touch. Her father looked at him and turned to Solomon and Marta where they stood in stunned silence outside the car. 'Solomon, have you locked up?'

'Yes, Umfundisi.'

'Right, you go in the back with Ellie, try to keep

her comfortable – but you know what the road is like. Marta jump in front with Ishmael and sit next to the door please. Try to keep him from fiddling with everything – and from falling out.'

'Yes, Father,' she said. She could not believe her luck, sitting in front! She glanced back at Ellie and noticed how her dark skin glowed with the fever and her eyes were weak and glazed. And her gratitude turned liquid in her stomach. When her father came round and opened his door, she asked, 'Is she going to be alright, Father?'

He looked over at her, 'We will do our best, for now she must get to hospital and she must not worry. So you will have to keep Ishmael quiet here in the car, while Narina and her father are at the hospital with me. I will leave them as soon as I can, but it may be difficult.'

'Yes, Father.' She had sat up straight in the front of the car, and pretended to show Ishmael where they would go on the map. He did not believe her but turned the map around and around in fascination, all the way to George and the hospital, where they had to wait. Eventually both Ishmael and Marta lost interest in the map and then Narina arrived. Ishmael did not even look at her. Still they had to wait and Marta told Ishmael stories from a book which lay on the front seat when he got restless.

But he was soon wild from sitting still so long in the sticky breathlessness of the car, watching the mist rolling in from the mountain. He became sullen, but was too frightened of the loud, shadowless street to climb out and run away. Being frightened made him mad and he clambered around on the seats, leaving smeared handprints on all the windows till Marta cried, knowing what a row there would be. But when Father had come back to the car, he had only taken one look at her face and at Ishmael's heightened feverish color and said nothing. He had simply driven home as fast as he could.

11

At the gate he let them out before parking the car. Two steps from the car, Ishmael had collapsed into his crouch, covering his face and crying at the light.

After the shadow games and a drink, they had played in the forest, where they had chased each other with relief, trying to forget what had happened before, in the car and the garden. They climbed trees and galloped on imaginary horses until late in the evening when Jacob had come to call her in to supper. Ishmael had stood square between her and Jacob; had eyed him up and down and then dashed into the forest without a word.

'What was that all about?' Jacob had asked.

'I don't think he knows many people.'

'Oh,' Jacob said, 'Ishmael,' he called, 'Ishmael, she will be back tomorrow.'

Ishmael had come out from under the trees then and stood shyly just at the edge and waved as they walked away. Marta turned to wave, too.

'Marta,' he had called, 'Marta, don't forget me in the morning.'

Just then Narina had come and taken Ishmael by the hand and led him squirming into his new house.

'Jacob,' Marta said, 'Ishmael is afraid of the sun because he has bad blood. And his ancestors will find his shadow.'

'Marta,' Jacob rounded on her, 'Marta, never say something like that again.'

'But he told me,' she was surprised at his fierceness.

'And father will tell you there's no such thing as ancestors finding your shadow.' Jacob paused and looked at her face and spoke more quietly. 'Probably he is just afraid of the sun, because he has lived in the dim shelter of the forest all his life.'

'Yes,' she had agreed meekly, thinking of their shadow games.

'But he will learn not to be afraid. Like I did with the sea.'

'Yes, probably he will learn.' And they had raced home; Jacob had let her almost win.

The morning dawned with news from the hospital that Ishmael's grandmother had died. Father and Mother had gone to the funeral with Narina, but they had not taken either Marta or Ishmael, though Marta knew to be good and quiet for Narina for a while. If Ishmael felt the loss at all he did not show it and he was not good or quiet. That made Mother worry about him, and she often talked to Narina about it, but Marta did not want to hear any of that and was glad when Father insisted Ishmael be given a chance.

And so on Monday when the others were all at school and Ben was with Narina, she had slipped out of the back gate and gone to find Ishmael. She found him sitting under a Kalander making strange soft clucking, hissing noises.

'What are you doing?'

'Shhh,' he hissed at her and pointed up into the tree. Marta peered and peered.

'I can see nothing,' she said finally.

Just at that point a branch swung clumsily in the air and there was a blur of green and red.

'What was that?'

Proud to be able to inform her, he had forgotten his anger at her disturbance.

'That was the loerie,' he said, and beckoned her to follow him.

They followed the jewel-green bird all morning, copying its call, until it grew tired of them and flew over the river in disgust. Ishmael told her what he knew about the bird.

'You only see her if she wants you to see her,' he said. 'She does not like people.'

13

'But she lets you see her?'

'She knows me – they all do.'

'Who?'

'The birds.'

'Will they let me find them, too?'

'If you're with me.'

'Alone?'

'Maybe.'

It was enough at that moment.

'Why is she so careful?'

'She is the watcher. She used to be the watcher for the elephants, too. She used to warn them when people came into the forest.'

'How do you know?'

'My grandfather has always lived in the forest, and our ancestors came to this forest from the frontier wars.'

'He knew the forest when there were elephants?'

'Yes.'

'Will he tell me about them one day?' Marta was still afraid of that stern old man who thought Ishmael had bad blood and who lived all alone in the forest now. So she was relieved when he only said,

'If he wants to.'

But after that, Marta always listened for the warning voice, which underlay the lightness of the piet-my-vrou and the finches as the trees dappled and shaded the bright sun. And because he had told her about the loerie, she told him about the sea, which he had not seen.

The sea, like the forest, had always been there, she supposed, waiting before she had seen it. She remembered vividly; the smell warned her first – saltiness invaded the slightly sour dark smell of the fynbos: its leaves and wood and mud. Gradually the saltiness blew away the forest smell. Marta realised then how huge the smell was, that it came from something much bigger than the forest, stronger and open in a way even the garden could never be. And she felt rising in her

14

a mixture of excitement and fear, which she sensed also in the others as they came closer. Ruth, Jacob and Simon had all tumbled out of the car in their hurry and raced far away, dropping over the edge of the world leaving Marta standing by the side of the car alone. She cried out and took her mother's hand. 'What is it?' she asked, 'what is it?'

'It is the sea, Marta, it is just the sea.'

Her mother picked her up and walked more quietly over the edge of the world while Marta could hear her father calling instructions to Ruth and Jacob. There were wooden stairs there and when the stairs ended there was sand, which fiercely burned her feet, clinging to them as she lifted them back from its sinking sensation. The calls of her brothers and sister had made her look up from its strange feel between her toes and she saw the shining silver lying on the edge of the sand. She had run over to it, wanting to touch that silver, but then she stopped short. Its voice went on forever and hung in a salty mist above its own silvery vastness; the sky loved this big thing, came down really close to it. Marta felt her chest expand inside. She thought it might burst through her ribs so big it grew. But tears made it deflate again.

Jacob scooped her up and carried her into the sea. And, clinging to his neck, she laughed fiercely when she felt the water tug at her legs, so as not to cry.

'Isn't it great, Marta?' Jacob had yelled in her ear.

'It roars, Jacob, it roars.'

'Roar back,' he said, swinging her so that her legs swept through the foaming tops of the waves. 'Roar back!'

And she and Jacob roared and capered wildly, trying to match their thin voices to the wide rush of the sea.

Though the sea was so huge, it had let them roar with it.

They had stayed till after dark when Jacob and Simon built a fire and they all sat round it on the sand, huddled in old blankets, watching the flames dance and crackle on the driftwood. After a while, her father asked, 'Well,

Marta, what did you think of the sea?'

'It's big.'

'Yes, that's why I like to come here,' he had replied.

'Why?' Simon had joined them.

'To remember how small I am. How small my problems and troubles are, which seem so big to me.'

'Johannes,' her mother's voice warned.

'It's just perspective, Anita,' he replied, 'they will all need it here.' He turned to Marta and her brothers and sister again, 'So when you feel that your problems are too big to be manageable, or you think too much of yourself, spend a little time at the sea, will you?'

They were all quiet for a bit, till Jacob said: 'Solomon told me a story about the sea.'

'Is it a true story?' Marta asked.

'I'm not sure, it is hard to tell with Solomon and Bosman, especially when they get together and talk.'

'Oh, they came to get their monthly supplies this week, did they?' their mother asked.

'Yes, and when I told them we were going to the sea, they told me about Nongqawuse.'

'Nonkwa, what?' Simon asked.

'Nongqawuse.' Jacob repeated the strange name 'She was a great prophetess; and when she went to the river one day, three ancestors appeared to her and told her that a day would come when the ancestors would send a great wind from the sea which would sweep all the white settlers out of this land and into the sea. But before this could happen, the Xhosa would have to burn all their crops and kill all their cattle.'

'Did the prophecy come true?' Marta asked.

'No dummy – look, we're still here, aren't we?'

'Are we white settlers?'

'No,' Mother put her arm around Marta, 'we are missionaries – it is a very different thing.'

'Well, then it isn't a true story, is it?' Marta asked.

Jacob did not know how to answer. He liked Solomon

16

and Bosman's stories.

Father answered for him. 'It is a true story, and a sad one. It happened after one of the big frontier wars when the Xhosa were feeling hemmed in by the British settlers, who were taking more and more land. And their cattle were dying of lung-sickness but this movement – the cattle killing – caused terrible suffering for the people – many, so many, died. The prophetess was later imprisoned for it. Little is known about her, but she may have been a war-orphan herself.'

'Well, Solomon and Bosman's grandfather actually saw all that happen!' Jacob was not quite ready to give up on the drama of his story.

But Mother was packing up now, 'Time for bed,' she said. And they all went home, grateful for their bed and the warm soup Mother had left waiting for them in the Aga.

When Marta repeated this, Ishmael listened to her story with wide and staring eyes. Then he had run away, yelling, 'It's not true, it's not true!'

But later he was back: 'Will you show me, then?' he demanded.

'One day I will show you.' But she knew she had answered like her parents answered. How could she possibly show him the sea? She did not even know where it was.

'What will you do at the sea?'

'I will drive my wickedness into it – give it back to the ancestors.'

'How?'

'I will find a way.' She knew he would, too.

After Ishmael arrived, Marta no longer cared that she was too young to go to school with the others. She was glad when they left and she could slip out, calling to her mother that she was going out to play. She ignored her mother's worried look as she left home behind and ran

into the forest where Ishmael would be waiting for her.
They played every day, till the others came home.

Marta tried once to bring him into a game with Simon
and Ruth, but Ishmael had not understood the game –
or pretended not to understand – and made off, calling
obscenities at them all. Mother heard those obscenities
and tried again to banish Ishmael but Father had insisted
that it was their Christian duty to 'embrace the child'
and bring him to God through love. For, while Ellie
and Solomon belonged to Farleigh Mission Church,
they had been too old to come to services and had been
embarrassed by their grandson. So Ishmael had never
been to church.

'Is he even christened?' Mother asked in horror.

Father replied. 'You know I christened him, the night
he was born and everyone thought he might die.'

One Sunday, Ishmael was to be brought to God.
Father always said the grace of God shone particularly
bright on Sundays. And somehow, for as long as Marta
could remember, even when they were grey or rainy,
Sundays had been brighter than other days: they started
with sung grace at breakfast; everyone dressed in their
Sunday best, looking kinder and better than they did on
other days. After breakfast, Jacob and Marta went round
to Narina's house to escort Ishmael and his mother to
church that day.

Simon went with Father to lay out the hymn books
and ring the bell, Ruth to prepare the old harmonium for
her opening hymn. It was already playing when Marta
and Jacob returned with Ishmael and Narina. Ishmael
was as jumpy as he had been at the hospital.

'What is it?' Marta whispered to him.

'This house of God,' he asked, 'do the ancestors live
there?'

'No, silly,' she laughed.

He was a little calmer after that and did not seem to

notice the curiosity he aroused as people greeted Narina but looked only at him. Finally Mother ushered Narina and her whole flock of children in so that people would stop staring.

Throughout the service Ishmael was restless and fidgety on the hard wooden bench. Marta, sitting next to him, was aware of her father's anxious glances and her mother's frown. She watched Narina twist a handkerchief in her hands, entirely unable to look up. Ishmael squirmed.

Finally it was time for the sermon and all the children trooped out with Mother and Mieta for Sunday school instead. Bomani came over to Simon and Marta.

'Who's this?'

'This is Ishmael. Narina's son,' Simon answered.

'Is he the . . .'

But his mother did not let Bomani finish the question.

'Come, children, let us first sing 'What a Friend' and then we will have the story of Hagar and Ishmael in the desert.'

Ishmael sat up at once and did not take his eyes off Mieta all through the reading of the story but Marta did not think he had been brought any closer to God, because after a while he went back to looking out of the window. And afterwards, he could not or would not answer any of the questions, muttering to Marta, 'There is no angel watching Ma and me – we only have angry ancestors.'

The children went back into the main church for the closing prayers. And that's when it happened. Father was praying the usual prayer, remembering all the recently dead of the mission. Ishmael was instantly restless again and when Father mentioned his grandmother, he shot up off the seat and out the door before anyone else could react.

Marta ran out after him because Narina had only stood stock still, staring in fright at the other parishioners who opened their eyes at the disturbance. Father prayed on and they bowed their heads again.

Marta was barely out of the door before she called out, but Ishmael ran on. He ran through the gate which led to the river; that was forbidden, she knew. But she felt so confused by the failure of the grace of God to shine on Ishmael that she ran on with him. Finally she found him. When she stood before him, he said, 'Let's go and find the sea today.'

Whether it was because the stories of the desert always made her feel like one ought to do big and brave things, or whether it was because of all the looks Ishmael had had to endure during the service, Marta did not know why she disobeyed her parents that day, but she did.

Jacob had told her that the river went to the sea, so she led the way to the river and walked along it. They walked quickly and surely at first, but they gradually tired and there was still no sign of the sea.

The day grew long and the sun grew dim. Clouds were drawing in and mist was rising from the river. Marta shivered and wanted to go home, but Ishmael would not give in so easily. Finally he agreed to rest. They sat with their back against a willow tree and Marta stared mournfully down at her dress, which was not only muddy, but ripped in two places. Ishmael tried to help her wash the stains in the river but they only made it worse and got thoroughly wet.

'How much further to the sea?' Ishmael asked to distract her.

'I don't know, we're lost,' she answered and began to cry.

This time he made no jokes about the birds laughing at her, but looked uncertainly at the closing mist. They huddled together amongst the roots of the tree.

It was there that Father, Joseph and Jacob finally found them. Jacob had remembered Marta asking about the sea for Ishmael and known they would follow the river. They had walked along it calling and peering anxiously into the swirling water, afraid of spotting two small bodies. So at first it was pure relief when they had been found. The children were both gathered up into blankets and brought home, where they were given soup and a warm bath.

But in the morning Mother explained that Ishmael had been banned – 'at least for a while,' until Marta learned that she still had to obey her parents and not do dangerous and stupid things.

Shaken as she was, Marta clung for a while to mother's radiant Sunday world and did her best to forget Ishmael. However, Ishmael had lurked around the edges of the garden, had called and whistled from the trees. He left honey flowers, fire lilies, wood daisies and evening flowers on the door step. But Marta was closely watched and she would not go out to play with him, afraid of what she had done.

Then one morning she saw a red orchid disa on her windowsill. She went to the window and he was there, crouching beneath it. He was holding something out to her, twirling it to catch the light: a feather. It was green and blue, but as he turned it, the end glowed red.

'What is it?' she asked before she could stop herself.

'A loerie feather.'

And she had forgiven him and begged to play with him again. She took the disa to her mother, saying that Ishmael had brought it. That, and Christian duty, won her over.

He took her to a loerie nest and they watched quietly all morning till the birds came low enough for her to see their green faces, their crowns and their bright eyes, with the red rings and white lines, which made them look like Egyptian kings.

She soon forgot her mother's warnings and how frightened she had been at the river. As the days passed they roamed further and further from home. They climbed the highest trees and fell down with some regularity. And they did not obey the instruction to remain near the garden. So, her parents forbade her to play with Ishmael again and Narina began to look anxious and frightened every day.

'What is it, Narina?' she had asked.

'It is Ishmael,' she had answered. 'He will not even get up in the mornings.'

Her mother would go and talk to him and he would play remorseful and cry and bang his head against the door until she felt sorry for him. And then, for a while, Ishmael would be good, would play quietly till her parents relented and said they could play together again.

Nothing could keep Marta from him. He would call for her with his strange wild cry from the edge of the forest and she would leave whatever she was doing and find him. She listened for Ishmael all the time and always answered his cry.

But in the afternoons, after that Sunday when he should have come to God, he always disappeared, melted into the forest when her brothers and sister came home from school. And he remained always in the dappled world of the forest, and refused the brightness of Sundays, even when he sat in church next to his mother, still as a stone.

TWO

On the days when Mother forbade them to go into the forest they began to explore the Farleigh buildings. The smell of the carpentry almost made up for the noise of the saw. Sometimes they were given good bits of wood with which to build castles and forts, or on which to ride into the Wild West. One day such a ride brought them to Farleigh School. It was early in the morning and they were just trying to creep into the barn to ambush some marauding cattle thieves, when they heard singing.

'What's that?' Ishmael demanded of her.

'It's "Morning Has Broken".'

'What?'

'It's a hymn,' she answered. 'A *song*,' she added when he still looked puzzled.

'Who's singing?'

'Let's go see.'

They left the barn and Ishmael grimaced as he realized that the music came from the church building.

'It is school today, not church,' Marta said and pulled him along by the sleeve. The bell stood silent in the morning sun as the hymn rang out.

They tiptoed closer – the door was shut but if they climbed on the border stones of the flower beds they could see into the windows. The Sunday pews had been pushed aside to make room for four tables, around which four pews were now arranged. At the altar stood a crowd of Farleigh children singing, while someone unseen was playing the piano.

The hymn finished and most of the children bowed their heads for a little while as a voice said a prayer. Then they all turned and came towards the tables and benches. Some of them saw Marta and Ishmael's faces at the window and began giggling, others were handing out books and pencils from boxes placed near the altar, before which stood a single table: the teacher's desk.

The two outside now recognized the teacher as Mieta, Bomani's mother, who also took the Sunday school with Marta's mother. In fact Bomani was among the gigglers and pointers. Mieta came over to the window; without a word she beckoned the two in. They climbed sheepishly down from the border and went round to the door, where Mieta and all the children were waiting. Mieta ordered the children back to their seats and brought Marta and Ishmael to the front.

She did not shout, as Marta half expected, but instead gave them each a piece of paper and some crayons and set them at the end of the table where the smallest children sat. Bomani smiled at them as they sat down.

'Thank you, Mieta,' Marta said.

'It's not Mieta at school,' Bomani whispered, 'I do not call her Ma now either, she is "Ma'am" at school, because she is the teacher here.'

'OK.' Marta was pleased to be in school. She would learn and catch up with Ruth at last. She worked hard at her big 'M' and then had a go again at the other letters in her name, just like Ruth had shown her.

Ishmael was soon bored with sitting still and drawing. He quickly turned his 'I' into a tree and then began taking the crayons off the other children, trying to scribble on Marta's paper to get her attention. He did not like her to be so absorbed in something other than him. It was not long before he was sent out. He stood for a while outside and threw stones at the church door and the bell. Marta looked up, worried, but then it was time for a story and she turned back to Mieta. So Ishmael left and by the time school was dismissed, he was nowhere to be found.

Marta asked Narina about it.

'He must start school after Christmas,' Narina replied. 'He is late already. He is not looking forward to it.'

'But it was such fun!'

'He is too restless, he likes to be outside. He is not very obedient . . .' She trailed off, looking at Marta's earnest face.

Just then Marta heard the others come home and she ran to tell them about her day at school.

'Can I go to school, Mother?' she begged over lunch.

'Well, actually it is about time you went to school. We need to get you ready for it.'

'But I can just go – I started already, today and I did well – look, Mieta gave me a star!' Marta explained.

'You can't go to Farleigh School,' Simon butted in, laughing.

'Why not?'

'It's not for you. It's for Farleigh people.'

'But I live here, I am Farleigh people.'

'Yes, but you're white! You have to come to school with us – in George.'

Before Marta could ask any more Father confirmed that this was true. The law, he explained, said Marta could not go to Farleigh School.

The next day she went into town with Mother and Father. It made up a little for not being allowed into Farleigh School – both to have her parents to herself *and* to go into town, which was big and busy, a little frightening and very exciting. They went past the library, the white Moederkerk and the central shops, and stopped at last outside a brightly painted shop. In the windows stood school children in uniforms from all the schools in George.

Inside it was dark and cool. Marta sat on the narrow wooden bench, while Mother spoke to Mr. Patel's daughter, who was bright and glittery in the dimness. Mr. Patel's daughter then searched through the many wooden drawers to find the right size white socks, school knickers and sports shorts. Marta sat still on the bench, watching the growing pile and thinking of the knowledge she would have when she wore them. Miss Patel brought three blue school dresses and then Marta had to go with Mother to try them on. The middle one was best, Mother thought, it was only a bit big, the belt loose. Marta saw only that she looked like Ruth, going to school in the morning.

'How many of these would you like?' Miss Patel asked.

'Just the one – one new one because it is the first,' her mother answered.

Marta wanted to keep the school dress on, wanted to know how it would feel to walk out in the sunshine in it, but Mother said it would spoil the first day if she did that now. Marta knew she was right, so she took it off and walked out of the shop holding the big pink bag instead. Then they had to find Father – he was in the old library.

Marta found him, sitting in one of the armchairs. Mother sighed because he had forgotten them, lost in a book, but Marta climbed onto the arm of his chair and peered over his shoulder, still holding the bag with her school things. She peered at the book so hard she toppled into him.

'Hey, missy,' he said, catching her, 'how soon will you be reading Ranke's *History of the German Reformation*, I wonder?'

Marta peered hopefully at the many words of his book.

'Johannes,' her mother began. But he interrupted her, 'Anita, I must have my own copy of this.'

When they got home she had helped Mother hang the dress in the cupboard alongside her Sunday dress, and placed the new black shoes underneath it and rolled the socks into pairs and placed them on her shelf in the cupboard. She thought the dress looked dark and the socks small. She remembered Jacob coming home unable to sit because he had been caned, and Ruth's tears about girls in her class who would not talk to her. She felt scared; not the kind of fear she felt in the wide open, the frightened-of-the-sea kind of scared, but a fear which made her heart small and tight.

In the morning the others headed off to school without her again. Marta watched more carefully and saw how Ruth struggled to eat her breakfast – she had a Maths test – and Simon and Jacob argued about stupid things. Their school bags stood neatly side-by-side at the door. Then came the hurried brushing of teeth, and remembering PE kits and other extras at the last minute before they all walked together out to the bus stop, closing the gate behind them. Marta shook off the cold feeling it gave her by running to the dam to find the red weavers on the willows then playing in the irrigation channels, hoping to hear or spot Ishmael at the edge of the garden where the forest and the mountain began.

The mountain was magic (she knew it, though Father did not like to hear such things) and school lay on the other side of it – in a world which was not forest, not home and not sea, but shoved these familiar things aside and demanded everyone's attention. She hung limply over the gate and wondered what the others were doing right now – but then she heard Ishmael's call and the mountain's magic was back and the forest was all there was – till Christmas.

After Christmas she lined up her new red suitcase with the reflecting lights on its side. It smelled of leather and had come all the way from her grandparents in Germany. It stood next to those of her brothers and sister at the front door before breakfast. She said goodbye to her mother and to Ben and felt not at all like herself. Father was taking them in the car, in honor of Marta's first day.

She sensed a new self growing and this began with the climbing out of the car and walking, head down, to the boot to get the suitcases, which had all fallen in a heap, and then the abrupt dispersal to their various classes. Marta looked at her siblings who seemed like strangers to her now.

Jacob took her hand and said, 'Come on.' So she lifted her head, shook off his hand, but kept near him as they walked towards a door which said 'Sub A' in big black letters on a green card.

There was a pretty dark-haired teacher in the room, called Mejuffrou Niemand who invited her in to sit and draw 'until the bell went' and Marta was soon so absorbed in her drawing she did not notice Jacob leaving or anything else until her table was bumped by three crying children. She looked up: two dirty blonde girls and a boy, who all looked just like each other, were clinging in a dirty, snot-nosed tangle to a bedraggled and exhausted-looking woman. Mejuffrou Niemand was trying to pry them loose.

'Sannie, Mina – look! Would you like to draw with the wax crayons?' But it was to no avail – they had their faces in the skirts of their mother, who finally pried them loose and fled.

'Piet, take Sannie and Mina to wash their faces at our basin,' Mejuffrou Niemand tried to restore some order. There, they were finally distracted by paintbrushes which they began washing. They washed till they stopped crying.

Marta watched them and then noticed the other children in the class were giggling behind their hands. She wanted to go to the three newcomers but did not want the other girls on the carpet to giggle about her too. In confusion she returned to her drawing, trying to ignore the sniffs and the giggles alike.

Then her teacher suddenly called her name sharply:

'Marta. Marta, the bell has gone.'

She looked up wondering what that might mean and saw all the other children crowding towards the door. What bell? She did not have time to ask or even wonder. She joined the neat row of children heading out as her teacher smiled and sighed at the triplets, who burst into noisy tears again at the suggestion that they leave the basin and go outside. In what she knew from Simon was the quad, where the sun was already blazing fiercely down, stood row upon row of blue children rising like organ pipes towards the far end. Marta was glad the blue children stood there for where they did not, the light hurt her eyes. She kept her eyes on the blue pinafore of the girl in front of her and stood in a row with the others. There was a faint rustling as pupils whispered together: Marta wondered what they were talking about but was too shy to ask or join in.

Then suddenly all whispering stopped and the children straightened their backs and faced the front. She wondered why, but could not see, though she craned her neck and stepped to the side of her row. Immediately her teacher was at her side, pushing her gently back into place. Marta wanted to resist, but when she looked up at her teacher's face, she did not. Her teacher pointed silently to the front and up. Now Marta could see a grey, stooped man standing on the raised veranda behind a podium. He was speaking in a loud and fierce voice. Although she knew the words, they made no sense, so Marta began to examine other things instead, though

with her teacher's hand still on her shoulder she could
not move or turn her head. She looked instead at the
other teachers standing in a row, like the children, behind
the small, stooped man, with the angry voice. It was
loud and not good to listen to and, as she tried to think
of forest leaves instead, the voice changed suddenly.
Another man, dressed in black and bigger than the first,
had now stood up and said,

'Kom laat ons bid.'

Like clockwork all the blue children dropped their
heads. Marta looked at them in amazement – how did
they do that? Altogether like that. Then she felt her
teacher's hand on the back of her head, pressing gently,
but firmly, and she dropped her head too. Her neck
became sore eventually; the man spoke for so long. The
voice droned on and on, it rose and fell with emotions
she did not understand. She began shuffling her feet,
feeling the heat begin to prickle her legs, making her
itchy just behind the knee, but she dared not scratch.

Then everyone began singing. She was relieved and
looked up and around, but she did not recognise the
song, so she could not sing. This earned her some looks.
The teachers had all come down now and were standing
near the end of their rows. Then everyone turned on
their heels and began walking, still in rows, towards
the classrooms around the quad. Her teacher kept her
hand on her shoulder and led their small row back to the
classroom where everyone was placed behind a chair.
There Mejuffrou Niemand told them each to unpack
their pencil cases and then hang or stand their suitcases
against the wall in the corridor outside the classroom, so
that no one would fall over them as they moved about
the classroom. Marta complied quickly, wanting to get
on with more interesting things. But having to part with
their suitcases made the triplets cry again.

'Oh, come on, they'll only be outside the door.' She

was ready to be impatient again and scornful until she remembered Ishmael and his fear of the sun and knew she did not know their world. The others were laughing; making the triplets' tears worse.

She took Sannie, who seemed the strongest of the three, by the hand and said, 'Look, where my suitcase is, I can just see it.'

Sannie looked and nodded, sniffing.

'I can move mine and a few others along a bit, and you three can have those places opposite the door. Then you can see that yours are safe.'

The triplets were happier with that solution but two of the other girls who had to move their suitcases were huffy until Mejuffrou Niemand thanked them for their kindness. Then suddenly they had smiled sweetly at the triplets, though they rolled their eyes when her back was turned. Back in their seats Piet put his thumb in his mouth, clearly overwhelmed by so much strangeness. Sannie arranged his pencil and ruler for him. Mina watched.

Marta smiled at all three and sat with them when they were all asked to come to the carpet and sit cross-legged while their teacher read something to them – from the Bible. It was the story of Joseph and his brothers – which Marta knew – so she decided to examine her classmates instead.

They were all strangers, except for the triplets, who were sitting beside her, fingers in their mouths a little apart from everyone else. Marta let her eyes scan the others, who were all looking at their teacher, except one. She had blonde hair and two beautiful ponytails as well as a thick, heavy fringe, from behind which two bright blue eyes were looking out of the window; she was clearly not listening either.

Marta did not know that eyes could be so blue or hair so straight and shiny. Her own hair was reddish brown and hopelessly curly and untidy. It never stayed long in its plaits, no matter how tightly Mother did them. Suddenly the girl seemed to sense Marta looking at her and she turned her eyes to Marta and smiled. Marta wondered whether they'd be friends. But then, as the blue eyes slid over the triplets, the expression changed to disgust.

Marta had never seen anyone look at another human being in that way. However, she could not think about it further because she had to get up like the others and take out books to learn to shape an A. At the tables Marta saw that she was sitting next to the blonde-haired girl. The girl made her feel uncomfortable, but both set to work with a will, drawing an A and an apple next to it.

'I am Rochelle,' the blonde girl whispered.

'We shouldn't be talking,' Marta whispered back.

The girl ignored this, 'What's your name?'

'Marta,'

The teacher called in a warning voice, 'No talking in lessons.'

There was peace for a bit. Then Rochelle began again, 'Marta? That's a really common name. We have a maid called Marta.'

Marta kept her head down, and then felt obliged to say, 'Rochelle is a very pretty name.'

'It's French,' Rochelle told her.

Interested now, despite herself, 'What does that mean?'

'It means my grandparents fought for their God and brought Him here from France where Catholics were killing them.'

'My parents do that.'

'No, they do–'

'Girls!' their teacher's voice behind them cut short their discussion. 'You two will have to clear up after everyone has gone out for break.'

At break the triplets wanted to stay in with Marta, but Rochelle waved them away imperiously. Marta did not know what to do.

'Why can't they stay with us?' she ventured finally.

'They're forest people,' Rochelle said, as if that explained everything. It did not, but Rochelle seemed very sure of herself.

School turned out to be full of such explanations and there was much that was very difficult to grasp. Writing was difficult and slow, compared to thinking and speaking, so her work was often untidy and smudged. Her page about Noah and his ark was grey by the time she had finished. She had forgotten all about the writing as she had got involved with drawing the animals coming out of the ark, and God standing smiling by, lifting his hands in blessing as they walked. Only the loerie she had drawn looked back at him.

At the end of the lesson she had taken her book proudly to the front. The teacher took her book, while Marta waited for a gold star.

'Who is this?' her teacher's voice low and shaking with anger.

Marta's throat tightened; she looked. She had been pleased with her animals, with Noah's curved stick with knobbles, where branches had been. It looked real and the wooden ark had each plank carefully marked, as wood would be.

'It is God,' she explained in a strangled whisper.

'Go-o-o-d?' the word was drawn out low and long. 'And do you, Marta Reben, know the face of God?'

She was afraid to answer; she had always thought God must look like her father on Sundays, but now she remembered that they had been told to leave the face of God blank.

The teacher spoke again, 'Marta, you must not imagine that you can know God's face. We can know only his word – and look how you have spoiled that!'

She had had no answer, had only dropped her head in shame because she had dared to think God looked unkind with a blank face. She held out her hand for the stinging leather strap and knew that school's God was very different. She cried only a little when no one could see and she could not look at her smiling God again.

She hated school soon – it was always taking her by surprise like that, just when she thought she was learning, it turned out she had it all wrong. Not even breaks were manageable. The boys played around the back of the assembly hall with marbles or cars. Their games made sense, but girls were not allowed to join their games.

The girls stood about in small groups and giggled about things she did not know. They had laughed when she had told them about the tree spirits, and called her a forest person, like the triplets, who were really hard to play with or talk to. Those three spoke only to one another in incomprehensible mumbles, still cried easily and though they were always grateful to Marta and hoped for help from her, they were not really friends. Rochelle remained as unpredictable as she had been that first day.

One Monday about a year later, a new girl arrived. By Friday, Rochelle had absolutely no time for Marta, was too busy telling the other girls about the new girl, whose name was Sara.

'Where was she before?' Someone asked.

'In Knysna, her father runs a fancy private school there. It is English, but her mother is properly Afrikaans.' Rochelle always knew everything. 'They live in the forest but they are not forest people. She's one of us.' Marta tuned out and thought of the triplets, how scared they had been. So when the new girl came, she barely looked up, not wanting her to feel stared at and so more

34

embarrassed and scared.

But Sara was not afraid or embarrassed. She swept into the room as if she owned it, dropped her bag carelessly near the others at the door, and greeted Rochelle, who immediately began the introductions, leaving Marta out, to punish her for not taking part in the gossip earlier.

Then the first bell rang and they all had to go out to assembly in the quad.

By some mischance, Marta stood behind Sara, who stood behind Rochelle. Briefly Sara turned around and said, 'I am Sara.'

'I'm Marta,' she replied, before Mr. Heyns came and silenced them all with his Bible reading.

Marta saw only that the new girl had beautifully straight dark hair and shocking green eyes in a tanned face, before she swung round with an oddly familiar movement. Marta felt hopeful all through that assembly, thinking maybe this new girl could be a friend. She had smiled at her when they turned around to get back into class.

Sara was placed on Marta and Rochelle's table. Mevrou Lategan set them all some work and then spoke quietly to Sara to find out what she had learned already. Afterwards, she stood up and left the three girls to copy work neatly from the board. She sat down at her desk and began calling the children one by one to do some reading for her. The class was peaceful; the sun shone in and made the dust on the carpet dance when someone walked to the teacher's desk or back.

It almost felt like home on a Sunday afternoon, Marta thought.

'Marta Reben,' her name rang out in the quiet room, and she walked quickly to Mevrou Lategan's desk. She liked reading.

When she came back she smiled happily at Sara who

was looking up and watching her. In return she only got a cold, blank stare, after which Sara turned pointedly away from her and got on with her work. She stumbled with the surprise of it, which earned a gasp from the teacher and a titter from the class at her clumsiness.

The bell for break brought no relief. Sara's response to Marta had not gone unnoticed, and the other girls crowded round her to find out what Marta had done. Marta stood baffled and then wandered about, hoping to find an older sibling, hoping for an explanation. She found Ruth, who let her sit with her and her friends to eat lunch, but she was not allowed to say or ask anything.

Back in the class, Marta tried to ignore the whispers and titters. It was news time, unfortunately. They all sat on the carpet and had to think of interesting things which had happened to them over the weekend. A boy was telling a complicated story about an accident he had seen, when suddenly Rochelle leaned forward and hissed, 'Kaffirboetie' at Marta. The other girls tittered appreciatively.

Marta swung round, 'What?'

'Kaffirboetie!' Rochelle said it more loudly this time.

Mevrou Lategan looked up from helping the boy write his news on their news sheet. 'Girls,' she said warningly.

'Yes, Miss,' they said. But once more Marta heard that word; she did not understand it, but the tone was unmistakable. The shock of the day and her anger and hurt boiled over. She turned round, sat up on her knees and swung a fist. It connected with Rochelle's face, who toppled over crying loudly. All the girls were up on their feet now, except Sara, who was bending over Rochelle.

Mevrou Lategan called out, 'Marta, what was all that about?'

Marta was stunned by what she had done. She sat back on her heels and stared at Rochelle and Sara.

'What happened?' Mevrou Lategan had come closer now and was also bending over Rochelle, who was crying loudly. When she had prised away her hands, everyone could see that she was not badly hurt. Satisfied with that, Mevrou Lategan focused her attention on Sara, who told her what had 'happened'– Marta had turned around for no reason and hit Rochelle.

When this was questioned, Sara conceded that Rochelle had perhaps accidentally bumped into Marta. Marta was sent out into the little corridor to think about her bad temper and the rest of the class got on with their news pages.

When the bell rang for break, Mevrou Lategan called Marta in. 'Would you like to tell me what happened?'

Marta told her.

She sighed and muttered something about having known this was not a good idea, under her breath. Then she turned to Marta, saying, 'You were right to be angry about Rochelle using such a word, it was very wrong of her. But you should have told me and not hit her.'

'Yes, Miss.'

She asked Marta to tidy the book shelf and strode to the staffroom.

On the way home Marta asked Jacob what a Kaffirboetie was.

'Why do you want to know?'

'The girls called me that, today'.

'Which girls? I'll–'

'You'll nothing,' their father interrupted. 'Marta, the girls have simply found out the kind of work I do, and their parents do not like it.'

'Why not?'

'Because they believe that people should only work and live and care for their own kind.'

'Their own kind?'

37

'Whites with whites, blacks with blacks.'

'Oh.' Marta had always thought her father's work good. 'But Jesus tells us to care for the poor, doesn't he?'

'Yes.' And then, after a pause, 'I think they would rather I cared for poor whites.'

But Marta, thinking about how Rochelle treated the triplets, did not think so.

'They're just mean,' she said.

'No, they believe that God ordered people to live separately from each other – and what we do goes against that.'

'But it's stupid,' Jacob joined in.

'Don't judge,' her father said wearily.

Marta secretly agreed with Jacob; not being friends with Ishmael, with Bomani and Narina would be unthinkable.

'They're mean to everyone who is not like them,' she explained to her father and told him how they treated the triplets, going against the silent agreement between the Reben children to leave school behind and not talk about it at home. 'They are just mean, Father,' she insisted.

'You may be right,' her father conceded. Ruth put her arm around her. Silence descended again.

Sara was moved into the other class and no one was punished for using bad language.

Marta soon forgot all about Sara, but the blank-faced God stayed and was often angry and very decisive about what He liked and didn't and all the teachers seemed to know what that was, though they did not know His face.

God refused the Reben children flags on Republic Day, when everyone else was given a little flag to wave or fidget with during the long boekevat and prayers and singing of the South African anthem. She put her hands behind her back for singing; they did not feel so empty there. She glanced at Jacob over in the big boys' line and saw that he was not singing but had his lips pressed

38

tightly together and his eyes were brimming with anger. She stopped singing too, then, but she was not as brave as he – she dropped her head so that people could not see that she was refusing to sing God's song for their country.

Fortunately God at home was less decisive, less angry about her deeds. He was more often disappointed or puzzled but ready to guide rather than punish, and often He was kind, even pleased with her. And He still had her father's face.

The end of the year came at last and the Christmas holidays began. Holidays meant cousins from the Transvaal. Like them, their cousins were a family of seven. Like them, just different enough at school to cause suspicion. Like them, relieved to have holidays without that cloud of being at odds with others. Christmas holidays were the longest and they had nativity plays in them and acting; but one summer there were questions – about Mary and her baby.

'Why she was not sent away then, Mother?' Marta heard Ruth ask her mother. 'Like Narina?'

Jacob had answered, 'Because the Romans and even the Israelites were not as vicious as the Dutchmen.'

'Jacob,' her mother had said warningly.

But he had gone on, 'No one rejected Mary for it, she had her baby and that baby came from the seed of Bathsheba. But Ishmael is colored. No one wants to accept him.'

Then Mother had spotted her and set them all to do some chores around the large table in the kitchen while she made supper. Father came in and read stories to them which everyone laughed at, except Marta who was not really listening and who soon slipped down to 'play' with Ben and little cousin Joe. Really it was to think about what she had heard. She had never questioned

Ishmael's existence before; he belonged simply to Narina and the forest. Now she realized that he had no father – many of Farleigh's children were born 'out of wedlock' as her parents put it, and she knew that meant their parents were not married. But Ishmael was more than that, Ishmael was 'colored.' For the first time she thought about his color – how different he looked.

'Colored' in the world outside Farleigh was a bad thing, because, after the winter holidays, the triplets had come back with news of their uncle's farm the other side of Oudtshoorn and Piet had drawn a picture of his cows. One of the girls had said,

'I have seen your uncle's farm. He keeps kaffir cattle, doesn't he?'

'No, he doesn't.'

'Yes, he does – they are ugly and colorful and patched, not like cows should be at all.'

'They are the cows of stupid black herd boys; they are not proper cows at all.' Others had joined in.

And then the girls had begun chanting 'kaffir cow, kaffir cow' until Mina had cried and Marta had felt sick, watching and not knowing what to do. She did not understand why the girls sneered or why colorful cattle were something to be ashamed of. To her they were beautiful, luminous as the forest orchids.

In the glaring quad of the school the orchids would not survive, they needed the quiet shade of the forest. At school, in this quad where the girls had to play, everything was bright and hard – even the ground which was covered in concrete squares. Like the road it was hot and jittery and though it created beautiful still pictures of water far away, it was really dry and hard and noisy.

Then there was the long, hot athletics day, spent yelling and shouting the chants, which had been practiced so long beforehand at breaks and meant sandwiches could not be eaten. Marta wondered at the noise of it,

40

the drumming feet on the grandstands which had first frightened then exhilarated her. Still, she had not entirely understood what any of it meant, or why there was now suddenly enmity between children who had been friends before, just because some were in the red 'house' and others in the yellow. The 'houses' yelled names at each other as they practiced shouting on different grandstands.

When athletics day came, the houses competed with fury – to the point where a red girl fainted just at the finishing line to the jeers of the yellow grandstand. Marta's feet became red and raw from running bare on the gravel and Ruth crawled under the high-jump instead of going over. Mother was there, selling biscuits and drinks from one of the windows in a classroom with other mothers and Marta spent some time wandering about quietly drinking a rare fizzy drink and so, despite her sore feet, it was a good day. Yellow won and red lost – Marta wondered whether this was because of the war against the reds, which the teachers were talking about.

THREE

Throughout the bustle and confusion of school, the afternoons were still Ishmael's. He would be waiting for Marta just beyond the gates of her father's missionary school every afternoon, when she came back from her school, too. One day, at the start of the holidays, she found him scowling. 'What's the matter?' she asked curiously.

'I have to leave here.'

'Leave?'

'Yes, your father says Farleigh School has taught me all it can teach me now. I have to go to school in town.'

'What, with me?' Marta's eyes widened. She could not imagine what school would be like with Ishmael in it. 'Don't be cross, Ishmael,' she said.

'I don't like things to change.'

'I know, but I will be there.'

'Do you promise?'

That evening at supper, Marta asked her father about it.

'When can Ishmael come to school with me? Is it soon?'

'Marta, Ishmael can't come to school with us,' Ruth was scornful of her little sister's ignorance.

'Yes, he can, Father said so. Father told him he's too big for Farleigh School now.'

'Yes, but he must go to a different school.'

'Why?'

'He's colored.'

That word again. Marta stared at her sister and turned to her father, who looked to their mother for help.

'It's true, Marta,' her mother said, 'Ishmael cannot go to your school.'

'Where must he go, then?'

'Fingo village,' Narina answered as she brought the soup from the kitchen and began ladling it out for them.

'Narina, I don't think–' her mother began.

But Father said, 'Eyes closed!' and all talking stopped for grace and then for soup.

On Monday morning, Father asked Marta if she would come with them for Ishmael.

Her mother said, 'Johannes, is that a good idea?'

'He might like someone with him,' he answered. Mother gave in.

Outside Narina was waiting in her best purple dress and a hat with flowers on. Ishmael looked strange in a white shirt with a stiffly starched collar and a pair of grey shorts from Simon.

They climbed into the car. Ishmael and Marta sat in the back and Narina sat in front when Father opened the door for her, though she was embarrassed. Just before they started, Father asked one more time, 'Are you sure, Narina – Fingo village school?'

'Paul Radebe is an old friend,' she said.

He took a breath to say something, thought better of it and started the car.

Marta glanced over at Ishmael. He looked like a startled blue duiker, eyes darting from one adult to the other and then to the window. He sat in unearthly stillness, though Marta could see breaths short and sharp, shuddering in his thin chest.

The starched shirt was chafing his neck and his
new shiny shoes dangled from the seat. Marta tried to
remember whether she had ever seen him wearing shoes.
No – not even at Easter or Christmas when Narina had
managed to get him to church.

They drove all the way to George, where they had to
slow down. The high street was full. There were people
everywhere. At the garage was a black man in a Father
Christmas outfit. Marta felt sorry for him, 'He must be
so hot,' she thought. But he called out to all the children
passing in cars, smiling and giving sweets to those
whose parents stopped for petrol.

He stared long into their car and stopped smiling.
Ishmael shrank back and even Narina grew anxious, 'I
should sit in the back.'

'Nonsense,' Father was short – Marta saw how white
his knuckles were on the wheel.

Soon he swung off the high street and the road
became winding and full of stops and potholes.

The noise of the busy town centre was behind them,
they got to where it was quieter still and dustier, with
fewer trees lining the streets. Eventually there were no
trees and the houses were made of corrugated iron or
stretched sacking, with some gardens still bright with
flowers in halved petrol drums and others derelict and
bleak. Thin dogs and chickens roamed the streets. Here
and there people were talking together, turning curiously
to see the car.

Some recognized her father and waved, though the
stares turned hard when eyes found Narina. Amidst it all,
children were playing football on the un-tarred roads,
using beer cans to mark the goals and whirling the dust
as they ran, shouting and laughing and punching the
air. Marta watched Ishmael watch them; his back was
stiff, his eyes glittering, but he kept himself back in the

shadow of the car, not leaning towards the window.

They came to the school building; it was a small, dun-colored building and some of the windows were broken. To the side, on a bare and dusty piece of ground, there were goal posts and from two rusty poles near the gate hung a sign. Marta could just make out the word 'skool', which she recognized from her own. How different it was from the building that was her school; quite beautiful with its Cape Dutch front and the large oak tree, under which grew grass, which was cut and well kept and the borders full of bright flowers. She could feel her heart grow tight, but she said nothing and her father and Narina were also silent. Then her father spoke.

'Well, Narina, here we are.'

'Yes, Umfundisi,' she said.

When they got out of the car, Marta could see the creases on her father's clammy shirt at the back from the long hot drive and Narina straightened her skirt. Then they opened the doors for Ishmael and Marta, too.

'Come on,' her father said cheerfully, though Marta could tell it was not real, 'time to enter.'

Before Ishmael could make a dash, he had taken him by the arm and kept him by his side as they walked through the rusty gate towards the building, which was leering at them now, daring them to enter its dismal doors. But her father walked briskly up to the door, opened it and walked in. Inside was one big classroom and at the far end stood a large desk with smaller tables and chairs in neat rows in front, though some of them stood skewed with bent legs. Behind the bigger desk was a blackboard and there were no pictures on the walls, though there was one notice board on which an old child's drawing was pinned as well as a lot of papers with the government crests on.

A tall black man now appeared through a door at the far end.

'Umfundisi Reben,' he said with a warm voice, 'welcome to my school.'

'Mr. Radebe,' her father replied. 'Thank you for seeing us. You know Narina. This is Ishmael and this is my daughter Marta.'

'Marta,' the man addressed her smiling, shaking Marta's hand and clasping her wrist with his free hand.

'Ishmael,' he said. Perhaps it was Ishmael's eyes that warned him; he did not shake Ishmael's hand.

Narina watched this and cleared her throat. Marta saw beads of sweat on her temple, which was pulsing.

'Paul, thank you for seeing us. I have come to enrol my son, Ishmael.' She handed him the papers she had been clutching all the way.

'Narina, you cannot do this,' he said, his voice uncomfortable, his smile no longer welcoming, but light and scared all at once.

He moved to sit behind his desk and folded his hands carefully, looking down a moment and then up again, his gaze focused behind their heads somewhere. 'Everyone knows he is colored.'

'But his papers . . .' Narina began.

'The papers will not be good enough.' He glanced at them. 'Father unknown?'

Narina did not respond but said, 'Paul, he is my child. I came to this school. You and I – we were at Fort Hare, don't you remember? We *taught* together. How can you refuse to take my child into your school?'

'Look at him, Narina.' He was unhappy but would not say any different.

'Would it really make such a difference, Mr. Radebe?' It was Marta's father who spoke up now.

'Yes, Mr. Reben. Yes, it would.' He did not call him Umfundisi now. 'The inspector is very, very particular about enrolments. And very strict; I would lose my job. My wife, my children . . .' He released his hands and gestured vaguely and helplessly around the room.

Her father wanted to argue, but Narina was already leaving.

'I understand,' she said softly, yet every word was clear, 'I understand. Thank you.'

'Narina,' her father said, getting up, but she did not turn.

The two men shook hands hurriedly and only then did anyone take notice of Marta and Ishmael again. Marta was watching everything in stunned silence, but Ishmael suddenly yelled incomprehensibly, yelled and barreled off his chair, crashing through several of the neat desks and hurled himself at a window, which smashed, while he sailed out. He scrambled a little on the loose earth and then was off, still roaring his rage incomprehensibly. Narina walked on, her back like stone. Father said to the principal, 'Let me know how much for the window,' and began straightening the desks.

The principal said nothing but helped straighten the desks. Only Marta ran to the door and called after Ishmael, but he did not come. She went as far as the fence, though the other children, who had been playing in the street, were now crowding round giggling and pointing at the window. Some of them were imitating Ishmael and laughing.

Marta ignored them; they were like Rochelle when she was head of the pack. They would be no help, she knew. She did not ask whether they had seen which way he went. She stood silently at the gate and stared down the street in each direction. There was no sign of Ishmael.

Narina came to get her, 'Come, Marta. We must go home.'

'But Ishmael–'

'Ishmael will find his way home, you know he always does.'

'But has he ever been here, Narina? He does not know this place! How can you find your way home from a place you have never been to?'

'He always comes home, you know he does,' Narina assured her, yet in her eyes Marta could see fear just like her own. She understood the need for calm, for staying quite still, in case the whole world should turn into disaster. Keeping still was all one could do.

Narina's inhuman calm led her father to agree silently with Marta and he drove slowly, scanning everywhere – through all the streets of Fingo village, then Blanco, stopping to ask whether anyone had seen Ishmael.

All the while, Marta cried, softly, softly, not to disturb the precarious balance of things. Narina said nothing and still Father searched the crowded streets for sign of Ishmael. Finally, he looked at Narina.

'No, Umfundisi,' she said firmly, 'please do not tell the police. They would be too glad. Just take me home please, I am sure he is there or will be soon. I don't think he can get lost in the forest.'

'Well, we shall see. I do not like the thought of a child alone in the township *or* the forest. I shall search with your father, he is still the best tracker at Farleigh – he may find signs of him.' And he dropped Narina and Marta home with Mother and left for Millwood.

Her mother took Marta in her arms without a word, and held her back when she wanted to go with Narina, who went to her little house to see if Ishmael was home.

'Let her go,' she had said, 'Narina wants to be alone now.'

'The forest will take care of him, won't it?' Marta asked her mother.

'It is not just the forest Marta, it is people.'

She looked at her mother. 'People?'

'People.'

Her father had driven away fast. Marta sat quietly in

her room and pretended to read. She listened and listened till he returned.

Jacob came in to see how she was.

'Why could Ishmael not go to the school his mother had been to?'

'Ruth told you yesterday. Ishmael is colored, which means he cannot go to the Fingo Village School, he must go to the school in Blanco.'

'He couldn't come to my school?' She still could not give up on the idea.

'No, because . . . here and now everyone must go to a school which is for his race. The blacks must go to Bantu schools, the coloreds to colored authority schools and Asians to theirs and whites to theirs.'

'Does it make so much difference – where you belong?' she asked softly.

'In this country, yes, it makes all the difference in the world.'

Later that night her father went out to see how Narina was and whether Ishmael had come back. He found him sleeping in a tightly curled ball in the corner of his mother's front room. His new shirt was torn and streaked with blood and his eye was swollen. Johannes Reben looked at Narina, 'What happened – did he tell you?'

'Not a word, Umfundisi, you know what he is like, not a word.'

'Does he need anything? Mercurochrome? Plasters? Aloe vera?'

'Thank you, I have what I need.'

And he had known that she could stand no more and left.

He tiptoed into Marta and Ben's room and bent over Marta's still, straight form. She was wide awake, straining to hear the night and all it contained, straining with all her might to reach Ishmael who she knew now did not belong entirely to her world.

'He's safe home, Marta, you can sleep now.'

The relief brought more tears – a flood of them – and her father took her to her mother, where she, like Ishmael, curled in a tight ball against her mother's warm form and finally fell into an exhausted but restless sleep.

Her dreams were haunted by the events of the day. The small school building was suddenly monstrously big; the principal had long spidery legs, a furious red face, and though his eyes had been full of pity, he was adamant – Ishmael cannot go to a Bantu authority school, Narina, he must go to Blanco. And again Marta watched helplessly as Narina wanted to flee with humiliation, wanted to go home and never come out again. Until Ishmael said to her, with clear eyes and a loud voice, 'Mother, I am going; they want me to go there, I will.'

And in the morning it was Ishmael who led the way, past their house from the forest to the waiting taxi her father had ordered, and then to Blanco.

'Narina, are you sure you don't want me to come?' Father asked again.

'I think this one will be better if it's just me, thank you, Umfundisi.'

'I don't like it, Narina.'

'No, Umfundisi, but there is nothing you can do.'

In the afternoon Marta heard Ishmael's voice calling, high and insistent as it had never been before. She ran out to find him. He was sitting with his back against the gate post when she found him, his face was bruised, one eye swelling shut.

'Ishmael what happened?'

His voice was dull as he told her, his eyes glittering in a way which frightened Marta:

'We went to the government offices. There were other people there. And they greeted us with smirks, they smirked at my mother and she did nothing, Marta, she did nothing.'

'What did you want her to do?' Mother had followed Marta, and for once she was glad.

But Ishmael was spitting fury again. 'She should not have gone in there when she saw them all looking and laughing behind their hands at her bastard child.'

'Ishmael, where did you learn such words?'

'That's what they called me; that's what I am.'

Marta had not heard that word at home before and sat frozen now, looking from her mother to Ishmael, thinking of drops of blood on her and Ishmael's arms.

Her mother broke the silence; she took Ishmael gently by his arms, 'What happened next, Ishmael? Where is your mother?'

Before he could answer, her father's car drew up and Ishmael stiffened like an animal sensing danger and hissed, 'School will never make me do anything I don't want,' before leaping down the veranda steps and disappearing.

Marta watched her father slowly climb the stairs. He looked up at them.

'What's the matter, Anita?' But Mother was twisting a tea cloth in her hands and calling after Ishmael.

'I am not sure – perhaps I should check on Narina.'

Marta and Father sat silently on the steps.

'Father, what is going on? Is Narina hurt?' Marta's voice was small.

'Let's wait and see what your mother says when she comes back.'

But when Mother came back, she said nothing to Marta. 'Johannes, you need to call a doctor.' She went to the hall cupboard, took out towels and also something from the medicine cabinet in the bathroom.

'Mother, what is it?' Marta asked in a frightened voice.

'Narina is hurt, Marta – that is all I can tell you now.'

'Was it the people at the government office?'

51

'Yes. Now, can you call Mieta from the church for me, please?'

Mieta and Mother left, leaving Marta with Ruth and Jacob. They did not come back for a long time. Meanwhile, the doctor arrived and Father took him round to Narina's house. The children waited.

The house and the forest felt as loaded as they did before a storm. Marta could take it no more; she went out and pursed her lips for the loerie's call. But no Ishmael answered. Finally Father came back, his face white and jaw clenched.

'What happened?' Jacob asked.

'Narina was a student teacher, some years ago. Things did not go well for her and she had to leave. '

'But what had she done?' Ruth asked with a frown, trying to imagine Narina as a teacher.

'She had Ishmael and she could not marry his father.'

'Why?'

'There are laws.'

Marta stared a while, only half hearing the questions and answers between her brothers and her father. Gradually things fell into place: the thundering addresses in assemblies, the knowledge that certain things did not happen, the whispering behind hands, the calm certitude of Rochelle telling her 'the facts of life' as she called them – and that certain things could not happen; were not allowed to happen, by God. But they did; they had. Ishmael had been the result. And this.

Her father put an arm around her and said softly, so that she would know he did not agree with what he said, 'Narina crossed a line, and no one on either side has forgiven her. Today they punished her.'

'What did they do?' Simon's voice was smaller than Marta had ever heard it.

'Unspeakable things.' Father covered his face. 'I should have gone with her.'

The children sat around their father, unable to look at each other with this new terrible knowledge between them.

'Go to bed,' Father said at last. 'There is nothing we can do tonight.'

Marta held back till the others had left the room.

'What about Ishmael, Father?' she managed at last.

At that moment Mother came back. 'He is with his mother now, Marta. He is safe.'

'Go to bed,' her father urged gently as he hugged her tightly. 'I will come to say goodnight in a bit.'

When her parents came to her bed, she asked one more thing. 'We have, haven't we?'

'We have what?' her mother asked.

'Forgiven Narina.' Marta could not look up.

'We had nothing to forgive, we're from a different world.' Her father tipped her face up towards his. 'What is that you've got in your hands?'

In her hands she held the feather which Ishmael had left on her windowsill when she had not been allowed to play with him.

'Ah. Your Turaco feather.'

'Turaco?'

'Yes. That is the Latin name for your Loerie.'

'Oh! May I bring it to Ishmael?'

'Yes.'

'Wait a minute.' Her mother was standing behind them. 'I have a case you can have for it, before you bring it to him, so the wind cannot blow it away.'

Her mother came back with a long, dark blue narrow box. It had a small silver button, which if pressed, popped the lid up. The box was inlaid with white satin and had gold writing in the lid. In two places were loops. It was the case in which her mother's watch had come – the one Father had given her for their anniversary.

'May I really have that for our feather?'

'Yes.'

Carefully Marta placed the feather in the box, tucking its end into one of the loops, while her mother held it.

Then Marta took the box, and went with Father through the dark forest to bring Ishmael the gift. Though she really was too big now, Marta held her father's hand as they walked, stepping carefully on the uneven ground, slipping now and again on the dank mud.

Ishmael stared at the box, 'What is it?'

'It is the feather – the Turaco feather.'

'What?'

'Turaco – that is the book name for the Loerie. My father told me.'

'Turaco,' he rolled the word in his mouth. 'Turaco.'

'Look: it opens,' Marta answered and showed him the small silver button.

The feather glowed softly on the white satin, lit by the light of Narina's meths lamp.

Ishmael snapped it shut quickly, and held the box reverently while they spoke.

'I have to go to school in Blanco now.'

'I heard. How was it?'

'Who cares? It was school. I hate school.' A pause. Then, 'Come, I'll show you where the elephants have stripped a witels.'

'Tomorrow.' Father said, coming back from the other room, where he had spoken softly with Mieta, who was sitting up with Narina. 'Stay here, near your mother now.'

Ishmael scowled, but Father took Marta by the hand and when she turned at the door, he had snapped the box open again.

In the morning no one spoke about it. Mother made breakfast herself. Ruth put music on to fill the silence and then everyone dispersed to the day's activities. Marta played a listless game of Ludo with Simon and

Ben, waiting for a chance to escape to the forest, but Mother was watching with eagle eyes today. 'Ishmael and Narina need to recover,' she said firmly, and she kept Marta inside all day. That was the last Marta heard of the matter.

It should not have been possible for things to return to normal, but they did. Christmas passed and soon it was time for the next school year. For Ishmael it spelled a new freedom. He lost what small restraint there had been on his behavior at the gentle Farleigh School and Marta was swept along by his new and fiercer wildness, his conviction that all authority was to be defied. She was entranced by the idea of missing school as freely as Ishmael did, awed by his lack of fear. He roamed the forest, the coast, all over the mountains, and *knew* things; he understood things few other people knew existed. He had established his scorn for the school on the very first day and now attended only to cause trouble for the people who had looked at him with prurient contempt.

He no longer waited for Marta at the gate every afternoon. She would have to find him somewhere in the forest around Farleigh. She would drop her bag in her room, call a brief 'hallo' and then run to the river, calling Ishmael. She usually found him at the Homtini.

He had made a rope swing one morning and hung it from a wild pear tree on the bank of the river. Wearing only his shorts, he was glistening wet, but his eyes were still and bright.

They swung all afternoon. They landed in the golden water and splashed to the side again. Eventually they worked out how to swing themselves all the way over to the other side.

Ishmael went first. He pulled the rope as far back as it would go, then stood up on his toes, gripped it as high as he could, swung his legs tightly around the rope as it flew through the air above the river. He threw back his head and yelled. Marta yelled with him. He let go just as he swung close to the other bank, landed with a splash, but waded to the far side.

'Come on,' he called back to her. *On, on, on*, said the echo. He called again. And then whispered, 'Marta, come on, the ancestors are calling you.' Louder: 'Come on, Marta, come on.'

On on on on, the forest rang.

Marta looked fearfully at the long rope and the branch from which it hung. But then she looked at Ishmael dancing with impatience on the far side of the river. She waded in and caught the rope and dragged it behind her to the place where he had stood. Gripping the rope, she stepped back and swung, curling her legs around the rope as Ishmael had done.

She landed with a splash on her backside in the water, but she had reached the far side.

'Welcome to the land of the turando!' Ishmael said.

'The what?'

'You know – what your father said was the name of the loerie.'

'Oh, you mean the Turaco.'

'All right then. The land of the Turaco, then.'

They roamed deep into the gloom of the wild trees. It felt like they were the only people in the world.

Most days Ishmael would roam ahead of her. Sometimes it took Marta till dark to find him. Without him, there was no kingdom of Turaco, only trees full of angry ancestors.

She complained.

'You should call,' he said.

'I do!'

'I never hear you.'

'I know!'

'Well, call like this – kow, kow, kow, kow,' he called with rising tone and pitch.

'That's the loerie.' Marta said.

'I'll always hear that.'

They practiced until they were satisfied that they would always find each other.

The next day Marta called as she flew over the river on their rope. There was a faint answering and she followed it. She moved through the forest quickly, not seeing today the luminous orchids in the gloom, or the bright disa in the clearings, only intent on his whistle.

The sound was close now, and soon closer still, but she was tired. She sat with her knees drawn up against the cool bark of an ironwood and whistled again.

The answering whistle seemed to come from around her feet.

Marta searched around, interspersing her whistling with calling. She jumped in fright as Ishmael's face appeared from behind a fern.

She had no time to be cross with him as he immediately beckoned her closer.

'Look at all this,' he gestured. Marta looked: there was a great hole hidden by the undergrowth. Carefully so as not to disturb any of the small forest spiders, she pulled the ferns aside and stared into the musty darkness.

'Let's go in.' Ishmael urged.

'But we don't know what lives down there,' Marta was uncertain.

'Are you afraid?' he mocked.

Promptly Marta lowered herself through the opening, feeling with her feet for the floor. There was none.

'It's deep, Ishmael,' she whispered.

'Let me, then. I'll pull you back.'

But her fingers slipped from his hand and the edge of the hole crumbled and she fell.

'Marta!'

'I'm alright,' but she felt her ankles gingerly and

shifted quickly as Ishmael's feet brushed her shoulder. They discovered that they were in a tunnel, but it was too dark to see much else.

Their hands closed on rusted pickaxes here and there and pillars of ironwood held up the roof.

'What is it?'

'It is a cave,' Ishmael offered.

However, when Marta spoke of it at home Jacob told her it must be the old Millwood mines they had found.

At school, Rochelle told her they were haunted and full of mad forest people, but in all their time there, Marta and Ishmael saw no one else, though now and again they saw the spoor of elephants when they came out. It caught Marta's breath every time to think of those great creatures near them. The two never saw more than trail, and for the moment the lure of the tunnels was adventure enough. Sometimes there was an odd smell of cinnamon and apples, which made her think of Christmas, but this was pushed out of her mind by Ishmael looking for gold. So she forgot to ask anyone about that smell.

Marta collected candle stubs from home and she and Ishmael began their search for gold in earnest. They collected pieces of rock and examined them closely in the river, having prised them from the ground.

'It's gold. Look, it's gold!' Marta cried, holding in the palm of her hand the small square shining gold rocks.

'It's perfect,' Ishmael breathed, 'it comes already in ingots.'

They stowed it carefully in a bag, which they hid near the entrance of their cave. Every day the hoard grew.

'We should find out how much it is worth.'

After some hesitation, 'Yes, we probably should.'

So the next day Ishmael waited for her again at the gate – clean and dressed in his school uniform. He had already fetched the bag.

'How do you get home so quickly from school?'

'From where?'

'Ishmael, you will . . .'

'Sssh, here is your father.'

They followed him into his study. Father was glad to see Ishmael again.

'Ishmael, how are you?'

'I am well, Umfundisi.'

'And how can I help you two today? You're looking very solemn.'

'Father, can you tell us how much we will get for this?'

They held out the handful of gold to him. He took it and examined it briefly.

'Nothing.'

'What?'

'But it's gold! We found it in the mine.'

'It is not gold. It is pyrites – also called fool's gold because lots of people–'

But they heard no more. Ishmael roared again as he had that first day at school, and roughly hit Johannes Reben's hand so that the pyrites scattered to the floor. Sitting hunched with his arms wrapped around his knees, he refused to look at anyone.

Marta knelt to gather it up. She did not know what else to do. She had never seen anyone treat her father like that.

Finally she said softly, 'Come, Ishmael.'

Listlessly, he got up and followed her out.

They walked in silence to the gate. Ishmael opened it, instead of vaulting it as he usually did.

But then something came over him. 'Come.' He grabbed the bag and began running.

They ran and ran all the way to the big road. There they crossed at the Kom Se Pad and ran on to the edge of the forest where it overlooked the sea. The evening mist was just creeping through the light of the setting sun over the sea that roared and smelled of salt in its own restlessness.

Ishmael stared at it; he roared back, 'When will you ever let me have anything?' He took the bag, poured all their gold into his hand and gave Marta some.

'What are you doing?'

'Throwing them into the sea! The ancestors can have their damn fool's gold back!'

They shot the stones one by one out over the sea with their catapults. The small stones flew up first and caught briefly the dying light. They sparkled and shone as they arced gracefully into the mist below and the two children were silent as they watched the twinkling fall of their treasure.

The moment was alive as no other. And then it was over.

'Now they're dead,' Ishmael said, 'like your father's garden. Like Millwood mine.' It hurt her when he spoke like that and they did not go back to the mines. But Marta never forgot the bright flight of the stones, the lovely fool's gold as it fell into the sea.

The next day Marta found Ishmael at Dolphin's Point again. He was looking speculatively out at the sea, throwing pebbles. When she arrived he turned to her.

'Let's make something fly.'

'How? What?'

He let fly another pebble into the sea with his catapult.

'Oh,' she said, disappointed.

'No, you don't understand: big things. I will make big things fly – we have to build a bigger fling than this,' he gestured with his catapult. 'I want to set heavy things free, to let them feel the wind, to let them not be stuck in their one place. I want to set a tree free and myself – I want to show the ancestors I can. I want to drive something into the sea.'

'"Oh, I have slipped the surly bonds of earth,"' Marta whispered, remembering something Jacob had had to learn by heart at home.

'What?'

She repeated it.

'Yes,' he said, 'like that.'

'It is a pilot speaking in a war plane,' she said, but Ishmael was not interested in her explanations; he had headed back into the forest to find what he needed to make his giant catapult. Marta saw that he had no idea how to do it so the next few breaks at school she spent in the library, looking up siege weapons and copying out the drawings. She showed them to Ishmael and he took them, his eyes alight, studying them with more patience than she had ever seen him display. She wandered off, looking for dolphins on the sea's horizon, leaving him with the papers. He called her back.

'Marta, we have to build one of these.'

'What are you going to fling?' She was suspicious now and suspected that this new scheme of his would involve a lot of work.

'I am going to fling the old Kalander, the dead one here at Dolphin's point.'

'The one that was struck by lightning in the last storm.'

'Yes.'

'But it's huge!'

'Yes.'

Marta caught his enthusiasm then, and they worked harder even than they had worked in Millwood mine. They borrowed tools from the Farleigh carpentry and measuring tape that sprang back as soon as they had made their mark, snapping at their fingers. It was hard work and even in the winter sun they sweated as they sawed and measured and lifted and hammered their Fling. It was beautiful, Marta thought, its lines already

61

soaring up into the sky in their clearing. She stood back from it one evening in June and could not believe that they had made it.

By the last week of term they had collected enough information on angles and trajectories and power to complete their giant catapult. They worked on it every day. Ishmael 'borrowed' a tarpaulin from Bracken Hill farm to protect it from the rain; they worked beneath its sticky darkness many days, when the rain soaked and soaked all day and their impatience could barely be held back any more.

Then it was finished. Fling was complete.

On the last day of term Marta heard Ishmael's call early in the morning. She crept out before Ben would notice and found him under the willow tree near the dam.

'What is it?'

'I want to fling the Kalander this morning.'

'We can't do it this morning. I have to go to school.'

'I am flinging it this morning. Are you coming or not?'

'But Ishmael–'

'Do you want to be there? Do you want to see it free? Do you?'

She nodded, her eyes wide with anxiety.

'Then be there.'

She walked with the others to the bus stop. Marta was restless; she did not know how she would escape to get to Ishmael.

When the bus arrived she heard Ishmael's call and with a despairing call in response she ducked off into the forest, despite Ruth's calls and threats. The bus drove away.

Marta was breathing hard but she scrambled up and ran to find Ishmael, who had Bomani with him.

He smiled when he saw her.

'Doesn't it feel good?'

She thought of what the others would soon be doing at school and it did feel good. It felt so good she had to dance and whoop.

Ishmael and Bomani joined her and then they walked to Fling. In silence they took off the tarpaulin and wheeled it to the edge of the cliff. It was hard work, even with the help of Bomani. Then they had to get the tree to the edge too, ready to be loaded into Fling. They stared hopelessly at the huge trunk and the many branches.

'We'll have to saw some of them off,' Marta pointed out.

Bomani fetched the saw and they took it in turns till the trunk had clean lines for flying – as Engineer Ishmael called it now. Then they had to get the clean lines to Fling.

They used the sawn off branches as levers. It was dangerous work, and hard. The trunk rolled and toppled but they did not give up. The three rolled it when they could, stemmed its branches and ran whooping away when they let it topple next to Fling at last.

With the help of their levers they lifted the tree into the cradle and secured it. Panting, they stopped to rest and Marta shared her lunch.

'We have to learn that verse you said,' Ishmael said.

So Marta taught them what she remembered of the airman's poem.

At midday, Ishmael decided it was time.

They pulled the cradle back. Ishmael and Bomani held it while Marta slipped the loop of rope over the wooden end. They paused, looking at each other with shining eyes.

'Ready?'

'Ready.'

Ishmael pulled the loop: they chanted together, '"Oh I

have slipped . . . and touched the face of God'".

The tree flew up and somersaulted into the white wintery sky. It flew wide over the sea and seemed to hang there for a moment, before plummeting down, down, down.

They watched it fly as they spoke the verse over and over and their breath shaped the words white into the mist. They felt the sea air touch their hair and knew it touched the tree too, before it fell into the water.

After a period of silence Ishmael turned to Marta and Bomani.

'The Kalander has set us free. It has gone to the ancestors in the sea. Now no one can touch us.'

'No, they can't,' Marta agreed. Bomani watched them both in silence.

'No one can take that away. I have given the ancestors what I owe them, now they must leave me alone.'

'They can't take that away from us. We made a tree fly.'

Marta did not care what would follow for having skipped school, though she knew Ruth would tell her father, knew there would be no escape.

School would be out early today so Bomani slipped back home, where he had feigned a sore throat to his mum before she left for school. Ishmael and Marta circled back to Farleigh. Marta wondered at Ishmael. 'You do this every day?'

'Nearly,' he said, unconcerned. 'I hate school.'

'Don't you get in trouble?'

'No.'

'Does your mother know?'

'She guesses sometimes.'

'Don't you get in trouble then?'

'Yes – with Grandfather.'

'Don't you mind that?'

'No.'

'How do you do it?'

'They can't do anything to me. I set the Kalander free,' he was ignoring her question.

'Well, my father can do plenty to me. I'll be grounded for this.'

Ishmael looked at her face. 'Wait here,' he said and disappeared for a while. He returned with the blue watch case. 'Here,' he said, 'take it and remember: we are free.'

F O U R

Marta waited in the forest above Farleigh for the bus.
She saw it come and then followed Ruth and her brothers
in the cover of the trees and crept back home unseen,
arriving at the same time as they did. She knew it was no
use, though. Ruth had gone straight in to talk to Mother.

When she came out Marta hissed 'Tattletale,' but felt
bad when she saw that Ruth had been crying.

'You could have been hurt,' she said and slammed the
door to her room. When Father came in, he spent a long
time in the room with Mother.

Ben asked Marta with big eyes, 'What will you do?'

'Nothing.'

'What did you do?' he then asked and Marta told him
about Fling.

'I wish I had seen it.'

'It was beautiful. It was the freeest thing I ever saw.'

Supper passed in ominous silence. Afterwards Father
read a chapter from Winnetou in an uncharacteristic
monotone and Mother sat with her hands in her lap. No
darning, no knitting, no letters to write.

Marta dared not look up – she knew this was her fault
but she had not been reprimanded so did not know how
to fix it.

Finally she burst out 'I'm sorry.'

Her father looked up, 'Don't interrupt Marta, please. Let me finish.'

He finished the chapter and said goodnight in his No Argument voice. Usually at the start of a holiday they got two chapters.

'Boy, are you in trouble,' Simon said in the bathroom. 'I have never seen him like this. They don't know what to do with you.'

'It was just the last day of school. We never do much work then anyway,' Marta said, defensively.

'I don't think it's the skipping school they're so worried about.'

'What then?'

'Your running around with Ishmael all the time.'

'What's wrong with that?'

'He's a bad influence,' Ruth said primly. She looked down, perhaps feeling guilty about having told now.

'What did you say?' Marta's fists clenched as she stepped closer to her older sister.

'Marta, don't you know that he is the naughtiest boy in his school?'

'He hardly ever goes,' Marta retorted, 'how can he be naughty then?'

'He respects no adult, he never listens – even when he gets *caned* he doesn't listen. He lies to his mother all the time, and he doesn't care about his education. He steals, too.'

'That's not true, we borrow stuff – we give it back when we've finished.'

'It's like Solomon says,' Ruth went on ignoring her sister, 'he's got bad blood.'

At that Marta shoved Simon aside and tried to grab her older sister's throat. 'Take that back! Take it back!' she yelled. Jacob held Marta by the scruff of her pajamas as she tried to get at Ruth and then carried her, still kicking, to her bedroom.

'It's just dangerous for children to be alone,' he said placating her. 'You don't know what might be in the forest.'

Ruth left the bathroom and Mother appeared at the door. 'In your beds, please.'

She waited till they were each in their bed and then she came and sat on the edge of Marta's bed.

'Marta, why did you go with Ishmael today?'

And Marta told her about Fling, then.

Mother listened quietly.

'It was so beautiful,' Marta finished, 'it flew and nothing got in its way.' She was close to tears now.

'Why didn't you speak to your father or me about it this morning?'

'You would have said I must go to school and then I would have to disobey you.'

'Have to?'

'I could not have missed it.'

'Why did Ishmael want to do it this morning?'

'I don't know.'

'Did you think to ask?'

She looked at her mother blankly.

'What will you do with me?' she asked.

'Well, you're grounded for the weekend. No playing with Ishmael, no going out at all.'

'Yes, Mother,' she responded meekly.

'Now, think about what you have done. Ask forgiveness and then get some sleep, and we will find chores for you in the morning.'

'Goodnight, Mother.'

And she felt under her pillow for the blue watchcase.

It was the longest weekend of Marta's life. The hours crept by. She read, she wrote a story, she practiced the piano and tidied her room and tidied it again but still the time crept. Her mother did take pity on her finally and asked her to help tidy the pantry. They had to take everything out, wash the shelves and the jars and then replace them all neatly.

Then she tidied her father's bookshelves in the lounge and lost herself a little in his many great books with their marbled covers and gold edged pages. There was one called *Der Ewige Brunnen* that was full of poetry. Marta skimmed the pages and found to her surprise that she could read it, though she had only been taught to read Afrikaans at school. This did not look so very different. As she browsed, she came across Schiller's *Freude*. She read it over and over, till she knew by heart:

> *Freude schöner Götterfunken*
> *Tochter aus Elyseum*
> *Wir betreten feuertrunken, Himmlische dein Heiligtum.*
> *Deine Zauber binden wieder was die Mode streng geteilt*
> *Alle Menschen werden Brüder wo dein sanfter Flügel weilt.[1]*

And she knew that was how she had felt, when she watched the Kalander fly. Time dragged less after that.

On Sunday evening her father announced that they would be going away this holiday. Marta stared at him. Then she leapt up and ran from the room, threw herself down on her bed and cried. She was the reason everyone was to leave Farleigh and she could not bear it.

Jacob knocked softly on her door and came in.

'Hey Marta, what's the matter?'

'What's the matter?' she stormed. 'We're leaving and it's my fault.'

'We're not leaving. We're just going on holiday.'

'We've never been away before!'

---

[1] *Joy, spark of Gods divine, fire-imbibed, we enter, heavenly, thy sanctuary*

'No. But you must have heard others in your class talk about their holidays.'

'Yes,' Marta grimaced, 'but for us, holidays are here.'

'Well not this time. Things can't always stay the same.'

'Why not?'

'Because the same is dull.'

'Where are we going?'

'We're going to see our cousins, remember? They came to see us last long holidays.'

Marta grimaced again. 'Where do they live?'

Jacob explained, using maps and a globe to show her exactly where the Eastern Transvaal was and gradually Marta forgot that this was a punishment and that she would not see Ishmael for three weeks. Slowly the world was back as it should be – just bigger – and Marta was excited to leave.

'We will go and see God's Window in the mountains, and the Blyde River Canyon and the potholes,' Jacob enthused. He showed them to her in his geography book.

The next day her cousins arrived in a Combi. They had already been on holiday to Cape Town and were on their way back home for the last three weeks of their holiday. They would stay one night before they all drove up in convoy.

Marta tried to picture a convoy while they all sat inside playing monopoly but she could only imagine a wagon with big old wheels and a tent on it, swaying from side to side. She decided to wait and see, just as she would wait and see where her cousins lived in the far North of the country. It would take all day to get there. Marta could not imagine driving so far. She did not know what the world looked like on the other side of the mountains. She stared at the pictures in Jacob's atlas, studied the flat Karoo in surprise.

Marta played a little shyly with her cousin Lily, who

came from the other side of this flat world and was closest to her in age. She showed her the garden and the trees, told her about Ishmael. 'Would you like to meet him?'

'Yes.'

'Okay, let's find him.'

'Marta,' Ruth warned her. 'You're not to–' but Marta was already out the door.

She took her cousin to their back gate, beyond which was the forest and whistled and called. He came but stood stock-still when he saw that she had someone with her.

'Ishmael,' she called, 'this is my cousin Lily. It's okay, come and talk to us.'

Ishmael came slowly, his eyes rolling whitely like a horse being asked to cross a path he did not want to cross, or was afraid of. His head was back and his nostrils flared.

'Where have you been?' He asked.

'Grounded,' she said.

'For Friday?'

'Yes.'

'They don't want you to play with me, do they?'

'No.'

'Will that stop you?'

'I am here, aren't I?'

'Not alone.'

'Obviously. Let's play something.'

Lily was equally afraid, of Ishmael and of the dark forest, with its strong pervasive smells, whispering trees, singing birds and all its strangeness. Ishmael and Lily glared at each other but Marta did not see that: she was too full of the wonder she had discovered through Jacob and wanted to tell Ishmael about it.

'What?' He stopped her excited speech when she told him they were going away.

'Yes, we're going to go and see God's Window and the Drakensberg—' but he was gone.

He would not come back. She leapt off the gate calling after him but Lily began whimpering behind her. Marta stood between them and did not know which one to choose, to whom she belonged any more. So she took her cousin to play inside with Ben and her own little brother and then ran out and into the forest, calling for Ishmael. But Ishmael was gone. He would not come.

Marta called and whistled but it was useless, no Ishmael appeared. Narina found her curled on her own in the corner of a classroom in Farleigh.

'Come on baby, everyone is looking for you.'

'*I'm* looking for Ishmael.'

'Your father has said not to play with him for a while.'

'That is upsetting him.'

'Yes, it is. But he should not be so bad, then. And he should not take you with him. He should know better.'

'Sometimes I think he knows better than anyone, Narina.'

'I know you do, little one. But you mustn't. He is not right.' And she gestured at her temple.

'Narina, he is your son!'

'Yes. And I am glad he has a friend like you,' Narina appeased the child.

'What will he do all holiday without me?'

'I don't know.'

'Does he know I still want to be his friend?'

'I don't know.'

Marta had a thought and scrabbled to her feet. 'Wait here for me Narina. Wait here – please don't go anywhere.'

'I'll wait.'

Marta ran to her room, knelt by her bed and pulled a shoebox out from under it. She took out of the shoebox

72

the watchcase her mother had given her for the feather.

Marta opened it briefly and looked at their feather. There it lay, glowing like a jewel in the lamplight.

There were footsteps along the corridor. She snapped the box shut, and crept quickly out of the window before Ben and Joe came into the room to find the two swords and shield sets Ben had been given last Christmas.

Lily tagged behind them. 'Can I be the princess?'

Marta felt a brief twinge of guilt but dove into the dark courtyard and got back to the classroom just as the carpenter was locking up. Narina was as good as her word; she was there tidying books, waiting for her.

'Will you give him this? Will you ask him to take care of it for me till I am back?'

'Yes.'

'I will be back, Narina. Tell him that.'

They set off before sunup next morning and though still sleepy, Marta sat up to wonder at the mountain's exposed sides as they drove through the gashes the road had made in it. 'Convoy' turned out to mean just the two cars together, one behind the other, always in sight of each other. It was very disappointing. They drove through the endless round of the world beyond and the flat and bright veldt of the Karoo. Marta wanted to crawl away and hide from its brightness but Jacob comforted her and said there were more mountains further on.

'And trees?'

'Well, there is bush,' he offered.

'Which is what?'

'Bushes are smaller than trees.' He was not certain how else to explain.

It was dark when they arrived at their cousins' house so they could not see much. They had been paired up for sleeping but they waited in the kitchen, drinking warmed milk and eating rusks while their mother and aunt made up beds for them. Ruth and their big cousin helped.

Then they fell into their camp beds next to their cousins and lay still, knowing how tired everyone was after the long trip. As Marta lay there, she felt the air smelled empty and she missed the sound of the trees.

By the morning she forgot this, intent on exploring the house and garden. They had no pets because their oldest sister was afraid of them but they had lots of fruit trees and behind those there was a mountain, just like at home.

The three weeks went by very quickly. They drove to all the places Jacob had said. They had picnics and sang all the songs they knew on the way home. Their uncle had taken the seats out of his Combi and they all sat together on old mattresses in the back, except Ben and Joe who sat in the boot and called things down to them.

At God's Window Father was anxious and made them all line up against the cliff wall while he took them one by one to the edge, holding their hand to let them look down.

It was beautiful. There was mist in the valley miles and miles below and the wide open sky above it. It felt like they were looking through the clouds from heaven down onto paradise.

'It's like Sunday every day.' Marta said when it was her turn.

'What was that?' Father asked.

She repeated it and when Father still looked puzzled, added, 'the light – look.'

'You're right,' he said. 'It's the grace of God. It does feel like that, doesn't it?'

'Oh, it makes me want to fly,' Marta said, thinking of Fling.

Father's grip on her shoulder tightened again, 'Right, step back,' he said, 'Marta, don't be silly. Lily wants a turn.'

Marta wanted to stay; she wanted to look down into that valley forever. She wanted to remember every stone, every pebble, so she could tell Ishmael about it. But she had to step back holding Father's hand – something she was too old for – so that Lily could see too.

Lily looked and cried. 'It's so big!' not seeing how beautiful it was.

Marta snorted in scorn and earned a fierce look from Father.

Mother looked at Marta's face. 'Come,' she said, 'help me unpack the basket.'

They walked a little way down to where there was space for all of them to sit on the blanket.

'You're struggling a bit with Lily,' her mother stated.

'She's afraid of everything. Even when we played catch in their garden yesterday, when Simon caught her she cried.'

'So that was what that fuss was about.'

'Yes. She's a coward and a crybaby,' Marta complained.

'Well, be patient with her,' Mother said, 'here come the others.'

Marta felt a little better.

The last week came and the older cousins had come up with a plan for their final evening together. Fritz, the eldest, had had a part in his school play and ever since had dreams of the big stage. He chose to practice on his cousins and siblings. He wrote and rewrote scripts for several sketches. Ben and Joe and Marta and Lily had to do a dramatic version of *Hansel and Gretel*. Aunt Sarah had an endless supply of dressing up clothes, plastic brooms, swords and anything else they might need. She altered a skirt so that Lily could be the witch.

The afternoon before, all rehearsals stopped. Fritz insisted that they all rest and he patrolled the corridors and timed their loo trips. Then there were regimented bathroom sessions for each pair, followed by sandwiches standing up in the kitchen with no peeping into the lounge, which had sliding doors into the dining room. They were closed.

The dining room had been almost stripped. The table stood right against the wall and the chairs had all been taken out and placed in between the lounge furniture for the audience.

On the table stood bowls of cheese curls, chips, jelly babies and popcorn. Deep red Fortris juice glowed in glasses. Bright paper plates had been set out and paper napkins had been folded into hats and scattered around the table.

Fritz had found a bell and rang it in the corridors. 'Five minutes till curtain up. Everyone in the green room.'

'The green room?'

'In here.' Ruth explained, going into Fritz' bedroom.

'Why is he calling it the green room?'

'Because that's what they call it in the theatre. It's just the room where all the actors wait for their call.'

'Okay, little ones,' Fritz said, 'you're up. Take your places.'

'Not while you call me little one.' Marta sat down on the floor, crossed her arms and hunched over.

Fritz rang the bell furiously. 'But it's your call. Jacob calls you little one all the time.'

'Jacob's my brother – you! You are just my cousin. And I hate you!'

'You hate me?'

'Yes, you're bossy. Stop ringing that bell!' And she was on his back, grabbing for the bell ringing arm.

'Hey, hey, hey. Pre-show nerves?' Jacob took Marta round the waist and swung her off. 'One more night,' he whispered in her ear, 'now go. Ben and Joe are waiting and Lily is close to tears.'

She went; shouted her first line angrily and was rewarded with laughter. She had forgotten the audience over her irritation with Fritz. Their laughter made her afraid.

Ben took her hand, 'Come, Gretel, help me find the bread crumbs.' His big anxious eyes reminded her of what to do next. As they wandered about 'the stage', she remembered being lost at the river with Ishmael and saw again in her mind's eye the looming Kalander and Iron woods and there was no need to act – not fear of the witch, nor joy at seeing their 'father' again.

Afterwards they got to sit in the lounge and eat cheese curls while they watched the others. Fritz and Jacob were wonderful in their sketches of 'Oubaas' the old farmer and 'Lena' his servant, who always got him out of trouble. Marta forgave Fritz all his shouting and his bell ringing because he was so funny. By the end of the evening she knew she loved all her cousins and all her brothers, and Ruth too!

Early the next morning, they set off and drove the long, long way back home. It was dark when they arrived but still Marta and Ben ran all over the house and the yard, exclaiming at their familiar things looking so strangely different. Then they fell into bed and Marta breathed happily the air thick with fynbos smells.

In the morning Marta went out the back gate and whistled and called for Ishmael but there was no answer. She looked everywhere, at the river – even at the mine. But he was nowhere to be found.

Just as she was giving up she found him sitting quietly at the foot of the old wild pear near their swing. He leapt down from the tree and landed softly next to her.

'You came back.'

'Yes, I said I would.'

'I was not sure.' Then despite himself, 'What was it like?'

And she told him, about their final night, about the dizzying potholes where you could lose your sense of everything in the swirling water and the endless rings in the rocks. She told him about the Blyde River Canyon, where those same rings were huge and rose above the river in glowing red and gold towers. God's Window she kept for last.

Finally she had told him everything and was looking at him with shining eyes.

'Ishmael, it was the light of God's grace everywhere – every day,' and, forgetting that he did not understand German she began to recite Schiller's poem.

'Was it?' he said softly. He got up. 'Was it?' That time it was yelled and then he turned and ran.

'Ishmael,' she called, 'Ishmael!'

'Go back to God's Window!' he yelled. 'Go away, we don't need you here! I've got Bomani now!'

Marta searched for him as she had searched for him countless times before.

Finally she stood in Narina's kitchen doorway.

'Where is he?'

'I don't know; I'il help you look.'

Narina and Marta searched together till sundown, but found him nowhere.

'Is he angry with me?' Marta asked. 'Did you give him the feather?'

'Yes, I gave him the feather.'

'What did he say?'

'It's Ishmael. You know he says nothing unless he has to.' But Narina was pale. 'He has been wild most of the holiday, without you. The education department came to find him and gave us a warning. If he misses any more school, they will have to take him away.'

'What do you mean? Take him away? Where to? He

78

belongs here; he can't be anywhere else. What do you mean, Narina? Where is he? What happened?'

'He ran away.'

Narina sank down amongst the roots of a tree and cried out.

And then she turned to Marta, 'Go home, child, go home. Your mother will be waiting for you.'

'But–'

'Go home!'

Her voice was so fierce, and her eyes so far away, that Marta was frightened and ran, not minding the branches that snatched at her legs and her arms and even her face as she ran blindly home.

'Marta, what is the matter?' Father asked when he saw her come through the gate.

'Ishmael is gone,' she answered, 'and Narina does not know what to do.'

'We found Ishmael.' Something in his voice frightened Marta.

'What is it, Father, where is he?'

'The doctor is with him,' Father replied. But before Marta could ask any more, he said, 'you had better show me where Narina is.'

So she took him, not running but walking quietly and quickly. Every moment mattered; they did not have time for falls.

When they got there, Narina was still sitting in that hopeless way, leaning back against a tree, staring up into the darkening leaves as if seeking help but knowing none would come.

Father went to her and squatted down near her.

He spoke to her but Marta was too tired to listen properly. They spoke about Ishmael and Narina cried. She cried like a child cried, abandoned to the despair within her. No grown-up had ever cried like that before in Marta's life. She took Narina's hand but was shaken off. Father stood up then and put his arm around her, silencing her questions for now.

Then he spoke, his voice gentle but also firm. Marta knew that voice; it was a voice one had to obey.

'Narina,' he said, 'you cannot stay here all night. You have to come back with us. Ishmael will stay for tonight. He will sleep now, the doctor said. In the morning we must make decisions.'

Narina did as she was told though she walked as if the life had left her legs. Her eyes were dull with crying.

All three walked in silence, busy with their thoughts; so tired that every step required concentration. The forest was a menacing darkness of angry ancestors again.

Back at the house Mother was waiting with the doctor, who was no doctor Marta had ever seen before. He spoke a long time with Narina and her parents while Ruth made sure that Marta had something to eat and a bath and went to bed. She did so quietly, though she was aware that missing this opportunity to protest meant she would not know about where Ishmael had been and why he needed a doctor until morning. Mother only told her that he was unhurt and not to worry, and for once Marta was so tired that she obeyed.

In the morning there was no one in the kitchen and when Marta asked, Mother told her to wait until the whole family was there so that she could tell everybody at the same time. But Marta did not wait, and ran out to see. In the garden Caleb was digging a row of small holes. The rabbit hutch was lying on its side, the ground was covered in blood and the smell was sick and sweet. She wanted to run but she crept closer instead. She could not help it.

The small mangled bodies stared at her accusingly. Their faces still looked so normal, showing no pain. She reached out for them, whispering, 'I am sorry, I am so sorry.'

Caleb turned around, 'Klein mies,' he said, 'klein mies, you shouldn't be here.'

He took her stiff hand and led her back to the kitchen.

'Marta, did you go out?' Mother asked.

Marta could not answer. Mother took her hand from Caleb and sat down with her arm around Marta. All the children were in the kitchen now. Mother spoke.

'Ishmael's mind is ill. Father found him in the rabbit hutch. He had killed all the little rabbits, wrung their necks and then cut them open.'

'No!' Father caught Ben on his way out. 'You'll not go outside.'

'Their hearts were strung along the fence.' Mother told them all in a quiet voice, un-dramatic but not sparing them either. They would soon enough see the mess and the freshly dug earth.

'Why,' Marta cried, 'why?'

'We do not know. That is why he is with Narina and the doctor.'

Marta did not want breakfast. She barely drank her milk and was listless at school. Her classmates left her alone after the first attempt to get her to play only brought a snarl. That was the first time Marta had felt that the inside world was breaking too. The outside world she had known was a broken thing, full of anguish and anger and love and loss – but that the inside world could break too, she would never have guessed. Ishmael's had broken so completely and Narina's, and her own a little in sympathy and guilty loss.

She remembered her own words that had made Ishmael run away – God's grace and words about joy he did not understand. Was this his bad blood, finally? Was this why his grandparents had beaten him? Was this why he had no father?

Dimly she remembered overhearing the conversation between her parents, Narina and the doctor.

'He was brought up very strictly, doctor. He knows right from wrong.'

'Could you explain what you mean by strictly?'

'Well, my parents made sure he knew about sin. Sin and atonement.'

'Sin?'

'Yes, doctor.'

'He is only a child.'

Father had intervened. 'Ellie, his grandmother, took the teaching of my predecessor to heart, doctor. He thought children should atone for the sins of their parents.'

Sin and atonement. Sin and atonement. Sin and atonement. The words repeated in her mind till they lost all meaning and she thought her head would explode. She felt lost in all her worlds that day. Ishmael, who made the world big and strong and fearless, had broken it. And she understood that least of all.

But when she got back, Ishmael was quiet; too quiet. Marta was afraid but she was wrong. The doctor was satisfied with him and when her father did not want to press charges he said he would not notify the police and they would leave it at that.

The adults left the room. Marta sat with Ishmael, watching him as he slept and could not imagine him doing what he had done. It would not go into her head.

'Ishmael,' she called out, wanting him awake, wanting to see him as he had always been.

But Ishmael would not turn and talk to her, would not talk to any of them and the next morning they moved him back to Narina's house so that Jacob could have his room back.

Marta visited him there but Narina thought that it might be better if she stayed away – then he might want to get out.

So she stayed away and listened for his call. None

came. And when she could not wait anymore she ran out to the river and swung over to sit in their cave. There she wondered what she could do to fix this. But she could think of nothing.

Then she heard the call of the loerie. She stiffened with hope, crawled carefully to the cave mouth and searched as hard as she could. But there was no sign of him anywhere. She slumped against the wall. Finally the tears came.

Rain and early evening were drawing icy fingers along the hillside before she came out of the mine without gold. There was something under the fern. She bent to pick it up. It was her mother's old watchcase. Marta picked it up but was too afraid to open it. She ran home, clutching it close.

It was all she had with which to face his silent absence.

FIVE

The months passed. The grass grew over the small
mounds in the garden. Ishmael became quieter than ever
and kept far away from Farleigh, though Narina took
him to the doctor every week. Marta left him for a while,
thinking she might imagine how he felt but not sure how
she would speak to him. Rabbits haunted her sleep still.
But after two months she could not bear it any more. She
copied out Gillespie's poem: 'Airman', folded it carefully
about the loerie feather in its box and left it on his bed in
his mother's house. After that they went to Millwood and
Gouna again. They never spoke about the rabbits.

Ben began school the next year. He hated it so much
and was so often in tears that Ishmael agreed to let
him see the swing and come into the forest with them
occasionally.

Then it was winter again. The path from Farleigh to
the road was cold and misty most mornings when all of
the Reben children walked down to the bus stop together
in the half dark before the sun came up. They walked
quickly and close together to get warmer. The bus lights
were eerie in the mist and half dark. They drove over the
mountain as the sun came up over the sea. As the light
grew, Marta knew they were leaving home-world and
going into the school world and she knew how Ishmael

must have felt stepping into the garden from the forest. The days were still bright after this and the oak trees in George gradually turned bronze and dropped their leaves to reveal their bare essence. The air was sharp-bitter as they drove past Paccaltsdorp and Blanco where people burned what they could for warmth.

When they came home they all sniffed deeply, waiting eagerly for the moment when Father would crouch over the fireplace in the lounge and make the first fire. When they smelled the sweet apple wood burning, they ran up the hill, dropped their bags and huddled happily round the blaze. Mother brought in soup, which just on this one day they were allowed to eat around the fire. This was how Marta loved winter, cold and misty, its mystery spreading in the trees, making the forest strange and fearful. Only Ishmael did not fear the mist, was never lost in it but knew his way in its bewilderment as well as he did on sunny days. But Ishmael was home less and less that winter and Marta felt the world grow dim with his absence in the early winter darkness each evening as she swung over the Homtini River with Ben.

Then things changed at school, too. The school gates which had always stood open all day were now closed at 7:30 when school began and the teachers huddled in anxious groups at break and talked to each other in hushed tones, while the children played games of more than usual aggression: 'border games' they were called. These games were not stopped as Marta's 'steal the treasure' had been.

Republic Day came at the end of May and this year the preparation for it seemed even grander than usual. The choir practiced long and solemn songs. Simon sang a beautiful, sad solo in one, his high bright voice soaring above the others. It made Marta think about Fling and the 'Airman' all over again.

They were waiting for choir practice to begin, sitting in the hall, chatting quietly, when they heard the music teacher arguing with the headmaster.

'But he has the best voice,' they could hear the music teacher say.

'Yes, but we cannot let him sing in our church.'

'But none of the others can sing that descant.'

'Well – we will have to do without. The dominee will not have him in the church, with his missionary family ideas.'

'He is a child. He will sing and only sing,' tried patience rang through the voice.

'He does not belong in our church.'

'Well, Mr. Heyns, why don't you lead the choir then?'

'Don't be preposterous.'

'You're interfering with my work.'

'I am protecting our culture.'

'Our culture? Since when has it needed your protection beyond the rugby field?'

'There is no need to be aggressive, Mr. Liebermann.'

'Well, the rehearsal is yours then.'

Footsteps departed hurriedly and Mr. Heyns came into the school hall alone. He stood a moment, blustering and then opted out.

'Children,' he said, 'there will be no practice today.' Then he spotted Marta and Simon, 'I need to see you two and your sister, now, in my office.'

He turned on his heels without waiting for a response and left again.

The choristers looked at one another, shrugged and went to wait outside the school gates for their parents to fetch them.

Ruth, Simon and Marta walked towards the office.

'Are we being kicked out of the choir?' Simon asked hotly.

'I think so.'

'That is so unfair.'

'Are you going to say so?'

'Yes.'

'You'll get six of the best.'

'I'll take them.'

'I want to see that. You wouldn't say that if you'd ever been caned.'

'Perhaps not.'

Marta looked from one to the other. 'What is the matter?' she asked. 'What is going on?'

'Wait and see,' Ruth soothed her, out of habit.

'Tell me. I am not a baby anymore.'

'They don't want us to sing in their church because we belong to a different one.'

'But we're Christian! Like them!'

'Yes and we've sung in other churches. But apparently we may not sing in the mother church.'

'But it looks so beautiful. I was looking forward to seeing it inside.' Marta thought of the lovely white spire reaching into the sky surrounded by the dark tall cypress trees.

'Well, you can't,' Ruth retorted as they arrived at the door to the principal's office. She knocked.

'Come in!'

They stepped diffidently inside.

'You wanted to see us, Sir.''

'Yes, er–' He shuffled a few papers on his desk, cleared his throat and then stood up, came round his desk and stood before them, looking down with false kindness.

'You do understand,' he began, 'That I cannot let you sing in the mother church on Republic Day, don't you?'

They did not answer. He blundered on, 'You do not belong. We let you attend our school but you cannot come into our church and be part of our service.'

'Yes, Sir,' Ruth whispered, looking down.

Simon looked up angrily and Marta saw tears welling in Ruth's eyes, as she felt her brother's disappointment.

They trooped out. So simply it had happened. Marta could not believe that just like that they had been asked to leave the choir after weeks of practicing.

'Ruth–' Simon began.

'Simon what did you think we could do? He makes the decisions; nothing is going to change his mind. Wait till you've been here as long as I. They are not like Mother and Father. You cannot talk to these people.'

'You could have tried.'

'Why didn't you?'

'You're the eldest, you should have spoken first.'

'That's nonsense. You're the one singing the solo.'

They stared at one another caught in this thing they did not understand, accusing each other because there was no one else to accuse, because there was no one else to fight. Something of this must have dawned on Simon as he broke away from them then, running blindly.

'Simon,' Marta called for him.

'Leave him. He doesn't want us now.'

The sisters walked to the gate where Jacob already stood waiting, having finished orchestra practice early as well. All three sat in silence. Jacob had already heard what had happened from other children and there was nothing that could be said.

Their father was often late because he forgot what time choir and orchestra practices finished. But today it seemed he was especially late. The Reben children sat away from all the others and felt eyes burning holes in their backs. No one spoke.

Finally, everyone else had left and still they sat waiting without Simon. Jacob went to look for him in all the usual places but he came back empty-handed.

Mrs. Swanepoel, the principal's secretary came out to them. 'Could you tell your father when he comes, that Principal Heyns wishes to see him.'

'Yes, ma'am,' they said.

Just then Father's car came around the corner and she could tell him to come with her to the principal's office herself. Something in her tone made Johannes Reben get out of the car at once and follow her. Jacob, Ruth and Marta watched them walk in uncomfortable silence.

He came back with Simon, whose face was a furious cloud, despite his swollen eyes.

No one spoke all the way home.

Simon was sent straight to bed and the others sat about doing their homework in unusual silence. Supper was a tense meal and they did not sing grace but listened to one spoken by their father, who struggled with the words.

The food stuck in their throats and though Mother tried to ask about spelling or Maths lessons, no one managed more than one word at a time. Finally Mother asked Ruth whether she would read the next chapter to everyone in her room. Ruth led them all out of the dining room, where their parents sat in their own awkward silence.

In the morning Simon feigned sickness but his father spoke sternly to him.

'You must face the consequences of what you have done.'

'What did he do?' Marta whispered to Ruth. Her sister shrugged and Mother gave them both warning glances.

'Are you sure this is the best thing,' Mother asked their father as they set out for the bus.

'Yes,' he said.

'Should you not take them today?'

'I don't think there is any need for that. Mr. Heyns has already spoken to me. What more will they do?'

When they got to school, Simon had to go straight to the principal's office.

Once with her classmates, Marta discovered that

there was to be no assembly that morning in the quad. Mr. Heyns was to address the whole school over the intercom as he usually did in the afternoons.

'Why?'

'We don't know. Something really bad has happened.'

They did not need to wait long. As soon as the class was settled in their seats attentively staring up at the small box above the blackboard, Mr. Heyns' crackly voice could be heard.

'School – yesterday our school suffered a terrible onslaught. Somebody, somebody we have allowed into our school despite his difference, tried to set fire to our school.'

There was a disbelieving gasp around the classroom. Their teacher stood up in front and held up her hands – but no one spoke. All wanted to hear the next words.

'He was discovered in a classroom setting fire to the bin.' There was a dramatic pause.

'And this is how we punish those who attack us.' Another pause. 'Come on,' the voice said, 'come on.' They could hear a shuffling noise. A chair was being pushed and then footsteps. Then a swift swipe of the sjambok came down and they heard the stifled whimpers of a child. Again and again the sjambok hissed until the boy was screaming. Finally it stopped.

And Principal Heyns' voice came again, a little breathless this time.

'Now, Simon, apologize to the school.'

Marta froze rigid in her chair as she heard her brother's crying over the school intercom, the screaming and begging still ringing in her ears.

She heard titters from behind her and shot up from her chair and fled to the toilets, where she locked herself in a cubicle.

Her teacher came after a while. 'Marta, I am sorry you had to hear that and I am sorry that was done. I am sorry this school is the way it is. Please come out.'

But Marta would not. 'They laughed,' she said, 'they laughed at him.'

'I know. But it was because they did not know what to do – it was a very strange thing.'

Then she heard other voices, 'Marta, Marta we are sorry we laughed.'

Still she would not emerge until her teacher called Jacob, who came shyly into the girl's toilet while the teacher waited outside.

'Marta, don't let them win. Don't let them see how much they have hurt you.'

'What is Simon doing?'

'Simon is back in class.'

'How can he?'

'How can he not?'

Marta opened the door, came out. Jacob briefly hugged her. 'Never let them win, Sis,' he said fiercely, leading her out. And because he had not said, 'little sis' this time, she went out with him.

Her teacher was there too.

'Thank you, Jacob,' she said as she held out a clean cloth for Marta to wash and dry her face with. She helped Marta retie her plaits, too. As they walked back to class she explained what they were doing so that Marta could do the work without any fuss in class. She handed Marta a small soft ball. 'When it feels like you just have to scream, when it feels too much, you will squeeze this and remember that Simon is back in class, too.'

Marta looked at her gratefully and got through the day. Rochelle leaned over once or twice and showed her which exercise to do next. They smiled awkwardly at each other.

When the bell rang for break her teacher spoke softly to Marta. 'You are very brave, Marta.' But Marta stayed in to tidy the bookshelf.

After school, the bus fell silent as Simon came slowly up the steps with his brothers and sisters. The two front rows had been left free for them. They struggled home from the bus. Simon could barely walk. At home, when they explained what had happened, their mother was speechless, but Father got straight in the car and drove to George to 'have words' with Mr. Heyns. Simon had been unrepentant; they heard their father report to their mother later that evening.

'We will take them all out of thát school. They will never go back. Not one more day.'

'No, Johannes. We will take them out, but they will finish the term. We will not be humiliated again by this.'

'Can you manage that, Simon?'

He nodded as he came through the door.

Simon had been changed by the events of these two days. Marta could see it. His face had lost some of its boyish roundness and his shoulders seemed wider, straighter than before.

His father stood up and said to him then, 'I am sorry, Simon. I did not know they would treat you in that way. I did not imagine such things were still possible.'

Ruth and Marta took it in turns to fill towels with new ice for Simon to sit on.

They went back to school till the end of the year. Decisions had been made but not one of them wanted anyone at school to get one more moment of triumph out of Simon's humiliation. No one dared to speak to them about it and in assemblies they each made a point of staring at the headmaster so hard, with such an air of interest and facile obedience that he faltered repeatedly in his addresses to the school but could say nothing.

They were model pupils with a deliberation that made it a mockery and they did so without agreement but with a concerted effort that was stronger than anything else

Marta had ever felt in her family – a drawing together in adversity, which made her feel almost invincible. This was how Ishmael had made Marta feel at times. The other children at school, sensing something of this, drew away from them. Without a word two camps were drawn up.

But on Republic Day Mother would not let them go to school. And when the school phoned to ask about their absence, she told them they had eaten something bad and were all sick. The school may well have been relieved not to have the Reben children in that day. They sat about feeling bad about the lie their mother had told for them, feeling anger at the school and relief at not having to be there. On the radio they could hear the voices of politicians raised and crowds cheering and then the singing of the anthem. The day passed quietly but Marta sensed a new restlessness in it. There was no sign of Ishmael, though it was nearly week end. In the afternoon she and Ben could take it no more and went for a long walk across the Homtini and into Gouna forest. But it was not the same. The people who were turning the mine into a museum were there and the two children had to be careful. They kept away from the paths and with the noise of the people they were surprised when suddenly they heard the warning call of the loerie.

Marta held Ben's arm.

'What is it?' he asked.

'Danger,' she told him, 'or elephants.' She drew him towards a wild pear tree and they both climbed it. Marta looked carefully around and breathed deep to catch any smells at all but all she could sense was the smell of trees being chopped and the old engines being oiled.

After a while they climbed down. They walked home via Kom Se Pad, where they found elephant dung.

'See! What did I tell you?'

He looked at her with shining eyes.

'They are still here, Marta.'

'Yes, they are.'

'It's like Christmas,' Ben said.

Marta nodded, but she missed Ishmael.

In June they went back and faced the last three weeks of term. School was now filled with days in which the army came and the headmaster and the history teachers seemed bigger than usual and walked with a heavier tread about the school. Everyone would be marched into the quad and would stand in silence and be harangued for hours in words Marta did not understand, and then they were taken to the sports fields and in class groups were shown hand grenades and how to defuse them – to hold them close to your body until you were out in the open and then to throw them far away and fling yourself flat on the ground and let it go off, far away from other people.

The evacuation drills were disturbing and frightening too. The teachers put on a front of calm which silenced the children, except the triplets who continued a tradition of tears. They struggled so with everything life threw at them because they did not understand. For them, each of these moments was real danger and it often felt like real danger to Marta too. Masses of children moved out to the sports field in silence, flinging themselves down on the far end of the rugby field, full of dubbeltjies and blackjacks at the edges, which took a long time to remove from their white school socks in the afternoons.

The siren went again in the middle of Maths one day.

'Put down your pencils,' Ms Naude said calmly to the children but already Marta could see the lips of the triplets wobbling. 'Hold each other by the hand,' she commanded them and took the one closest to her. 'Stay close.'

They went out onto the crowded veranda of the school. It was so full of silence that it hurt Marta's ears, with only the sound of school shoes walking carefully and quickly. It was more unsettling than the quiet in the forest before a storm. But she smiled at the triplets, who had stopped crying now that everyone was walking.

'It is just a practice,' she said to them, as she had heard Mrs. Naude say many times when they could not settle down.

Another teacher overheard her. '*Just* a practice,' he hissed at her. 'It is a practice that could save your life. And you will never know when it is not a practice. Danger lurks everywhere, little girl, and the best you can do is follow orders.'

'Yes, sir,' she said. 'And keep calm?'

'You're a Reben, aren't you?' he asked.

The triplets were crying loudly now and the teacher had the grace to look embarrassed as Mrs. Naude came up and hurried them on. Marta felt furious and was glad when Mrs. Naude put her arms around the girls while she jogged with Piet to their designated collection point on the rugby field.

Marta sensed the teachers' fear beneath these exercises. She spoke to Ruth about it but Ruth had no answers. She said only that they were practicing for attacks by the 'swart gevaaar', which Simon scoffed at and Jacob left the table to go and work in his room, alone, where one could actually concentrate, he said.

Then one day Simon and Jacob came home with army uniforms. They smelled, so Mother washed them twice before she would let them into the wardrobes.

'Why have you got those?' Marta eyed the dark shapes on the washing line while they were doing homework at the table on the veranda.

'They make us practice now for being in the army.'

'In the army?'

'Being soldiers.'

'Will you be soldiers?'

'Every boy has to be,' put in Ruth.

'Why?'

'We are a country under siege,' she quoted, turning back to her books.

Marta stared at her brothers. She could not imagine them like the man who had come to tell them about the grenades.

'When will you practice?'

'Every Wednesday.'

'What will you do?'

Jacob said, 'We'll see,' but Simon snorted angrily.

'Father said to keep the peace,' Jacob said warningly.

On Wednesday, assembly looked strange in the quad because the boys were all in their khaki uniforms, their legs covered in goose pimples in the cold wind and their black berets rolled into their shoulder straps.

Many of the girls giggled and stared at the boys. But Marta was determined to invent a reason to get out of class, and slip to the field. She wanted to see what they would do.

So, when after break she saw them all file out to the athletics track, she asked whether she might leave the room. Her teacher answered irritably, 'It's just been break.'

Marta hung her head humbly. 'I know. I am sorry.'

But she was allowed. She ran quickly out to the gravel road behind the fields and came through a hole in the fence to the back of the stands. She crawled underneath and found herself a spot under the stands from which she could watch them.

They marched without music. They marched and were yelled at and then they marched again. They were quite stupid about it. They got it wrong a lot. Marta soon got bored. She was about to leave when suddenly she heard the sergeant's voice raised, almost to squeaking.

She stopped and sank back onto her knees to watch.

A boy, she could not see who it was, was standing in

front of all the others and the sergeant was shouting at him

'What did you say?'

She could not hear his answer.

Nor could the sergeant because he yelled his question again, louder.

Another boy stepped forward and answered more loudly, looking up into the sergeant's face this time.

Something about the way he stood made Marta think it was Jacob, and she realised the first must be Simon.

The sergeant stood stock still for a moment. Then he exploded.

'Do you see that tree, at the far end of the field?' he asked them both.

They looked at each other and nodded.

'Do you see that tree?' he roared at them. This time Marta could hear their answer.

'Yes, sir.'

'Fetch me a leaf.' He pointed at the tree.

They ran. Then they slowed to walk because after that they had to fetch another leaf and then do press-ups.

Finally Marta crept away. She knew she would not tell anyone ever that she had seen that, least of all her brothers. She felt ashamed and knew they would feel it too but did not know why.

On Saturday evening there was a knock on their kitchen door.

'Marta, will you get that please?' Mother was making supper and Marta was helping. She went to the door and there stood Bomani, his face a rigid mask.

'What is it, Bomani?'

Mieta, his mother, stepped from behind him.

'Marta, can we see your mother, please? And your father.'

'Father's not yet back, but Mother is here.'

Marta called out to her mother but she was already behind her, wiping her hands.

'Bomani, Mrs. Mbulawa, come in. What is it?'

'They came again, Mrs. Reben, they came again. And we don't know where Joseph is, so they did this.'

Mieta turned Bomani around and lifted his shirt.

Marta slipped round to see.

Bomani's back was dark with bruises and there were raised welts from his shoulder down to his waist, where the trousers were now aggravating them.

Mother did not flinch and her eyes briefly warned Marta to stay calm. She asked Marta to get a bowl of clean water, a cloth from the cupboard in the hall and the arnica lotion from the bathroom cabinet.

Marta did it all silently, determined to be like her mother in this.

While she worked, Mother, who had given the bowl to Mieta and had asked Marta to make tea, asked what had happened. Her voice was calm, though her eyes kept flitting to the window to look out for Father's return.

They dressed Bomani's back and he endured all with a stony face. Not one tear. Marta admired him, though he felt like a stranger.

Then he had eaten the soup and bread he was given and they sat more companionably at the kitchen table, reading the comics in the newspaper and waiting.

And Father, when he came home and heard what had happened, had gone into Fingo and Tembulethu. He tracked for three days the devious route by which people disappeared and phoned and waited outside offices. He had been patient, brought biltong, had pleaded and bullied and finally found that Joseph had been taken and charged with growing dagga and disturbing the peace, after he had been found at the school where a meeting of 'dissidents' was being held. There, evening classes were teaching things they should not and people gathering in groups of more than three had been forbidden.

Marta did not understand much of this but she knew

the anger she felt whenever she thought of Bomani's back.

The police came to Farleigh again. Marta saw them arrive as she was sitting on the edge of the dam with Ben, chatting and practicing pebble hopping across the water. They glanced at each other, got up and circled round to get to the back door where Ruth was making tea in the kitchen.

'Why are you making tea?'

'Because Father asked me to.'

'For them?'

'Yes.'

'They beat Bomani.'

'I know, and Father knows. He is talking to them. Now go and play.' She was trying to sound like Mother.

Instead, they sat anxiously in Ben's room and waited. Father did not come to talk to them when the police finally left, or to Mother. He went out.

At supper he was quiet and it took all weekend to lift the shadow from the house.

In all this time there was not a word or sign from Ishmael. Narina said she thought he was staying with some friends in Paccaltsdorp but her eyes told Marta she did not know and that it tore at her every day and that she went back to her empty cottage full of fear.

Not long after Bomani's back had been tended in the kitchen – when their own winter holidays were about to begin but they were still at school – there was news of a big happening. All day news trickled through of a huge gathering of black youths, marching to the Orlando stadium, shouting slogans and holding placards ('Down with Afrikaans'), marching and singing, until the police opened fire and then there had been chaos. Marta listened with the others to the sounds of gunfire, screaming, shouting and the newsreader's high excited voice, faster even than a sports commentator, telling of violence and police trying to keep order. But it was hard to tell amidst the screaming what he was actually saying.

'What is it, Father?' Marta asked. 'What is going on?'

'The black school children in the north are rebelling against Bantu Education.'

The voice on the new television which sat like a black eye most days, silent in the corner of the lounge, spoke of a rising tide. As Marta watched those children running, crying and shouting with raised fists or with arms shielding their heads, she knew suddenly that they were the sea too and that each one had a sea inside them. Her fear of the children's running and screaming was gone and she could not take her eyes off them.

She dreamed that night of a wind from the sea on which these children flew to engulf her school. It was like Fling and the first meeting with the sea together.

Two days later Marta heard Ishmael's call in the afternoon. She left her homework and ran round the back of the house to find him in the forest.

'Ishmael, where have you been? I've missed you.'

But he was staring at her coldly. 'Oh, did you then?'

'Yes, where have you been?'

'Never mind,' he said importantly. 'What have you been doing?' he asked to distract her.

She told him then about Simon but he looked at her scornfully. 'You think that matters? Compared to the things going on here now? There are children in detention, police detention, getting beatings like that every day. Simon's beating is nothing compared to that.'

'No,' she said humbly, thinking again of Bomani's bruised dark back and Joseph's beaten face, when they finally released him on bail – and then her brother's. 'I suppose not.'

Then he told her that he was going to Port Elizabeth, where they were 'doing something' rather than 'taking it'.

'Your mother won't let you,' Marta countered fearfully.

'My mother? Oh, she'll let me – the old people have nothing to say to us. They let all this happen. They are weak and have no pride.'

He did not sound like himself at all.

'Who told you all this?' She tried to bring her Ishmael back.

'People, who know.' He was refusing to be drawn out.

She tried another approach. 'How will you live there?'

'My cousins live there. They will take me in, we will do something together. They are planning a big march and boycott, just like they did in the north.'

She could picture the news of a few nights ago: the chaos, the sound of gunfire, the children screaming, the many feet running, as the singing became fainter. She was not sure she understood it really. She knew that the children were fighting unfairness the way Simon had tried to, but bigger, much, much bigger and she knew that everything was very dangerous and people were restless and afraid and angry.

For the next few days she wandered about the house, feeling lost and afraid. She wondered what she could do.

Simon had been angry and thrown up his head and said, 'How can we sit here and do nothing while they – look at them Father – they are fighting it?'

'While you live in my house, Simon, you will do as I say. Violence is not acceptable and your mother will never forgive me for bringing her out here if you are hurt in this conflict, this hopeless struggle of a David against a Goliath. This is not just a battle here but also between America and Russia; and there will be no hope for anyone when they become more actively involved.'

Marta had stared at their angry faces locked onto each

other. On Sunday Father had preached about becoming like children, praying for the families of Orlando and there had been once again an uneasy peace between them all. Mother had said to him afterwards in the kitchen when they thought no one was about, 'You will be in trouble for even mentioning it, you never know who is spying on us again – and your brother's work in the Cape is no help.'

'No,' her father said humbly, 'it is no help, but what else do you expect him to do?'

'I know, I know. But it all makes me so afraid.'

When Marta saw Ishmael again, she only asked, 'do you know your cousins?' She was afraid of never seeing him again.

'It doesn't matter. This is big. This is the biggest thing I can throw.'

'What do you mean?'

'We're throwing the government.'

Marta looked at Ishmael standing before her as he had stood on the cliff with Fling. He looked big and fierce to her.

But she remembered also her parents' conversation and asked how it was possible.

'You white people don't understand,' he said.

It was the first time he had ever called her white and the shock of it stung but she only dropped her gaze. 'No, I don't understand. Will you speak to your mother?'

'Will you tell her for me?'

Then she knew why he had called for her and she left him, angry and lost.

Every night her father came home, his shoulders hunched more tensely and his eyes darker; he told of another child who had disappeared and more people in the parish who had been 'detained'. Every time she heard that word, Marta saw again Bomani's back and

Ishmael's wild eyes, saying he would fling something bigger than the old tree.

And then one evening, her parents sat them all down round the table in the dining room and said that Ruth would be going to Germany for a year when she had finished school. Marta was stunned. How could that be? And she was afraid for Ruth, who cried as her parents spoke.

In the morning, she spoke to Narina about it, about how small Ruth looked and how she would manage all on her own in a different country far away from them all. Narina said there were two kinds of people in the world, those that made people feel bigger and those that made people smaller and that Ruth was about to find out what kind she was.

'Ishmael is one of the big people, isn't he, Narina?'

Narina turned and looked at the anxious girl beside her as she did the dishes.

'He makes everything big, Narina – even I feel big and brave with him. He is being brave out there, now isn't he?'

'I don't know,' Narina sighed. 'I am afraid he is getting into more trouble.'

'Do you think we will see him again soon?'

'I don't know. My brother has not sent word. I don't even know that he has got there yet.'

'How long has it been?'

'About four weeks.' They were both silent.

'I would know,' Marta said then, putting her hand on Narina's arm for a short while. 'I would know if something happened to Ishmael.'

'You?'

'The loerie would call.'

They finished the dishes together and Marta walked Narina as far as the gate. She did not tell her of the dark hole in her heart every time she thought of Ishmael.

When they stopped at the gate, they saw a light flickering through the trees from Narina's cottage. 'Ishmael,' they both knew it. They ran towards her house.

And there he was: a strange sight. He was taller than Marta remembered him and dirty and fierce as he never had been. He had always kept himself so clean. Marta stopped and held back, remembering his last words to her.

But Narina stepped forward, 'Ishmael, you cannot light a fire in the middle of the forest like this.'

'Why not, Mother?' His voice was ugly as she had never heard it before. 'Why not?'

'The trees,' she faltered, 'the animals, you will disturb–'

He kicked the fire and burning branches rolled dangerously out of the reach of the fireplace. The dry leaves began to blaze.

'They matter, do they, Mother?' His voice was a hoarse scream.

'Yes.'

'Well I don't care,' he said. 'I don't care. The forest can go to hell, everyone can go to hell.' He reached down and picked up a blazing branch, brandishing it wildly.

'How are your cousins?' his mother asked softly.

He laughed a shrill high laugh. 'My cousins? My cousins? They are no family of mine they tell me. Bastard, they called me, bastard and mongrel. They would not take me in.' His arm dropped now. 'They said I should get help from my white father, as you did.' His eyes were as fierce and burning as the flames they reflected.

Jacob, Simon and Caleb worked several hours to stop the fire. In the morning Father suggested that Ishmael should go to his brother's mission station up north for a while. New surroundings might be good, might take his mind off things and get him focused on his schoolwork a little. Narina was willing to try. She took him up. Marta was not allowed to go, having her own new school to start. And Narina never spoke of it. She came back and for a while it was as if Ishmael had never existed.

Marta swung alone on the frayed rope over the Homtini and wandered long in Gouna forest. She listened for the loerie but she did not call. Finally, she sank down near the foot of the big tree and whispered, 'Elephants, you know him, you know everything, please take care of him. Don't let them get him and do to him what they did to Bomani. Make him come back.'

She hoped the loerie would answer but the forest was silent and gloomy. She went home.

'Where you have been?' Ruth asked her as soon as she came in.

'Out,' Marta said shortly.

'Well, we've been looking for you. We are all going somewhere.'

'I don't feel like going anywhere.'

'I don't think you'll be asked. It's quite an event.' Ruth pushed her gently towards the bathroom.

They drove all the way to Knysna and stopped outside the museum. Father struggled to find parking, but eventually he joined them.

'Quite full?' Mother asked her husband with a smile, leaning on Jacob's shoulder.

'Yes,' he said, taking her arm and walking into the building with her.

Marta watched them. 'Was Mother ill?' she wondered but the thought was soon pushed from her mind.

The foyer of the museum was full of people drinking wine and toasting each other's health. Knysna had finally opened a branch of the wildlife society and they would protect the elephants now. Marta stood rooted before a large poster, which told her so.

Protect the elephants? They needed protecting?

She turned and searched in the crowd for Jacob. He had gone out into the museum garden and was standing under a tree there, talking to the curator, whom she knew from school visits, and another person she did not know.

Marta slipped out and stood next to Jacob. She said nothing, knowing that he knew she was there, knowing he would speak to her when he was ready.

'So I could come in this holiday and do some work with the wildlife society on the elephants?'

'We always need observers. And someone who knows the forest well would be very welcome.'

'When could I start?'

'Come see me when school's out.'

'Thanks.'

'What is it, Marta?' Jacob asked when they had walked a little bit away from the others.

'Why do the elephants need protecting?'

'Because there are so few of them left.'

'I thought they could do everything. They have powers. They are invisible and are kings of the forest.'

'Marta, all those things are beliefs about the animals. The truth is that they are a nearly extinct species and we have a duty to protect them as the last free elephants, maybe in the world.'

It was incomprehensible. How would the elephants protect Ishmael, if they needed help from Jacob?

SIX

Not long after the last term at the old school had begun, there was news of Ishmael. The police were looking for him. He had run away from their uncle's mission. Marta once again overheard her mother in conversation, this time with Narina. She rarely listened to the conversations of adults now – they were complicated and did not yield much understanding of things. But this time she heard Ishmael's name and hoped to get some news of his return.

'Narina, you know that Ishmael is not settling in the Transvaal.'

'Yes, Nkosikazi, I hear he has been trouble.'

'Well, yes. My brother wants to return him to us, before the police get involved.'

'What will I do with him now?'

'What about his father?'

There was a long pause and Marta could hear the sharp intake of breath from Narina. She herself was shocked – she rarely thought of Ishmael as having a father. He was Narina's and the forest's. She listened more sharply, all guilt about eavesdropping forgotten in the interest of the story she was hearing.

'Should you not ask for his support, his advice?'

There was no answer, so Mother went on: 'Simon, Marta and Ben are starting at a new school after the summer; they could all make a fresh start together.' Her mother paused and then took a quick breath, 'Some of the private schools are accepting colored and black children now: Bracken Hills is one of them. So it is not as if it would seem unusual. No one could point fingers.'

'Yes, Nkosikazi, I hear the church schools are taking a stand against Bantu education.'

'Well, there you are then, it seems to be lying in the hands of a higher power. This way he could help keep an eye on him ... discreetly.'

'I don't think he'll do it.'

'But he should.'

'It is too complicated. He will be afraid of gossip, he will be afraid of hurting his family.'

'Isn't it a bit late for that? Is not now the time for atoning for the hurt he dealt you . . . and for dealing with the results of what happened?'

'He won't.'

'I don't understand. Why are you so sure?'

'Nkosi . . .' Narina began and Marta wondered at the weariness in her voice, 'it is a bad day when you realise that you have risked everything for a coward.'

'That's a strong word, Narina.'

'Yes.'

'It was a big thing he was risking, too.'

'Yes. His and mine.'

Her mother gave in. 'You're right. He should not have started what he was not prepared to finish. But perhaps he has had time to think?'

'He told me,' Narina's voice faltered, 'he told me that the best he was capable of now either way was guilt.'

'That must be a terrible place to come to.'

'He has chosen his path.'

'Chosen?'

'Yes. There is always choice – to think otherwise is to lie to yourself.'

There was a pause and then Narina's voice sounded more like her own again.

'And anyway, there is no money for that kind of thing.'

'We would find the money . . . and there are scholarships.'

'For Ishmael?'

There was no answer to the question.

'I shall speak to Johannes about it.'

'Thank you, Nkosikazi.'

Marta returned to her room and began doodling listlessly in her scrapbook, while images of Ishmael and policemen kept flashing through her mind. She suddenly wondered whether this was what it meant in the Bible when it said Mary stored these things in her heart. She did not know and there was no one she could ask.

A few weeks later, their cousins from the north came to stay and said they would bring Ishmael back with them. Marta waited all day for them to arrive. They were late and then very late; Marta could sense her parents' anxiety. At last there was a phone call and such a mixture of relief and concern between her parents that Marta finally crept away and hid in the old oak tree in the courtyard while more phone calls were made. She waited and watched.

When they did arrive she was afraid to greet them. She watched as one cousin after another clambered out of the Combi – but no Ishmael. Marta climbed out of the tree and went to the doorway as everyone filed in.

'Where is he?'

Father put his arm around her and took her back out into the garden. They sat together on the bench.

'He ran away, your uncle said, around Middleburg.'

'Will he ever come back?'

'Well, we have told the police . . .'

'Will he be in trouble?'

'No, they'll bring him here.'

'If they find him.'

'Yes.'

But when the tumult began and nine children filled the house and garden at Farleigh, there were times when even Marta forgot that Ishmael was still not home.

Breakfast could no longer be eaten in the dining room and was moved out to the verandah, and on sunny days even under the oak tree. They sang grace with a full choir and the house and garden were a sprawl of children all day. They all invaded the river and the forest now. Simon and Jacob had mud fights with Fritz and made rafts for Marta, Lily and the small boys, who went on adventures up and down the Homtini. They found crabs and small frogs and had their own mud fights when they scrambled down the slope to the deep river and saw what the older boys were doing. Only now and then Marta would stop and look longingly at the far side or strain her ears over the noise of her cousins for the loerie call of Ishmael.

He was the reason for the phone call and for the late arrival, she knew. But there had been no further calls, no news from the police, though she asked before breakfast every morning and though Father phoned, visited, searched and phoned again.

Narina and Marta watched him leave one morning.

'Why did he not come with my cousins?' Marta asked.

Narina smiled anxiously. 'I don't know.'

'And he has not yet come home?'

'No. When they find him he will go to the forest to live with his grandfather again.'

That made Marta suspect something was wrong. So one afternoon when the games were quiet and indoors because a storm was brewing and the mist was rolling in, she crept away and made her way to Narina's house. She called softly and there was no reply. But something twitched at the window.

'Ishmael,' she said. 'Ishmael,' she repeated as she opened the door softly.

It took a while for her eyes to adjust to the darkness and she stood outlined in the grey light of the door for a moment. A stone came whistling out of the dark and struck her on the chest. It stung and she nearly cried out but this rough greeting could only come from him and tears would only drive him, laughing scornfully, away.

'What was that for?' Anger was better; he countered that rather than running away.

'You're intruding.'

'I came to find you.'

'I'm here.'

'Why haven't you come to say hallo?'

'You're busy.'

'Yes, but you could have told me you were back.'

'I was told to leave you alone.'

'Who would do such a . . .' she began and then decided not to care. 'Fine – leave me alone then.'

He caved in so quickly, she knew at once he was lonely, too. 'No one is supposed to know I ran away.'

Instantly his stone-throwing was forgiven. He was the most interesting person she knew and she allowed him everything. She pretended not to know already and it was different talking to him about it, not just hearing it from adults.

'You ran away? I thought my uncle brought you back?'

'He brought me some of the way … but the car was loud and full of your cousins.'

'Yes.'

'I walked from Middlesburg.'

'That's a long way, I think.'

'Yes.'

'Come,' she said. 'Let's go out into the forest. The storm is making me restless.'

He looked at her. 'We need to be in the Kalander when it breaks. In the Transvaal there are many storms, I was out in them often. I have made friends with them.'

She was full of admiration for his bravery again, for his indomitable spirit, which walked all the way from Middlesburg and did not give up, which defied her uncle, her fierce, large uncle.

In her mind she heard again Ishmael's wail of despair when they told him he was leaving the forest. She had known that Ishmael could not live in a place without the forest and the loerie and the possibility of elephants. Ishmael belonged with trees.

They reached the big tree just as the storm began. They climbed into its branches, though they were soaked and though Marta knew this was a foolish and dangerous thing to do. But it was exhilarating to outface the storm, after being sensible for so long, to watch it hurl its white hot anger into the forest in forked bolts of light, magnificent balls of brightness. They were too swift to touch but she would never forget having seen them, knowing their power and laughing with it. All the while the sky roared.

They yelled back at the loaded sky from the tree tops, watching the lightning snake down and explode in white balls of fierce light.

'Look,' Ishmael called to her, as steam rose from the hot trees. 'The ancestors are coming out to scold the sky for its noise.'

They laughed, shaking the stinging drops out of their eyes, and waited for the storm to end.

Marta was late for supper that day but it did not matter so much, for she hugged within herself the secret beauty of the lightning. She had missed the boys' puppet theatre show and she minded, but not as much as she had minded Ishmael being lost.

His return made each day difficult again, full of choices because Ishmael would not join in anything the others did. And her cousins did not mention him, did not seem to miss him. Gradually Marta realised from half-heard snatches of conversations that he had been placed with one of the farming families. That he had bunked school and been beaten, called bastard and bushman and had run away. It had taken their uncle weeks to find him in the bush up there, weeks he could not afford to waste. He had also got involved in 'politics' again, she heard her uncle say at supper one day. The adults looked at each other meaningfully as they said that phrase. The words had a darkness all of their own which swirled about the air after they had been said. Marta felt her back tingle and she wished she were back in the forest.

Marta tried to divide her time equally between her cousins and Ishmael. Sometimes she wished he would just play with the others too. But then she watched how his back stiffened when her cousins came near his home and their voices could be heard, watched his eyes grow wide as he instinctively went on the alert. He was just like the forest animals, always alert, always on the lookout for danger.

One day when they were walking in Millwood, Marta was enjoying the silence, not having to talk – Lily did talk an awful lot – when she stumbled and fell to her hands and knees. She found herself looking into a softly rippled round print of an elephant foot.

'Ishmael,' she whispered. 'Ishmael, look.'

He crouched down next to her and traced his finger softly round the spoor. 'They're here.'

Then he began searching the ground all around. 'Let's find them, follow them, and see how they live.'

Above them in the trees a loerie began her clucking and gurgling.

Ishmael paused in his search to look up at the sound. 'I know. I am not afraid.'

But the loerie did not stop; her calls became more urgent and her hops more ungainly, before she swung heavily from the branch and flew away still clucking loudly.

Ishmael followed the disturbance of her noisy flight with his eyes a while and then said, 'We'll go this way – they'll be here.'

Marta followed without question, her heart beating in her throat and her knees prickling as they took slow, painfully cautious steps.

Then they heard it – the rumbling of huge stomachs.

Marta clutched Ishmael's shoulder just in front of her.

'We've found them,' she whispered.

'And now we had better find a tree.'

They chose a wild pear tree and climbed swiftly up into the wide branches. Despite the half-fearful excitement, Marta felt the rough bark under her hands and the small stinging whips of the twigs in her face with relief. Lily's tame games could never compare to the forest or to Ishmael. Only once they were several meters up did Ishmael allow them to begin looking for the grey giants. They peered carefully down through the leaves and branches and Marta struggled to see in the brighter light up in the trees, looking down on the twilit world of the forest floor. Gradually, her eyes adjusted and she found the grey patches amongst the green and brown. She caught her breath as she began to make out their shapes, the bony curve of their backs, the huge Africa of their ears flapping attentively as their thickly muscled trunks tore branches from the trees and swung the leaves into their mouths.

There were three. They watched them, in silent awe for a while until Marta whispered, 'They are the holy family of the elephants.'

'What?' Ishmael hissed in irritation. At that the elephants trumpeted in alarm, the big one swinging his trunk and sending a warning ringing out across the forest before they made off, tearing through the underbrush in alarm – away from the intruders and into the thick and ancient forest.

'Now look what you did!'

'It wasn't me,' she began but he had already begun climbing down.

'Are we following them again?'

'No point now. You'd better go home.'

'Shall we meet again tomorrow?' she enquired timidly.

'Two o'clock at the swing.'

She agreed meekly, knowing that her voice had sent the elephants away.

Ishmael scowled when she arrived, later than they had agreed.

'White people never keep their promises.'

'Don't call me white.'

'Why not – you are, aren't you?'

'Does it matter?'

'Yes,' he said brutally. 'It will always matter.'

'Why?'

'White people don't understand!'

Knowing the comforts of her life compared to his, she did not argue but allowed him his tyrannical hold on the moral high-ground. Still, she wondered why he needed to hurt her for it.

She knew it was something to do with her family: how no matter what she did she belonged to them and was safe with them even when they were cross with her,

Ishmael belonged only to himself. Narina tried but he was not hers in the way Marta belonged to her mother. Narina knew that and Marta knew how it hurt both of them to feel that distance, though not one of them had words for it.

Ishmael had learnt to swagger about his 'independence', his freedom, not having a mother who nagged him, he said, as he watched Marta run inside when she was called. Narina tried to nag him, tried to own him and be responsible for him but she could not manage it. Marta knew that everyone was afraid of him, even his mother.

Christmas time arrived again and gradually Marta was drawn more and more into her enlarged family. They practiced carols and poems for Christmas Eve and they worked on making presents, counting on their fingers how many were needed. On Christmas Eve afternoon when they should all be resting while Mother, Father, Uncle and Aunt decorated the tree and laid out the crib and the gifts in the lounge, Marta was frantically thinking she had forgotten someone. There were sixteen of them but she only had fifteen presents. She had made, at great cost to her fingertips, little needlework people for her aunt, mother, older sister and girl cousins and had made desk toys for her father, uncle and the older boys. For the younger cousins, she and Ben had made a ginger bread house together.

She was deliberating softly with Ben whom she might have left out.

Suddenly Ben's face brightened. 'It's you,' he called out triumphantly, 'it's you, you're number sixteen and you don't need a present for yourself.'

Marta felt stupid and grateful all at once. 'Of course. Thanks Ben.'

'Anytime,' he said and she did not mind the smug voice today.

Evening fell at last. The children were sent to the bath in twos by their smiling, insistent mothers. The two eldest stood sentinel outside the bathroom, calling time for each pair as they went in.

Marta stepped out of the bath, clutched her thin towel and ran along to her room where she found a freshly starched pink Sunday dress and sandals laid out under the neatly made bed.

She slipped it on and felt the new seams scratch her ribs and the hem irritate her knees, but today she would bear it. Today was Holy Night.

She was practicing the lines for her song in the nativity play, in her head, till Ruth interrupted by reminding her to put her recorder with all the others' instruments. Then she was picturing the fingering for the shepherd's march she was to play with Simon and Ben, after church for her parents.

But before any of that would matter, there was the service at Farleigh church. It was crowded and hot in church as always and it smelled of the packed-mud floor, freshly sprinkled to keep the dust down, and the crowding bodies. The church was soon full of small children giggling and squirming, too shy to talk to Marta or Ben on such a big occasion. The older ones were nowhere to be seen. The choir stood dressed in red at the back. The whole two front rows had been kept empty for them while everyone else crowded into the other benches. The blackboard had been cleaned and was standing to one side, the teacher's desk was covered with a white cloth and green runner and two tall white candles burned in the fierce sunlight. A multitude of garden flowers filled the church with an overwhelmingly sweet scent. The Christmas tree was magnificent, almost invisible beneath the tinsel and colored streamers made by the nursery children.

Narina stood quietly with the choir at the back,

betraying no recognition of the Rebens at this ritually important moment. Then suddenly the singing began and everyone in the church rose to their feet. The children came in, some walking with staffs and tea towels on their heads, others crawling, baaing enthusiastically and giggling as sheep. From a side door Mary and Joseph appeared, holding in their arms a doll, carefully wrapped in swaddling clothes. There was no familiar head of long curls amongst the sheep or shepherds, nor was there a tall green-eyed king from the orient. Marta felt her heart constrict and looked over at Narina, who was singing and seemed to all others entirely absorbed in the service. But Marta saw the tight corners around her eyes; eyes that so resolutely did not look for a son who was not there.

Afterwards there was the ceremonial handing out of gifts by Marta's father. Marta, like her siblings and cousins, now began to slump on the uncomfortable stiff bench. She tried to see who got the dolls that she had chosen this year to give away before Christmas. But now the farewells had been said and she was impatient now for the rest of Christmas and did not want to sit here and think about where Ishmael might be.

She managed to slip along the rows in the tumult and get to Narina, who shook her head at her and only said quietly, 'You know he does not like Christmas. Or crowds.'

'I thought perhaps now that he has been away from it, he'd like it better.'

'No, it has not made him any better.'

Looking about the busy church, Marta knew she could never understand that part of Ishmael. Christmas was happy and beautiful, and more so every year.

They drove through the soft evening air towards the Hoekwil German church, singing in a full choir in both cars. The small white church looked graceful and brave on the hillside, welcoming them all, through its dark wooden doors, to its carpeted serene stillness. Father kept his sermon brief to leave room for their nativity play and by the time they got to Bethlehem at the altar it was dark and the candles shone brightly now and the tree looked alive, as the Kalander had in the storm. The entire world seemed lovely and at peace in the red glow. Even the Christmas lights on the main street, along which Father drove, looked entirely holy. The mountain smiled at them, Marta thought, as they turned towards it, driving home.

Once home, Ruth helped Mother and Aunt Sarah to bring out the sandwiches and the ice-cream and everyone ate and felt quieter. Finally the doors to Christmas were ready to be opened. Father checked that all were present, waited for everyone to fall silent and only then opened the door. There stood Mother and Aunt, their smiling eyes reflecting tiny trees of light. Behind them on tables and boxes around the room lay the small piles of gifts for each one.

Uncle read the prophecy from Micah from the Bible again in German and they sang, softly at first and then swelling as each of them realized that it was truly Christmas at last.

Each child was led to their table of gifts and was lost for a moment in that bounty, delighted and turning only briefly now and again to smile their thanks at their parents. At some point it became time to rush off to their own rooms to fetch their gifts for everyone else and hand them out. Eventually they all sat down to watch the last Christmas tree candles burn down and the one who had correctly guessed the last candle to go out, poured drinks for everyone while Ben and Joe fell asleep under the table and Marta's eyes sagged.

Just at that moment when the world seemed whole

and safe and all manner of things were well, Marta
caught sight of a white glimmer at the window. She was
instantly alert and knew that it was Ishmael and that he
was in trouble. She stiffened and Ruth, who she had been
leaning against, asked what the matter was.

'Nothing,' she said. 'I just need the loo.'

She ran to the back door and called again and again.
She ran to the gate at the back leading to Narina's home.
Then she stopped and listened, calming herself and
straining her ears and yes, she could hear a faint sobbing
amongst the trees.

Marta walked to the gate, putting one hand on it
to climb over. It creaked and she stilled, knowing her
father's sharp ear for such things. Satisfied she had not
been heard, she climbed over, ripping the hem of her
new pink dress. She barely noticed, intent on following
the sound.

She found Ishmael curled into a ball, tighter than she
had ever seen anyone curled.

'Ishmael,' she whispered, 'what is it? What is it?'

But the only response was a dry, terrible sobbing.

Marta sat beside the crying boy and did not know
what to do. She was afraid if she called for help he
would disappear and she thought that this time it might
be forever.

So she sat there, her small hand on the thin, heaving
shoulder and waited for him, saying his name softly over
and over to herself.

As he quieted she found herself talking to him about
the trees. She half sang their litany of names for him, as
Narina had told them to Ben and Marta when they were
very small.

'The Kalander knows where you are tonight, the Vlier
and the Witels are whispering for you and the Kersboom
is waiting for you and the Kamassie will laugh again
with you tomorrow.'

When he finally turned his face to her she could just make out in the moonlight that it was smeared black with ash, she thought from the smell, and something else. His hair felt sticky where his hands had raked it.

'Happy Christmas,' she said to him softly so that he would know she said it only to give him time to collect his breath. 'Where have you been? We missed you at church.' she asked.

He looked at her. 'I cannot tell you.'

'Ishmael.' In her mind she saw again the chaos in the hutch.

'Marta,' he cried. 'Marta, I will never be able to tell you anything again. They will take me away. Goodbye Marta. Goodbye!'

But he did not move.

'Ishmael, what did you do?'

'I went to my father's house.'

'Your father? But–'

'I know who my father is. Your father told me.'

Marta stared at him and did not know what to say.

'Why didn't you tell me?'

'You were busy, you were happy.'

'Yes, but . . .'

'And your father and my mother told me I should go to his school and start again but that I must never expect him to know me as his child.'

'Ishmael, that's–'

'So I went to his house. I thought though he will not know me at school, perhaps he will know me on Christmas. I knocked on his door. He let me in. He spoke to me, he was gentle and quiet. But then his wife came in and she told me I had no right coming there. She called me names.'

'And your father?'

'He just stood there and did nothing. He was ashamed of me.'

'What did you do?' Marta kept her voice calm as Ishmael himself had taught her to be calm around wild and disturbed creatures.

'I left when he showed me the door and then I waited.'

'Waited? For what?'

'I waited till they had all gone to bed. He came out once more but it was only to pet his dog, to give it a treat before he turned off the lights. That dog got his love, got a treat for Christmas, Marta.'

The intensity of his voice shocked her now and she was afraid of what would come.

'And then I took a piece of wire, opened the garage and … and set their car on fire.'

'Didn't the dog stop you?'

'The dog? No.'

And then Marta knew what it was that made his hands and face sticky, knew that smell again, sickly sweet and rotting already in the warm night. She saw the mangled bodies of the rabbits.

'Ishmael,' she cried now, 'Ishmael what will we do now? Why?'

'He loved his dog, he loved his dog.'

Just then she heard Father's voice. 'Marta, Marta where are you? Bedtime.'

She sat stock still and listened without moving.

Ishmael, with an agonized cry, scrambled up and ran crashing into the forest, while Father found her.

'Marta,' was all he said when he found her.

'Father, I . . .'

'I know,' he said, 'I know,' and he pulled her gently up and with his arm around her, led her into the house, into the kitchen where Mother was.

Without a word her mother took her quietly into a bathroom.

Jacob was there. He said at once, 'I will fetch her nightie, Mother,' and was gone. He handed it through the door.

Marta saw her pink dress lying on the floor, felt the warm water as her mother washed the blood from her hands and arms and face. She did not cry, only sat and watched the brown swirling into the water and then away, down the drain, to the darkness beyond. The drain suddenly frightened her with its greedy gulping sounds and she clung to her mother.

Finally she asked. 'What will happen to Ishmael now?'

'I don't know. Your father has gone to wait with Narina and Solomon.'

'Is no one looking for him?'

'Marta, what good would that do? Who can find Ishmael in the forest? Not even you can. The forest is his best chance of finding his right mind again tonight.'

'Yes.'

'Mother, may I put one of the candles in the window for him tonight?'

'Of course.'

She lay in bed and watched the nightlight in the window. Ben was already asleep and Ruth popped her head in on her way to bed.

'Goodnight, Marta.'

'Goodnight.'

Jacob came and sat on the side of her bed softly.

'Hey, littleness.'

'Jacob, he is all alone.'

'Yes, but I think he needs to be, don't you? Would you not want to be alone, if you had done what he did? And he is in the forest; the forest has always been there and knows many things. The forest will hold him tonight.'

'Yes, he will go to the Kalander,' she said half to herself.

'Which . . .'

'You said he needed to be alone.'

'Yes, I did. Let the forest hold him tonight then, littleness, and sleep yourself.'

'And in the morning?'

'We will have to wait for it to arrive.' He looked at her rigid body, her huge eyes.

'Come; I'll stay with you until you fall asleep.'

In the morning the police arrived just after the slow Christmas breakfast to which everyone – for once – was allowed to appear gradually, still in pajamas, and nibble bits of Christmas cake as they sipped their coffee or Milo. Marta looked about the table and noticed that Jacob was not there.

'Where's Jacob?'

'He has gone for a walk,' Mother said steadily so that Marta would know not to ask more now.

Their aunt and uncle were looking uncomfortable. Marta wondered what they had thought in the months when they had had responsibility for Ishmael. None of the cousins were up yet, she noticed.

When the knock came, Father said to Mother, 'Anita, I think . . . get Marta dressed and ready.'

Marta spilled her Milo, which she was cupping in her tired hands as the events of the previous evening came flooding back.

'Johannes, must she?'

'If we hope for anything from them, we must cooperate, Anita.' His voice was gentle but steely.

Marta knew he was afraid, too and somehow that made things better.

And she said, 'Mother it is fine, I will speak to these people but I will not help them find Ishmael.' She looked fiercely at Father.

'You need not do that. Just tell them what happened last night.'

So when she was ready she told them. They were kind to her and spoke quietly and gently.

They were sterner with Father and as she watched those big hands writing in their small notebooks, struggling with the ungainliness of having to write on their knees, she almost laughed. Father did not clear table space for them in his office, where they sat and Mother brought them tea. They asked questions with their mouths full of rusk.

Finally came the question Marta dreaded. 'Where do you think he is now?'

'We do not know,' Father answered

'And you?'

Marta only shook her head and held his gaze steadily.

Just then, Marta looked out the window and saw Jacob coming back towards the house. He stopped, breathless and perplexed when he saw the police car standing with Father's truck and their cousins' urban car.

He glanced at the house and then went round and came in by another way.

'He knows,' Marta thought, 'he knows and he has seen Ishmael,' and she burned with impatience to go to him, to know.

But she hid her feelings from the police who finally wished them once again a Merry Christmas, though their voices did not mean it. They were angry to be out working.

'Where are they going now?' she asked her father.

'I will show them the way to Narina's house.'

She ran off to find Jacob in the kitchen alone with their mother.

'Where is he?'

'He was at the Kalander. He had spent the night in the tree.'

'And . . .?'

'And he was calmer.'

She nearly asked if she could go and see him but remembered that if she asked and was forbidden she would have to go against her parents' will. Just doing it was slightly better.

So she only said, 'Thank you, Jacob.' and collected a few things quietly and unobtrusively in the busy house, where cousins were now surfacing.

Just as she stepped out of the door, her mother caught her by the sleeve.

'Marta, you are not going.'

'But–'

'No, Marta. Narina has gone to him, she will do what is needed and you cannot do more now.'

Marta pictured the scene: Narina looking for him, calling perhaps, or would she know not to call? Yes, she would know. She would find him at last, still sitting with his back against the tree. She would give him the biscuits she had brought and the cold potato and piece of meat. He would eat them ravenously. In the morning light, would his mother still see the traces of ash and blood on his face and hands and all over his clothes?

'Come on, wash yourself,' she would say, offering him a cloth, which Marta knew she would have brought.

It wrung her heart to have to stay, to have to wait.

Would the police know? Would Solomon lead them to Ishmael? She knew the answer.

The silent forest could not help.

PART II

SEVEN

That is where it felt like things ended.

Marta sat in the courtroom far from Ishmael, unable to
reach him, unable even to speak to him. The shrill voice
of Mrs. Stander accused him of arson and attempted
murder, her eyes blazing with hatred for all of them. No
new-found father came to his defense, or even attended
the trial. Ishmael stood through it all, looking as small
as he had looked in the garden that first day, shoulders
hunched in futile protection from the blows that were
raining down on him, from words he barely understood.
Words *she* barely understood. What then, she wondered,
did he hear in them, standing with his head bowed in the
unbearable humming whiteness of the fluorescent lights?

Father, Narina and Solomon were up in front with the
witnesses who had been called during the week as the
trial had progressed. Narina was as bowed and small as
Ishmael and she winced every time Mrs. Stander spoke,
and would not look up. Ishmael's eyes burned with tears
he would not shed. Father tried to shield Narina and her
son alike but was helpless in the face of the judge who
was so sure of the law, so sure that this child, whose very
existence was a sin, needed correction.

It was Jacob who held Marta's hand as she sat in that frightening room with the old and rusty fans churning slowly in the sluggish January heat. She was not able to see the whole trial, for school had started again and her mother had insisted that she go; it was the beginning of the English school and she should not miss those important early days. Jacob took her. She felt lost all over again, as she had when she had started school several years ago, but it mattered less because of what hung over Ishmael.

'Where will he go this time, Father?' Simon asked one day in the car coming home from school. 'Can you send him to the Transvaal again?'

'I don't think so. They will probably send him to a reformatory.'

The word froze her spine, even in the brooding heat.

'What is that?'

'It is a school for boys who have committed crimes and can no longer go to ordinary school.'

'You mean a prison.'

'In a way – but it is also a school.'

'He won't be allowed out into the forest?'

'No.'

'Then it is more prison than school.'

'Yes.'

'And he will have to live there all the time, every day?'

'Yes.'

'And every night?'

'Yes.'

'There will be guards?'

'And teachers.'

'I don't think that will make it better for Ishmael.'

'No.'

'Will I be able to visit him?'

'We will see.'

With the outcome predetermined, Ishmael went to Tokai Reformatory for Colored Boys in Cape Town and though it was closer than Lydenburg had been, Marta knew that he would be in a different world entirely. She helped Narina pack his few belongings and slipped amongst them, unnoticed, the dark blue box containing the shimmering feather. She felt as if she would never see it, or him, again.

Month followed month – without Ishmael. Every time Marta walked to the Kalander, she looked for his face amongst the leaves. At Dolphin's Point she found only Fling's sad carcass and the drop to the sea was empty without Ishmael's laugh. Finally she stopped looking – stopped listening. But she still wondered where he was and what he was doing. No news came; no letters – not even a police report; and it was as if a door had simply closed.

Marta's family tried to be kind but she could sense, or thought she could, a relief that Ishmael's 'influence' was gone. She seethed in silence because no one spoke of it. Not Narina, not her parents and certainly not her brothers and sisters. The silence grew like ivy on stone walls.

Everyone was absorbed in surviving English school and preparing Ruth for her year in Germany. She was going to see Uncle Toby and family again (their mission station had been closed during Ishmael's trial and they were 'back' in Germany) and stay with one of Father's sisters, attend a music school, and 'find her feet in the real world'.

'What world do we live in here?' Marta asked her sister when she told her that.

'Well, this is just South Africa, isn't it?' Ruth had answered hesitantly, 'It's not part of Europe, where world history happens.' This made no sense to Marta, so Ruth finished with, 'I think Father and Mother just mean learn to live on my own more independently.'

'But you'll be with Aunt and Uncle?'

'Yes.'

'How is that independent, then?' Marta felt that there was far too much change happening already; she did not want Ruth to leave. Not having Ishmael or her cousins around was hard enough.

'We all have to grow up, Marta,' Ruth said, but her voice trembled and Marta stopped asking questions and hugged her instead.

Early one morning they were all woken up long before dawn to say goodbye to Father and Ruth. Father was taking Ruth to the airport in Cape Town; he would come back without her. Mother cried when she thought the others could not see her and the house was bereft. Marta was glad to get to the bus stop and pretend normalcy. The new school still felt nearly as strange as it had on the first day.

The first day at the new school had failed to convince Marta that things would be any better there. She felt lost as soon as Mother and Father left her and Ben at the gate to walk in 'as unobtrusively as possible' in the uncomfortably stiff green uniform. She could tell the children were greeting each other after the long holiday and crowding before lists to see whose class they were in but she could not understand them at all. She had learnt one or two words of English but they had taken flight with the rest of her senses during the events of Christmas, which overtook her again in the stream of children pulling her into a strange building.

She looked at Ben's face, stiff with containing his fright, too. She decided to take action, sure that like her he would have forgotten the small bits of English they had practiced last night. She managed to get herself jostled to the front of the board and found first her own and then Ben's name, as well as the numbers of the rooms they should be in.

'What about assembly?' Ben asked nervously.

'I don't know – but all these others are going to their room numbers.'

She took him to his room. 'Stay here – or at least stay with these kids, so that you don't get lost. I will find you here at break,' she promised, before diving back into the stream of children to find her own room number.

She wondered how Simon was getting on at the high school. And Jacob too. It was strange to think of him so big now – in matric, ready to finish school, like Ruth. It seemed such a long way off. She planted herself with a bravado she did not feel outside door number 11.

A bell rang shrilly and a harried looking teacher clip-clopped quickly along the corridor and paused to balance a precarious pile of books as she unlocked the door.

Marta was a muddle of indecision. She wanted to offer help but did not know how to say so in English.

Once in the classroom, Marta felt a little more at ease. Things were familiar; there were desks in double rows and the teacher's desk at the front with a faded blue carpet near it. On the boards around the classroom were cheerful bright posters and the blackboard was a perfect, smooth green, while several unbroken pieces of chalk lay in its trough. The smell of school was the same: no softening smell of sap in trees, of wood chips and leaves quietly decomposing in the sun, no far away whiff of sea in the closed room. Martha's shoulders hunched and her eyes grew bigger, drinking in the light, waiting anxiously, hoping to see things before they came to her – not to be taken by surprise. She knew that was how the creatures of the forest survived.

Her name was read out. She put up her hand and managed a strangled yes but found no pointing hand to tell her where to sit. Instead the teacher was clearly asking her something, but Marta could only stare at her mutely and shake her head. She watched the look of irritation flit across the teacher's face and felt the old familiar band of darkness tighten round her chest.

It was the start of the year, so all twenty-eight children waited till their names were called, before sitting down in the place assigned them.

Marta found herself next to a girl called Andrea and was amazed at her pretty pencil case and the variety of materials within. She wondered what they were all for. But various children had now been assigned tasks and were handing out a bewildering number of books to be named and have subjects written on them, as well as the obligatory pencil, eraser and ruler from the government. The teacher also took in the school fees, which went away with a lady who came back with important green slips, which she knew had to be returned to her mother, who would keep it in the beautiful silver box with the embossed cathedral on it, which still smelled faintly of lebkuchen.

Marta had to keep track of what Andrea was doing so that she penciled the right subjects onto each book in preparation for their being covered with brown paper and plastic that evening. Then the bell rang again and everyone sat stock still, looking expectantly at the dark-haired teacher whose name was Mrs. Henderson, Marta now knew. She smiled approvingly at the silence and then allowed them to get their lunches out and stand quietly next to their desks as they waited to be dismissed into break row by row. Before she dismissed their row, Mrs. Henderson spoke to Andrea, who rolled her eyes secretly but said 'Yes' and then jerked her head at Marta and they went out together.

'Rock Spider,' someone hissed as they went by.

'Boertjie,' another voice joined in the corridors.

Andrea scowled at them and they went away.

'Can't you speak any English?'

'I can – a small amount.' Marta answered in Afrikaans.

Andrea smiled condescendingly and followed this with a stream of words Marta did not understand. So she smiled and said only:

'My brother,' showing the corridor where she knew Ben would be waiting.

Andrea nodded and then ducked out a side door. But Marta had spotted Ben and did not mind.

'Ben,' she called, 'Ben!'

He turned and his face lit up.

'Let's get outside.'

They found a lucky bean tree and settled down amongst its roots to eat their sandwiches and compare notes about their classes. They decided for school it was not too bad.

'What is a Rock Spider?' Ben asked.

'I think it is what they call Afrikaans people.'

'But we're not . . .'

'I know, but how would they know the difference?'

The bell called them back into classes and they scrambled, not wanting to be late so soon.

Lessons were torture for Marta that late morning. The teacher kept trying to ask her questions, smiling encouragingly and then shaking her head in despair when Marta only stared at her in incomprehension.

This went on for several days before she kept Marta back one day and introduced her to Mrs. Bruce, who would come to fetch her for 'special lessons' once a day.

Marta was proud to understand that much. The special lessons took place in a cozy room at the end of one corridor and involved a doll's house, puppets and huge cards with picture stories. Ben came, as well as several other children who also never answered questions in class. Mrs. Bruce was lively and laughed a lot. She understood Ben and Marta and allowed them to explain themselves as best they could, telling them the English words quickly and gently as they spoke.

Ben and Marta were coming along fine they heard Mrs. Bruce tell Mrs. Henderson.

'Soon they'll be back in their normal lessons.'

'Nothing wrong with them, just overwhelmed by the language change,' was the verdict. 'They'll soon catch up.'

And they did.

One day towards the middle of her fourth week at the school, Marta was summoned from class. She did not know why she had been called but quietly followed the older girl, who walked with long, confident steps along the school corridors. Marta wondered whether she would ever feel that self-assured around a school building. She was taken across a quad and through a dark set of doors, where things smelled unmistakably of gym and Marta grew anxious that she had been called to do PE. Indeed, before them was a sports hall, and within boys were climbing ropes and rungs along the wall. Marta could hear somebody shouting encouragement. Mercifully they did not go in there but turned instead towards two doors in a dark corridor. The older student knocked respectfully but not fearfully, and Marta could just hear a voice telling them to enter.

They went in and were almost blinded by the bright sunshine in the room. They stood a while blinking before they could make out the small round woman sitting on a chair next to a black upright piano, shiny and new.

'Marta,' the small white-haired round woman said. 'Are you ready to begin piano lessons?'

'Yes, I think so.' Marta managed, staring mesmerized at her halo of white-blond hair, as her tongue forgot to stumble on the English.

'Thank you, Amanda,' the piano teacher said and the older girl left.

Marta sat down at the piano as directed and listened to the first instructions. She had longed to play the piano as well as Ruth could and played dutifully the notes she was shown.

At the end Ms. le Cordier played a light and tripping tune which made Marta think of Sunday mornings at Farleigh. When she had finished, she turned smiling to the rapt child.

'Soon we will have you play that.'

'Oh, I hope so,' Marta breathed fervently. And then she knew things would be all right at the new school. No matter what else happened, if this room was here, she would manage.

Ben had piano lessons too, though with Mrs. Chapman in the other room. But they both joined the advanced recorder group. The music rooms became more than lesson rooms. This was where a group of them began to hang out. Here they came and experimented with the various instruments, made dreadful noises on the electronic keyboard, or practised the music they were preparing for Arts Festivals or concerts or exams. Ben and Marta felt at home with these children who, like them, felt a little lost on the playground and preferred the library or the music rooms.

Most importantly, they were permitted to sing in concerts and perform their exams in the vast darkness of the Anglican Church. Simon, Ben and Marta were even asked to join the Anglican Church choir, which was run by the school's choirmaster. Simon's eyes shone with delight each day as they made their way to the church after school.

Outside the church stood a group of adults and boys; white and black and colored. All of them were chatting easily, sharing jokes and telling off the small boys who were playing football on the lawn in front of the church. The three Rebens stood a little shyly to one side. The other choir members asked them their names and welcomed them but did not press them with any other questions, allowing them time to get their bearings. At last Mr. Barry's bright yellow Mazda drove up and he leapt from the car, apologizing for his lateness and scattering pieces of music as he hurried to unlock the sacristy door for their rehearsal. Everyone hurried up the stairs into the choir stalls and collected their music.

'Leonard, would you make sure these three get a stall each and some music?' Mr. Barry asked one of the older gentlemen, who herded the three Rebens into the church and showed them each their place in the choir stalls. They picked up 'their' music like all the others and hurried downstairs into the crypt, where they were shown to their seats in the right voice-sections.

The rehearsal moved quickly and expertly through an entire Mass. Marta found reading the psalms difficult at first but then Joyce, one of the experienced choristers, showed her how the notation fitted with the words and things improved.

Simon was grimacing a little in the tenor section. He found it hard not to sing the melody anymore and struggled with a voice which was not yet fully in his command again.

It was a strange and lovely place to be singing in, though, and on the way home all three were unusually quiet, their minds filled still with the sound of the plain chant and the echoing stones of the old church.

On Sunday they were asked to sing in the Mass and, as it was much earlier than Father's service at Farleigh, they were allowed to go. They arrived early as instructed and were fitted with robes by Joyce but not given the white collars all the others had as they were still on probation.

'What does that mean?' Ben asked Marta, wary of strangers as always.

'It means they have a chance to change their minds about us.' she replied, as worried as he.

Leonard came to the rescue and explained that, if after six weeks they still wanted to be in the choir, they would make a commitment before the congregation and Father Rupert would put the white collars on them – then they would be full choristers.

The Rebens looked at each other.

'Will Father mind?' Ben asked.

'We'll have to ask him.'

The robes smelled of incense and Marta felt a tremor of awe as they lined up outside the church in order, ready to process in with the altar boys, the censer and Father Rupert. In their hands they held the red hymnals, which smelt old and sacred with years of lying on the dark wood of the choir stalls.

They gathered at the back of the church behind the christening font and waited for the service to start. As the first notes sounded from the organ, the congregation rose to its feet and the choir began to proceed slowly up the aisle, singing within the clouds of incense left by the altar boys, who seemed transformed from mischievous to angelic all at once.

It was strange and different after the simplicity of her father's church, though Mr. Barry played the organ with the same devotion Father had. Here they sang in robes and tiny bells were rung while everyone knelt for communion. Marta learnt to genuflect and cross herself and became so used to it that she felt impious forever after whenever the three names were invoked and she did not – though it earned her frowns at times, back in her father's church at Farleigh.

When the fog of sound at school cleared a little and resolved itself into words and comprehensibility, and the letters on the board and in books began to make some sense, Marta found herself enthralled by the 'whispering of wind in silver birches', of lessons in poetry. Just as the mist swirling in the forest lost its power to scare when the trees took on their own shapes and stood familiar in their names, so she found her way now in this new language.

Poetry was what she had been looking for. English words were suddenly more than merely words; they transformed the things they named and made them radiant with meaning, briefly incandescent, like fireflies. It was Schiller's joy, coming home again in a strange tongue. She read on and on, hoping, always hoping for such moments. They were rare but when they came they were like treasures glowing in the dark. They were Ishmael's Fling – phrases that burst free across a blue and kindly sky. Marta heard music in her head then. Music from which no one was shut out as they had been; before Simon tried to set fire to the school, before Ishmael killed animals and the government killed children. And at this new school she was permitted to join that music, was part of it in every way.

The tilting earth found its balance again. Marta began to find it easier to breathe, though she could not help listening to the high song of the wind in the trees, hoping it carried Ishmael's call.

The world turned out to be entirely more than she had ever dreamed possible. She learnt about Mesopotamia, about cuneiform script, about civilizations so ancient they were hard to imagine, but remnants of which could be pored over in the dim light of the library. She learnt how people – how life – had changed since, how the glory and horror of the crusades had gradually become the great magnificence that was the Italian Renaissance.

Gerald, one of the noisy boys in the class, asked belligerently why they should have to learn about people long dead in faraway places, who had nothing to do with them and could help them not in the slightest in their lives now.

Marta knew she would never forget the answer their teacher gave: that they needed to know that this small town of George was not all there was to the world. That they, their culture, had come here from a great tradition of knowledge and learning, of science and art, that they were part of the Great Western tradition and that they should always guard against forgetting the work of their ancestors: that the best way to maintain civilization was to know and care for it. To learn it and not to lose sight of who you were and where in the world you belonged.

Mr. Berg was almost misty-eyed at this point. Then he became very serious as he turned to the children. Here in sub-Saharan Africa, he told them, they were so far away from all that, from true civilization. And, more specifically, in South Africa they; this school, the universities, the libraries, constituted the last outpost of bringing this light into darkest Africa – everywhere else, that mission had been abandoned. England, France and Portugal had abandoned their posts here.

'We are the last hope of civilization in Africa!' he finished on a triumphant note.

The children were impressed. Even if they did not quite grasp his meaning, his deep voice, positively vibrating with emotion and passion, stirred something within them all. And for the rest of that day they learned a little more eagerly.

A while later, Mr. Berg came into class with several large cardboard cylinders in his arms; and would not tell them what they were.

'Wait,' he said, 'wait and see.'

Marta gave herself a crick in her neck trying to crane from her desk to an angle at which she might peer inside. Mr. Berg laughed and said nothing but soldiered on through long division. History was after break.

Mr. Berg dismissed them all but did not lock the class as usual and go to the staffroom; he stayed behind in the classroom.

Break seemed stupidly long that day but at last the bell rang. They filed back into the room and looked for the blackboard which was invisible under the yellow and ancient maps that had been hung in front of it. The class stared at it. They had never seen anything like it before. Then the questions (and comments) erupted.

'What is that, sir?'

'It looks more like Geography, sir. You must be in the wrong class!'

'What is it, sir!'

'*Where* is it?' Marta asked.

But once again they got only that same infuriating answer. 'Wait and see.'

He began explaining about Marco Polo who lived in Venice but explored the Far East, where he met and befriended the feared Genghis Khan. Mr. Berg took a red string from his pocket and asked Marta to hold one end over Venice while he unrolled it all along the shoreline of the Mediterranean and let it find its way to China, as he told them the story of the great adventurer. The class was silent now, and in that silence Mr. Berg walked back to his desk and took out small dark jars, which he said they should pass about the class and smell,

'What is it this time, sir?' Gerald asked cautiously.

'Spices from the East.' Each one held the jars reverently one by one and smelled in them a world in which cinnamon, cloves and frankincense grew, a world which smelled always of Christmas.

The class sat in enchanted wonder. And for weeks afterwards the game in the pool was Marco Polo and there were map-coloring competitions for his routes, the excitement over which was overcome only by that of projects on Michelangelo and the Sistine Chapel.

Marta was gratifyingly proud now that her parents
had come directly from Europe, and as such were a
part of all that magnificence, and so when she played
Bach on the piano, she too belonged to that world, a
little tiny bit. When Mr. Berg explained to the class that
her parents' part in the missionary work meant that the
wonder and beauty could come to Africa as well, it made
her proud, too.

Mr. Berg had gone on, explaining that Africa had
so little cultural beauty of its own. It needed, he said,
culture from Europe, to match with music and art the
natural beauty of this empty continent.

Marta remembered stories Bomani had told her of
his father's days as a herd boy, singing the cattle home
to their byre, praising them, knowing their life depended
on each other and singing to them, for them, about them,
celebrating that miracle of belonging together. Marta
had known that was like their hymn before breakfast on
Sunday mornings, that singing together made joy and
safety and beauty.

Mr. Berg could not answer her question about
Bomani and Solomon's stories and songs. He explained
instead that she did not understand the important
differences between Bach and a farm boy's singing.
She resolved to ask her mother about it but before she
could, something happened, which placed all else in the
background.

Marta, Simon and Ben came home to find only Narina
there.

'Where's Mother?' Ben asked.

'She's in hospital.'

'What?'

'What happened?'

'Why?'

'When will she be back?'

Narina held up her hands to stem the onslaught of questions and met their wide eyes with her own. 'She fell and couldn't get up; she was in a lot of pain. Your father took her in. He'll be back shortly with news. Try not to worry.'

No one felt like lunch.

'She said to do your homework and chores as usual,' said Narina. 'She doesn't want any idleness while she's away.'

They tried to smile at that.

'A fall's not so bad.' Ben said.

But Marta remembered now how tired their mother often looked. How she seemed to have gone out less and less recently for her walks. How she sang less and fell asleep in her chair in the evenings.

Father came home late in the evening and explained that Mother would need to stay in hospital for a while. That she would first need an operation and then radiotherapy.

'What are we going to do now?' Ben's voice was small.

Marta was glad he had asked. Like him, she looked expectantly at her father and older brothers.

'We will do,' her father said, after a while, 'what we always do. We will go on.'

'Yes,' Jacob joined him, 'and that means, Marta, please finish the dishes. Ben, help her to dry and put them away. And then, Marta,' he added before she could complain, 'you need to practice your piece for the Arts Festival, don't you?'

'Yes,' she sighed. It was a difficult piece by Bartok and playing it note by note, perfecting bar by tedious bar, occupied the remainder of her evening.

As she said goodnight to her father, she asked softly, 'What about Ruth?'

'I have spoken to her,' he said.

'Will she come home?'

'There is no need for that yet.'

But Mother was not able to see a single one of their several performances in the Arts Festival. Father did try to record them on the old tape recorder they used to make choir tapes to send to their grandparents, back in Germany, every year. In hospital, as Mother listened with tear-bright eyes to the distorted and crackling sounds of their tunes above the coughing and shuffling of the audience, Marta finally found the courage to tell her how her solo had gone wrong.

The house felt dark and gloomy even in Sunday's midday sun then, as they all set out for the hospital to visit Mother. They sat anxiously about her bed, not knowing what to say to this new person who lay on the bed, pale and thin. This person who smiled at them, who had no instructions for them, did not chivvy about homework or clothes on the floor or remind of practice required. She listened hungrily to news of their new schools and promised to be home soon.

But their father's eyes remained anxious. He drove them to school in the mornings in silence and was never late to fetch them, when they drove straight from school to the afternoon visiting time. Their mother lay in a gaudily cheerful room with pink floral curtains that floated against the green walls softly in the breeze as the smell of the forest drifted in on the sea-winds.

The holidays came again and Mother came home but she was installed now in a separate bedroom downstairs and she spent most of her time in that part of the house. Narina now chided after homework and clothes on the floor when she came in from Farleigh Nursery School. Their mother spent more time sitting in the living room listening, with a yearning face, to music and tapes of people reading aloud from books which came from the library for the blind in Grahamstown, for she became exhausted so easily and found even reading strenuous.

So much changed and no one spoke about it – Father, and Mother too, continued in a strained normality, which Marta found stifling. Ruth stayed in Germany with an uncle they did not even know and learned a little about the world, studying music at the conservatory there. It was odd not to have her about and hear her quiet instructions as one practiced piano, or her soft curses over Maths at the kitchen table, late into the night. Jacob was now the eldest and undertook his role with infuriating seriousness, commanding a regime from them all. Marta and Ben only avoided this by keeping away from the house as much as possible.

They took to playing Marco Polo along the Homtini River, or went on crusades or pioneered the American West. Sometimes they swung over the river and went for long walks, discussing everything from school to Mother's illness.

Ben looked at Marta in the middle of one such voyage.

'Is this more than agriculture, then?'

'What do you mean?'

'Us – talking about life and books and everything.'

'What do you mean: more than agriculture?'

'Well, you know Marc and them at school; they're always telling me that the only culture a farmer knows is agriculture, just like the Boere. That farmers are barbaric.'

Marta thought again about what Mr. Berg had said.

'Why did they tell you that?'

'Because I knew an Afrikaans song in class music today.'

Marta had no answer to this, so that evening she asked her mother:

'How do you know that you are civilized?'

'Civilized?'

'Not barbaric.'

'You don't know it – until you are tested.'

'Tested? How?'

Mother told her about life in the war and how people lost their civilized humanity in desperation, by forgetting exactly those things that Marta was learning from books and music about how to live.

'And what is the link between music and books and art and being kind?' Marta asked.

'That, I do not know. I only know that when I hear it, I want to be kind and do great and good things,' her mother replied gently.

Jacob joined in then. 'When I read Tolstoy I know what nobility is.'

'But knowing the right kind of music – does that make one kind?' Ben put in.

'No, not automatically . . . for some of us it helps,' Mother said slowly.

Then Mother told them of her older brother who hated the Russians for what they had done to her family home and to her father, who had died when the Russians invaded.

'He sees only the horror of what the soldiers did, the war-crazed monsters who sawed our piano in half in order to loot it, who tore books to burn for fuel as we were herded into a corner, shivering and afraid and far from the fire of our own books.'

'That was barbaric.'

Mother nodded and went on: 'But then once we were on the run there was a soldier, an enemy soldier, who searched for hours and risked his life to get my mother milk for our baby sister. You see, how you treat an enemy determines how civilized you are, how you treat the weak. Not what language you speak, or what wine you drink, or which songs you sing.'

She was exhausted after such a long speech and Father came to chase Marta, Jacob and Ben. 'Out! Enough for now,' he said, 'enough. Your mother needs her rest.'

Jacob, Simon, Marta and Ben continued the conversation long into the night. Finally Jacob said, 'What school calls culture, then, is like the teaching of the ancestors for Bosman and Solomon.'

Simon said thoughtfully. 'The wisdom of the past.'

That sounded about right to Marta 'But what is the difference?' she wondered.

E I G H T

Ever since he had spent his first holiday helping out at
the Conservation Society, Jacob had begun to spend
more and more time in the forest. Soon after Mother
was well enough to come home, he let up on 'watching'
Marta and Ben and went back to helping the foresters.
Marta hardly ever went into the forest anymore but one
day Jacob asked her to walk with him. Walking about
with him was so different from the way walking with
Ishmael had been – with Ishmael the forest was magical
and powerful; with Jacob it seemed fragile, delicate.
Jacob had taken to tracking elephants. On walks he
would stop suddenly, sniff the air and say, 'Is that the
smell? Is that it?'

Marta couldn't tell. She had never told anyone about
finding the elephants with Ishmael and resented Jacob
finding them too. All the same, Jacob knew where to
look on the trees, to spot where strips had been taken by
passing elephants – just like Ishmael.

'How do you know all this about elephants and the
forest?'

'Solomon's been teaching me.'

'Solomon? Narina's father?'

'Yes, shall we go and see him?'

She agreed, though she wasn't sure. She was still afraid of the old man, whose stories were always shrouded in violence and horror: frontier wars or the cattle killing were always fresh on his tongue. She now knew that he was not old enough to have experienced them himself, but told these stories because he seemed to enjoy their reactions. Jacob did not mind the old man's strange sense of fun but for Marta it would always remind her of Ishmael's pain.

On Sunday after church, they set out up the hill on their bicycles. It was a long ride but it was a clear winter's day: the forest was still, the air crisp and the rain holding off. So they cycled comfortably till they could cycle no more and then they pushed their mounts until they got to Solomon's small house. It looked as if it had been quite neglected since Ellie's death all those years ago, when Ishmael had first come to live with his mother and the Rebens.

They leaned their bicycles against the candlewood tree, brushed the twigs and dry leaves from their clothes and then knocked on the door. There was no answer.

'Are you sure he knows we're coming?'

'Yes.'

'Knock again.'

Still no answer.

Jacob put his hand on the door handle and pushed gently.

'Hallo, Solomon, it's Jacob and Marta.'

But the small house was empty.

Marta sat down on the threshold of Solomon's door. 'What do we do now?'

Jacob stepped carefully into the house, examined something inside and then came up behind her.

'Get up,' he said.

His voice was so preoccupied and without his usual big brother tone that she obeyed without protest. Jacob stepped carefully over the place where she had been

150

sitting, his shoulders hunched forward and his eyes on the ground. He was searching for something and kept himself very still. Then he leapt forward a bit.

'Here, come on, Marta,' he said. 'Solomon has left us a trail. He wants me to follow him.'

Marta, whose mind had suddenly filled with memories of Ishmael she wished she could shake, followed her brother. It was a very different brother from the one she had known before. Before, his tall gangly form had been awkward and perpetually getting in his own way. He had always been bumping into things, dropping things, getting bruised. Now he seemed to walk as if he belonged to the earth – the way Ishmael walked. Marta was glad for her brother and followed him, recognizing the signs of tracking in him. He seemed, as far as she could tell, good at it: alert eyes scanned the square-meter of forest before him, quickly spotting not only prints on the ground but crumpled ferns and bent twigs higher up too. He seemed to have forgotten Marta's presence, entirely absorbed in the task. Finally he clucked and muttered, 'The old man is getting careless,' as he picked a brown thread from the rough bark of a candle tree.

They came upon Solomon, sitting with his back against a witels, looking up into the sky, wrists resting on his knees. He was smiling and contented as Marta had never seen him before, remembering him largely from rows with Ishmael. This was a different Solomon, she could see.

He turned his face towards them when Jacob called his name softly and said, 'Well done.' Jacob put his hands in his pockets and leaned against the tree.

'It was nothing,' he said.

'What are you doing out here?'

'This was the tree.'

'*The* tree?'

'Yes, the tree.'

'What are you talking about?'

'Tell her. Tell her the whole story again, Solomon.'

Jacob and Marta found comfortable places to sit while Solomon poured himself some tea from his old battered thermos. When they were all three ready, he began.

'I was just a lightie, then – but I remember it as if it was yesterday.'

'What?' Marta asked.

'Shhh,' Jacob admonished her.

'The last great, bigfeet, er, elephant hunt in the Knysna forest,' Solomon said. Marta could feel the old dislike of naming the giants by their real name in him.

'I know who the bigfeet are,' she said.

'Yes,' Solomon acknowledged her help, 'Yes, it was a big, big day here in the forest. Major Pretorius had got permission to shoot just one more for a museum in Cape Town and he made a day of it.

'It was a cold winter morning when we gathered. The sea-clouds were still clearing from the forest on the mountainsides. Ag, the trees looked sorrowful and their leaves wept mist – as if they knew what would happen that day.'

'They knew,' Marta breathed, sure of it.

'I had to make breakfast for all the white people who had gathered to watch. The major liked to show off to the ladies, so he had a big breakfast arranged at the camp. We were up long before dawn tending fires, frying bacon and making coffee.

'I had looked carefully at the major's gun the night before; I had never seen such a big gun before, or one that worked so smoothly. I watched my father clean it.

'Then everyone set off. I was with all the beaters, though I was supposed to stay behind and tidy up camp. But no one paid much attention to one small boy in the excitement and drama of women twirling their parasols at the major and the men readying their express elephant rifles,' he rushed the words together, 'and pretending to know the forest, the bigfeet and tracking all at once.

'Of course, it was my father and the other beaters who really found the herd. They were grazing in Goana's morning sun. Then I heard the loerie call. But almost none of the cows looked up or even paused. They should have listened to her warning. Man, they should have listened.'

'Perhaps they didn't . . .' Marta began, but Jacob shook his head at her. Solomon did not seem to hear the interruption.

'We beaters were sent around behind the herd to bring them towards the guns. The major and his party waited, keeping hidden and as silent as white men can. We crept round, the herd grazed on, as if it were any other peaceful morning. I don't know what got into me that morning but I wanted to shout, to warn the bigfeet. These huge creatures that I had been afraid of all my life . . . suddenly, suddenly I could see how small they were . . . compared to Major Pretorius and his guns.

'The loerie called the whole time we were creeping round and finally one, one elephant responded. He looked up. It was one of the younger bulls and he trumpeted. The herd began to move. But the young one who had sounded the alarm did not know what to do, how to deal with the alarm – he must have smelled us, people, all around him. So there was little direction in the herd. They were milling around, not trumpeting, just restless and finally one cow broke; and she broke in the direction of the guns.'

Marta gasped, but said nothing.

'At last this one cow noticed what they were up against and she began a charge against the guns. They shot at her but she kept coming. Then during all the confusion, because everyone was on the move now – the beaters, the, the elephants … only the people with the guns stood still, waiting.'

Marta could not take her eyes off the old man.

'Then a great bull came out of the forest. Major Pretorius, like the fool he was, shot him in the back, which set him off. He charged through the forest. Someone shot him in the head, and he let out a mighty bellow, but still he went on. I tried to keep track of him but before I could follow him, some of the spectators started yelling and pointing and there was another big bull, charging towards the major.

'The major was laughing; he was enjoying all this. I did not understand that, and thought he must be drunk with shooting; otherwise he would be afraid like everyone else. He shot this bull too, who turned away and into the forest. Now, for the first time, the major moved. He turned and followed the bull.

'They had now shot three bigfeet, though none were dead yet. The noise was deafening with the old giants crashing through the forest, guns going off, ladies shrieking and us beaters calling to each other about the action from the trees.'

'From the trees?'

'Yes, we had climbed – it was the first thing we had each done when we first came across the herd.' Solomon looked at Jacob and Marta: 'My father always said, "first thing you do, son: always first choose a tree to climb." While there were still bigfeet in the forest, it's what you did whenever you stopped.'

'So you spent the last great elephant hunt hiding in a tree?'

'Will you let Solomon tell the story?'

'Sorry, yes, of course. Please go on.'

'As I was saying, the noise was terrible. The dogs were baying, the elephants were crashing through the trees, trumpeting, calling each other, but the birds were all silent now, even the loerie.

'Just as we thought, the herd had moved away from this side of the mountain. The baying of the dogs rose higher than it had been before; it seemed they had become hysterical. My heart was in my throat. I had not seen my father since the first charge. Word came soon that the dogs had found a calf and had surrounded it. I decided to climb down and find out. The other beaters signaled to me that this was a bad idea but I wanted to see for myself.

Suddenly there was a sound above the noise of the dogs and I knew the mother had found them. Her trumpet was high and shrill as I had never heard one before. There was a great fury in it, fury and terror and love. Then we heard her attack the dogs. They yelped now amongst their baying and you could hear the thuds as they fell, where she swept them away from her calf. Now that mother was in sight it had begun its own small, fearful trumpeting too.

'The noise was deafening and all you knew was noise and fear and wrath and the smell of gunpowder in it all and the strange laughter of the major. Then the rest of the herd helped the mother and calf and the dogs turned away, afraid and whimpering now. Some of them were yelping with pain. The bigfeet made into the forest, mother and calf safe with the herd again for now.

'My father found me then. There was silence in the forest now as everyone regrouped, except for a whimpering. "What is it?" I asked my father.

'"It is one of the dogs," he said. "Come, let's find him."

'We found him; his back broken where the cow had tossed him against a tree. He looked at us and my father took out his knife and put an end to it. After that the forest was silent. It was a young dog. I was shaking then.

'"Come," my father said, "the day is not done."

'And already another trumpet call told us more was

happening. We came back just as the first shot rang out – the old bull had found us, had found Major Pretorius. The two had faced each other for a moment, and then the first shot hit the grand old man of the forest.

'He stumbled, but walked back into his forest. The huge gun sounded again but still the old bull walked on. Man, he was a grand old man, that bull. When the third shot was fired, he fell just before he reached the trees. Pretorius laughed again and jumped up swinging that heavy gun high.

'The bigfoot raised his head one more time to look at the man who had killed him and then died without a sound.' Solomon's eyes looked far away into the past, remembering the awful moment.

'I thought then that must be the end – he had come for one large bull and he had got the biggest, hadn't he? But he reloaded that terrible gun of his, and, still standing on the old bull's body, he resumed his post, signaling to my father to keep beating.

'I don't mind telling you that I was crying by then. And my father tried, he said, "Baas Pretorius, baas, you have the big one. Baas, it is what you came for – that is the best the biggest bull you have ever shot, you cannot top that baas."

'But that major was trigger-happy now and his bloodlust was hot. He shot another bull – it took six bullets. My father and I had moved away, though, because I was being sick in the bushes by then.

'Suddenly my father shushed me. We listened.

'It was the sound of a small elephant in distress. We crept to the edge of the mountainside and peered down into the ravine below us. There was a small calf, stuck and afraid. My father said: "Help him, Solomon. Help him."

"How?" I said.

"Come on," a stranger's voice said behind us

suddenly. It was one of the other hunters, "let's help that little chap." So we went down to see what we could do. Mostly the little one was just frightened and a little tangled in some roots and undergrowth.

'While we were trying to figure out how best to untangle the little beast, the mother's trumpet call sounded above us. We all stopped dead in our tracks, looking at each other. Then my father went on untangling the root that had caught the young elephant's foot. The hunter nodded at him and told him to keep going while he kept watch. I was rooted to the spot, my blood running cold; I could not even climb a tree. The hunter held his gun ready to chase her off, if necessary. The cow was now coming down that steep slope dangerously fast. Her voice was fierce and she did not care what she dragged down with her. The hunter shot his gun in the air to warn her away but she kept coming.

'"I'm going to have to hit her, she's not being put off," he said.

'My father nodded. The small elephant was free now but frozen to the spot and like me he was lost to fear. But his mother, being shot, now turned away. Trumpeting her anguish loudly she made off into the forest.

'"Right, well at least he's free now. Well done my man," the hunter said. "Come on, let's get away so that she can come to him. Go on little fellow, go on." But the small animal stood motionless, trembling.

'I knew how he felt. My father took a look at both of us.

'"You want to stay here with him," he said, and it was not a question.

'I nodded, still not able to speak.

"You may . . . but in a tree," he added firmly. "You can watch that he's safe from a tree." He selected this tree for me.' Solomon's hand slipped from his knee to the roots of the tree they were sitting under. Jacob and

Marta looked up at the branches with new eyes. 'He made sure I was safely up it, had a sandwich with me and then he left to do the long, hard and messy work of the hunt.

'You know, they killed five, five bigfeet on that last hunt.'

Marta and Jacob sat in silence and nodded, thinking of what the forest must have been like before. Before . . . when the elephants were still there.

Marta could not help asking, 'And what happened to the little one? Did you stay with him all night?'

'I did.'

'And?'

'And his mother did not come back; she died of her wounds, miles away. The herd came for him at dawn.'

'Oh, Solomon,' Marta said, forgetting that he was Ishmael's wicked grandfather. The old man looked at her, and his eyes were again the eyes of a child confronting death. Marta thought how alone he must have felt that long night in the tree and then it was all for nothing.

'I should have been kinder to him,' he mumbled.

'Who are you talking about, Solomon?'

'Ishmael. I should have been gentler on Ishmael.'

Neither Jacob nor Marta knew what to say to that. The old man's mind seemed to be wandering.

'Leave me here a little,' Solomon said, 'you two need to go home. Your mother will worry.'

'Are you going to be all right, Solomon?' Jacob asked.

The old man had never spoken so quietly, had always been gruff and hard to please. It had taken Jacob's own donkey stubbornness to stay with him and learn from him.

'Yes, yes, I am fine. More fine than I have been in a long time. Tell Narina to come and see her old father some time.' He turned to Marta with this.

'I will.'

'And tell her . . . tell her that Ishmael will be all right.'

'How do you know?'

'I watched that little bigfoot – he had a hard time, but he turned into a good, a good . . . elephant in the end. He lived his life here in the forest. He did not ever trust people much – none of the last herd did, after that. They stayed in the forest, they hid you could say – but they lived. Tell Narina that.'

'I will,' Marta promised.

'Now go.'

'Yes, Solomon.'

Brother and sister made their way home in silence. Just before they went inside, Marta said, 'I am sorry Jacob; I always just thought he was a mean old man.'

Jacob paused for a moment, 'I think to most people he was. And he was very mean to Ishmael.'

But Mother had taken a turn for the worse and it took till the end of the week before Marta could tell Narina the whole story and by then Solomon had died. He never got up from that tree again. He died sitting there remembering that last hunt.

As Mother was too ill to be left alone for long, it was Jacob who took Narina and Marta to visit Ishmael at the reformatory, to give him the news of Solomon's death. Joseph had stopped by the mission school in the morning to tell Narina. Father had held the funeral and the body had been cremated as Solomon had wanted. The ashes were put in a small wooden box embossed with a simple leaden cross. Narina, Marta, Jacob, Ben and their father fetched the urn from the funeral directors and then drove as deep into Gouna as they could. Then they climbed out of the car and walked in silence to the white pear, where

Solomon had spent the night on the last great elephant hunt and where finally he had come to die too. They stood silently for a moment, and then Narina opened the small casket and scattered her father's ashes amongst the roots of the tree.

Marta watched Narina's face as she worked. It was drawn but composed. Father put his arm around her.

'Narina's an orphan now,' Marta said softly.

'Yes, she is. But she still has us. We're here.'

Now Narina struggled with the box; her hands shook and she could not seem to get the lid back on. Gently Jacob took it from her and closed it.

'Thank you, Jacob.' She held it tightly on her lap all the way back.

The next day Jacob, Narina and Marta set out for Cape Town. It was a beautiful drive, even at the end of winter, along the coast to the reformatory in Cape Town.

'Are you afraid of seeing him?' Marta asked Narina.

'A little.'

'I am too. Does he know we're coming?'

'Your father spoke to the chaplain and the teacher. I think they will have told him.'

The reformatory was set against the sides of the mountain. The surroundings were as beautiful as the building was bleak. Inside the compound there was little vegetation – a few acacias and scuffed dusty ground. It was unnervingly silent when they drove up.

'Where is everybody?' Marta wondered out loud.

Just then a bell rang shrilly and both Marta and Jacob sat up, expecting noise to erupt from the building now. But nothing came until, at the side of the building, they saw at last a thin line of ragged boys emerge slowly out to the dusty yard.

They lined up between two adult men holding sjamboks in their hands and waited their turn at the tap. Then they were given a ball. The two men lounged beneath the acacia trees and the boys played a half-hearted game of football. The goal was empty.

The three in the car sat watching. Not one of them had made a move to get out. But one of the men spotted the car and came over, slapping his sjambok idly against his boot as he walked.

'Come on,' Jacob said. 'Let's go.'

Hesitantly they made their way to the large gate, topped, like the walls all around, with rolls of razor wire.

'What do you want?' the man asked insolently.

'This is Narina Gqwashu. She has come to see her son, Ishmael.' Jacob spoke. Marta watched him squaring his shoulders, wanting to be bigger, braver than he felt.

'Do you have an appointment?'

'Yes, well, no, not exactly. We spoke, that is my father, the Reverend Reben, spoke to Mr. Schwartz' assistant, as did Mrs. Gqwashu.'

'You can wait in his office.'

They were let in through a smaller gate inside the bigger one. Marta tried to spot Ishmael amongst the boys playing in the yard but could not.

'Where is he?' she whispered to Narina.

'I can't see him.'

'Do you think we don't know him anymore?'

'No. No, he's not there, that's all.'

The boys feigned a studious indifference to the visitors, though it was obvious they were watching.

Jacob, Marta and Narina were led into a dim, shuttered office with a cheap linoleum floor and chipped green paint on the wall. There was a single table in the room, with a half-empty coffee cup standing amongst the untidy papers; a wilting sandwich bled an oily stain onto some envelopes. At the far wall stood a steel filing cabinet and three kitchen chairs. A broken fan hung its head on the floor near the wire mesh dustbin. The air was sluggish and choking.

'Take a seat. Mr. Schwartz will be with you shortly.'

Narina sat down on one chair, Jacob on the other while Marta went to the window and looked into the central courtyard. There was a single figure sweeping. Then she saw that in the shadow was another – one of the guards again, slapping his sjambok against his side as the others had done. Something about the sweeping figure seemed familiar. Marta leaned towards the blinds, lifted a hand and slipped it between two of them, widening the gap to see.

'It's Ishmael,' she whispered.

'What?' Narina asked.

'It's Ishmael,' she said more loudly and she fumbled to get the blinds up and the window open, calling his name all the while. The figure in the courtyard froze then spun around to look at the window where Marta was now leaning out so far she nearly fell.

A smile lost its way across his face as he saw his mother and Jacob behind her. Then he bolted. The guard had been on the alert as soon as Ishmael had frozen and was ready for this, neatly tripping him up with his sjambok before bringing it down square between his shoulders, after which he bent down to grab the boy by the collar. Ishmael struggled and got another lash with the sjambok for his trouble. All the while Marta was yelling at the guard to stop.

'Can't you see you're making it worse?' Jacob hissed furiously.

Narina was at the door. It opened in her face and through it stepped a large, balding man, with long black curls sweeping down the sides of his bulging, mottled face, which was half-hidden by a dark pair of round glasses.

'Mrs. Gqwashu,' he beamed, as if no one was being beaten in the yard 'you have come to visit your son at last.'

Nevertheless, he ushered her back into the room hastily, shutting the door behind him. 'Take a seat, take a seat.'

He had to raise his voice because the guard struggling with Ishmael had begun to shout for help. Outside, the remaining boys were being commanded back into their dormitories and locked in while all the focus was on Ishmael. Every one of them was shouting and rattling the bars at the windows.

Order was swiftly restored, though Marta was sure she could still hear the swish of the sjambok and the sound of whimpering which followed it. She was not silenced so easily though.

'Why did your guard have to beat him?' she yelled. 'Let me see my friend, let me see Ishmael!' She was not intimidated by this mountain of a man.

Jacob had to threaten to send her out to the car before she would keep silent.

Mr. Schwartz smiled grimly, 'Please wait a minute. I will see what I can arrange.' He went out. After a brief, whispered conversation with the guard outside, he returned. 'Mrs. Gqwashu,' he ventured, then caught himself. '*Miss* Gqwashu,' he corrected with a grin. 'You have come to give your son news. Sadly you have travelled a long way to no purpose.'

'What do you mean?' Jacob interrupted.

'Mr. Reben,' the mountainous man said, 'we tend to speak to the parents of the offenders.'

Jacob gave up. Marta seethed.

'I'm afraid you will not be able to see your son, Miss Gqwashu. His behavior has been too poor for us to permit a visit.'

Jacob began again, 'But his grandfather . . .'

'He has been given the news,' Mr. Schwartz said calmly, 'so there really is no need for any of this to go on any longer.'

They stared at him in disbelief.

'I am sorry for the wasted effort. Had your father spoken to me at greater length, instead of with my assistant, we could have explained all this.'

Marta was in tears. Narina had stood up to go and Jacob was holding her arm, leading her out, hissing at Marta to pull herself together and get out to the car.

Mr. Schwartz accompanied them as far as the gate, where a guard took over and opened it. He let them through the gate and then locked it without a word.

Jacob opened the car and got out some water for Narina. She leaned against the car and her face was pale.

'What do we do now?' Marta asked. She was already speculatively eying the fence, remembering an excursion years ago when she and Ishmael had crept into the Boys' Town compound in George.

She had thought that was awful but it was a palace compared to this, she knew now. It had been for white boys. She turned away from the fence to her brother.

'I don't know.' He sounded cross but his eyes told her it was only because he felt as helpless as she did. He turned back to Narina.

'What should we do?' He asked her

'We must go home. There is nothing we can do.'

'Are you sure, Narina? If you want me to, I will go back and try to reason with Mr. Schwartz.'

'There is no point,' Narina said.

But Marta was back at the gate ringing the bell furiously.

'We can't give up so easily, we can't.'

At that moment a middle-aged man came up the slope pushing a bicycle. He was dressed in a grey sweat-soaked shirt and dark trousers. He had glasses and a shock of dark hair falling over his forehead. It irritated Marta that he somehow seemed familiar but she could not place him. He was clearly in a great hurry but he

164

stopped when he saw them. Then a smile broke over his weary face. He wiped the sweat from his face and dropped his bicycle.

'I am so glad to have caught you,' he said. 'Please don't go yet.'

'Who are you?' Jacob asked.

'Never mind that now – have you seen Ishmael?'

'No, we were not allowed to see him.'

'That is what I was afraid of. You must tell your father. He needs to get Ishmael out of here as quickly as possible.'

'Why – who are you?'

'I am a chaplain to some of the boys here, from Lutheran Mission congregations.'

Suddenly Jacob narrowed his eyes. 'Are you . . . no you can't be . . .' He tried again. 'Are you our uncle Simon?'

'Yes, I am.'

'The one who is always–' but Jacob stopped Marta just in time.

'Yes, yes, the one your mother worries about all the time. The one who causes trouble. This kind of trouble. You must tell your father that Ishmael must leave this reformatory – he needs to be transferred to Sterkfontein in the Transvaal. It is better there. Mr. Schwartz is a monster. The way he treats these boys will undoubtedly drive Ishmael mad.'

'But,' Jacob asked, 'can you not arrange such a move better?'

'Me?' their Uncle asked, 'Me? I am lucky not to be under arrest myself – I should not be here. I must leave. If any of the guards see me here they will phone the Special Branch again. It has been good to meet you two. Send my love to your parents.'

And he swung himself up on his bicycle and left, careening down the hill with greater speed than safety.

At that moment a guard emerged. 'Is something the matter?' he asked.

'No, no, all is fine,' Jacob answered, recovering his wits.

'Was there someone here talking to you, holding you up?'

'No, we were just getting a little water.' Jacob glanced at Narina.

'It will be dark soon. You want to be back on the road before then,' the guard said.

'We were just leaving.'

Marta had to ask. 'Can we not at least say goodbye to Ishmael?'

The guard laughed derisively, and that was the last sound they heard before they drove away from that place.

Jacob drove faster than he should but neither Marta nor Narina said anything. His knuckles were white on the steering wheel. They sat all the way in silence, though it took nearly four hours to get home.

At home Mother was back in hospital, having had a bad reaction to a new drug she had been prescribed. Ruth had been summoned back from Germany. Their father looked haggard and worn. Jacob could not bear to tell him what they had seen at the reformatory. But when Narina had gone back to her own lonely house and Jacob had retreated to his room Marta told her father everything.

'It's awful, Father, everything there is awful. Is there nothing we can do?'

'I will phone your uncle in the morning,' he said heavily.

'Mother won't like it.'

'No. But she would understand and she would agree.'

'Yes, she would.'

In the night however, Father was called to the

hospital. They thought Mother would not make it through the night and the phone call to her uncle was not made.

Mother recovered from that bad spell and promised to return home soon.

NINE

Despite the terrible week in hospital, Mother was
declared to be in remission soon after and was allowed
to come home. Ruth's return was a comfort for them
all, even Jacob, who had grown tired of being the eldest
and had spent more and more time in the forest with the
forestry students, poring over maps and marking them
at the end of every trip. He was helping in the search
for the remaining elephants. He finished school without
paying it much attention. Ruth was accepted to the music
department of Rhodes University in Grahamstown and
left again.

Marta moved on to high school soon after that and the
change seemed unremarkable. She continued with much
the same lessons, though teachers changed, and though
her movement about the school had become as confident
as Amanda's, she had not noticed when. She was lead
flautist for the orchestra and took the younger children for
recorder group in the afternoons. In the library she read
with joy all the books related to Russia she could find.

How she longed to see the spires of St Petersburg,
how she wondered how life would be if these names,
so strange and hard to read, were familiar, were home
to her ears. Life went on, swallowing the changes till

they seemed a part of the unchanging whole. Simon, Marta and Ben took the bus to school as they always did, though increasingly it was only Marta and Ben on the way home, as Simon stayed to work in the library or attended meetings of the student council.

Marta and Ben walked home from school – they had got off the bus earlier than usual, both tired of the noise and the barbed laughter. It was the start of the brief September holiday and they could no longer wait to be rid of the noise and stupidity. They had not needed to say anything at all but got up almost simultaneously and stood quietly waiting for the bus to stop. There were catcalls – but that was fine. After one incident, where someone had dared to mock Marta's friendship with a jailbird, there had been torn shirts, bruised faces and several detentions all round. Now they dared only laughter and that was in groups; no one actually mentioned Ishmael to Marta's face anymore.

Walking home through the forest, past Karatara where they said goodbye to the triplets, helped. Most of their peers were afraid to walk there – were afraid of the forest-people, who had been moved out of the forest; and now were unemployed and lost in a bright, open world they did not understand. The schoolchildren mocked their crazy eyes and their parents were afraid of the possibilities of drugs being sold there. The triplets, however, lived there and were bullied at school for it but were never followed into Karatara itself. They had continued to struggle and were still in the junior school, though they would soon go on to the vocational college. They looked forward to it, Piet told Ben.

'We'll be with people more like ourselves.'

'Will you come see us soon?' Sannie asked Marta.

'Yes, soon – on the weekend?'

Sannie and Mina skipped happily to their house and Piet ran to catch up with them.

Marta and Ben walked quietly, saving their breath for the steep climb through the forest up to Farleigh. Their path took them past the last straggling houses, where the outcasts who had been neglected by their own lived. In a shanty in the backyard of the last house, sitting on an old kitchen chair, they saw Narina's half-uncle, Bosman, Solomon's Khoi brother, and waved to him. He waved back, too far away to see who they were, driven only by a lifetime's courtesy which brought no consolation at all. He lived alone now, since Ishmael had been taken away and Narina refused to speak to her family anymore over her fidelity to a son, whose only response to a world where no place could be found for him had been to try and break it. Today they did not stop to chat as they normally did. Bosman had befriended Jacob since Solomon's death and all the Reben children liked the strange old man who knew trees so much better than anyone else. But today they were both too restless to speak.

An army officer had visited the school again that day. He had explained about the Angolan war – how neighbours helped one another and if your neighbour's roof was burning, you helped put the fire out to protect your *own* roof. The other boys had all been full of enthusiasm about their turn in the army, about what they would do when school was finally over and they got to be men. Jacob had got his call-up papers as soon as his matric results had arrived. Still not sure what he wanted to do, he could not defer his army time for university as Father had hoped. And now Marta knew Ben was thinking of Jacob, of his faraway eyes whenever his brothers or Marta asked him about what he did now. So she walked silently beside him, accepting his silence and simply focused on getting home and forgetting that anything else existed.

Only in the forest, when the smell of the open road and of the town had been overwhelmed at last by the smell of fynbos in spring, did they stop and breathe and smile at each other.

They walked and climbed, shifting heavy school rucksacks around on their backs and finally reached the southern barn on the slopes of the final steep climb. They flung themselves down in the straw, shrugging their rucksacks off and splashing their faces at the cold water trough where the flies buzzed soporifically in the midday sun. They waited for their breathing to slow down at last and as they waited they heard faintly a scratchy high-pitched cawing. They sat up and listened. Both determined a direction and went in search of the sound.

The barn contained three separate hay stacks and as she scrambled about, Marta wondered when last they had chased each other through it or built dens from the bales before they were taken off to faraway fields in the winter. She shook off these thoughts and listened intently for the sounds they were tracking. She thought she could hear something to the left. There was an excitement in her that she had not felt in a long time.

She located the sound – it was coming from the far left corner of the barn where the surplus bales from last year were still stacked high, as this year Father had not had time to bring them out to the small-holders at Karatara. She wondered whether it would be a wild cat with her kittens that had found a safe shelter there. She decided to approach from above and began climbing up the side to reach the source of the sound from inside the dark barn roof.

Marta climbed carefully, not wishing to disturb the heavy bales and injure whatever unseen creatures lived among them. She reached the top and paused again to listen. The high-pitched sounds seemed weaker now – whatever it was must have been aware of her. She was halted for a moment by the thought that some creature was trying to avoid her and the danger she was to it and she almost called the search off then and there. But something made her go on – she did not want to be empty-handed. She could not hear Ben call at all anymore and guessed he felt the same. All the same, both searched on in intense silence.

Marta was guiltily glad that she found the source of the noise first, in that high-up far left corner of the barn. Marta carefully shifted a bale and curiously peered down into the gloom. It was an owl nest. Two chicks were inside, screaming their hunger. She half-pulled back in delight and fear of disturbing the nestlings, who stared back at her odd human face from impossibly dark eyes in a small sea of scruffy fluff which barely covered their pink and wrinkled nakedness.

'Ben,' she whispered urgently, 'Ben – they're up here.'

He came scrambling up. She tore her eyes away from the chicks for long enough to turn towards him with her finger on her lips.

'What is it?'

'A nest,' she said, 'an owl's nest.'

And he had knelt down with her to peer carefully over the shifted bale at the two chicks.

'They're ugly,' he said.

'Yes,' she said, 'but also sweet.'

'Sweet?! Listen to that.'

So they climbed down and found a place on the middle stack from which to watch as the mother flew in, disturbed by their presence but preoccupied with checking that all was well with her roost.

For weeks they returned again and again to watch. School's wearisome routines were endured only through the hope of these moments as the chicks grew and the mother cared for them with a fierce and tender patience. Daily they climbed off the bus early to the taunts of the others, who had no idea of their find; daily they stopped at the barn to see how the birds were coming along.

And then one evening, when school choir had

rehearsed till late, they came home as it was getting dark. Walking past the forest, Marta had been made anxious by a loerie call.

'Listen to that, Ben,' she said. 'Why is she calling now?'

'You still believe all that stuff?'

She did not know what to answer, only hurried on, driven by an urgency she could not explain.

On the road to the barn they found the mother owl. She lay on the road, her head twisted in a way even an owl's should not twist and her breast slit neatly open, the beautiful soft white feathers soiled and her blood spilling onto the hard ground from the empty rib-cage. They stared at each other in horror and then without a word ran all the way to the barn.

The barn had been disturbed, too. The bales had been flung out from the very top of the stack where the nest had been. They lay in tattered heaps all round the left side of the barn. Marta's heart tightened with fear as she searched. Neither of them said a word. They searched and searched.

Finally Ben said, 'Marta, stop. It is no good. He's back.'

'Oh it can't be him, it can't. Ishmael,' she cried, 'Ishmael!'

But as they stared at each other, half in anger half in horror, they both heard it. The soft, shrill, hopeless cry of the owl chicks. They knew it well now.

Their search resumed. At last Ben found the crying chick. It sat nestled closely to the bedraggled, limp body of its sibling. Ben called Marta, as though afraid to be alone with these two.

Gulping with horror she crouched down, afraid to touch it. A long moment passed where she stared into the terrible silence of a hopeless and frightened chick and the darkness of those wild, unblinking eyes. Ben climbed up the stack to see the damage: the nest had been shaken loose and was hanging rather precariously. Marta had sat down hopelessly with her back against the stack and was sobbing.

'Ishmael. Oh, Ishmael. Who let you out without warning us?'

Her silent sobbing pierced the still afternoon.

'Hey, maybe it was not him,' Ben said, but he knew it was hopeless. It bore all the marks of Ishmael's bizarre violence, which frightened everyone – even his mother. Only Marta loved Ishmael beyond question and without needing a reason. Now he had destroyed something she had taken into her protection. Ben sat up on the haystack and looked down at his sister, wrists swinging aimlessly between his knees. As he watched her crying over the strange boy, who had only ever caused trouble, he tentatively reached out a hand to comfort her. But when she hunched further away from him, he got up, crawled to the other side of the stack and walked home without a word to Marta. She remained and watched the small, frightened chick, wondering what she should do; torn between the chick, and her brother, knowing that once more Ishmael had come between them.

Marta sat and thought for a long time, with her back against the rough wooden poles which supported the roof of the barn. She did not realize that she had begun talking to the chick.

'There is no one left to take care of you now is there? I would, but you look at me with horror in your eyes – you remember only Ishmael now and what he did to your brother. Did you hear the terrible laughter from my nightmares? That gulp in his throat which is the worst sound in the world? Would it be kinder to let you die here?'

But as she became aware of her thoughts and her voice, she realized that now she had begun to talk to

174

the chick it would be impossible for her to let it die. Something had to be rescued from the horror.

And so she convinced herself, finally, that it would be best to take the small frightened bundle home. She took off her jumper and carefully made a nest in which to carry it, her rural family's strong taboo against touching wild animals with her human smell keeping her from picking it up with her bare hands.

She nearly forgot her school bag and had to repeat the whole procedure of picking the fragile, screeching bundle up with the heavy books on her back and being careful not to topple. She was crying now; the distress of the bird was hard to face and she was afraid of what she was doing, afraid also of a pair of watching eyes, full of both glee and despair in a way she did not understand. A voice from memory taunting her, 'White people don't understand'.

To shut out that voice, she talked incessantly to the little chick, wanting it to settle down, wanting it not to be so afraid – not to make her so afraid. She was afraid of what Ben would say, knowing that he had run off, knowing that he would want to share the care of the chick but might be too proud to ask now, having run off.

She was afraid of Ishmael being back. Was he back? Yes, she was sure. Why was he back? Had he been released? Had Uncle got him out permanently? Why was she frightened like everyone else about it – instead of glad? What had happened to her? Ishmael was back and she was more concerned for an ugly small owl chick. She was afraid of her family's disapproval of the interference with wild animals. She did not know that she would be able to explain to them why this one mattered so much, why she felt she had to make good what had happened, why she felt responsible for Ishmael's deeds. Except perhaps that somebody should.

She walked round the house and entered by the

kitchen door, hoping to be unseen, hoping to catch her mother alone and be able to speak to her before anyone else. She was in luck; her mother sat alone in the kitchen, her hands curled about a mug, eyes staring far away into the middle distance of the vast red kitchen floor.

'Marta,' she watched her mother collect all of herself to speak to her and wondered in that moment for the first time where her mother went when she was not simply 'Mother'.

'Marta, what is that?' Now her mother was all there, was getting up to see. Marta moved quickly towards her, before anyone else should hear them.

'Ben and I have been watching them carefully – they have been in the barn. Today we found the mother dead – she had been wounded with a kettie and then . . . and then . . .' Marta could not go on.

She looked up at her mother, 'Ishmael,' she said, 'Ishmael.'

'I know,' her mother said, 'I know he has run away again. The police have already been and Narina has gone home.'

'What will they do to him?'

'I don't know. You need a box for that, and some newspaper. You'll need to make a nest to keep it safe and warm.'

Mother walked slowly into the pantry and found a shoebox on the top shelf, which she brought down to Marta.

'He will prefer it dark,' her mother said.

Marta had carefully deposited the little bird inside the box. It was silent now. Marta was afraid that it was just defeated.

'What will I feed it?'

'For today, perhaps some pronutro and tomorrow you will go to the library and find out what it needs.'

Marta was glad of her mother's calm decision and

she allowed the rhythmic tearing of the paper and then mashing a boiled egg to lull her into a kind of hope and quietness. The little creature did not eat much and she had had to clean out the newspaper and tear some more almost immediately, but it kept her busy and her mind off Ishmael.

'Find a quiet place,' her mother admonished gently.

Thinking of all the nestlings found by their grey cat, who was a formidable hunter, Marta found a secure place in her room, on the shelf above her bed.

Her night was restless with not thinking about Ishmael and sitting up and checking that the little creature was still alive. Towards midnight it began to hiss at her when she lifted the lid carefully to look in on it and for the first time that day she smiled again.

Morning brought the problem of where to keep the little bird safe while she was not in. During the night Marta had kept the door closed and the cat had made do with Ben's room after that. Ruth, home for the holidays, had sniffed at its ugliness, but had not demurred beyond that. At supper, Ben had only looked at her once with burning eyes but then later he had come up to her room and asked how it was doing.

'Come in and see,' she replied.

He came in without a word and stared for a while down at the little creature.

'It is not hurt?'

'I don't think so,' she said. 'Just frightened.'

'Well,' he replied, 'aren't we all?'

'I suppose so. Yes.'

'I hope it lives till morning, anyway. Goodnight.'

Though he left abruptly, Marta knew he would help if she needed it now.

The weekend arrived, meaning she could tend to the poor creature herself. However, when the school week began again, she had no one to take over.

Weekends used to mean Ishmael but that felt so long ago. Marta did not know exactly when things had changed. He may have run home again, may have escaped from the Tokai reformatory. But he remained far away. And no amount of phone calls or brief visits to the police or mental health institutions with her father and Narina revealed where he was. And she knew now that mostly the government wanted to pretend that mixed-race people, like Ishmael, did not exist. She wished that she did not have to think of him in that way, that he could just have been a friend whose life had gone wrong, wished that politics, which she knew she understood only imperfectly, did not have to poison everything.

'Even you,' she said softly to the bird, miraculously still alive and eating more readily, the strange slop she was feeding it. 'Even you, though you should belong to the forest, are poisoned because Ishmael did this to you – but I will not let you die. You must know that on a different day he would have been gentle and kind, he would have stood with me here helping you live.'

That evening their uncle phoned.

'Johannes,' he said; his voice urgent and loud over the phone. 'I need Narina to be a witness in a case against Mr. Schwartz of the reformatory.'

'What do you mean?' Her father asked and then he closed his study door.

Marta tried to listen from the other side and was nearly knocked over when he returned and explained that Mr. Schwartz had been abusing the boys; putting them in isolation and making them do extreme physical labor, while not allowing lessons to proceed as they should. About two weeks ago, when Ishmael had finally attacked one of the guards for whipping one of the smaller boys, Mr. Schwartz himself had whipped Ishmael so hard that his own shoulder had dislocated. Ishmael had escaped, having first used the whip on Mr. Schwartz. When the

police had finally caught up with him it was to find
Uncle Simon Reben standing in their way, ready with a
lawyer and a case of child abuse against the reformatory.
In the meantime Ishmael was hiding in the abandoned
tunnels of Millwood mine. Uncle Simon and his lawyer
friend had been collecting evidence from all the inmates
and their families for years and Ishmael's dramatic escape
had finally drawn everyone's attention to the case.

'Narina, will you go?'

'What will happen to Ishmael now?' Marta
interrupted.

'I am not sure yet. He will have to stay in the
reformatory, I think. He does not sound like he is stable,
does he?'

'Don't speak about him like that!' Marta could not
help her anger.

'Think of the bird,' Mother added, casting worried
glances over at Marta.

'I will go with you, Narina,' Marta said.

So they found themselves back in court but this
time Ishmael was not the accused and though the case
was deemed inconclusive, the board of directors took
Mr. Schwartz away from his post as 'master in charge
of young offenders'. Simon Reben took the post when
it was offered him. But Marta, although she paid
careful attention to all that was said, and knew that the
reformatory would be better now, knew also that she had
not been able to talk to Ishmael once in all that time and
that he was still not free.

All she knew to do in her helplessness was channel
all her thwarted need for action into caring for the bird.
It made a new life for her. This life swung between early
mornings and late nights out catching insects, lizards and
other small creatures to feed her owl, and going back and
forth to the library, finding out what her bird needed and
how she could get it.

For the first time in the long years since Ishmael had gone and Mother had been ill, life for Marta seemed to have some purpose beyond the dull constricted routines of school. Now things mattered again, whether she got home on time mattered and her reading in the library mattered. She called her Lady Grey, knowing that the bird would be lovely one day, no matter how scruffy and ugly she looked now. And she had loved the story of the brief nine day queen, who thought she could save a war-torn country.

The bird depended on her and she could do something about that and for seven months that made all the difference. It made up for seeing Ishmael disappear a second time, it made up for everyone's silence about that. It made up for the strained normality in a house where their mother was dying.

The bird miraculously, and with endless patience, learned to fly and then to hunt. Marta had cut bleeding chunks of meat for her, had thrown them for her to find and, eventually, catch before they fell on the ground. She and her bird were constantly together. And through the bird, Marta found her way back into the forest.

Marta unearthed in the school library a copy of T.H. White's *The Goshawk* and had read and reread it. She consulted with Bomani about how best to make the equipment she needed to train her bird from bits of tackle and other scraps. Ben and Bomani soon lost patience with it but for Marta it became an all-consuming passion. As soon as she got home from school, Marta would go to the shed where the bird stayed and slip inside; talking softly to the bird, which would come to her wrist, which she guarded with her father's old welding gloves. She would put her home-made jesses on Lady Grey, leash her and they would go out together. They would settle somewhere in the garden where the dogs would not bother them and Marta would read and talk to the bird about her day. Lady Grey listened sleepily, head cocked on one side. When she grew restless, Marta would begin with the commands and signals and the evening became a battle of wills between the two creatures.

Watching her bird fly; learning to understand her and seeing how she, in turn grew to understand Marta, felt like singing, like finding the right harmonies for a tune. It was both smaller and greater than choir. Greater because it was between different worlds, not just voices; smaller because it was quiet and intimate, just the two creatures – human and bird, the harmony soundless.

Then one Friday afternoon, Marta came home from school to find the bird gone. She had always left the window of the shed ajar, allowing Lady Grey some cool air during the long school day. The bird had always been back when Marta got home after the long walk from the bus stop. Often there would be the familiar soft swish of her wings overhead as she swooped down to Marta's outstretched hand. As soon as the bird had alighted, Marta would forget homework and the annoying way in which some idiot at school had persistently been stupid about her hair. Simon and Ben had watched her walk, half in envy and half in relief that they did not have the added chore of taking care of a demanding and, Simon insisted, half-mad bird (Lady Grey had been sharp of memory and unforgiving about his attempt to tease her when still a fledgling and struggling to hunt).

But now she was gone.

TEN

The next morning Marta was up with the birdsong and slipped quietly out of the house to begin her search again. In the misty grey light of an autumn dawn, she breathed deeply the smell of winter coming and felt a chill of anguish. What if she did not find Lady Grey? The thought was overwhelming. The bird was her consolation for all else that had gone so very wrong. Ishmael, her mother's illness, even school's continual idiocy.

Just at that point she heard a familiar call and saw the dear shape weaving in and out of the trees.

'Lady Grey,' she called reproachfully and the bird returned cheerfully to her wrist. Marta's eyes smarted with gladness but she withheld the tears and her voice as she only gently chided the bird with soft nonsense words of affection.

In the afternoon, the bird took off again. This time Marta lost no time in following her and soon she was running through the remains of the summer's undergrowth, stumbling as she breathlessly looked up to follow the path of the owl. They came to a lopsided cottage with a partially caved in roof and the remnants of a garden about it. Marta stopped in surprise. She knew the forest well, she thought, almost as well as Ishmael, and this cottage had stood empty for years. Now there was smoke curling from its chimney and Marta could see that the garden had been cleared a little. Not much had been done however, as if the person doing it didn't quite want to admit to having done it. Her owl swooped into the eaves and determinedly putting her usual horror of meeting strangers aside, Marta stepped up to the door, hand raised to knock.

As she did so she heard a voice rumbling inside.

'Well, lady owl, what you are so excited about? Is it outside? Shall we look?'

Before Marta could knock, the door swung open to reveal a large man with shaggy dark grey hair and piercing green eyes. On his wrist sat a quiet and content Lady Grey. Both humans were silenced by consternation; the bird looked silently from one to the other. The door slammed shut.

'Miss Owl, you know we cannot have people here.' Marta heard the man remonstrate with her bird. Angry now, she raised her fist to the door and banged.

'You have my bird. You must give her back,' she called furiously and in tears again.

The bird, distressed by the noise, bated and then took off. Marta saw her fly out through the window under the eaves again. But she did not come to Marta's triumphantly outstretched wrist but instead perched in a tree just at the edge of the garden and watched the two humans in pointed silence.

The old man opened the door a hand's-breadth. 'Your bird?' he questioned. 'What does a girl like you know of such birds?'

'I know this one is mine,' Marta retorted, still angry, and hurt now that the owl had not returned to her hand.

When there was no response she turned and sat down under the tree, beneath Lady Grey. She sat amongst the roots, despondently leaning her head back against the bark, her wrists dangling from their rest on her knees. As she sat there she remembered her mother's exhausted face, her own long days of searching and the fear of loss overcame her again. She threw her head forward into her hands. At this the door of the cottage cautiously opened and the dark grey head appeared, whistled desultorily for the bird, but then the man came and hunkered awkwardly down by the crying girl.

'So where did you find her, then?' he asked quietly.

'In the forest; after a storm.'

'Shaken from its nest, huh?' His voice told her he knew it was a lie.

She looked up, stung by the disbelief in his words. 'Actually, yes. The other one was dead.'

She saw again the moment before her; those large frightened eyes and the piercing emptiness overhead, as well as the anxious warning call of the loerie in the ironwood. The birdlet had lain in the straw and fluttering above it in the evening air as she sat were the white moths, disturbed and anxious as the loerie would have been.

She could not tell this stranger the truth of how she had found the birds and why she had to take it home against all reason, why she knew she was responsible for this one.

He seemed to sense some of that and relented.

'Well, you have done well with her,' he offered after a pause. 'She's very capable.'

'Yes,' the girl answered, afraid of what was coming next.

'You know you have to let her go.'

'Yes. No. What if . . .'

'That is for Miss Owl to worry about now, not you. Look at her.'

'She's not Miss Owl.'

'No she isn't. But it is what I have called her, when she has visited me.'

'She's Lady Grey.'

'You have been doing the Tudors, then?'

'Yes.' Bristling with embarrassment.

'Well, she was a brave woman, too.'

The owl was weaving among the branches above them. She flew to the next tree, perched and looked back, then flew on. Then looked back.

They both shook off their own thoughts for a moment and concentrated on the bird between them.

'She needs you to say go.'

'But I cannot, not yet. She's not ready. I'm not ready,' Marta whispered.

'I know. There is no readiness. Nevertheless, you must and you will.'

'Soon,' she agreed, 'soon.' She wondered why she was listening to this man. Something about him was familiar.

They left it at that. Marta slowly stood up, stepped clear of the tree and raised her wrist. The bird returned and held her eye steadily for a moment. This happened rarely, Marta knew. Birds of prey did not like to have their gazes met. But Lady Grey looked and then flew off, swiftly gaining height in the darkening sky, not turning again for a long while.

Marta watched till she lost sight of her bird. Dry-eyed, she knew that however often the bird returned, it would never be the same again. She was her own being now and free of Marta.

After a while the old man spoke. 'Would you like some tea?'

They went silently into the cottage. The slanted, pale light of an autumn afternoon fell straight onto a painting that hung alone on the rough whitewashed wall of the kitchen. Marta stared at it. It glowed in the dim kitchen:

below a stormy orange and grey looming sky stood a mountain which held within its lightning-white trees and rocks a golden city, from which spilled light to the river below.

'What is it called?' she asked.

'It is Rembrandt's *Stormy Landscape*.'

'Where is it?'

'It is nowhere,' he said roughly at first before relenting, remembering that she was there by his invitation. 'I am not sure where Rembrandt painted it, but I think it could be St Augustine's City, or one of the cities of refuge.'

But she was not listening, she was reading instead something written on a small yellowed piece of paper, tucked into the corner of the frame:

Der Seher Johannes schreibt: Und ich sah die heilige Stadt, das neue Jerusalem, von Gott aus dem Himmel herabkommen, bereitet wie eine geschmückte Braut für ihren Mann. Und ich hörte eine große Stimme von dem Thron her, die sprach: Siehe da, die Hütte Gottes bei den Menschen! Offenbarung 21, 2–3 [2]

The old man continued, 'Look, here, where are they now? There were six of them, Hebron was one, I think and there was one near Mount Ephraim.' He looked through the thin pages of an old Bible lying on the kitchen dresser.

Marta, staring at the words, asked 'You speak German?'

'A little.'

'Why?'

'I spent some student years in Holland – and Aachen.

---

[2] *And I heard a loud voice from the throne saying, "Look! God's dwelling place is now among the people." Revelations, 21, 2-3*

Do you want to know about the cities?'

'Yes, sorry – go on.' She did not take her eyes off the painting.

'In the Old Testament,' he explained and when she said nothing, he read softly, '"These six cities shall be a refuge, both for the children of Israel, and for the stranger, and for the sojourner among them: that every one that killeth any person unawares may flee thither."'

Marta whispered softly under her breath words she had heard somewhere at school, in a history lesson, she thought. '"The soul takes flight, to the world that is eternal . . . invisible. But there arriving she is sure of bliss."'

'Yes, something like that – if bliss is safety.'

'Safety?' She was being persistent now, she knew this often irritated but she wanted to know. And she could see his back stiffening as he fussed with the tea things. And now she noticed how fastidiously clean the kitchen was, for all the neglect outdoors.

He did not answer yet but Marta knew he would; he was getting ready – she just needed patience like one did with the loerie. So, she sat as still as she could and watched him only surreptitiously. He fussed quite a long time. He cleaned the cups first and the tray and bent a long time to find a milk jug, though the milk in the old, fat cornered fridge was in a jug too. He poured some over into the smaller one, found an ornate sugar bowl with a daintily wrought pewter spoon and placed all these carefully on the tray before carrying it all two or three steps to the table where she was sitting.

He sat down heavily on the old, intricately carved wooden chair and in silence poured the tea and milk and offered sugar which she silently refused. Finally he took a deep breath to begin, as if still gathering his thoughts, though she could tell from his eyes and the set of his shoulders that he knew what to say, just not how.

'In the Old Testament', he began, coming back to that anchor from which to reel his story out, 'six cities were designated as Cities of Refuge, where those who had done wrong, without deliberate intent, could find sanctuary from the arms of the law and start again.'

She remembered now one of Father's sermons about places of refuge. He had spoken about the mission stations. Now in the times of unrest, he had said they should be sanctuaries for any who needed one. So she nodded.

The old man went on, 'And St Augustine developed this idea for his City Of God thesis, the New Jerusalem where, through the compassion of Christ, everyone, no matter how sinful, may start anew and live blissfully in the constant presence of God.'

He turned to her, driven out of his habitual wariness by the idea. As he spoke, his deeply shadowed eyes lit up with a faraway hope and a longing she had never encountered before. She had seen glimpses of something a little like it, perhaps, in the speakers who came to school to speak about God's chosen people and the land which had been given to them. But the light in their eyes had disturbed her. And Simon had explained that it was their fanaticism which was frightening.

Here she did not feel that need to flee. There was a difference, but she could not put her finger on it. Instead, she turned her attention back to the gentleman.

He had fallen silent. Abruptly, he stood up, took the picture from the wall, brought it to the table and showed her how the light worked and how dangerous Rembrandt had made the terrain so the city was difficult to reach.

'Why?' she asked, 'why is it so hard to get to?'

'I think,' he said slowly, 'I think,' he said 'because you have to convince yourself that you deserve the sanctuary, God's compassion – and that *is* very hard.'

'Isn't the point of it all that it need not be deserved –

that it is grace?' She couldn't help asking, knowing she risked his displeasure. These were the conversations with her father that she missed since her confirmation.

He smiled briefly at her. 'Yes,' he said, 'yes, it is grace, but one must accept that.'

'And that is the trouble?'

'Yes – once you have got your hands dirty.'

He picked up his teacup again, having returned the picture to its square of sunlight against the whitewashed wall.

'My name is Wilhelm, by the way, Wilhelm Charles Stander.' He was still standing, almost ceremoniously. 'And you are?'

She got to her feet, driven by his air of ritual. 'I am Marta Reben.'

'Daughter of Johannes Reben of Farleigh?' There was an almost imperceptible flicker of the eyes.

'The same.'

'Well Marta, I am pleased to make your acquaintance,' and with the slightest bow of the head he extended his hand to her.

She shook it, surprised by this gallantry. She found herself just stopping short of the habitual curtsey of the unconfirmed.

Just then her bird returned, settling with a flurry on the back of a chair.

Marta looked at the fading sunlight. 'I must go,' she said.

They finished their tea in silence but peaceably now. At the door Marta hesitated for a moment, and then she took a deep breath. 'I'll see you tomorrow?'

'I shall look forward to that.'

Smiling, Marta held up her wrist for the bird, which flew over calmly now and they went home together.

Marta did go back the next day, drawn by the light of the painting. Her owl came with her, a half tame and half wild thing. She wanted to see that light again, to gaze and be lost in the world of that painting but Wilhelm did not invite her into the house at first. He was painting in his garden. Politely she lingered there with him, watching him paint in silence, bringing him fresh water when he needed it and, finally, making tea for them both. While she waited for the kettle to boil, she had time to look at the painting again. She did not dare lift it off the wall as he had but stood before it a long time. The sense of wonder she had felt the first time still lingered around it and she stood waiting for it to burst out and pour itself through her veins as it had done before. Finally a little warmth spread through as she looked, remembering Wilhelm's words about the City of God. She turned from it then and made and carried the tea out on the same tray he had used the day before, careful to do everything as he had. He watched in silent approval.

While they drank, Marta, at his bidding, examined his barely completed painting, tracing mentally the fall of light on the broken flowerpot in its centre and the late roses from amongst the weeds, which he had captured – also the fynbos flowers coming in from the forest over the wall, which was crumbling in parts. The light was earthly, real.

'Well,' he said, suddenly close behind her shoulder.

'I like the light.'

'Yes, so do I, though it is hard to paint.'

'To make it like Rembrandt did?'

He did not answer and she knew then that they must speak of other things. But Rembrandt's grace would always be there between them – like the bird, who visited both occasionally. And it would keep her coming to his cottage for a long time.

'I know what we could do. Wait here,' he said and disappeared into his cottage. Marta waited, wondering what he was planning. He emerged with another easel and set of brushes and a small white flower palette. It felt odd to be painting outside and not in a classroom with the familiar smell of paint and glue and fresh paper. Instead, her nostrils were filled with the sour smell of the forest. There was freedom in it, though Marta knew her skill was poor. But as she stood in the dappled light of that garden surrounded by the forest, doing her best to mimic Wilhelm's stance and confident strokes, she remembered catching butterflies with Ishmael. How she had waved a small net, a gift from faraway grandparents, as she now yielded the brush – stroking the canvas to coax the light onto it – as she had silently coaxed butterflies to open their wings and show her their bright glory.

She bit her lip with the vivid memory. Seeing the old man as he loaded his paint with water to make the light luminous, she remembered a small, fine-boned boy who waved the scent of flowers into the air, sweeping his arms from the flowers to the sky to invite the butterflies to fly.

A late butterfly settled on the rose she was painting. It startled her a little; she did not attempt to transfer its presence to her canvas, but instead left the small white patch of her surprise above the flower. It made the picture luminous, and drew the eye, despite the shortcomings of the brush-strokes.

When she left he asked her casually, as if it did not matter, to promise to tell no one of her visit to him. She wanted to ask why but then looked up again at his face and did not, only nodded and left without another glance, knowing that he watched her go.

Marta found herself near the cottage whenever she went for a walk. She always felt restless these days. School had dulled into a troubling routine of incomplete homework and inattentive lessons. Home felt odd without Ruth and Jacob, and Simon was too often now distant and faintly contemptuous of his younger sister and her daily concerns. And with Mother's illness the house was quiet and anxious. Ben listened to her and they shared their annoyance over school, but his own large-eyed fears amplified her own and she preferred the company of the silent trees. She was drawn into the forest all the more strongly by that small cottage, rundown and broken within the trees, in which there hung a luminous painting of a divine city safe in a storm. Wilhelm was not always in and she pretended not to mind but in truth she looked forward to talking to him more and more. Increasingly she would find opportunities to slip off and visit him, telling no one, keeping the secret as promised.

One afternoon she came home from school to find her father pacing outside, his dark eyes wide in a drawn face and his hands, usually so calm, wringing the air before him. His helplessness terrified her. She turned to go into the forest but he had seen her.

'Marta,' he called, 'Marta, I am so glad you are home. Go and see for me how your mother is.'

She baulked and looked at him.

'Why?'

'Just go in and tell me what is happening.'

Then seeing her frightened face, he added, 'Narina is there.'

Fuming at his demands and at his fear, Marta went in, her own heart clenched. Crossly she yelled, 'Narina,' as she came in, 'Narina, where are you?'

'Here,' Narina's voice sounded as it always sounded and Marta's heart pounded a little less. She followed the voice into her mother's room, where she had known it would be.

Narina was holding a bucket and her mother was retching into it and sobbing softly but uncontrollably.

'Come, Marta,' Narina said calmly, 'come and help. Hold your mother's head for her, she is weak.'

Marta dropped her bag, climbed onto the double bed from her father's side, knelt next to her mother and held her head as renewed retching shook her mother. Then there seemed no more and Narina gave the signal to let Mother sink back onto the damp pillows in exhaustion. Marta wiped her face with the tissues scattered about, while Narina emptied the bucket.

Her mother was sinking into sleep. Marta let herself rock back onto her heels and watched. She had been frightened by how small her mother's head had felt beneath the wet, patched hair as she held it over the bucket. Now she looked at the thin shoulders with the hollows between them and her weak neck and wanted to cry. She wanted to throw her head back and howl as she had not done since she was too little almost to remember. But she did not; she slipped off the bed and began tidying the tissues away, throwing them into the bin and straightening the bed clothes as far as she was able to. Narina came back in.

Marta turned, but Narina walked over to the window.

'Let's let some air in.' And opened it.

'Narina,' Marta could barely suppress her fury now. 'Narina, what happened? What has made her so much worse?'

'She's tired,' Narina answered, 'she wants to go.'

Marta stared at her.

'The news from the hospital today was bad.' Narina added.

'You mean she . . .' Marta started.

Narina took her by the shoulders, looked into her eyes and then held her close. 'Yes, baby, the new course of chemo is not helping.'

But Marta struggled away, took one look at her mother's still form, already so far away, so far from the mother she had known, and ran from the room.

She kept running until she got to Wilhelm's cottage at the edge of Millwood forest.

He was not in and the house stood as quiet and deserted as it had stood before he moved in. That he was not in and had unreasonably not told her he would be gone, fuelled a wild anger rising in her. Furiously she circled the small house, looking for a way in, remembering her escapades with Ishmael, remembering his fearlessness. She found a small window at the back propped open. She wrenched it further open and wormed her way through, kicking the toilet shut and landing on it with a thump. She grazed her arms and her cheek but did not feel it.

She stalked about his small domain, staring at everything angrily – his books and paints and a few things in the kitchen. What good were they, she wondered, what good could they possibly be? Where was he?

She decided mulishly to make herself at home, without his permission. She did not know why she had run to this house. She could not look at the painting in the kitchen now, though she knew somewhere in her mind that she had come for that. Angry with herself, she put the kettle on, ignoring the play of light on the overturned clean glasses.

She did not know that the old man had felt the same way that day. He had come to the forest to be alone and yet in the afternoons he found himself looking out of the window, searching for her curly head amongst the trees more and more and felt disgruntled when she did not come. So he had taken himself off for a walk.

Marta calmed down as she drank his tea. More quietly now and guiltily she snooped about the dark little house, in a small room kept dark with heavy curtains over the little window. It had on the floor a moth-eaten and faded carpet, in the centre of which stood an old wingback armchair. Ranged around the walls were rickety shelves weighted with books, standing and piled and nearly falling off. Next to the chair stood a tall, slim lamp that looked ready to topple over, a large tasseled lampshade perched precariously on top. The lamp had been left on and cast a soft glow over the whole dingy room and the coziness made Marta long for rest. She sat down in the chair, closing her hands about the warm cup. She slipped out of her shoes and curled her legs beneath her, leaning back against the goosedown cushion and letting her head fall against the wide wing on its side. She sipped her tea and tried to think through what had happened.

Events would not settle in her mind into any kind of order and she became restless again, feeling her anger and fear rise. So she sat up a little and read idly through the titles on the shelf. *The Divine Comedy* sounded interesting. Gingerly she took it from the shelf and opened it. She stared in horror at the picture that confronted her: contorted bodies, faces drawn in fear, arms becoming trees and at the edge, wolves with bright eyes, waiting. This was the very image of the dark forest – the one people all around her feared, the one that made them afraid of people like Bosman who lived in it and loved it and made it their home. Why was it here – what was this book – hell? She dropped it; divine comedy? Divine? Funny? She ran from the room, spilling her tea in the process and dropping the old book with a crash. She did not care, she had come here for comfort and what had she found?

She stumbled in her hurry down the dark corridor, trying to find her way to the kitchen, where she bumped into Wilhelm.

'Whoa there,' he held her arm. 'What's the matter?'

'That book, people trapped as trees, the monstrous forest. What is that? Who would put that in a book? And call it *The Divine Comedy*? Why? Why would they do that?' She could not stop the torrent now. 'It's all the horror that is hidden, that should stay hidden – that we read to get away from.'

She struggled away from him wanting to be outside, wanting to know that the forest was just the forest and not a nightmare.

'Marta,' he said her name for the first time. 'Marta, calm down. Shall we have some tea?' He was groping after a ritual which would contain this burst dam.

It did but not in the way expected.

Feeling foolish and embarrassed now, Marta hung her head and said, 'I had some tea – I spilled it.'

'So,' he was amused, 'you broke into my place, helped yourself to some tea and then spilled it in my library – potentially over a precious old book?'

'Yes.'

'Well you had better help clean that up. Bring a cloth – they're under the sink.' And he led the way back to the library.

The book was unscathed, but the old frayed carpet needed careful washing. Fresh tea was brought into the library. Wilhelm sat on the chair and Marta was allowed to pull up a footstool from under the table.

'You know, if there is one thing *The Divine Comedy* still offers us it's the knowledge that whatever we may have done in our lives we can imagine poetic justice for it. Punishments to fit our sins – and there is something satisfying in that – especially when, like Dante, we imagine that for our enemies. We think we know what justice is – and often we find devising just punishments amusing – most of us only do it in our heads, but still.'

Marta, still feeling shaken, asked. 'But what about the unjust punishment – the arbitrary illness and pain?'

'For that,' he said, 'we must turn to tragedy. You have read Shakespeare?'

'Shakespeare?'

'Yes. Do you know any?'

'We've read some of the sonnets, and *Romeo and Juliet*.'

'Well, there you go – their suffering was greater than their sin, wasn't it?'

'Yes, but they are also annoying and stupid.'

'That is true. Have you read *King Lear*, though?'

'No.'

'Let's read that then.'

And they spent the afternoon reading aloud, taking parts in turn.

They would spend many afternoons reading and talking about what they had read. He was delighted with her interest in art and literature. She in turn was thrilled with his library, which he allowed her to use at will and so she spent many hours there curled up happily, sometimes taking books home for the long nights, when she lay listening to her mother's ragged breathing, waiting and not waiting for those inhuman cries of pain which would tear the tenuous peace of the night.

She would read then, not to make the world go away but to find again a way that she could be at home in it. To see the things that made it lovely. Because you could turn from the books with different eyes and see your world as you had not seen it before. She knew it was here at this terrible time that the dance of words moved beyond the beautiful to the sublime.

She paid no attention to the rumors about Wilhelm and his estrangement from his family, or to the nagging uncertainty about his name and where she had heard it before. The girls at school giggled about the 'fancy old headmaster' of a private school and said he was 'going native' in the old style. She thought she knew what that meant and did not think it a bad thing. She asked no one. Her visits to his library were an escape and she was afraid that questions would bring an end to them.

The two of them would begin with faint awkwardness, he pretending to ask about school as he ought, but soon they would speak of the real things – about books.

'People are afraid of you,' she would say to him eventually.

'Yes,' he said, 'people always fear what they don't understand.'

Even braver one day, she asked, 'Do you miss them?'

'Yes,' he said, 'I miss them.'

'Then why –?' but she got no further; he had already begun noisily to wash their brushes. So she took up their water jars and emptied them outside. As she stood outside, she heard the loerie call.

He stepped to the door, seeing her stand so still.

'What is it?'

'The loerie.'

'What about it?'

'She's calling. I wonder what the trouble is.'

'What do you mean?'

'The loerie calls to warn of trouble in the forest or when elephants are near.'

'What nonsense,' he said, angry beyond reason. 'The bird is called the Turaco and calls because it's calling its mate, or because it's evening, or because *birds call*. It has no knowledge of trouble or danger.'

'But the loerie . . .'

'It is called the Turaco, Marta.'

She did not know what to make of his anger and decided to leave it at that. She remembered that Narina had always said there were some things no one could fix for you. You had to fix them for yourself.

And she was grateful for his lack of questions, too.

So she did her best simply to be nice, even when he was gruff and ungracious, which was often.

ELEVEN

Bach's *Cantata No. 180* woke Marta. It was barely
dawn and the Outeniqua mountains were still shrouded
in mist as she stepped to her window and looked to see
what kind of world greeted her today. The music told
her that Ruth was home and Marta remembered happily
that she had arrived late the previous evening in time for
Mother's birthday. Jacob too was home, on a rare leave
of absence from the army, and he had made every effort
last night to be a part of things as usual.

Marta padded down the corridor quickly and quietly.
In the kitchen the kettle was still hot and she made
herself a cup of coffee and walked softly through to the
stoep, where she knew Ruth would be. She stopped in
the doorway, looking at her older sister sitting curled
up in the heavy armchair in the pale light of morning,
made soft by the mist from the mountain. She felt a lump
in her throat she could not understand. Ruth's face was
resting between both her hands, the fingers lying lightly
flexed about her cheeks and her eyes were round and
dark with the music.

Marta softly picked up her mother's footstool and
placed it near her sister and sat down, resting her head
near her sister's elbow. Ruth did not acknowledge her

but Marta knew they were glad of each other's company. They sat in silence, letting the music fill the morning as the light rose slowly and with difficulty from the mountain and spilled into the valley and crept up the long path to their own home. Finally as the last notes sounded, the two girls were sitting in the full light of the morning. The morning glories turned their bright heads towards the sun and the mist was retreating from the tip of the mountain. Their coffee was cold.

'Mother wanted to hear that this morning,' Ruth whispered. 'She said "no one else understood the soul's longing for God like Bach, don't you think?"'

'Oh, Ruth.'

'Shhh, let's just leave it for now. It was so lovely.'

They went together to the kitchen and boiled the kettle again. Ruth began the preparations for the Sunday breakfast.

'Shall we lay the table outside?' she suggested and once again Marta did not mind her older sister's bossy tone but did as she was told.

Marta cleaned the table and then opened the dark wooden chest that stood outside her mother's room, taking out the heavy white tablecloth that bore her great aunt's crest. She swung it out over the table, placing the emblem near the top of the table where her mother would sit.

Then she fetched the dark wooden placemats and placed them around the table, along with the silver cutlery and the white plates, which she knew had been in the family longer than she had, having been wedding gifts to her parents. She fetched glasses and mugs. From the kitchen she could smell fresh coffee and bread. Then, with a pair of rose-cutters, she stepped softly onto the glittering grass, walked to her father's rose garden where she cut five white buds and some greenery, which she placed in an arc around her mother's place. Then she

201

went to wake the others. When she returned to their table, Ruth was already tucking candles amongst the flowers she had placed around her mother's setting. Jacob came out with Father's Bible, placing it next to his place opposite Mother's and then they all stood about the table and waited for Father to bring Mother out to breakfast. They waited a long time.

'It is hard this morning.' Simon said. Last night they had been quite late, waiting for Ruth's arrival on the last train from Port Elizabeth. 'Let's sing something.'

They sang *Die güldene Sonne*, Mother's favourite morning hymn. As they sang the world felt whole again for Marta, as it had not since Ruth had first left home and she knew, as she had not known for a long time, that a kindly God was looking down on them, whatever might happen. Their mother came out of the house, stood in the doorway, leaning only slightly on their father's arm and smiled at her five children singing for her on her birthday. Jacob, without missing a note, lit the candles around her place. Simon pulled her chair out and when the song finished, their mother was installed in her place and bade them all to sit. Their father read from Isaiah the promise of eagles to lift the stumbling and said grace. They sang once more the traditional family birthday hymn and then Ruth and Ben brought in the baskets of eggs and freshly baked rolls while Marta poured coffee.

Breakfast was her mother's favourite meal and all were glad that they could have it out here, though halfway through she needed a blanket and a jersey. After breakfast, Mother sat in the lounge softly listening to the radio church service, while the others went to church with Father. Marta stayed to do the dishes.

She went about her task quietly so that she could hear if her mother called and also so that her mother could listen undisturbed to the service on the radio. When Marta finished she cleared the table of crumbs to prevent bees and put the flowers from her mother's place in a vase. She brought them into the lounge where her mother was sitting.

The service was just ending and her mother turned as she came in. 'You've brought the flowers.'

It always surprised Marta how well her mother understood what was going on around her despite her limited vision. 'Put them here on the little table in the sun, Marta, they will smell more in the warmth,' she added.

When Marta stepped close to her mother and had put the flowers down in the bright sun near the window, she suddenly found her hand caught in her mother's.

'What is it, Mother?'

'Oh it is so dark. I am afraid.'

Marta felt stricken and wished she were not alone with her mother now. But wishing would not change things, so she crouched down, keeping her mother's hands in her own and said. 'We are all here now, Mother. We are all here for you, Mother. Even Jacob is here.'

'He goes to the border soon, doesn't he?'

'Yes, but he is here now.'

Her mother said no more and Marta held her hands until her face and the shaking in her hands quieted. Then she began telling her mother softly what she could see outside. Suddenly her voice caught as she spoke. She was sure she had seen the jewel green of a loerie amongst the leaves of the poplars her father had planted before their gate.

Loeries never came so far out of the forest. And yet when she listened, she could hear the thrilling, urgent clucking of the bird. But she could see no danger. She clutched her mother's hand tighter. It's not the loerie, it's the Turaco, she told herself. It sings because that's what birds do.

'What is it, Marta?' her mother called and as Marta

turned to her, she saw that the pain was back. Her mother's face was grey and drawn and she bit her lip, her breath coming in rattling gasps.

'Mother,' Marta whispered, 'what can I get you?'

'Just stay with me.' Marta could barely hear her reply through the rasping breaths. So Marta stayed. She wiped her mother's face with the wet cloth that always lay ready and gave her a little water.

'Is there nothing else I can do?' she asked.

'No, Marta.'

When the spasm was over, her mother smiled wanly and whispered. 'It is too long, Marta, too painful. I can't do this anymore. But you are all so young.'

'Oh, Mother, we will manage. Don't stay if it hurts too much.'

Her mother patted her hand. 'Thank you,' she said, 'thank you.'

'Do you want to rest?' Marta knew how the pain exhausted.

'Yes.'

So she pushed the chair back into a lying position, rearranged her mother's cushions and blankets and turned her to face the sun.

'Will you put Bach on again?'

'Yes.'

And so Marta left her mother lying with her eyes closed in the pale, warm sun as Bach's melody poured into the air.

Schmücke dich oh liebe Seele,
Laß die dunkle Sündenhöhle
Komm ans helle Licht gegangen[3]*

She went out briefly, to see whether she could find the

3 *Deck yourself, my soul, with gladness*
Leave behind all gloom and sadness
Come into the daylight's splendour

204

loerie, whether she could see what had brought the bird so far out of the forest. But there was nothing except an April chill in the air, a warning that winter was not far off.

She sat on the gate a while, humming softly the melody spilling from the house across the deep mountainside and mingling with the slower, heavier singing from her father's church. One of the dogs came up and barked fiercely at the gate, jumping up and yapping hysterically.

'Shut up, Toyon,' she said irritably. But when he didn't, she asked, 'What is it?' and opened the gate to step beyond. Toyon shot through and sniffed excitedly at the ground, and then he put his tail between his legs and crept back into the garden. She laughed at him and looked for what he had sniffed at. It was scuffed by his paw marks at the edges but it was unmistakably an elephant spoor, round and rippled like a small dry lake on the path.

Marta stared at the spoor for a while, instinctively scanning the forest nearby, even as she felt an indescribable joy rising in her. But the loerie was silent now. She decided to speak to Jacob about it and went back inside to check on her mother, who was sleeping peacefully.

The family returned with several guests and ordinariness returned with them. Marta found no moment in which to speak to Jacob but was grateful for the bustle of guests needing hospitality. Her mother's pain and fear distressed her but she did not know how to speak to anyone about it. And somehow, Sunday passed as Sundays did, with a quiet calm, with long walks and late afternoon coffee and cake for visitors, who had been to the big tree so as not to tire Mother out too much with talking.

One of the visitors was their neighboring farmer,

Ianni Stavros. He walked with Marta at the end of the row between the tall trees.

Marta looked up at the treetops, which were quiet today, not hissing or gesturing their usual disapproval of people.

'They are quiet today; they don't mind us so much.'

'Yes,' he said to Marta, 'they know your mother is struggling.'

Marta was about to protest awkwardly, not used to adults other than Bosman who spoke in this way about the forest. But when she looked at Mr. Stavros's weather-beaten old farmer's face beneath the battered hat, with a rare loerie feather, she remembered how often her mother had walked through the forest, had found the people in it who needed her and said nothing.

After a while she said. 'Yes they do know her.'

'And they remember. They know also that she is tired.' Briefly he put his arm about her shoulders then and helped her over a muddy patch amongst the dark trees.

When they got back, Ruth had already helped their mother to bed and so the evening was spent at the braai, a bit away from the house so as not to disturb her with their conversation, which rose and fell as the wind in the treetops.

That night the world tilted again, the way it had when they took Ishmael away from the accused box and Marta had known that she would never see him again. She realized for the first time that her mother would die and die soon. They had all been so caught up in caring for her, in knowing what relieved her best, that Marta had not paid attention to this central fact. She wondered whether the others had known. Though she was lying down she felt dizzy.

She knew the world tilted and turned but she

wondered whether it should be doing it so fast. Her dreams were vivid and left her feeling hollow in the morning. This world where she belonged had begun in the forest, at the moment when she first learned the names for things from Ishmael. Her sense of herself had grown from knowing where the Kalander grew tall and where buchu was bitter on the hillside and where the wide sea made flowers tiny in the wind.

She had learnt that her mother's past was far away in Germany. History belonged there and the war – and though as she grew older, she had known that this was childish, she knew that her world still turned on that sense that the war and cruelty were history, were far away and in the past. Suffering belonged there; was rooted in her parents' stories of the past. Its intrusion here was unreal and pulled everything out of kilter.

She remembered now being taken to the old Milkwood tree, called the Post Office tree, where sailors had posted letters for hundreds of years in an old boot. She had stared for a long time at the tree, its old bark and wild branches and the boot to which the sailors had for so many years entrusted their letters. She could not imagine that kind of trust, she could not imagine needing it with her family so close around her, though she had known her mother needed it daily, when she turned a hopeful face to her father's hands as he came home from the town and post office.

So the world grew. From the trees, birds and the disa it grew to include the sea and the ships sailing on the sea, and her frontier rolled back towards Cape Town and the landing of the ships from the Dutch East India Company and the building of the castle by Jan van Riebeeck, whose long oily locks, thin moustache and deep black eyes unsettled her from the pages of her history books.

Then the world beyond the sea had taken on more shape, too. Gradually the link between her mother's stories of her home before the war, the grandeur of the oak trees, the sea and the lake, the midwinter hunts and her grandmother's entertainments turned into life stories and the gap between the two islands, the one here and the other built of her mother's memories, filled in.

How horrified she had been to find that part of what filled that space was ships that held people. People to be sold into slavery. And now the world included America, where the slaves went to pick cotton and sing, according to school. She wondered what they did in South Africa – 'farm labor', she'd been told – some people apparently treated their slaves well. But she could still not fathom the thought of owning other people. You owned your family in some ways, or they owned you – but strangers? More difficult still, to understand the role the Bible played in all that. The same Bible her gentle, forgetful father read and preached about, the same Bible her mother read to them in the mornings before they all set out for their day.

Marta vividly remembered the lessons on Noah. First the flood and then the story of Noah's son, who had seen his father's nakedness and was punished, made to become a servant for all eternity, which Mejuffrou Niemand had said explained Africans.

Marta had not been able to stop herself calling out. 'But, it was a mistake. He didn't mean to see his father's nakedness.'

'Marta we don't call out in class,' her teacher had warned.

But she had been too engrossed in the unfairness of it to care. 'And, and it was Noah's fault – he was drunk.'

At that point she had been smacked on the hand and sent out of the classroom. She remembered the punishment now, and remembered again standing outside that room and realizing that the same thing could have such very different meanings. She had wondered how

208

that was possible and had found no answers in her head, though she puzzled all the rest of that lesson and break spent inside the classroom.

Did they actually see different things? She tried to think of ways to ask but could think of none except directly. And when she asked, she learnt that there were also things that nobody really wanted to see at all, like the injustice of God, which she thought was all too clear in that story. Injustice not only to Seth, who had been trying to help his drunken father but to all the people of Africa, who had to be slaves for it.

Marta squirmed now, remembering her outrage and her struggles with symbolic stories misinterpreted and explained to unsuspecting children as literal fact. And she traced her thoughts on the topic further. She remembered now her first Latin lessons.

The Romans kept slaves and the Greek architecture and philosophy would not have been possible without their slave economy. Must good things be built on the suffering and labor of others?

So Europe had gradually sailed closer to her own world, which had itself pushed northwards through history lessons. The free burghers, who had freed their slaves and wanted their own freedom, did not want to be enslaved to the British – another version of that word, which meant something else again? Enslaved did not mean the same as being kept in a dark ship in chains and then having to work and breed like cattle.

Sometimes she wished the world would keep still beneath the words. But it did not and sometimes she knew it could not. The world beyond the life of things and plants and people, to which gradually had been added the knowledge of Jan van Riebeeck's landing at the Cape in his three graceful ships. Linking the world of history, war and the impossible past. This world here, now, of loerie feathers in the dark shade of the forest and the big smell of the sea, out of which ancestors should, but did not, rise to the rescue, could not ever be one thing only again.

She had felt growing in her the knowledge that her world and the world of Jan van Riebeeck and his castle, of border disputes and the post office shoe, would converge. And when they were one piece she would be grown-up. But she had felt also in all she was taught, an urgent need in the grown-ups to pull everything in the world apart, not to have anything converge or become one with anything else. Teachers flinched when she asked about the word 'enslaved', when she asked about beauty built on 'un-freedom' and they sent her out when she asked what their own arts festival was built on. She sensed that teachers kept things separate and feared questions that exposed the links of the chain the government tried so hard to hide.

One day, not long after she had begun at the English school, her mother had found her spinning the globe in the living room and then stopping it with a finger placed at random on its surface. Marta peered at the place where she had stopped and tried to remember what she knew about it.

'What are you doing, Marta?' her mother had asked.

'I am seeing how much of the world I know, how much of it is in my light,' she answered.

'Well, and . . .?'

'China is still dark, there's only this little bit of light around Marco Polo.'

'I see.'

'And Africa is dark, Mother, we live in Africa; why is so much of it dark? There are only tiny pools of light – Egypt and here and some of the ports around the edge. And that was for slavery so I am not sure it counts.'

'Counts?'

'As light of knowledge.'

'Right.'

'Mother, why? Why is Africa left dark?'

'I suppose because we do not understand much of its history.'

'Well, how hard have we tried?'

'Actually I think it is because we Westerners do not think it matters. In the West I think people believe it does not affect our progress, is not part of us, our history or our understanding of the world.'

'But it is, isn't it? It is for me. I live here.' She paused, while her mother considered an answer. But she could not wait; she blundered on, 'I would not be me if I did not live here, if I did not love the forest, if I did not know the stories about it that I do.'

She did not say, 'It matters, Mother it matters. It is where Ishmael still lives.'

'You're right, Marta,' her mother had finally ventured. 'The facts of our lives are the anchors of our identities. It is how we know who we are.'

Mother always made her thoughts real.

'The facts of history are the same thing for nations: they define the limits and boundaries. Events are the landmarks by which countries have become what they are.'

'But I have two sets of anchors, don't I?'

'Yes, I suppose you do.'

'Does that mean I will always feel lost?'

'Perhaps,' her mother had said slowly, 'perhaps, but it might also mean that you will have a heart ready to listen to others who are lost.'

'Like Father and Uncle Simon?'

'Yes – like them.'

Talking to her mother had always been the surest of her anchors, more than the facts of history, more than the smell of fynbos, more than learning the notes and singing the whole song. These themselves only became real, steady things, when she had told her mother about them.

She remembered how it had felt that first day at English school, when all her carefully acquired anchors from Afrikaans school had turned out to be leg irons, reasons for the others to despise her. And she remember how lost it had made her feel, how afraid that the tilting earth would never stop making her too dizzy to move. She realized now that she would lose the surest of her moorings.

She switched on her bedside lamp. The house was silent – but she could not shake off the fear. She remembered the loerie's call and the spoor she had not told Jacob about. She remembered how cold her mother's hands had been. So she sat up and began to read. Always when her own story threatened to be overwhelmingly chaotic, she turned to other stories, stories where nothing was random and everything had meaning. There was consolation in that, however small. She read until her eyes closed once again.

In the morning, Mother was dead. Father woke them before dawn and they all crowded into her bedroom and father said the Prayer for the Dead from Luther's Hymn book. Then they all stood about helplessly, too helpless even for tears.

Finally Father said, 'She is at peace now; no more pain, we should be grateful for that.' And then, 'Girls, I think we could all do with some tea.' And he pulled the sheets up over their mother's face, before disappearing into the bathroom, where they could hear him heaving.

They gathered again in the cold kitchen, made tea and waited. Waited for the dawn and for the world to wake up; though it seemed impossible that it should do so.

When the time came, Father phoned a funeral parlor

and organized for 'the body' to be fetched. Then he asked Pastor Carolus whether he would assist at the service. Ruth and Marta saw to the flowers, Jacob phoned relatives in Germany and Simon chose hymns and their settings. In this way the days between death and the funeral passed.

The funeral was a relief and a comfort, followed by the difficult task of picking up the strands of life and going on. At school people were kind and awkward. The flowers eventually wilted and Jacob had to return to the army and Ruth to university. Jacob phoned when he arrived at base to say that he was being dispatched immediately to Caprivi. Simon cursed and raged at the news and Father prayed specifically for Jacob every morning now. But to no avail.

Eight months later, Father got a phone call that Jacob had been injured.

At Christmas, when Jacob came home to mend his leg, it was sweltering and dry and so much seemed to have been lost that Marta was surprised when gradually sense returned and shaped her next three years. Mother's death had changed them all. Ruth came home only to spend every day with her boyfriend, Peter. And Jacob, who had been away for two years in the army, disappeared into himself completely. She watched him disappear further on every leave of absence, his face gaunt, his eyes withdrawn. The boy, who had told her Solomon and Bosman's stories, had sung and laughed on weekends, was now taciturn and abrupt. He left the room when she stood up to play the piano.

Father said he was still Jacob – just hiding – that the old and the new Jacob needed time to become a person again. He said not to ask him questions about the army and the border just yet. He would tell her when he was ready. But Marta wondered whether he would ever be ready. She knew also that there was nothing she could do about it. It was something he had seen and done and she had not. She could not share it until he spoke. He was like Wilhelm and she would have to wait for him to be ready to speak or not.

So she watched him quietly, brought him what he needed and saw with horror the bandages changed and the leg that would never again be entirely straight. And she brought him the cards he wanted, and watched as he played solitaire with that blank stare she did not recognize.

'What is he doing?' she had asked, frightened by this new brother.

'He is playing the world back into order.' Narina said. Narina often said things like that; strange sentiments nevertheless imbued with a curious, poetic reality.

When things got to this point, Marta would leave. She would go to Wilhelm, pretending she wanted to know whether he had seen Lady Grey recently. But in reality, she would just sit in his library for a while, pretending that nothing had changed at home. They would talk about the owl a little – she was an almost entirely wild bird now and doing well, but she did come to 'talk' to both Wilhelm and Marta now and then. Marta liked that better than the jesses and lures. It was something real – to have a creature's trust and loyalty, without any need or bond beyond that. Wilhelm understood that. He also understood her need just to read, to be away from the world for a while. He made her tea and let her read freely in his library, occasionally placing books strategically so that she might find them. These days, with her distress about Jacob, they were *All Quiet on the Western Front* and the war poets. Marta understood and was grateful, wondering what it was like to be a pupil at his school.

But at night, Narina went home and she heard Jacob's high pitched, inhuman cries of despair, which made her start up and run out into the corridor, where her father would already be standing. And he would send her back to bed, while he went into Jacob's room and spoke to him as a mother speaks to a small child. Marta stood in silence on the cold corridor, listening to the murmur of voices and missed her mother again, as in the first week.

'Marta.' It was Ben, calling softly from her door a little further down the corridor. 'Do you feel like some Milo?'

Marta didn't but nor did she want to be alone. 'Yes.'

In the kitchen Simon was already filling the kettle. Ben found the rusk tin, which Ruth now kept filled for them in Mother's place, when she was home from university. They sat down together at the large round table, waiting in silence for the kettle. Then they walked in single file, as they had done for years and, without any need for agreement, went into Ben's room. Simon and Marta slipped under the blankets at the foot of Ben's bed and all four for a while cupped their mugs and waited for their feet to feel warm again.

'How long do you think he'll be like this?' Marta finally asked.

'Father says a long time,' Simon answered.

'Will you go?'

'I have to, don't I?'

'It'll be different – to go as chaplain.'

'Yes.'

'What do you think they're talking about?'

'We cannot know. Father saw some stuff in the war in Germany – perhaps it helps Jacob.'

'Maybe.'

'Is this what it is like?' Marta asked.

'What is like?'

'Life after school. Adult life – you know all that stuff

the teachers keep warning you about?'

Simon and Ruth did not know what to say. Marta asked impossible questions.

'Is it full of this silence around things people know but won't speak about?'

The murmur of voices in the other room had died down now and they heard their father softly closing the door and go quietly back to bed, pausing at their doors, listening, hoping they were all asleep. It was such an unlikely hope, so willfully blind, that Ruth for once answered Marta.

'Yes – and no. It is not all there is. There is more and it is good to feel yourself grow to understand a bigger world, too.'

'Yeah,' said Simon, 'which is why we need more rusks right now.'

In the morning, Marta went for a long walk along the river and a swim. She took *War and Peace* and lay on the pebbles in the dappled shade to read. For a long time she did not open the book but lay on her back, looking up at the sky and over at the river. She loved this spot; the river golden brown and flecked with bright flashes of pyrites, the trees giving way to the sunlight on its banks. She had always imagined the river carrying news of the forest to the sea. And it was even now still a link between these two, which had been the boundaries of her world.

She wondered when she had first realised what they marked and how much came together here. The forest, the sea, the cattle-killing, Narina's troubled world, the bright world of her parent's faith, school, political unrest, the family, this warm misty world, her parents' Germany and the many words, swarming around every luminous piece of it.

She wondered when she had first noticed that each bit

cast a shadow no light could touch and her own shadow was dark and bigger than she was. That everything was both itself and its shadow. That everywhere was two places at once at least. And she needed to find out how to live there and where she belonged. And it would be much harder to learn that now, when she could no longer tell her mother the bits as she discovered them.

She picked up her book and took the question to Wilhelm's library. Since her mother's death and Jacob's injuries, she did not like to bother Father, who had always been a little impatient with her odd questions and her inability to accept things the way they were; which he had said on numerous occasions would only land her in trouble like her Uncle Simon. She had decided to take that as a compliment, though she was sure her father had intended otherwise.

It made her feel better to think of Ishmael with Uncle Simon, who had been so straight-eyed and serious throughout the trial of the creepy Mr. Schwartz. She knew from Narina that Ishmael was doing better now at school. That he had learnt to read well and that he wrote to his mother occasionally, letting her know how he was.

In Wilhelm's library that day she read Celan's *Fugue of Death* and then she read Rilke's *Duino Elegies* and then she read on and on. She wondered where the words got the power to take pain out of the dark to a place where it was bearable. She did not understand but she knew it was the most important thing words did. And so she read late into the night every day. She read through Ruth's marriage to Peter and she read through Simon's departure for the Department of Theology in Pietermaritzburg. She read through Jacob's healing and his joining of the Forestry Department and she read through her own final years at school. And when the time came for her to leave school, she chose to keep reading.

PART III

TWELVE

In the crowded student union building, Marta stood awkwardly against the wall, clutching a folder she had been given by the students' association. She watched the others. How did they do it? She wondered how they knew each other so quickly and found things to talk about. Her own mind blurred red with the wings of a bird she feared she would never see again and her new small niece's eyes watching her leave that last evening; at that moment she hated them for leaving her so poorly prepared for this.

She wanted to ask why that girl with the long dark hair kept moving her hands over her face as if she had a veil over it, or why that huge brute standing against the far wall seemed to have dancer's hands as he spoke, though his feet were planted widely as if prepared for a rugby scrum. But she knew from experience that these questions did not go down well, that people were disconcerted by them and would much rather talk about the Cathcart Arms and what Ed had done with the lampshade. She did not understand.

So she was standing against the wall on registration day, drifting off in the afternoon sunlight's dust dance and thinking of home: the cattle coming home in the evening; Narina taking out the ash and laying the fire for the next morning in the kitchen; and the weavers chattering and swallows coming in as the rays of the sun sank down the mountain side and the shadows of trees stretched to meet the singing sea.

She was nudged from this reverie by the sudden movement of the people at the table near her, 'What?' she said, confused and lost.

'It's R now, R has been called.'

'Oh.' And she joined the queue of people whose names began with R shuffling towards the door.

'Did you not hear?' The student in front of her asked.

'No.'

'You were miles away, weren't you?

'I was.'

'I could tell.'

Marta smiled, embarrassed and yet somehow pleased that this tall person had noticed her.

'What are you signing up for, then?' He asked amicably.

'English.' she said. 'History, Latin; possibly French and Philosophy. What about you?'

'Law.' he said.

'Oh.'

'So I'll be doing History and English as well – for the first degree, anyway.'

She felt pathetic at how much that brightened the day. But she liked his face and the easy way in which he spoke without triviality. They moved together through the door to the long row of tables lined up along one side of the football pitch.

'Fun,' he said with a grimace and steered her towards the first table.

A young woman with long tangled locks, several strings of leather with indefinable beads round her neck and a loose long Indian dress confronted them.

'You want to join the National Union of South African Students, NUSAS?' she asked. She was pointedly looking at Marta, not the young man, who was dressed in formal trousers and a shirt.

'Yes,' he butted in, enthusiastically, 'make that two new recruits.' he said.

She looked at him sceptically but then wrote out the names they spelled for her on a list and sorted out the introductory materials for them.

Behind her stood a young black man in jeans and a green T-shirt, sorting piles of papers and clusters of cheap Bic pens. On closer inspection some had NUSAS etched along one side, the others BSM. The young man who was sorting them snorted derisively as they signed.

The woman at the desk turned to him. 'We agreed.' she said.

'Yes.' He was sulky. 'We agreed to cooperate for this one day.'

Marta watched the tension between them. They seemed almost like siblings to her, fighting companionably. Then the pile of material was handed to her. She was glad to see that there was a wad of paper also, which was pressed into her hand with the NUSAS logo printed across the front in black on a deep blood red.

She moved on.

'The first meeting is on Sunday afternoon,' the student called after her, 'at 2:30. The address is on the welcome letter.'

She moved along more of the tables, taking in only half of what they told her. Then finally came her course registration, where she was told she needed to go to the English and History departments to choose tutorial times. After that there was only one more table, at which sat what she supposed must be a mature student, for his hair was already receding and his face was lined with fatigue.

He was leaning in his chair so the back feet bit deeply into the grass. He chewed the back of his pen and looked very bored. Despite this she thought that his eyes took in everything about her, though they rested only briefly on the pack of papers and letters she held in her hands.

He motioned her over as he brought his chair upright, rolling his eyes.

'Name?'

She told him. He glanced up as she said her surname and she noticed now how sharp his eyes were, how thin the moustache that darkened his stretched upper lip.

She automatically began spelling her name, but he stopped her. 'That will not be necessary,' he said. 'Just give me your home address and your student address in that order please.'

He was polite but she sensed sharpness as he looked at her, which made her wary.

'What is this for?' She wished the student in the trousers would catch up with her.

'University admin,' he answered shortly.

She dared ask no more but looked over at the other tables and wondered at the slight distance between the others and his, and she noticed too how the students helping at the other desks did not look over at him and smile as they occasionally did to each other and he had no assistant.

She turned away before he had finished noting down her telephone numbers and said, 'I'm sorry, I have to go now.' She walked away as quickly as she dared though she wanted to run, feeling herself as panicked as the little blue duiker when the loerie called.

He called after her. 'Never mind, Miss Reben, we know your family well.'

At this she burst into a run, across the grass, scattering her papers as she did so, the empty forgotten bag swinging wildly at her hip. She did not stop until she was inside the building out of his line of sight. She felt his eyes, those cold, small eyes still biting into her back even so. Ducking into the toilets just to the right of the door, she splashed her face and leaned her forehead for a moment against the cool tiles. Then she looked at her pale face in the mirror. Her cheeks looked sallow and the shadows beneath her eyes were darker and fuller than they usually were.

'Come on,' she said to herself, 'pull yourself together.'

This earned her an odd look from the leggy student who came out of one of the cubicles just then. She smiled wanly.

The student smiled back, 'It's alright,' she said. 'It'll feel like home soon, you'll see. Wait till after the first rave.'

'Thanks.' Marta said and did not ask what a rave was.

Then she tidied her pile of things, having wiped her hands on the back of her trousers, rather than on the dirty towel hanging over the railing, took note of what was missing and decided that none of it was urgent enough to go back to the lawn where the pencil moustache could see her. Then she examined her map so that she could find her way to the English department.

'I'll need my timetable.' she realized and began looking for it. It was nowhere to be found. She sighed, wondering whether she would find it on the lawn. She doubted it.

She stacked as many of her things into her shoulder bag as she could and then wandered out, keeping her eyes on the ground, searching for her papers. She wondered if she would have to rejoin the queue, or if there was another way of getting another copy of her timetable.

She sidestepped a shadow, her eyes scanning the lawn.

'Hey, Marta.' A voice hailed her.

She did not look up. 'I've lost my timetable. I can't talk now, must find it.' She walked swiftly on, her eyes on the grass and the possibility of gusts of wind.

Suddenly she felt a hand on her shoulder. She shuddered and spun round.

'Your things, you dropped them.'

Feeling contrite and embarrassed for the second time that day, all she managed was a blush and stammered thanks.

'Shall we have coffee now?' he asked.

'I have to book tutorials with my other departments.'

'Sure,' he said. 'We'll do that on the way and have coffee somewhere in town. It's better than the stuff they serve in Kaif anyway.'

'OK, thanks.'

He smiled at her. 'What set you off in such a rush?'

She examined her timetable with more care than necessary. 'Oh, I don't know, I just wanted to get out of the sun for a bit.'

She could see he did not believe her.

'Do you know where the English department is?' she asked to distract him.

'This way.'

'You're not a first year?' She was surprised.

'No, but I need to catch up some credits.'

And they set off, continuing their easy banter as before.

Callum helped her find a suitable spot for her tutorials. And then he signed up for the same one.

'I thought you were in your second year?' Puzzled.

'I failed history last year.' He told her as they made their way up the stairs of the Humanities block from the dark dungeon of the Modern Foreign Languages Department. History was several floors up.

Most of the tutorials were full already but she

managed to find one more with a space in it and wrote her name in.

One of the professors came out of his study just then. He smiled at her and came over to ask whether she was looking forward to the course. However, seeing Callum, he scowled and turned away.

She turned questioning eyes on her new friend. 'What was that all about?'

He shrugged, 'I failed, didn't I? They don't approve of me.'

Marta was surprised at how easily he accepted both his failure and the disapproval of the professor. 'Doesn't it bother you?' She asked.

'What?'

'That you failed?'

'Oh dear,' he mocked, 'am I really going to have coffee with a nerd?'

That stung. Marta had not thought that such categories would apply at university as well. Her back stiffened. 'No, you're not. Thanks for your help with my things and the tutorials. I'm sure I'll see you around.'

'Hey,' he called after her, 'Hey, I was joking! Come on, don't be like that.'

He trotted to catch up with her, ran around her and walked quickly backwards in front of her. 'If you would only stop for a minute I could beg properly, on my knees,' he implored, and his brown eyes shone mischievously.

She laughed then, forgave him and they had coffee at The Copper Kettle. On the way back, they stopped at the university bookshop, and she bought *Hamlet* but no other required reading material, as Callum said she might find some of it more cheaply if she kept an eye on the notice boards at Kaif. *Hamlet* she wanted for this first weekend, which her sister had warned her would be long. He dropped her back at Allan Webb Hall in time for supper and left her with a promise to see her the next day.

She spent the rest of the evening and most of Saturday vainly trying to make her room feel a little more comfortable, but found little to make it less brown. Her few small drawings and the single poster she found in town only emphasized the bare expanse of the pale walls; her books looked a little lost on the dark bookshelf and her few clothes only took up half the cupboard. Her towel on the hook of the door remained the only splash of color.

All the same, by Sunday, things were beginning to feel less strange. She had gone to the big first years' rave along with the others from her corridor, mostly to avoid the noisy second and third years who had come back and were filling the residence now with noise and life, which made it feel almost like home and yet was utterly different.

She had struggled through the preparations for the night. The others already seemed like lifelong friends, comfortable sharing and borrowing clothes off each other, getting dressed in each other's rooms and posing in the bathroom mirrors for each other, critical and friendly and together.

They walked in a giggling bunch altogether to the Great Hall, where the rave was to be. The warden warned them repeatedly to stay together, not to go wandering off and not to come back through Eden Grove alone. And in any case, to come back to the front door, along the well-lit street.

Dire warnings about a rape last year and a flasher who had been spotted in the botanical garden followed. The girls all looked serious, some of them even frightened. Nevertheless they went together, Marta at the back with Didi and Avril who had come from Die Baai and like her were doing English, which she had discovered when she found Avril sitting on a washing machine as it churned, reading *Hamlet*. They had finished reading the third act together loudly above the noise of the washing machines.

As they crossed the square before the library and sidled into single file at the far end to make their way down the narrow stairs leading to the high street, they could hear the music.

'Oh, yeah!' said Didi and jived down the stairs. It made Marta laugh and the knot in her stomach loosened a little. Her father had shown her how to dance but it had been foxtrot and waltz, not this. Not this free movement on your own or opposite your partner, smiling and contorting rhythmically, while the lights flashed and the music thrummed through your feet. How did Didi manage these steep stone steps so easily and dance, too? Didi saw her face and linked arms with her.

'You scared?' she asked.

'A little.'

'Ja, me too. We'll stick together,' she said, 'we'll dance with each other, OK?'

When they got to the hall, they were asked to show their student cards and then their wrists were stamped before they were allowed into the throbbing darkness.

'Drink,' Avril said purposefully and steered Marta and Didi towards a table along one side of the hall. It was punch of some sort, sweet with bits of floating pear and bright cherries, which Marta swallowed whole. Then Didi had her by the arm and was dragging her towards a small space on the dance floor.

'Come on, I love this song!' and she began dancing.

Marta felt hot with embarrassment but found that she was copying Didi and the music was easy to keep up with. She relaxed and smiled back at Didi, who, satisfied that her friend was OK, turned her attention to a tall, dark-haired man, who enveloped her enthusiastically with his long arms and lifted her from the floor. She laughed and her eyes were brighter than ever.

When he had put her down, she turned him towards Marta and introduced him.

'This is my boyfriend,' she said, her voice bubbling with happiness, 'Marc.'

And turning to him, 'Marc, this is my friend Marta.'

He stretched out a long, narrow hand and shook hers warmly. Then he turned again to Didi.

'How are you? How are you finding things? When are you going to get bored and come home?'

Marta was puzzled. Didi turned to her and put her finger on her lips.

'He sneaks in; he has friends who fix it for him – just to see me.' She was proud, clearly of this tall man, who braved the university authorities for her.

Marta felt a twinge as she watched them, felt lonely and thought she heard far beyond the music the wind in the trees and a fearless voice laughing, saying 'Look at the Fling, look at it go!' as a tree tumbled through the salt air into the wild sea below.

'How does it feel,' she wondered, 'when someone takes risks just for you, just to be with you?' She could not imagine it and watched with new eyes as her friend danced with the tall man.

Lost in thought as she gyrated alone amongst the many people on the dance floor, she was shocked into spinning when she felt a pair of hands on her waist and a voice surprised her from her thoughts.

'Hallo, Marta. The night is improving already.'

And then she was looking up into Callum's brown eyes, so close to hers that she could see the small gold flecks dancing in them as the lights flashed bright white periodically.

'Hi, Callum.' She did not want him to see how glad

she was. Then she realized something. 'How did you get in? This is for first years only, isn't it?'

He was smug and held up a badge.

She could not read it in the jittery light. 'What is it?'

'The student newspaper.'

'You write for them?'

'Yes, I am here covering the event. You had better have a good time so that I can say the university has done its duty for its new arrivals. Dance with me,' he said and swept her into his left arm and spun them both towards the centre of the room with practiced ease. He two-stepped with her and no one stared, for he did it so gracefully and with such conviction that it did not even feel odd.

When the music stopped he did not let go of her hand but, tucking her arm securely into the small of his back as he turned, led her first to the drinks table and then outside when he had secured some punch for both of them. The fresh air was a relief after the many pressing bodies, though something about his quick understanding of how she felt bothered her.

'Ah, that's better,' he said, sipping his drink as his eyes smiled at her over the rim of the polystyrene cup. 'How do you like your first rave, then?'

'Well, I was a bit nervous about dancing,' she said.

'Don't be,' he said, 'you dance beautifully.'

'It helps to have a good partner,' she said shyly.

'It helps to dance with someone so light on their feet,' he returned.

She looked at him, helplessly, not sure how to respond.

He laughed then and said, 'I did not know anyone who was so eager to read would dance so well.'

And then she knew what it was about him – he was what her mother would have called gallant and she laughed in delight at having solved the puzzle.

'What?' he said.

'My mother would have called you gallant,' she said.

He preened a little so she added. 'And my father would therefore tell me to be careful of you.'

'And do you always listen to your parents about these things?'

She thought she knew enough of these games to know that the answer should be 'Of course not', lightly said if possible. But it hurt to think of her parents so far away, so she said nothing.

He took her empty cup with his and threw both expertly into the bin some three meters away and said, 'Let's dance again.'

They danced a while more and then she danced with Marc while Callum danced with Didi, and there was a group dance at some point which made her very dizzy and then they walked back all together, chatting. Callum held her arm at times, when she was dizzy or the ground uneven and she liked to feel the sureness of his hand.

At the door, while Avril searched for her keys, Marc held Didi tight and said, 'See you soon.' and they kissed.

Marta turned away. Callum still had his hand on her elbow. He turned her to face him, saw her stricken face and so only leaned a little closer and said softly, 'Thank you. It was a wonderful night.' He kissed her gently on the cheek and said as he left, 'See you on Tuesday.'

'Wow,' Avril said over Didi's head to Marta, 'where did you find him?'

'At registration. He helped me find my way about.'

Well, I would think he's a keeper.'

For the first time Marta saw how like Narina Avril was, how much she already had an adult's body and eyes that were older than her face.

'No, Avril,' she said all the same, 'I have actually come here to get a degree, not a husband.'

'My granny would say "There's no reason not to keep a lookout for both."'

And Marta laughed – they both did then, while Didi went to her room.

'Do you want some coffee?' Avril asked and they crept softly downstairs into the kitchen of their dungeon corridor, made two mugs of Ricoffee and sat together on Avril's bed drinking and talking.

'Are you really looking for a husband already?'

'No, it's just something my grandmother says – and she should know.' Silence. 'No, I want a degree and then to teach. I have a bursary from the Colored Education Department, but don't tell the others that. They will call me a sell-out.'

'A sell-out?'

'Yeah. For taking money from the government, from this government, after years of boycotting, protesting against it. But there was no other way I would have got here.'

'Avril – will you go to the NUSAS meeting tomorrow?'

'No – I can't attend any political meetings, or I'll lose my bursary. And anyway, I would not have been a member of NUSAS but the Black Students' Movement.'

'BSM? But you're colored.'

'That does not matter here. And I still can't go.'

'How will they know?'

'They know.'

She got up to wash the mugs, which Marta took as a hint to leave her alone.

She went upstairs, her mind whirling. As she climbed into bed, she remembered vividly the school room from which Ishmael had run; remembered the principal's voice saying kindly but unshakably that Ishmael could not attend this school. And amongst such memories any thought about what Callum might have meant tonight seemed small and selfish.

She drifted off to sleep eventually, barely stirring when the other students returned.

Sunday morning dawned bright and fresh but before lectures had started it seemed a long and dreary day. Marta lay in bed and listened to the cathedral bells, shortly joined by those of the Catholic Church and others, further away. She knew the Methodist one would only chime much later. She thought of her father and curled guiltily under her thin university blanket.

'God, forgive me, I will go to church soon, but just now I miss my father too much to listen to someone else's sermon.'

She was glad when it was time for breakfast and the corridor became noisy. After breakfast she curled up on her windowsill, looking out at the shade of the oak trees on the knotted road as it struggled to the top of the hill. It really was beautiful, she thought as she returned to *Hamlet*, determined to read it through before the lectures started. She had chosen it rather than the intimidating anthology of poetry between the severe black covers. But as she leaned back against the frame of the open window, her mind filled with images of an old man standing in the afternoon light, looking at a picture of a city bathed in gold. Then she fell to reading.

After the big Sunday roast lunch, she wondered what one took to a NUSAS meeting, decided to bring nothing and set off with her street map alone. She walked briskly, not wanting to be late and afraid that she might get lost on the way. But she found the address easily enough, though the afternoon became dark as she walked. Clouds were drawing over from the southwest.

She knocked at the dark, small door, having been barked at by several mongrel-thin dogs which burst from the overgrown hedges or leapt madly at rusting gates of houses. The door was opened only a handbreadth.

'Hi,' she said.

'What do you want?'

'I've come for the NUSAS meeting.'

'Name?'

'Marta Reben.'

The door moved again, almost closing this time. She heard paper rustling and two voices conferring. A list was being consulted. Then the door opened wide enough to let a head come through, eyes scanned the road and she was let in.

'Quickly.' It was a command.

The hallway was dark even after the dim grey light outside, but as her eyes adjusted she could see a bare wooden floor, stacks of framed posters leaning against the wall and a rickety bentwood chair supporting a pile of coats, and a tall mirror.

She was led through a door sagging in its hinges to a dark room where several students sat already on ancient couches, carpets and each other. She felt a little out of place in her simple jeans and T-shirt and tied-back hair, rather than flowing floral dresses, long straggling tresses and leather sandals but she was greeted enthusiastically and soon drawn into the discussion about the government's refusal to negotiate with students, or with any of the black political parties about the homeland policy and the plight within them, the farcical nature of the tricameral parliament and finally the concern about the sixteenth of June exams, which black students were going to boycott – and consequently fail.

'Well, shouldn't they?' Marta asked. There was a stunned silence.

'What do you mean?' a shaggy haired young man sitting cross-legged on the floor finally asked carefully, as if she were a strange wild beast who needed to be approached with great caution.

'Well,' she said, 'does political action not imply choice and the willingness to bear the consequences of that choice? Doesn't that show that you mean what you say, that you are serious?'

'But we have a right to political action. It is a basic right – the university should not punish us for that.'

'But it is not a punishment; it is simply a consequence of missing an exam. Surely if you believe that will achieve something you will gladly bear that consequence!'

Her aggressor stared at her angrily. 'You don't understand, the authorities have no right–'

The girl who had opened the door and had sat at the desk at registration day said, 'Who is collecting notes for the comrades in prison next week?'

The scruffy cross-legged one got up to get a drink from the kitchen; as he did so he drawled, 'I don't attend enough lectures to be much use I'm afraid.'

But enough others volunteered. Marta even agreed to some English notes as one of the prisoners had to catch up an English credit. Naomi – for that was her name – thanked her warmly. That made her feel a little better, but the scruffy young man continued to snub her throughout the meeting, snarling at her later in the garden round the braai.

'Who are you, anyway?'

When she told him, he responded, 'I should have guessed. You're a Boer aren't you? Have you come here to spy on us?'

He drew right up against Marta and his breath made her eyes smart. His chest pushed into her arm, spilling her drink over her front.

'Please,' she said 'I don't know what you mean, my name is not Afrikaans: it's German.'

'German!' He roared. 'Well there's a surprise! Bloody Nazi, bloody fascist!'

Marta stared at him in shock, 'What do you mean?'

Naomi was at her side, 'Don't mind Nathan,' she said. 'He gets like that.'

236

She took Marta by the arm and led her back inside. In the kitchen she made her some tea, while others pacified the yelling dreadlocks

'Will you join us on rag weekend?' Naomi asked.

'What's happening?' Marta asked, trying to look composed and sure of herself when all she wanted was to leave these strange people. They seemed so serious about politics but did not want to bear the consequences of action. And were so closed to question. She listened to Naomi's diatribe against rag week and charity in general.

'Yes, I will come to the rally.' She was not yet ready to give up on her imagined heroes, or heroics she might herself perform in the name of freedom, just because one man was drunk and an idiot.

Naomi saw her to the door after that. 'You'll be all right, you'll get used to us. I liked what you said about being serious about politics, that's the spirit we want. You should think about writing for our paper. We meet most evenings above the students union.'

'I will,' Marta smiled gratefully and left, hurrying through the wet and clammy streets to get back to her dining hall before supper was entirely over and her absence noted.

Someone called her name. She turned. It was Callum.

'Hi, Callum,' she called and waited for him to catch up.

'What are you doing out here on a Sunday evening?' he asked her.

'There was a NUSAS meeting – you know: they told us at registration.'

'Oh, yes,' he hit his head, 'I forgot. Did anything important happen?'

She told him about the puzzling afternoon. He listened sympathetically and very attentively. It was soothing and his gallantry made her forget how disturbing she had found the afternoon. Now she laughed with him about it.

'Tell you what,' he said, 'at the rally; wait for me; we'll go together and I'll look after you.'

'I don't need looking after,' she bristled.

'Of course not – but a friend won't hurt, will he?'

'No. Thank you for walking me back again.'

'My pleasure,' he said and gave an exaggerated bow out there in the street. She loved that he was so flamboyant and did not care who saw him being extravagant. His confidence was mesmerizing and unsettling.

It was a relief when lectures started properly on Monday. After the distressing meeting and the unsettling walk home with Callum, Marta was glad to think that life here too would soon have a rhythm she would recognize. Despite this, at breakfast, when maltabella pap was served, she felt an aching stab of longing for home, for the trees and the mountain brooding in the mist. Blessedly, breakfast was fairly silent, mostly first years – and of those, only the ones who had a 'dawny' – first lecture of the day.

Marta had no dawny, but was glad to have the first peaceful hours of the day to herself. She wandered gradually over to the central campus and sat on the library steps waiting for the next lecture time. It was quiet so early in the morning and Marta soon began to daydream. She thought of the friendship of Goethe and Schiller and the letters of Rainer Maria Rilke to Lou; she thought about talking all day about *Hamlet* or *The Lady of Shallot*.

Then she plucked up enough courage to enter the huge, stark library – and stopped short. The books were on *steel* shelves, functional, standing in close grey rows on a linoleum floor. Marta stared: where were the wooden shelves? Where were the kindly, elderly and wise librarians, who knew every book? Where was the awed, carpeted hush of learning?

She turned around and left, dreams of pursuing truth crushed. She sat on the library steps and laughed at herself and her dreams of wood-panelled libraries with stained glass windows. She looked more soberly at the red bricks reaching up to the library steps in elegant patterns and the young trees newly planted, just beginning to cast some shade in the early morning light.

She went to lectures, which she struggled to follow; she took notes but the words would not fit into meaning for her. She soon felt despair creep over her, but she read on doggedly and went to most lectures. She avoided much of the res life though she went out with Didi and Avril. But most evenings were spent upstairs at the student union preparing the student newspaper with Callum and the others on the editorial team.

The thin-lipped man from registration came to talk to the team, asked them questions and finally warned them that they were being watched. He was particularly harsh to Callum, who came close to being smacked across the face during the questions. The girls fussed around him afterward.

'He's from the police, the secret service, not from university admin at all. How could the university have let him onto campus?' They raged, but Callum waved them silent.

'We can beat them,' he said. 'We have right on our side. All revolutions the world over have won eventually!'

And so Marta went to the rag week rally, having spent all week avoiding the common room, where they were making tissue flowers for the float. On Saturday morning the floats all went out into the dismal grey and looked a sad, garish sight, soon made sorrier by a drizzle that made the colors run into each other until they were a pale kind of sludge, hanging sadly from the exposed chicken mesh beneath them.

But later that day she met Callum and Naomi and they went together to the hill behind Kimberley Hall, where beneath the straggling bloekom trees the NUSAS and BSM had gathered for a giant rally. There were speakers and poets and there was a great deal of singing that Marta did not understand, but she took photos and scribbled notes all the same.

In the noise and the heat that had risen after the morning rain, she felt dizzy and strange, yet elated.

Callum smiled at her and stuck by her side, even when the entire cohort began marching towards town. They walked, singing, with linked arms, down Prince Albert Street and then turned into and marched along Somerset Street to the university administration building. They stopped at the arch, for there were caspirs and policemen with dogs lined up, preventing their entrance back into the university grounds. The policemen stood quietly, holding the dogs barking fiercely and straining against their leashes. The leaders turned to the crowd and gestured for silence. Then they began singing again.

They did not sing the songs they had sung before but *Nkosi sikele i'Afrika*. The police shifted uncomfortably and there was a brief, eerie pause: then they opened fire on the crowd with tear gas. But everyone sang on, peppery tears now streaming down their faces. One of the dogs broke loose and attacked a girl who had been taunting it. Pandemonium reigned and everyone ran – mostly towards the university building, where they would be safe – the police did not chase them on to campus ground. But the girl who had been attacked by the dog needed to go to hospital for stitches. Others were taken into custody – one of them was Eshile whom Marta recognized from history lectures. He had tried to pull the dog off his victim.

All exhilaration was gone then, leaving only fear as they ran; and Marta was horrified at her own lack of courage in fighting for her beliefs.

Callum comforted her. 'We'll get better at it. We have only just started.' He took her back to his room where he stayed with her till everyone who was still free, gathered at the students' union. They were all too shaken to do anything just then and Marta and Callum soon left.

Eshile was not seen again for a month. Work was collected for him but it was impossibly hard to tell where he was being kept. When he did come back he was haggard and bruised. Marta thought of Bomani back at home, at her mother's kitchen door and Mieta crying. She felt again the surge of guilt which had settled deep in her stomach since the rally. Guilt over her lack of courage, and guilt over her new happiness with Callum while others were suffering so.

Callum was very quiet in the weeks following the disastrous rally. He seemed to have lost much of his flamboyance and worked quietly at the newspaper offices, did not join in the drinks afterwards anymore and generally kept to himself. Only for Marta would he still occasionally come out of his shell as they walked back and crept into his room.

She asked him one day what was wrong and he said only that work was getting heavy but she thought it might be something else. When she thought of her own concerns about how her father and siblings would feel about what she did, she kept quiet and did not press him, knowing how hard the balance between selves might be.

The 16th of June was the next big gathering. There had been exams for a week already and Marta felt bleary-eyed and overwhelmed but Callum had asked repeatedly and anxiously whether she'd be there to help cover it for the newspaper, and so there she was. It was early and a bitterly cold morning as the students gathered, stamping their feet for warmth. Now and again someone would begin to speak, to commemorate Hektor Pieterse and other victims of Soweto before losing momentum. It was a subdued crowd that walked in complete silence to the university offices to demand a day of remembrance, a day of no exams. They walked through the arch, watched by the silent cordon of policemen and dogs once again.

The silence was ominous, threatening. The two sides watched each other, subdued but seething, when suddenly a signal seemed to be given and the students were attacked, despite their orderliness. They fled in all directions and to her horror Marta saw the university administration block shut its door before the students could get in. Thinking it must be a mistake, she ran up the steps to bang on the door. They remained shut and when she turned, she was confronted by a burly policeman who struck her once across the shoulder with his panga before Callum could get to her. He was yelling something incomprehensible.

She crouched down cradling her smarting shoulder and curled up out of the way, huddling against the doors she could not believe were shut. Callum crept closer. 'Marta, are you OK?'

'Yes, I'm fine,' she said, 'it just hurts – but look what they are doing down there.'

They had crept to the wall together and were kneeling up, peering over it. A policeman was beating a screaming girl whom Marta now recognized as Juanita from her Philosophy class.

'Why?' Marta cried. 'Why?'

'Because the ANC has called for the country to be made ungovernable and this is how the police "restore order".' Callum was quoting the newspapers.

'This restores order?'

Another policeman had called off the one who was beating Juanita and she remained on the ground.

Students were gathering round to help and the police were moving away. The doors to the university remained shut.

Callum took Marta by the arm and led her gently round the university building until they were in his residence, where he gave her some sweet tea and examined her shoulder. It was bruised but her thick sweater had prevented any serious damage. Callum sighed.

'Come on,' he said as she finished her tea, 'I'll walk you back.'

In the morning he was gone. His room was empty and his things had been packed. He had spoken to no one and no one knew where he was.

Letters arrived for him that his warden brought to Marta at the student news office. She stared at the official envelopes.

'Open them.' Naomi said, 'Perhaps they will give us a clue as to where he is and why he left.'

They were from the police department, Marta recognised the crest. Naomi suddenly became grim. A cheque fell out of one of the envelopes, addressed to Callum – for R600. Marta stared at the cheque, not wanting to believe what it told her.

The police had recruited Callum after he failed his first year. 'They apparently do this a lot.' Naomi explained to a stunned Marta. 'They pay your tuition and give you a stipend in return for "keeping an eye" for them on the student political organizations.'

'But he was so committed.' Marta could not yet give up hope that they might be wrong.

'Seemed so committed. Seemed. They only pick good ones.'

A week later Marta received a note from him, apologizing for all he had done and explaining that he

could not give her his address as he did not want the
police to find him. He had not realized what he had done
until that day before the university buildings, he wrote;
and then could do it no more. Nor could he face anyone
again. He hoped that one day he could be forgiven.

Marta did not finish reading, but stuffed the letter
in with her other things and then saw that the yellow
Mazda, her lift home for the holidays, was idling outside.
She ran down the stairs. She would try and understand
by the Homtini.

THIRTEEN

Marta went home in some anxiety. Her bruise was still quite visible. It had spread down her left arm and she feared her family's reaction, sure to be anxious and overblown. Further, her exams had not gone as well as she had hoped. Her mind had been elsewhere and she had in any case found many of the questions quite incomprehensible. So she was subdued in the car on her way home and left Graeme to do the driving as well as the talking. He did not seem to mind – and lectured her most of the way about some tribe or other in South America. He was an anthropology student in his final year. She thought, they're probably allowed to talk this much by then.

But then Graeme asked about 'that student', who disappeared. It seemed everyone had heard about Callum. She simply pretended not to know anything, to have only heard the same passing vagaries as everyone else had.

'But didn't you work with him at the student newspaper?'

'Working with someone doesn't mean you know them – or anything about them, really.' she answered shortly, then felt bad. He could not possibly know how these questions echoed her own whirling confusion about Callum. So she asked Graeme about his course instead and he told her about a dig he was going on near Sterkfontein for a holiday job. It *did* sound really interesting and Marta was sorry that she was only going home for the holidays instead of doing something productive.

He dropped her home and she paid him for the petrol and did not think any further about any of it. She breathed deeply; she had forgotten the smell of fynbos and the trees and now these familiar aromas rushed in on her with a dizzy intensity. In a moment Ben was there, picking up her bag and telling her all the bits of news of Farleigh. She did not realize how much she had missed it all until she found herself back in Narina's kitchen. But she was too restless to stay and wait for tea to be brewed. Ben sensed this and suggested they walk about the garden, so he could show her all that had changed or stayed the same.

'Home, the mountain – everything looks so great!' she enthused, hiding her anxiety about being back. 'Things are going well?'

'No. It's not good,' he said quietly. 'The mission in Berlin is ready to withdraw. Father tries, but he cannot convince head office to stay here any longer. They are getting a lot of media flak in Germany. It has become entirely inexpedient for them to stay here in the "current political climate" and they wish to hand all stations over to "the community".'

'The community? That almost sounds like a good idea.'

'Sure. Except that "community" is not exactly clearly defined at the moment. But the mission does not seem to care – as long as they can get the hell out of here.'

'And that makes Father feel like the betrayer?'

Then she noticed that in the carpenter shop the lathe

246

stood still and the sawdust lay undisturbed on the floor and in the corner lay an incomplete chair. Marta looked at Ben, who shrugged.

'No one will supply wood to us at the moment while things are so unclear – and lots of our people have left now. They go to meetings all the time, where they are told that missionaries stole the land from them.'

'Well,' she ventured, 'there is some truth in that.'

'What, you, too?' he asked incredulously.

'Not Father, of course, but historically speaking . . .'

'That's not the point,' he interrupted. She could see he did not want to discuss politics and she did not want to argue on her first day.

'Shall we go to the river?' she asked, 'My legs could do with more of a stretch after that drive.'

He accepted the conciliatory gesture. The house, she feared, would be empty without her mother and Ruth would only return later. Narina would be there with baby Maia, dropped off by Ruth before work, but that would keep. Marta did not know entirely why she was a little afraid of seeing Narina again but she couldn't shake the feeling and did not feel up to questioning herself. For a few moments she just wanted to enjoy being home and let it feel like home – not alien.

They walked in companionable silence along the still golden river, though the trees were nearly empty and there was an early chill in the late afternoon air. In spite of herself Marta was listening for the loerie's voice but they saw only the wood doves and on the far side of the river the vervet monkeys playing an early evening game.

'Better?' Ben asked after a while.

'Yes.'

'Come on, we had better get home. Father will be wondering where you are.' They walked back in the orange light of the sunset on the side of the blazing mountain.

Johannes Reben had been wandering about the homestead looking for his youngest daughter. Her suitcase had been left in the hallway so he knew she was back. Then he heard their voices and there she was, walking back from the river with Ben.

'So you greet the river before you greet your father,' he said with a wide smile.

'Well,' she laughed back, glad of the banter, 'the river was there, you know.'

Then she was almost entirely lost in her father's hug. He had always been a big man and much of his work had been physical, despite his bookish bent. He did not see her wince slightly as he squeezed her against him but Ben did and resolved to ask her about it later. It was an unspoken matter of pride with the Reben children to bear their father's burly hugs.

Marta recovered herself and walked now with her father's heavy arm on her shoulders without a murmur. 'It's good to see you home,' he said.

'It's good to be here,' she responded and meant it warmly, now that she had been to the river and some of the anxiety about returning to this place had eased. This place, where time seemed to stand still while she was away, changing, growing.

He smiled, 'Were you worried about how much *you* might have changed? And home not at all?'

'Yes.'

'You'll see, we have some changes too', he said softly and his voice seemed far away.

'Narina,' he called then as they approached the kitchen door, 'Narina, look who's here.'

Narina came blinking out of the kitchen, drying her hands on her apron and then clapping them in delight. Marta broke free from her father to hug the woman who had taken care of them all for so long.

'Narina!'

'Marta!'

'What's for supper? I'm starving!'

'Fresh river trout and baby potatoes.'

'Great. Come on, what are you all waiting for?'
Marta ran ahead to hide both her aching shoulder and the remaining awkwardness.

In the high chair in the kitchen baby Maia was gurgling and already eating. Ruth looked up and smiled at her younger sister. 'How are you?' she asked as Marta bent down to hug her.

'Fine,' Marta said and hid her wince in pulling a face to make Maia laugh, which she did, as well as patting Marta with her food-covered spoon.

'Here,' Ruth laughed, handing her a tea towel. Marta wiped her face while everyone took their places.

'Do we have enough for a sung grace?' Johannes Reben asked.

'I think so.' Ruth began and the others soon joined the canon. It felt good to be singing again.

Supper felt almost like old times. It was the first time Marta really talked to Ruth's husband, Peter. She was a little surprised to find that, in fact, she liked him. Before, she had largely thought of him as an intruder, part of the unwelcome developments in the family, relentless in their onset since Ruth had first left home. But now he seemed part of the family as he chatted to Ben about the teachers at the school he too had attended. And when Jacob came in and had hung up his stick, the evening became almost raucous. Father was so delighted to have so many of them home that he brought out some of his good wine and became increasingly expansive.

'Children,' he finally said, 'dear children, drink all you like: *I'm* going to bed.'

'Goodnight, Father,' they chorused.

Once he had gone the conversation became more serious.

'What happened this morning?' Jacob asked Ben, who was on study leave and so spent the early hours of the day at home.

'Well, the discussion with Brother Meiβner was long. Father did not say much but he did not look happy. I think head office really will close Farleigh down.'

'What, even after all the work we have put in to make it self-sufficient?'

'Well,' Peter slowly put in, 'it isn't just the money.' He appeared to choose his words carefully.

Marta watched her brothers accept his terms, listen to him, while she still wanted him to keep out. But as she listened she realized that he was another brother. Ruth had gone to check on Maia and though things were so serious, they were peaceful. As though everyone in the room belonged. After the 16th June demonstration, the interminable worry about Callum and the constant vigilance at the student newspaper, Marta felt glad to be back in the comfort and safety of home and gradually drifted off.

Ruth came back and gently told her to go to bed.

'But I want to stay and talk about Farleigh and what's going to happen to us all.'

'We won't solve that tonight,' Ruth sounded just like Mother.

Marta reluctantly got up from the corner near the fire where she had curled up, and made her way to her room. It was good to be there too. And tonight she was too tired to imagine what life would be like without Farleigh.

Her bed smelled as it had always smelled and through the slightly open window, even in winter, she could hear the wind in the trees and the soft noise of night life. She stood for a moment at her window and wondered where Lady Grey was. Then she turned and, wincing, climbed back into bed. She had to lie on one side or on her stomach to be comfortable and she gingerly lifted and lowered the blanket. But she fell asleep quickly.

In the morning she was awoken by a gasp from Ruth, bending over her with a cup of tea.

'What happened to your shoulder?'

Marta half asleep still, tried to grab the blanket and pull it back up over her exposed shoulder but groaned with the pain and let her arm fall.

Ruth put the tea down and sat on the bed, which caused further groans from Marta.

'What happened? Tell me.'

It was a relief in the end to pour it all out. Ruth listened without interruptions.

Finally, Ruth looked prim, 'I warned you about politics at Rhodes, didn't?'

'Yeah you did. And I can do without your gloating, thanks!'

'I'm sorry but honestly, what did you think I was talking about?'

'Just because things might go wrong, doesn't mean you shouldn't get involved.'

'It does if you're sensible and . . . and . . . and focus on your studies.' Ruth's eyes shone with triumph at having found the teacherly phrase.

'We'll never agree on this.'

'OK, let's drop it then. Does it hurt still?'

And she went off to fetch some arnica.

'Will you tell Father?' Marta asked as Ruth helped her rub in the ointment.

'No, you will.' Ruth responded. And then Maia came toddling in so the conversation ended.

They gently played ball with Maia for a while and she came out to the garden with Marta, where they had a little walk around. Charmed by her little lisping attempts at speech and unsure about how to talk to so little a person, Marta decided to 'teach' her niece the names of the flowers, and birds when they heard them sing. Maia was thrilled with everything they found. Each bright thing, each feather, each leaf brought forth new gurgles of delight and the bright eyes looked up at Marta, wanting to know what each one was, what its name was. Then she would blow bubbles in her eagerness to copy the words her aunt told her. It was strange to think of herself as an aunt, to think that this small new life was in some way connected to her. That she was part of the rolling generations of Rebens.

Marta looked up at the garden and the mountain beyond and drew again deeply into her lungs the smell of the forest from the fading mist. For a moment the world stood still. Marta knew she would always remember this moment, especially in light of what happened afterwards.

She heard a roar, an inhuman wild roar that instinctively made her clutch her small niece to her. The child did not protest but clung to Marta. Then her father's study door burst open and he emerged, phone still in his hand, trailing its cord where he had ripped it from its socket. He flung it across the grass now, and then, all energy gone, leaned against the doorframe and wept.

Marta held Maia close, wondering for a moment whether to go to her father or to take the child away. The problem was solved for her by Ruth and Ben, who came out, Ben towards her and Ruth towards their father.

'What is it, Ben?'

'He got the mission's final answer. They will withdraw from South Africa entirely in two years.'

'And Farleigh?'

'Will be sold to the government.'

'How do you know all this?'

Ben looked down. 'It's still a party line.'

'Right.'

Marta thought for a bit, and then she could not help herself. 'Isn't this what he was expecting, though?'

'He's been expecting it for so long, I think, that he did not believe it would ever happen. And their reasoning is so mean-spirited, so limited, and so expedient. So political!'

'Is that always bad? Politics?' In her head Marta could see again the marching students, the police dogs and the pangas, the doors of the university closed.

'You know this is a different kind of politics. It's not fighting for freedom, it's just to do with public image and money, I suspect. Since the press on missionaries has been so poor, they are not getting as much support as they used to from Germany.'

'Even with so many of them fighting for freedom here? Fighting now for equality? Like Uncle Simon, in and out of prison?'

'I think the general feeling is: too little too late.'

'When did you get so wise, Ben? You're the baby.'

'Since I've been the only one left at home,' he said grimly.

Marta remembered then conversations at countless NUSAS meetings about multi-racial versus non-racial: the arguments, the conversations and the futility.

'What will we do now?'

'I don't know, yet. I think Father has some vague plans but no more than that.'

Marta turned away from him, not wanting him to see the tears start in her eyes. The child was squirming now and Ruth had taken their father in but returned now to ask Marta to make some tea. Glad of something to do, Marta handed Maia to Ben, who took her off at a gallop around the garden towards the cows, just being let back out from milking.

Marta went in and found her way half-blindly to the kitchen. The world was spinning and she had to hang on to the sink with one hand as she brought the kettle over to fill it up. Narina found her there, took the kettle, filled it up and made her sit.

'Put your head down,' she said, 'put your head down.'

Waves of nausea swept through Marta and the rushing in her ears spun the kitchen and Narina far away. Narina caught her before she fell to the floor, made the tea and by the time it was ready to be carried through, Marta had recovered enough to join Ruth and her father and drink some tea. They drank in silence. Johannes Reben held his empty cup and stared at his hands. His daughters looked at each other.

Finally Ruth said, 'Father, you were going to check on the yearlings today and then go on to Paccaltsdorp and Karatara to see some of the old people who will not make church on Sunday.'

'Yes,' her father stood up blankly, 'yes I will go and do that.'

Marta stood up too, 'I will go with you.'

'Are you sure?' Ruth asked with some concern. 'You still look very pale.'

At this her father seemed to wake up. 'What's wrong with her?'

'She's just had a bit of a tough time, Father; she'll tell you on the way.'

Marta was furious with Ruth for pre-empting her in this way. She stalked out and would not glance at her again.

'Take a jacket,' Ruth called all the same. 'You know how cold it can get up in Karatara.'

Marta did not answer but went to her room to pick up a fleece. She was afraid a jacket would be too heavy on the now tender bruises.

She climbed carefully into her father's bakkie and watched him climb in heavily, too. He smiled wanly at her and said, 'We have not done this for a long time, have we?'

'No, we haven't.'

'Do you remember the time when we first met Ishmael?'

254

'Yes.' Marta's throat closed in anxiety.

Her father looked at her. 'All right. We won't talk about Ishmael then.'

Silence.

'Tell me about your term,' he said, 'what was Ruth talking about?'

Then she told him, haltingly but not without a note of pride, and as she spoke she saw from the corner of her eyes his hands tighten convulsively on the steering wheel. Anxiously she peered at his face – it had settled with some effort into its pastoral expression. He was determined to let her speak, to be reasonable, though he did not feel it.

Seeing this, her voice faltered but he had gathered the gist of it.

They sat in silence for a while, as her father watched the traffic on the motorway.

Then he said, 'You know this is probably all because of your Uncle Simon?'

'No, Father. All the people in NUSAS are watched. Especially those who are active members, who go to meetings, who write for the student newspapers.'

'Yes, Marta, but they knew your name. That Callum – he was detailed to watch you. They know our name because of Uncle Simon. Don't you remember the police snooping about when you were younger, asking questions?'

Marta did remember. Especially during the holidays when her cousins were there, the police seemed to swarm around them; asking questions about family holidays.

'How are Uncle Toby and them?' she asked, playing for time in this sticky conversation.

'They are settling in Berlin now.'

'Don't they miss Lydenburg at all?'

'Probably they do – but what can you do? You have to get on, don't you? That station was just closed.'

'As we are about to be?'

He stared moodily out of the window for a while.

'Father,' Marta reminded him softly, 'what about Uncle Simon?'

He resumed his story. 'Do you remember how he helped Ishmael and the other boys at the reformatory?'

'Yes – he was great.'

'Yes, well. He couldn't keep his hands out of politics after that. And he was hounded. The Special Branch claimed he was inciting the boys to rebellion.'

'Was he?'

'Probably, in all honesty. He was fired.'

'What does he do now?'

'He's in and out of prison, most of the time. He's supposed to be under house arrest but he keeps meeting with people.'

'Why didn't you ever tell us any of this?'

'Your mother and I agreed not to tell any of you about him, for your own protection.'

'Oh?' Marta sat up. Dimly she remembered half-heard conversations between her parents during the school riots.

'How long has this been going on?' she finally asked.

'Since he first arrived here – about five years after Toby and I began work here.'

'He came also as a missionary?'

'Sort of. He came to a street mission in Johannesburg. And then he branched out. He offered pastoral care to political prisoners and then began a campaign against their treatment in prison. They repeatedly tried to shut him up and asked the mission to withdraw him. But he came back illegally. He has himself been imprisoned several times and . . .'

'Is that who you went to see, those times when you had to leave so suddenly?'

'Yes.'

'I can't believe we never knew!'

'Yes, I was afraid that incident with Ishmael would draw you all into that, but Toby managed to smooth things over – got Simon the post for a while, promised it would keep him quiet: looking after the boys.'

'But it didn't.'

'No, not really,' he smiled. 'It seems to run in the family. I should have warned you away from the politics, the way I did Ruth when she left. There was so much else happening then – I should have known you would not be as quiet as she, that all this would be an issue as soon as one of you joined a student movement.'

'Have I made things worse?' she asked softly.

He did not hear her and went on berating himself, the world, anything. 'Of course they would send someone to spy on you.'

'Spy on me?'

'Well, yes. Not just you, perhaps. And you walked into that.'

'But Callum never asked about any of my uncles.'

'No, but how much did he ask about your family? Did that seem normal to you?'

'No. I was just glad to be able to talk about you because I missed you all so much.'

'Ach, Marta,' he said and involuntarily grasped her hand where she was using it to steady herself as they drove on the bumpy Paccaltsdorp road.

Now it was Father's turn to watch from the corner of his eye. He winced when she did, too afraid to ask to see her bruises.

'I don't suppose the university authorities did anything?'

'About what?'

'About students being beaten.'

'They closed their doors, Father.'

'Ah, yes, they closed their doors. And this Callum – he has disappeared?'

'Yes, he left me all the reports he wrote on me. He did not send them.'

'And what have you done with them?'

'They're in my bag.'

'We should probably burn them.'

'OK.'

'And no more politics when you go back, please.'

'Father,' was all she said and hugged him, carefully from the side as he brought the car to a stop outside a ruined-looking house.

Then it was time for what she and her siblings had always called her father's 'pastoral chats' with the old and the dying. He went patiently into house after house and drank tea sweetened with condensed milk. At the last one he stopped her briefly.

'Marta, I must give the final rites here. Do you want to come in – perhaps sit with his mother and sister? Or would you rather wait?'

'I will come in.'

Marta had felt a strange awe come over her as the morning progressed. She watched faces light up as her father came in, she watched hands unclench as he took them gently between his own and prayed softly over sickbeds or simply sat in the weak winter sun with the old people, who were lonely and too fragile now to come to church.

In this final house, the air was fetid and Marta nearly gagged as they entered the small, dark room. There was a candle burning near a bed on which lay an emaciated figure. So thin, it was no longer possible to discern any individual features or gender. A skull lay on the thin worn pillow.

Marta watched her father walk in and not falter once as he took in the small room and spoke softly to the woman taking care of the man – for that was what it was – lying on the pillow. The enormous, glazed eyes rolled in their head towards him. A woman was busy dressing ugly sores on his legs; the smell came from these rotten wounds. But she cleaned them gently, as if she smelt nothing at all. Marta watched her hands and gradually she too forgot the smell. Then her father took his seat on the chair that had now been placed for him at the bedside and took the hand of the person lying there.

'Good morning.'

A weak voice replied.

'How are you today, Khwezi?' her father asked and though the words seemed so obviously wrong, Marta could hear the real question in them, could hear the compassion and the readiness to spend time with this ill person.

'I am ready, Umfundisi.'

'And your family?'

The woman was now burning a small brush of buchu leaves and allowing the smoke to billow about the room as she waved it. It cleared the air and Marta felt she could breathe more easily now.

'Yes, Umfundisi, we are all ready.' She swiftly took off the overall she was wearing and called softly down the corridor.

'Bring chairs,' she told the face which appeared.

'I'll help,' Marta said and between them they fetched all the chairs from the kitchen while her father prepared the sacrament on the bedside table of the patient.

When they were all seated about Khwezi's bed, her father began the ritual words, so familiar to Marta but here and now they sounded like they did on Easter morning in the cemetery overlooking the valley to the sea. As her father sang the words for the preparation, someone got up and opened the curtain. Outside, with their hats removed, stood several of the neighbors, silent and listening.

'Marta help me hand out, will you?' Her father's steady voice asked.

259

It took a long time. The people all came into that small room where the patient lay with tired, bright eyes watching them. There was not enough sacrament but still they came for blessing.

When the ceremony was over the sun was high in the sky. The neighbors walked away in small companionable groups, while Khwezi's mother stood on the step waving her thanks. In the room Marta's father took the patient's hands again.

'Now I am not afraid,' Khwezi said, 'thank you, Umfundisi.'

'Khwezi,' her father replied, 'thank you. *Hamba gahle.*'

Marta and her father were silent as they drove now to Karatara. It was a good silence now, Marta thought. They no longer eyed each other carefully but looked out at the landscape and the mountain the bakkie was climbing slowly.

At Karatara they picked up Joseph and Rasta. Joseph told them how he had gone hopefully all the way to Port Elizabeth to find his son, Bomani, who was at Turfloop University in the North. Bomani had not come on the expected train but Rasta had been there, wanting to come home for a holiday from his cleaning work at the St George's hospital. He had organized a lift for both of them from Port Elizabeth as far as Karatara. Joseph had hoped that Bomani would spend his holiday at Farleigh, working in the carpenter shop as he had when he was a teenager.

'But,' he said, as he sadly shook his head, 'ever since that first beating Bomani got at the hands of the police, he was full of talk about the students' movement and the news that the university was under threat of being shut for all the rioting. How can they get any learning done, Umfundisi,' he said, 'with all that going on?'

Marta's father glanced briefly at his daughter.

'No,' he said slowly, 'it is a serious problem. We need justice, but we need educated people, too.'

'Yes,' he said, 'yes. But Bomani tells me that when they march he knows that we will get both.'

'Will you?'

'We can hope, Mr. Reben.' No honorific this time, Marta noticed.

'Joseph, do you know where Bomani is?'

'No. Somewhere up north, I expect.'

'Can you find out? We need to get him home for the holidays. They will not be the same for Mieta without her son.'

'Can you help, Umfundisi?' His voice sounded like that of a hopeful child. Marta was embarrassed, looked out and then tried to distract the trembling old man.

'How is Maleka?' she asked Joseph, hoping to distract him from this university talk.

'She is well. Her baby is coming along nicely and she is working at the nursery school now, over in George. She's home for the holidays. I'll tell her you asked. She will be glad.'

Back in the bakkie Marta shifted closer to her father to make space for Joseph, while Rasta leapt on to the back.

And then it felt like the years slipped away. Joseph and her father talked over her head as if she were still ten years old and would not understand a word. They simply seemed to forget she was there as they talked about the cows, the carpenter shop and the fences.

Marta was ready to drift off into her own dreams, as she would have when she was a child, when Ishmael's name arrested her attention.

'How is he shaping up, Joseph?' her father was asking.

Joseph glanced over at Marta. 'Bomani says he is doing well, yes.'

'They see each other?'

'They keep in touch.'

Marta sat stiff and pale, despite the heat prickling her spine. Father changed the topic.

'You went up to the elephant searchers yesterday, didn't you? Are they still causing difficulties with the farmers?'

'It is tense, Umfundisi, between them. Not comfortable with each other.'

'And Jacob is helping?'

'Yes,' Joseph laughed. 'He is one of the experts on the fynbos.'

'Who would have thought it? Hey Marta,' her father tried to include her now, 'elephants again – great herds of them. Jacob dreams big.'

She nodded but sat rigid, unable to give her father the opening he wanted. This was one thing too many for one day. Elephants back in the forest, but no Ishmael. She felt the world begin to spin again.

'Hey,' Joseph said, from miles away, 'hey, what's up – you look pale.'

He opened the window for her and the breeze made things a little better.

But when she got home she fell straight into bed, shaking and feverish now. It was only a winter flu. She was ill for three days and then gradually began to feel better. By then plans had been made to find new homes and to close Farleigh down. It would remain only as a forestry station, and so many people needed new homes.

Jacob came in to see Marta one afternoon. He sat at her bedside and talked about his work with the conservation department.

'They are finally agreeing to acknowledge the fynbos as a conservation area. We are still struggling to get agreement on the elephants. The government is afraid of litigation if the elephants destroy anyone's property.'

'But the forest itself is doing well,' he continued, when he saw how she looked away.

'How can you be part of this?' she burst out. 'How can you do this? We're losing our home to the forestry department. Farleigh is no more – and you are part of it.'

'Marta,' he looked at her, helpless, 'what do you want me to do? Change the government? Change the Mission's policy?'

'You could fight!'

'We did, all of us. Father, Brother Klaus . . . for a long time. We cannot save the mission station but we can save the forest and the elephants perhaps.'

'Who are we? I never know who "we" are anymore.'

'In this case, it's everyone working with us at the wildlife and conservation society.' He was visibly uncomfortable.

'And what will Father do?'

'I don't know.'

'Well you've thought of everything else!'

'Father will choose for himself.'

'He is lost – we are all lost without Farleigh. It was home. It *is* home.' She was angry now, yelling.

Ruth came in, 'Jacob, what's wrong?'

'Don't ask Jacob, ask me how everyone is leaving. Father is leaving Farleigh. Ask me how everything is changing and no one is doing anything about it!'

'Marta, what do you think yelling will achieve?'

'Oh, stop being so damned *reasonable*,' she spat the word like a curse. 'Stop – go away, all of you go away!' And she flung her hot head back into the pillows and sobbed. How would Ishmael ever come back, if Farleigh was no more?

They judged it best to leave her. Only Narina peered back in when she was asleep.

Marta stirred when she heard the door and was relieved to see Narina's face.

'Oh, Narina, I have behaved so badly, I shouted at everyone.'

'Yes, baby, you did. But they understand. Do you want some soup?'

'I would love some.'

Narina brought her hot vegetable soup and sat with her as she sipped it slowly.

'What will happen to us?'

'Well – you have to finish your degree.'

'But, Father . . .'

'Your father has already decided to work at Karatara.'

'And where will he live?'

'He will work that out–'

'But did you hear him cry when he heard? Have you ever heard anyone cry like that?'

'Yes – people do when they lose what they love. And then they manage. Your father will manage. And he will manage all the better for knowing you will.'

'Yes, Narina.'

She wanted to ask then about Ishmael but somehow the memory of her bird, Jacob's elephant work, Bomani's absence and her own smarting shoulder were too much right now. She would not know what to do with information about him now, how to fit him back into her world, for all her heart burned to know how he was.

In her mind also still hung the image of Callum, whom she had trusted in the new world of the university and who had turned out so very much not what he seemed. Her head still felt like bursting whenever she thought about it.

That evening her father came in to her room. He sat on the edge of her bed, his folded hands hanging down between his knees as he leaned his elbows on his thighs.

'Well, are you better now?' he asked.

'Yes, much better.'

'And your head?'

'That will take some thinking.'

'Yes, I thought so. You know that young Callum of yours, whose papers we still need to burn. You're angry with him?'

Silence.

'I thought so. But you need to remember that he did not turn you in. And he left university rather than go on doing work for the police. Meeting you, meeting the people who work, however dangerously,' he smiled at her bristling, 'who work for justice and freedom, changed him. A callous boy perhaps to start; who hoped to make his way through university in this way. Probably his family is quite poor, you know . . .'

'How would you know that?'

'Because I know the police prey on bright young people from poor families who could not afford university education otherwise. Some people will do anything for an education – for a chance at a better life. It is not so different to what you're fighting for.'

'Father!'

'OK, you're fighting for it generally and he only for himself. But you can understand the desire?'

'Yes.'

'And what will you do now, after such close brushes with the police, in so many ways?'

'Concentrate on my work,' she promised

'Good,' he said. 'I don't want you having to spend your holidays in prison, the way Bomani has to.' He took a piece of paper out of his pocket.

'Bomani? You've found Bomani?'

'He was arrested after a march and they are not releasing anyone till after July. He will miss all of the holiday and half the term. Joseph is scared he will lose his bursary now. And you, you should be worrying about similar things.'

'Why?'

'Because your results are not what they should be.'

'You *opened* them?' she cried.

'Stay calm,' he put a hand on her arm. 'We opened them to see whether you would be up to coping with the news.'

'How bad?'

'You need to work.' He passed her the paper.

Marta stared unseeingly at the faint printout.

Father still sat on the edge of her bed, his head hanging down, his elbows resting heavily on his knees.

'What is it, Father?'

'There is more bad news.'

'Yes?'

'Do you remember the triplets?'

'Yes? They are at agricultural college now, aren't they – up north?'

'Yes. And they were doing holiday work on a farm right up near the Limpopo.' Father stopped, not sure how to go on.

'What happened?'

'The farm they were working on was attacked. They have all three been killed.'

Marta found no words. The world seemed blank. Then she remembered Piet's voice, calling goodbye to Ben. And Mina, laughing on the road to Karatara, reminding them to visit.

'But I never even visited them, after I had promised the last time we saw them on the bus.' It was all she could think of, that promise and how happy Mina had been about it.

Father put his hand on her arm. 'Will you be able to go to the funeral? You have been asked.'

'Of course, it is the least I can do.' And then the anger came. 'But who would kill those three? They have never, never hurt anyone.'

'It was one of these farm murders – they happen a lot up at the border, you know.'

266

'Why?'

'It is part of the armed resistance now, the liberation struggle.'

She stared at him. She had known about these "farm murders", had read about them but had never really made the connection between horror stories in the newspapers and what she thought she was doing at university.

'Not all those who fight for freedom are innocent victims,' Father now said softly. 'Now can you see why I don't want you to get involved?'

In the morning after the funeral, Marta went for a walk. She wandered out of the gate and down to the river which she crossed for the first time in years and walked into Millwood forest. She did not know what she hoped to find there, knew only that nothing that had given her comfort before was there any more. No owl swooping above her head, no mother to return to and tell about gold or feathers. No Ishmael to talk to ever again. And now the triplets were gone, too.

Finally she sat down at the foot of the great Kalander and cried.

'Marta,' a familiar voice, 'what is it, child?'

And there was Wilhelm bending over her. 'What is it?'

She told him everything as he sat on the roots of the great tree with her. He listened in silence.

'What can I do?'

'Well, you will do whatever needs to be done next. As always.'

'But how can I go on fighting for a cause that killed three innocent people? How do I decide which side is more just?'

'It may not be quite that stark a choice . . .' he began and then looked at her face, knowing she could not hear so much now, and said only, 'I do not know. Only you know how you must choose.'

'It's hard,' she sobbed.

'Yes, it is hard for your family, too. They see only the danger to you. The rest is just politics to them.'

'But my father helped find Bomani, like he found Joseph before.'

'Yes – but that is helping people he knows. He does not see that as politics.'

'But it is – everything is political, here. Everything!'

'What will you do?'

'I don't know,' and after a while, 'I cannot hide in the forest the way everyone else does.'

'Everyone?'

'My father, Jacob – even you!'

She got no answer.

'I have to do something. This forest, it swallows the world and makes you forget that it is out there. And that's wrong – there are people getting hurt, everyday getting hurt by this government. How can you stand by?'

'There is no need–' he began.

'Yes there is,' she burst out. 'Yes there is need. You think you can hide in the forest from the politics but still Bomani got arrested, the triplets are dead, Uncle Simon is back in prison and Ishmael . . . Ishmael . . .' She could not finish.

'Ishmael?' He asked.

'It doesn't matter,' she said, exhausted. 'Jacob thinks fixing the forest will make up for everything else. But how can anything be fixed when the whole country is broken? When there are no good sides left?'

'I don't know, Marta,' he said, his voice low and shaking. 'All I know is this – if you ever need help, I will be there.'

'How could you possibly help?'

FOURTEEN

Marta completed the second half of her first year at
university quietly and focused on her studies. Half the
first years did not make it back for second year. Didi was
amongst them.

'What is she doing?' Marta asked Avril.

'She married Marc. She's pregnant.'

The memory of Callum and the triplets kept her
away from deep and serious involvement on the now
strident and often violent student politics. She chose
the company of books over the company of people – as
she had before. And so she returned in January 1987 for
her final year determined to stay focused on her work.
A state of emergency had been declared the year before
and the town and university were swept nightly by large,
fiercely bright lights, and the quiet of the night was
disturbed by the dark growling of the caspirs patrolling
the streets and townships.

But then in April there arrived in the Modern
Languages department, a tutor fresh from a French
university, who stirred up the dust in her again and
turned her mind once more to bigger things than her
own achievement. His name was Pierre and apart from
the obligatory work in the language laboratories (which

Marta had also taken on for a bit of extra money), he also took the final years for a course in Eighteenth-Century Drama. They read Racine's *Berenice* and talked first about its reception, how it had been mocked for lacking truly tragic drama and then read Racine's response:

> *Bloodshed and death are not absolutely indispensable to a tragedy. It is enough if the action is impressive, if the characters are heroic, if the passions are aroused, and if everything is charged with that feeling of majestic sadness which constitutes the true pleasure of tragedy.*

'Isn't that beautiful?' and because of his accent, and because of the floppiness of his fringe, the class largely agreed.

Marta remained sceptical. 'I'm not sure it's a truly great tragedy, though. Yes they suffer, but they do so because Titus chooses expedience over love. History tells us that he hardly saved Rome from any downfall, and even within the play the Roman populace is not seen as a great and noble people, so his choice is not between duty and love but between expedience or power and love. That is less noble, less convincingly tragic.'

'Is it?'

The class turned to her, aghast. She had contradicted Pierre and he was French! And so beautiful! She scowled at them.

But he motioned for her to continue.

'Well,' she said, 'Shakespeare has tackled the same theme.'

'He did?' Pierre was mocking her, she felt sure, drawing her out to set her up in front of the class. She suspected that he found her entertaining.

'Yes, in *Antony and Cleopatra* – and they made very different choices.'

'And had the decency to die for them?' He had cut her off. 'Let's return to our reading.'

Reading in class was painful. Marta knew that most of them were mangling the language and she longed to hear it as it should have been spoken. But Pierre only rarely read, indeed sometimes she thought he was barely following. He did not correct them much. 'Here is indeed the death of tragedy,' she thought.

After class, Marta stayed to challenge him on having evaded her question.

'Ah,' he said, 'I had hoped you would ask.'

'Well, I am asking.'

'You argue too much from life. Common sense will not make the grade anywhere in the world of academia,' he said.

'What do you mean?'

'There are theories which you should be learning, schools of thought about these things, if you're serious about understanding literature in the modern world. And you have the brain to make it – even in Europe – but you must learn to be rational at all times about these things. You lack the sophistication we expect of students there.'

Instantly Marta was back to her first few days at English school, hearing the softly hissed 'Boertjie, bosboertjie' and the laughter at her accent. And she felt tightening in her chest, the knowledge that she would never be good enough.

He saw how crestfallen she was. 'But you may learn it, it is not too late.'

He gave her some books and invited her for a cup of coffee once she had read them.

They were dry, arduous reads – most of them – but she could see the equation of them, the cool touch they had for all she revered. And how that would develop her taste into something far more sophisticated and restrained. She devoured them. Here after all was someone from the home of culture, someone who was prepared to share with her that golden apple. He would show her the way to be as rational, as sophisticated as him and would cure her of her provincialism and lift her to world class. She would never have the wrong taste again; she would never buy the wrong wine or drink white coffee but live as graciously as her aristocratic great-grandmother had done. She would go to Europe and never be an ignorant provincial again. She would shake the superstition of the forest, the convoluted trouble of this country and leave its backwardness in the sea between continents forever. She would be free.

And Racine would lead the way. Racine, with his fine distinctions and his impeccable restraint for just the right level of tragic evocation on stage. She saw that Wilhelm had been wrong to encourage her to feel everything with such intensity – feeling was not what Literature was about but judgement and thought and cool distance.

Pierre showed her this even in moments of intimacy – wry, witty distance was the proof of a superior mind.

But then one day Pierre himself lost his cool sophistication. He was inspired and he swept them all along with his vivid idea of what they should do with this play.

He wanted them as a class to put on a performance of it. 'An experimental version of this 17ᵗʰ Century play, at the festival fringe this year.'

'Racine as street theatre?' Marta asked sceptically, but he was expansive now.

'I bet it has not been done before.'

Marta wondered whether there might be good reason for this but kept quiet.

He smiled. 'Ah, but you see, here it is, an idea that has inspired me, that has moved me beyond the usual rational composure.'

'That's enough to make you want to try such a project?'

'Well imagine it: an extraordinary idea, the product of consideration and of trying out new ideas on old material. What if we did a Brechtian production of *Berenice*? One that made people think about the choices in the play, rather than indulge in the emotions. Let our audience know that they too have made choices – political ones – whether they like it or not. Silence too is an action.'

Marta remained thoughtful, silent.

'And in such a context where people are constantly finding the political invading the personal! It'll be electrifying! We could use projections of current news – the war in Angola, the raids in the townships. And no costumes – just as we are.'

And Marta sensed in his words her own old enthusiasm and was swept along into believing that *this* mattered, mattered more than anything she had done before. It was only a play and yet it mattered more than everything else. They rehearsed and rehearsed, Pierre now carefully attentive to how they said every line, though they spoke them in English now, which Marta grudgingly admitted, was a good idea, given their likely audience. Pierre, now that he had a project, was inspiring on a daily basis and carried them all along through the difficulties of finding rehearsal space and tackling the festival authorities for a slot.

They began their rehearsals, often without Pierre, who was invariably late. They stumbled and stuttered their way through and felt that they might never be ready for anything at all – least of all the festival.

'Do we even have permission to put it on yet?' one of them finally asked.

At that point Pierre bustled in, and announced triumphantly, 'We have a slot! It will be hard; basically street theatre in the foyer of the monument – but we're on the program! So let's make it good. We have to give the authorities a kick. We have to make our point.'

A deep voice spoke up from the dark storeroom at the back of the lecture room. 'No, you don't. If you do this it will have to be Racine's voice making a point. You must let the play speak for itself. You cannot push the context otherwise you will only be rabble-rousing.' Professor Jenkins stepped quietly into the room and came closer to them.

Pierre turned to protest but Professor Jenkins held up her large, ringed hand and said, 'Do you want to confirm what they'll be only too ready to believe of student actors? Or do you want to have people who listen and are moved by what they see, who think as a result of it about the choices between loyalty and the truth of experience, between personal joy and public duty?'

The young people looked up warily, a little frightened by her sudden intensity.

'Well – there you are then,' she said abruptly in response to their silence.

Pierre took over again. 'Act one scene four then – from the top, please.'

This moment confirmed the importance of the play absolutely for Marta. But she did not know how to explain that to her anxious father, when she told him of the plan on the phone. He was concerned about the state of emergency and the powers of the government to hold people without charging them. His brother was back in prison already and the police had been snooping about Farleigh again and the remains of his parish.

'We are so far away, Marta, if things go wrong for you. You don't want to be interrogated, believe me.'

She could hear how stricken he was. The money clicked over in the phone box phone and someone knocked impatiently on the door. She felt helpless and urgent and furious with the world all at once.

'I will call you tonight,' she finally said, 'after you get back from Uncle Simon.' She was afraid to say the word prison on the phone, sure that at least the one at home was bugged.

'And you, will you stay in? Study – that is what you went there to do, remember,' his voice was hoarse with fear.

'I will call you.' She did not answer his question directly and put the receiver down.

The door ripped open behind her.

'At last!'

'Yes,' she muttered, 'sorry about that.' Marta slipped out before anyone could see her face, hoping to have gained her composure again by the rehearsal. They rehearsed mostly in the evenings, when all could make it.

She missed supper again, too. Returning to her room only to pick up her copy of Racine and a coat, she began the long walk up to the Monument. The evenings grew dark earlier now and she wanted to walk up in the light, did not want to walk alone in the dark with her father's frightened voice still ringing in her ears. She stared out over Grahamstown, with the cathedral spire stretching up and the Methodist church just near it. On the slopes of the far hill, the smoky smudges were Rhini and Fingo village on the other side, closer to the green glow of the botanical garden and just in the last of the sun was the glint of Kotsch creek. She grimaced, hearing her father's voice again.

Marta scrambled quickly up the last of the increasingly steep hillside to the back of the Monument Theatre. She wondered how it had been swung that they should be able to do this here. In her heart of hearts she did not believe it would happen. Their small production in the Monument foyer! Still, she thought, stranger things do happen, as she made her way round the large, ugly building to find the entrance at the front and wait for her friends. It was always windy up there she thought as she stared at the exposed and dry rocky hillside, the squat ungainly building and vast parking area and pretty hotel. Suddenly she felt homesick for the wooded kloofs and the constant twilight in which nothing ever stood so exposed and bare to the wind. She missed the singing of the trees and the constant hint of mist. She decided to wait inside.

The cafe was still open but she had not brought any money, so she sat instead near a window and watched for the others. They straggled gradually in.

Avril came first, smiling as always. Marta wondered how she managed that feat, given how hard things were. She greeted her, glad of company at last.

'What's the matter?' Avril asked.

'Oh, nothing.'

'Rubbish. You phoned home?'

'Yes.'

'Your father . . .'

'Yes.'

Then Thari arrived, and Dennis, and soon thereafter the others, too. They were nervous and cheerful all at once. After the rehearsals in classrooms and common rooms, a rehearsal here was both exciting and intimidating. The space was enormous and echoed ominously. It was freezing; the cold wind from outside had followed them in now and they sat shivering on the cold stone steps.

'You had better warm up.' Pierre arrived in a swish of scarf and a flutter of papers which spilled gently from his overfull leather case as always.

How he lit up even the bleakest room, Marta thought, feeling the flush of warmth at his arrival race through her, before she had even joined in the warm-ups.

'Right then,' Dennis yelled, 'let's get to it!' and he began running up and down the steps with maniacal energy.

The others joined in calling their vowel sounds. Pierre stood back and smiled. They looked a most unlikely bunch and yelling as they ran up and down the steps did not improve the image. But when they finally stopped at his calling, they were flushed and warm and ready to begin rehearsals.

'Right,' he said, 'look around you, look at the space you have to fill.'

They looked solemnly about them.

'And there will be people,' he said, 'not all of them will be watching. Some may just be having a drink, some may be waiting for the next show or discussing the last one or want to *talk* – you have to beat all that. You have to rise above it, break through it, shatter it entirely. You have to captivate, you have to command; you have to own this hall as if you've lived here your entire life. I need you to be *riveting* in here.'

When he said it like that Marta and all the others wanted to be riveting and believed that they could.

'So let's take it from the top, then. A complete run through without pauses, please. Silence between scenes. Orientate yourselves carefully with your blocking before we begin.'

They looked about and judged the angles from the steps, where the audience would be, and then went to their places. The glass wall loomed dark now and the wooden Union Jack seemed like strange rigging in the high, whistling wind.

Dennis and George began and Marta was soon absorbed entirely in the story. Thari was tormented and Marta sensed her own anguish grow with Berenice as she watched him and played her own part.

The rehearsal went well; they needed few interruptions. Minor orientation changes were required, but that was to be expected, and the voice practice they needed was only a matter of time. The troupe was in high spirits as the lights went down.

Then all seven piled two deep into Pierre's old Peugeot and he drove them back to their various residences. The lights were sweeping and the caspirs were out. So their goodnights were stricken and anxious.

Pierre caught her arm and whispered intensely, 'Get some sleep, dearest.'

As promised, Marta phoned her father. Uncle had been conscious at the prison hospital but listless and disinterested he said. He would fetch him home tomorrow but he was worried. Always worried.

'How is Ben managing?' she asked.

'Ben has his exams.'

'And you?'

'Well we are finally packing,' he said, 'but, we've lost the house in Karatara; it has taken too long. Someone else has it now.'

'What will you do instead?'

'We will move to George – it'll make it easier for Ruth to drop Maia off with us in the mornings.'

'How are Maia and Ruth?'

A caspir drove past and Marta could not hear the rest of what he said about Ruth's firstborn. But Marta smiled so that he could hear when she spoke, 'Why don't you bring her to the festival?' she asked. 'That would cheer her up – she really misses theatre.'

'I'll think about it.'

They said goodnight after that. Marta wondered whether her father would take the time. Since Mother had died and his brother was constantly in trouble, he had been so absorbed in his work, so sure it would all fall apart when he left that he hated going anywhere else, hated being away from the land and the parish. And now he would have to go, to leave the land and the people on it, his people as she knew he thought of them.

She decided she should speak to Simon about it, but not tonight. She was exhausted. Then she wondered bleakly whether it was best to leave the family out of it entirely. Was she really endangering them as her father said?

At the next rehearsal she got her answer. There was a police car waiting when she and Ashley arrived at the monument. Dennis was waiting for them with Avril. Thari had gone in when he saw the police car drive up. Dennis and Avril sauntered over to the two panting up the hill.

'Act normal, act normal. I don't think it's for us anyway.'

They went in as usual and began the rehearsal. A large, blond policeman was standing threateningly over the seated, absorbed shape of Pierre, who was struggling through a lighting script with a theatre technician. He had assured them that at least some spotlighting would be available and possibly some kind of sound system but he was made anxious by the presence of the policeman. Pierre stood up to speak to the policeman, leaving the theatre technician to go through the final section alone. The rehearsal soon fell apart, though Pierre signalled them to keep going. But the policeman was taking things down and pointing at them and they could see from Pierre's increasingly animated hand movements that he was getting angry, though trying not to let either them or the policeman see.

The policeman left at last, satisfied it seemed. Pierre stood a long time watching his retreating back. Then he turned to them and vented a stream of violent fear and fury on them.

'Why did you stop?' he bellowed. 'You have to go on, no matter what you see happening, you have to go on! This matters! You know that. The audience is disturbed, the bloody army arrives; you go on. Do you hear me? You go on no matter what, you go on! Nothing stops this show!'

279

They were not a little disconcerted by his vehemence. Though they had experienced versions of it before in class, they had never seen him like this; there were tears in his eyes. 'Promise,' he said, 'promise me, even when I can't be there you will put this on – to the end.'

They had to promise each individually before he would let them finish for the night.

Later, Marta sat huddled with a cup of Milo under the blankets in Avril's room. Usually they met after rehearsals in Stanley Kidd, which was closest to the Monument, but tonight the two girls had been too tired.

'Do you think this play is really going to be a problem?' Avril asked.

'I don't know. At first it seemed so unlikely. I mean it's French and ancient. Hardly anyone will understand it, even in translation. Perhaps it is how we have chosen to do the ending?'

'We? You, Marta, you chose to make Berenice scornful at the end, which makes the whole duty thing questionable.'

'Perhaps; there are so many possible reasons for scorn at the end, though.'

'Possibilities are not popular here and now, are they?'

Marta could not suppress a grin entirely, 'No they're not.'

'And are we going to change it for that reason?' Avril was rising to the moment, too now. They had cowered long enough; now was the time for defiance and it was rising in both of them.

'No.'

'We will have to take what comes. They do this to every student group that performs at the festival.'

Pause. Silence. Then more soberly, 'Yes. I just don't think I am ready for that. I am afraid I will lose my bursary, too,' Avril said.

'Oh, Avril, I am sorry.'

'No, you are right, you know. You have been all along, about *Antony and Cleopatra*, about *Berenice,* even about the BSM and boycotting exams – if it matters enough, we must take the consequences. I just hope I am ready for them.'

'I'm not sure one can be ready.'

'There's a divinity which shapes our ends, rough-hew them how we will.'

'Yes,' Marta said, 'yes, and watching the fall of a sparrow.'

'Let's hope all this knowledge of literature will actually be useful one day!'

'Avril!' Marta feigned shock – anything to cheer them up a bit. 'Perish at the thought it isn't already!' They both laughed, half uneasily.

'Get some sleep,' Avril said, 'get some sleep. We have exams.'

'Yes, and a performance – only one month away now.'

They rehearsed many more nights and their exams passed almost unnoticed. Soweto Day arrived and looked to pass peacefully just this once, though the police were ready and looking for trouble at the commemoration march. At the end the detainees arrived, the university had made bail for them. And everyone had enjoyed an exam-free day. That afternoon, as they gathered for rehearsal, Pierre had a surprise for them.

'Come,' he said, grabbing Marta's hand impulsively, 'instead of rehearsing a play you all know really well today, let's go somewhere.'

And they climbed into his Peugeot, stopped at Checkers to pick up some food for a picnic and then headed out to Kenton. It was a bleak drive through the winter landscape but when they got closer to the sea, Marta cheered up. She felt small again with her bare

281

feet on the sand, breathing the salt smell of seaweed and seeing the wide emptiness of the hazy horizon.

Avril was anxious. 'Shouldn't we be rehearsing? There's a bit in Act two that is really not smooth yet. Dennis always stumbled on those lines.'

Marta looked at her, 'Avril,' she said, 'forget all that, and look where we are. Do you think the sea cares at all about our performance?'

'No.'

'Well – there you are then. That is your answer.'

'But . . . how can you not care anymore – one glimpse of the sea and you forget it all?'

'No, I do still care. I know it's just a human caring, though. That the world will go on regardless. That what we do matters only to us.'

'And you find that . . . what?'

'Comforting.'

They ate their picnic in silence, watching the sea and the gulls on the deserted winter beach.

The festival began in the loud arrival of 'Vaalies' and the colorful arrival of the market crowd on the village green. The stalls of the yearly village around the cathedral grew and Marta stood by and watched with a growing excitement. She loved the festival; she loved its noise and bustle, the many gigs happening and the vibrating tension that surrounded many of the shows. A part of her thrilled at the increased police presence.

'If they're shooting at you,' she thought, 'you're doing something right.'

She thought of her family and her heart shrank in fear; she felt it contract and settle in the pit of her abdomen as a hard ball that would not be moved. What would they do, if things went wrong? She did not even know what going wrong actually meant, she realised. 'It's all kept a secret! Because what you don't know can frighten you more than what you do.' But the knowledge was not comforting at all.

Her father had been angry the first time she had stayed on for the festival, in her second year. But she had found a job as an usherette and had convinced him that this was good. And then when that month had passed safely he had been fine about it this time. She had not told him about the continued play and she felt guilty about that, very guilty. She wished she could be sure that he would feel proud of her courage. She hoped she would have courage to the end.

She sat on a wall and watched the street kids try their charm on the new arrivals. They waved them into parking and then offered to watch the cars, they offered to carry and shift things, they told stories and they even sang and danced. A part of her loved watching them, glad that they had a good audience for once but a part of her hated it because she did not know how many of the stories about them to believe. Were they all gathered up at the end of the day by what was essentially a pimp in a Mercedes, who made money from the 'cute' urchins and kept them in poverty, as was whispered in Hall? It was a whole world she knew, which happened right here in front of her, but she did not know how to read it. They were so good at it, so clever and yet their plight was so real, despite their deception.

How did they smile so much and giggle, she wondered as she watched them guide a Jaguar into a parking space outside the OK Bazaar.

Three of them then clustered hopefully about the driver's door. He was obviously deliberately stalling, pretending to search for something in his cubbyhole. But they were patient, smiling and showing how much they admired the car and would guard it for him till he came back. Finally he gave up, casting irritated glances at them. He got out and shooed them away.

'I have nothing. Go away you little good-for-nothings.'

The boys' faces fell. Usually the festival-goers were a good crowd. They muttered under their breaths.

'Hey!' he shouted at them, 'Don't be so cheeky.' But they kept muttering.

The Jaguar driver now noticed Marta sitting on the wall, watching him. He had the grace to be embarrassed.

He shrugged at her, grinning awkwardly. 'Lazy little bastards,' he said, 'missing school to make some easy money.'

But she did not return the expected smile, would not comply.

'Really?' she said. She got off the wall and walked away from him, thinking of her own silences.

How many lies we tell ourselves just to keep from facing up to the huge silent truth of our lives, she wondered.

She distracted herself from these hopeless thoughts, which were bringing on the familiar vertigo, by wandering about the make-shift village as it grew. There was so much to look at here and she tried to imagine the life that came with being a stall-holder. Such a life – it seemed so tenuous to her, so dependent on good will. She watched the bright wares come out: T-shirts, saris, sweets and puppets. She found the finger puppet lady again and bought some further additions for Maia's collection. Ruth had told her how she loved the stories. But there were other puppets, too, proper stringed marionettes, lovingly carved and painted with dazzling color. Puppets were the thing this year, she could see, and wondered how these things happened. She looked at them rather sadly. She could never afford them.

'Hey, Marta,' she turned, it was Avril. 'Having a wander?'

'Yes, a wondering one.'

'Mind if I join you?'

As they meandered they were slowly overtaken by growing smells around the village. Candy floss and boerewors. But they finally succumbed at a samoosa stand.

'Do you know these are part of an Indian wedding feast?' Avril asked Marta.

'No – how? Tell me the story.' They settled back on the wall about the gravestones at the back of the cathedral.

'Well, the bride and groom link arms and eat a samoosa together – they might feed each other even.'

'Hmm.'

'It means they will share the sweet and sour of life.'

'That's beautiful.' Pierre was standing behind them and as he spoke he placed a hand gently on Marta's shoulder. With a quick glance to check where Avril was looking, Marta bent her head to let her cheek brush the top of his hand and then turned round.

'Isn't it?'

'Yes.' He bent his knees and crouched before her, took a samoosa from the packet on her lap, took a bite and neatly popped the rest in her mouth. They smiled conspiratorially into each other's eyes before he straightened and said, 'Ladies, shall we take a little walk?'

Avril's eyes were full of questions but Marta begged with a small shake of the head, not now, as Pierre linked arms with both of them and offered them a running wit on the activities of the market.

Avril soon excused herself however with a look at Marta which clearly said 'I will be waiting' and left to find her way back to the library.

'Will she tell anyone, do you think?' Pierre asked.

'I don't think so. She is my friend.'

'I am sorry, I could not help myself, you looked so,

so–' He seemed to be searching for the right word, 'so radiant in the sun and so wonderfully innocent sitting on the wall with your friend, I could not resist. I have never been able to resist you.' He turned to her impulsively and then looked solemnly at her face. 'Who could resist this?' He teased a strand of her long hair into the sun.

Marta was anxious that someone else from the university should be around and distracted him.

'Look at these marionettes, aren't they beautiful?' They were indeed beautifully made, with carved wooden heads, expressive and angular, while their bodies glittered in brilliant, royal colors.

'Oh, she would be a Berenice.' Marta said, taking the limp limbs of one hanging on a rail just to the side of the shop.

'What beautiful sorrow.' Pierre agreed, putting his arm around Marta's shoulders.

He turned her to face him. 'Do you want her? Oh please say you want her.'

'Why?'

'So I can give you something, idiot. I want to give you something, a memento for tonight.'

And without waiting for a reply he waved his hand imperiously at the store keeper and said, 'this one please.'

The store keeper was delighted with her first sale of the festival and wrapped the puppet tenderly in tissue paper before cradling her gently in a paper carrier bag and handing it all to Pierre.

He carried it for her, swinging it jubilantly at his side as he walked her back up the high street. They parted ways carefully at the corner before he turned towards his flat and she went up the hill towards her residence.

'Tonight,' he said warmly.

'Tonight,' she answered shakily.

'You will be ravishing,' he assured her as he swung away from her.

Their first performance went well. The milling crowd, waiting for the big performance of *Antony and Cleopatra* in the theatre stopped, intrigued, and gathered around to listen. People talked afterwards; she heard them in the bars and on the streets and on the way down the hill. They had liked Racine's masterwork, it had moved them and made them think.

There had been a moment of absolute silence before the audience clapped and that all important pause was all she needed that night. The review next morning spoke of the contained ending, the ambiguity of Berenice's choice and the wonderful juxtaposition of this performance with Antony and Cleopatra's headlong hurl into oblivion just beyond the door. It spoke of the new meanings the plays gained in light of the current political situation of South Africa.

Of course, the crowd was much bigger the next night and some of them were clearly waiting without tickets, as Pierre had encouraged them to do on his posters. The show began and the crowds drew closer again. It was thrilling for the cast to sense the expectation in their audience. Their lines took on a significance they had only glimpsed in rehearsal – here, now, in this conflicted time the battle between love and duty, between public responsibility and loyalty to a crumbling empire – their love seemed wrapped in a luminous pain which called to the people assembled there. Marta struggled to keep the cool distance, the slice of ice in the heart, which Pierre said all true artists must possess to become masters of their craft but she could feel the tug of the lines within her.

'Unrelenting time moves for my rapid thoughts with leaden wings!' she cried as she paced, waiting for news of Titus.

In a blur she saw the people watching. They were a mixed crowd, so unlikely in this country. Their faces showed their own pain that night. She could see as they dropped their public masks while the show went on. And she spoke for them the words of Berenice, her plea for the heart above duty, for love beyond the confines of a law that forbade it out of sheer – she did not know what – sheer fear? And her realization fed into the words of Berenice as she spoke them and the audience was riveted. The tension was sharp and tender all at once. So it was every night that the audiences grew and never grew restless. Until the final performance, that is.

Then everything changed. There came a shifting among the people at the back, sudden pools of emptiness in the crowd. In those pools materialized policemen and soldiers. They stood, legs apart, watching them, eyes boring, drilling, while their bodies passed fear through the crowd. But there was no stopping now. Marta and Thari drove the play to its conclusion:

> *There was still time. You could have left me then*
> *Unnumbered grounds could have consoled me then.*
> *I could have blamed your father for my death,*
> *People and senate, the whole empire, Rome,*
> *The whole world, rather than so dear a hand;*
> *Their hate, long since against me unconcealed*
> *Had long prepared me for catastrophe.*

The soldiers stirred but the policemen signaled them to hold. Marta's mind split – she was Berenice, with all her heart now she was Berenice and she spoke directly to these soldiers, to these policemen. She spoke the lines now for Narina, whose love had been forbidden by men such as these, she spoke the lines for Farleigh and her father, who did his duty so thoroughly and as Avril moved across their stage, she spoke them for Avril too, whose bursary commitments and desire to teach, forbade her now to speak her mind.

288

She thought they would interrupt but she watched the chief even as she was Berenice. They did not interrupt because he was suddenly caught by her words, by Thari's words, by Titus's agonized choice. He was rapt as he should not be and in that moment, in the midst of all that tension and fear, she felt an unexpected peace. All her worlds merged into this one moment where words he had come to destroy spoke to the lost heart of a policeman who had come to arrest them. It mattered, it mattered because it was pure and simple and real and so it was political, not because of a hunger for power but because at its heart were people. Farleigh and Racine and the ungovernable country all came home to her, all the pieces fitted for that one moment and she came home to the world.

In the silence of the audience another tension now grew and the words held them all, even – or especially – because they knew disaster would follow. But no one moved while they spoke. Oh if only the moment could hold forever, if only . . . and Berenice's words took on a yearning that was almost unbearable. The audience did not clap as the final words were spoken and she left, no contempt today but only tenderness for the imperfect choices of this tilting world.

As she walked off stage, the policemen came to their senses and stepped forward. One put a hand on her arm and the silence of the crowd changed again.

'Madam, I must ask you to come with me,' he said. 'Respectfully,' he added, seeing the look in her eyes.

'Yes,' she said, 'I know.'

Pierre was hustled forward as well and they, all of them, stood surrounded. No one in the audience said anything. They turned away, embarrassed by their own inaction but unable to act, unable to shrug off the years of acquiescence. Marta did not blame them, and she felt again that hard knot of fear inside her as she thought of the phone call her family would receive. What would they do?

But she had no time to think. They were brought to the back of a caged truck, the usual prison vehicles. Now I know what they look like inside, Marta thought, stupidly. She remembered how they had stood outside the courthouse; she remembered the arrival of one during a march not long ago. She tried to sit next to Pierre but was pushed to a seat opposite him instead. He did not look up once but sat all the way with his head in his hands, elbows resting on his knees.

'What have I got you into?' he asked, his voice agonized.

Ashley spoke for all of them then. 'We chose to do this.'

'Brave young people,' he muttered but he would not meet any of their eyes, not even Marta's.

At the police station they were taken to separate rooms. Avril and Marta were separated from all the men.

'Pierre!' Marta cried.

'Dearest,' he said, 'oh my dearest,' and then he was gone.

Marta and Avril did not have long together either. They sat in silence, did not think to decide what to say but sat dumbfounded, still half high on the effect of their performance, still not entirely able to face this frightening new reality.

'What do you think will happen to us?'

'I will lose my bursary.'

'Oh Avril, I didn't even think of that.'

'It was worth it.'

'What will you do?'

'I'll work something out.'

'What will your parents say?'

'My mother will be angry, but she will understand. Your father?'

'I don't know. I don't know.' She felt the panic rise.

'Let's see what they want first. Perhaps it's just questioning.'

They waited a long time. The young officer even offered them tea, which they accepted after some hesitation. They were cold and the togas Professor Jenkins had found for them were not warm and made them feel exposed and vulnerable in the bleak emptiness of the police station. He brought them each a blanket too. They smiled gratefully at him. They heard arguments in the corridor outside their room but could not follow the voices.

Then an older man came in. He had not been with the others at the theatre. He eyed them with cold blue eyes.

'What's this, man?' he asked the younger man. 'What's this?'

Apologetically the young man took the blankets away. The old man snorted when the togas of the two girls were revealed again. Involuntarily the girls crossed their arms in front of their bodies. They were both shivering, Avril's hand trembling as it clutched her teacup.

'Take the maid away,' the older man barked at the young one.

He leapt forward to pull Avril to her feet. They stumbled into each other and the cup fell and broke. There was a frozen moment and then the old man's hand flew across Avril's face.

Marta cried out, 'It was an accident, you bastard!'

He turned his cold eyes on her. 'Oh, was it?' He hit Avril again. 'Take her out; let's see what they tell us.'

It was a long night; a night of questions to which she did not know the answers. Some of them she did not even understand. They asked about a weapons depot, and training camps. Bomb plans. Again and again she explained that she knew nothing but they did not believe her, or pretended not to. And nor would they let her sleep; even when she slumped in her chair they would wake her with a yell or with cold water.

Now and again they would come in and tell her that Avril had told all and that she might as well but she could just about remember enough to disregard that. She knew, if anything, that Avril knew less than she did about the activism the police were wanting from them. Finally, it all became downright farcical and so she laughed. This enraged the old man, who slapped her hard across the face, as he had Avril. When she whimpered Pierre's name once, they pounced on that and claimed to have his signed confession.

Then they changed tack and said he was out, that he had deserted them and was on his way home already. She did not believe any of it anymore and only giggled moronically at them. They gave up.

Finally as dawn crept wearily over the horizon, she was allowed her phone call. That woke her up. She thought carefully about what she would say to her father as she was led to the phone.

It was not her father who answered, but Ben.

'Father is at the hospital,' he said. 'Uncle Simon has died.'

'How? Why?' She was bewildered.

'He hanged himself.'

'Oh, dear God, no.' Marta whispered.

'Why have you phoned at this strange hour, Marta? Did you guess?'

'No . . . Ben listen, I don't know that Father can take this now.'

'What's up?'

She explained briefly about needing bail money.

'I'll have to explain that to Father. I don't know when he'll be back. Can you wait?'

But suddenly she was too afraid to face her father's

voice even, could not bear to hear that voice here in this place.

'No, leave Father out of it.'

'Well I don't have that kind of money. What the hell do you think you're asking?'

'Just be quiet a minute, please. And listen carefully.'

She had remembered a voice in the forest, 'If you ever need anything.' She had not thought ever to use what she had taken to be a typical adult attempt at making things seem better.

'Ben,' she said urgently, 'Ben, find this name in the phonebook. Wilhelm Charles Stander. Call Wilhelm, tell him. Tell him everything. He'll come for me.'

'Are you sure?'

She nodded, and then remembered he couldn't see her. 'Yes,' she finally said.

'OK, where exactly are you? Grahamstown police station?'

'Yes.'

'What shall I tell Father?'

'Whatever you like.'

Then there was only waiting. The guard, who had changed from the young man of last night to another, with a less generous disposition, enjoyed keeping them awake with random noise though clearly the interrogation was over. She and Avril were in the same room again, with the same horse blankets, but they were still not given peace. Both were bruised about the face and Avril had clearly been beaten, for she struggled to move and cried out when Marta tried to hug her.

'Do you have any idea of where the others are?'

'No. They told me that they had confessed things, but I didn't believe any of it.'

'They said Pierre had gone,' Avril looked anxiously at her friend, wondering how she would take that news. But Marta shook her head.

'He would not do that.'

The day passed without really getting any warmer at all. And so the two girls shivered and dozed fitfully.

By evening, the guard came in grinning evilly, for his last check before shift change. 'Another night in here for you girls. No knight in shining armor to the rescue, but one little bird escaped.'

They ignored him.

The young guard of the previous night returned for his shift. He smiled at them but they did not smile back. Marta felt bad about that then checked herself. Why on earth was she feeling sorry for him?

The telephone rang. The guard answered and then beckoned Marta closer to the rails. 'It's for you.'

She took the receiver awkwardly – it barely reached that far and she was afraid it might be her father. But it was Ben again.

'Wilhelm is on his way – with money and blankets. He wants to know if there is anything else you need.'

'Yes, there are eight of us. Make sure he brings enough.'

'Bloody hell, Marta. Who is this guy?'

'Never mind, just tell him to come quickly.'

'As quickly as he can,' Ben promised. She hoped he really had told Wilhelm about her friends, too.

After that they were finally given a small period of respite. The guard even turned off the glaring overhead light, leaving only his desk lamp. How grateful one can be for such things, Marta thought as she drifted into a restless doze.

He also brought aspirin for Avril (at Marta's angry request) and an extra blanket to support her where she was in pain.

'She needs a doctor, you know.'

'I am not allowed to authorize that, ma'am,' he said.

'Can you hang on until Wilhelm gets here?' she asked Avril.

Avril weakly asked who he was but Marta could see she did not care.

Marta sat by her friend until she fell asleep, then went over to her own bed but could not drift off, for all her exhaustion.

Just after midnight, Marta woke to a knocking. When the guard finally stirred to open the door, she heard him. Wilhelm had arrived.

'Sorry to bother you so late. I have come for Marta Reben.'

'Yes.' The guard stood aside to let him in. 'You will have to sign papers and leave the money,' he said leading Wilhelm to the desk.

'Wilhelm,' Marta hissed. He turned.

'Marta, child, what did they do to you? You need a doctor; we will refuse to leave until you've seen a doctor.'

Marta smiled at him. 'It's alright,' she said, 'those sorts of rules don't apply here. Just please get us out.'

'Us?'

'Yes, Avril and me. And then Pierre, Mohsin, Dennis, Thari and Ashley.'

'Marta, I have come to get you.'

She could hear the anxiety rise in his voice. And it made her angry.

'I am not leaving without them.'

Wilhelm looked at her. 'Where are they?'

'Avril is right here; look, they have really hurt her. And she will probably lose her bursary over this.'

'Bursary?'

'She has an education department bursary. They are really fussy about any political activity.'

'Is she political?'

'No, she was in a play with me. Please Wilhelm; please don't ask these things now.' For the first time in the whole long horror of it she could feel tears welling.

'All right, let me see what I can do.'

'No,' she said. 'No. All of us or no one.'

'All right.'

It took a long time and as far as Marta could tell, a lot of money, but finally Wilhelm signed numerous papers and the guard slowly walked out of the guard room to unlock all the others and bring them together.

Wilhelm meantime hugged Marta as the door was finally opened and between them they helped Avril into a sitting position.

When she cried out unwittingly, Wilhelm said softly to her, 'It's okay, Narina, it's okay.'

Marta stopped as if she had been shot. 'What?'

'Nothing, I misspoke, I did not catch her name, what is it again?' he said too hastily, but Avril was in terrible pain, so she left it but kept looking at him; his face was so different, his eyes wide with memories.

The boys came through. They had been beaten and bruised and Mohsin was bleeding from a head wound.

'You all need to be taken to the hospital,' Wilhelm decided.

'Wait,' said Marta, 'wait. Where's Pierre?'

'He's gone, Marta,' Ashley said. 'He left almost as soon as we arrived. He had money on him and got a taxi straight to PE Airport as far as I could hear. It was almost as if he expected to need the bail money.'

'No, it's not true, he wouldn't …'

She would not rest until the guard took her to see his room and show her where he had signed for the money himself two days ago now. Marta stared unseeing at the page.

'Pierre,' she whispered, 'Pierre.'

'Come,' Wilhelm said, 'come on.' He took all the others out to his car and came back for Marta and Avril.

'We'll put Avril in front. Will you sit behind and support her?'

'Yes.' Marta's voice was dull.

They drove slowly and carefully to St George's hospital where grumbling nurses were made to dress wounds and support Avril's broken ribs.

'She will have to stay a day or two,' the doctor on duty declared.

The boys in the meantime got their wounds dressed, thanked Wilhelm and got themselves a taxi back to residence.

'Are you all right?' Marta asked them.

'Yes, no worse than a fight. We just want to get home.'

They left her alone then with Wilhelm in the hospital waiting room.

FIFTEEN

They drank the sweet, hot tea the nurses had given them and Marta sat still as she could while they examined her bruises.

'Did they do anything else to you?' the nurse kept asking.

'No, no I am fine. May I go and see Avril, please?'

'Finish your tea.' The nurse went out again.

That left Wilhelm and Marta alone facing each other across the ugly little formica table laden with out-of-date *Fair Ladies* and *Huisgenoots*. They finished their tea and when morning came, Marta found the courage to ask. 'Will you take me to one more place, please, Wilhelm?'

'Anywhere. Whatever you want, sweetheart.'

She gave him Pierre's address. He drove, watching her face, thinking of the years gone by.

They stopped. Marta slipped out of the car, ran limping up the steps and knocked on Pierre's door. She called as well and tried to peer through the mail slot.

A neighbor came out and said 'He's gone.'

'He can't be.'

'He left night before last. Do you want to go inside and see? I have his key, he left it with me.'

They went in. The small flat was empty. She stared

around, ran into the bedroom and found no trace of him.

'He was in a rush to get to the theatre, he told me. Then later Friday night he arrived in a taxi, loaded his stuff and left. He left some money with me to settle his bills and his keys to return to the landlord. He seemed in bit of a state, actually. Very frightened.'

'Thank you.' Marta turned away just as Wilhelm came up the stairs, wondering what was keeping her so long.

Marta ran past him, down the stairs and flung herself in the car.

Wilhelm and the neighbor smiled awkwardly at each other, shrugged apologetically and turned away. Wilhelm came slowly down the stairs. He paused and looked down at the huddled figure in his car.

He seemed not to not know what to do with this visible pain; the rawness of it out here, away from his forest cottage. He stumbled as he walked down the steps.

'You alright?' Pierre's neighbor asked.

'Yes, yes, quite all right, thank you. Just a sudden memory, you know how they can get.'

The neighbor didn't know and after one more puzzled look, went back into his flat.

'Focus on the child,' Wilhelm muttered. 'She is distraught. Everything else will happen as it does.' So he walked calmly back down to the car and climbed in.

'Are you managing?' Wilhelm asked gently, finding tissues in the glove box.

She looked up, 'I cannot believe he would . . . why didn't he leave me a message?'

'It sounds to me that he was very scared, Marta. He didn't know what to do. He did not understand what he had got himself into. Suddenly it was serious; it was affecting people's lives, putting them in danger ...'

'How do you know? You didn't even know him. You didn't see what we did, you weren't even here. No one

299

was even here.' But she was afraid of what he had said.

'I . . .' he began and then whispered: '"*Titus reginam Berenicem, cui etiam nuptias pollicitus ferebatur, statim ab Urbe dimisit invitus invitam.*"'

'What?'

'Racine quotes Suetonius in his preface to . . .'

'I know what it's from.'

'It is a frightening sentence.'

'That's just what Pierre said . . . Is that something they teach you in Europe?'

'What do you mean?'

'To use literature to excuse your actions?'

'Marta, I am not sure I follow you …'

'Why did you call Avril 'Narina' earlier?'

'Because she reminded me of someone.'

'I know someone called Narina.'

'Yes. The same person.'

'How did you know her?' Marta dreaded the answer already.

'I loved her a long time ago, when she was just a student teacher and I a teacher. We were part of a group of teachers working with black students and teachers and providing space for their lessons in our schools in the evenings. Of course the government did not like it much but it seemed the right thing to do.' He smiled uncertainly.

'Well, Narina and I . . . we managed to see each other a lot. She was so alive, you know, so full of energy and joy. And her students loved her so. We both taught history, so inevitably we'd meet alone, too, to discuss lessons and share material. We were a team; we worked together. I have never felt so close to another human being. She was so different from anyone else I had ever known. She lived such a rich life, so much more so than we did in my family.'

Marta stared at him, blankly. He faltered on.

'But then the police raids began and they were violent and brutal and, well, frightening. My family was furious with me, for endangering them – and my wife . . .'

'Why are you telling me this?' Marta interrupted.

'Because . . . because I thought it might help to understand how scared he was, your young man, how torn.'

'We were *all* scared.' In her fury she could barely see the door handle, fumbled furiously with it, finally tore the door open and fled.

'Marta' he called after her, 'Marta!'

But she ran, stumbled, and did not turn back. She slipped instead into an alley when she heard the engine start and then wandered, dazed, onto the central street.

Grahamstown's High street looked long and dreary as she walked. It was empty except for the odd beggar, curled in against night winds in doorways. She wondered whether this was how survivors of hurricanes felt. This sense of the uselessness of the world; of building cities, creating communities and preparing theatre productions that stopped no disasters and came to destruction in the end. The loveliness of buildings had gone and she felt that all they did was trap space, grant it unwanted shapes and hold people within who strove to be elsewhere but could not, could not furnish their own existence any better, for the walls were stronger than their will.

Half out of habit and half because keeping still set her mind racing, she walked through the arch into university grounds and then on, to the botanical gardens through Eden Grove.

She heard singing from the university chapel and some instinct made her wander nearer, drawn to it in spite of herself. She did not enter but instead sat in the shade of the oak tree outside and watched the white building with the wide steps. She did not need to go inside as she knew how she would feel and did not want

301

that old familiar warmth, that sense of home which she felt now to be a lie.

But she could not turn and go either, the voices singing those long-familiar tunes held her and she yearned for the old magic of that sound, of the warp and weft of melodies and harmonies of the glowing skein they used to weave about her world, laying the light of grace on Sundays.

Today she did not feel part of it, could not enter either chapel or sound. And she wondered bleakly whether she had exiled herself from her past for the rest of her life. She could not now imagine the calm rhythms that led one to church on a Sunday morning. She could not recapture now the joyful expectation of a Sabbath on Farleigh. She suddenly remembered that those mornings no longer existed. Everything was lost and the earth itself seemed to be lurching so much she thought she would fall.

Marta closed her eyes and pressed her head hard against the tree behind her, so hard that everything went away. When the music came back, she realized that the sermon must be over and communion beginning. She got up and went closer to the doors, which stood open. She sat down on the steps and listened for the bell, which signaled the moment of transubstantiation, the moment when the promise of 'God be among you' came true.

But today, as she strained to hear that softest tinkle, she was outside of it, not at that table, far removed from any possible redemption. How could any tired ritual matter here and now, when people were beaten and the doors of truth shut against them and the best and bravest ran away to save their own skins? She did not know how to piece her world together again – did not know how to make it fit once more inside her head or heart.

She watched the procession of people towards the altar for communion and how sanctimonious it seemed, their faces bathed in that facile Sunday holiness which never outlasted the sunset.

'What hypocrites they were,' she thought savagely.

She felt herself go limp against the wall and some sensible part of her mind got her up again and headed towards the residence, where she fell into bed and did not know the world again till suppertime. She had a shower and put on clean clothes, examined her bruises in the mirror and decided that any attempts to cover them would only make matters worse. She left her hair loose as the only compromise.

When she entered the dining room, she stood still a moment – it was empty. What was going on? There were some voices in the kitchen and she went towards them. The kitchen staff was sitting around their large table, drinking what looked like a final cup of tea in a spotless kitchen. One of them noticed her.

'Sisi? What is going on, Sisi?'

'Everyone's gone home. The festival – it's over.'

'Is there no one left?'

'No, no one. What do I do?'

'I don't know, Sisi.'

'There is a gentleman waiting for you.'

Against all sense Marta's heart lifted with hope. She rushed to the front door.

Wilhelm was sitting patiently in his car but he opened the door when she appeared and moved towards her.

'Oh, it's you.' She raged at herself, at the humiliation and her repeated stupidity.

'I need to get you home.'

'I never want to see you again.'

'I know. Shall we go and pack your things?' Deliberate, calm. 'Your brother said your father was dealing with another family emergency.'

Mechanically she agreed. They packed in silence and only on the way out did Marta pause and say, 'I have to hand in my key.'

'Would you like me to do that?'

'Yes, please.' Speaking was difficult with her swollen lips.

'Wait in the car for me.'

It did not take long and then they were on the road home. Marta sat in stupefied silence – even the waves of nausea had passed now, leaving only cold emptiness.

Once she started up. 'Avril,' she cried.

'Her mother was with her. She should be able to take her home tomorrow.'

She subsided again.

'I got their address and telephone numbers, in case you didn't have them.'

And he passed her a small piece of paper from his breast pocket.

The silence between them grew.

'You know, Marta', he began at last, 'I cannot begin to tell you how sorry I am for what has happened to you.'

She snorted derisively. 'You stood up for him,' she accused.

'When?' He was stalling.

'Outside his flat.' Silence, then she added, 'And you, you did the same thing.'

'Do you not think a man can regret what he has done – even after so many years?'

'What good does that do?'

'None at all,' he agreed.

'How could you have deserted her so? How could you not have been there for Ishmael?

'I did not know. My father, like yours, afraid of what I had got into, instantly organized a position for me, an exchange program with a school in Leyden and we were whisked off before I could tell Narina anything.'

'We?'

'My wife and I. She was also pregnant.'

Marta groaned in disgust.

304

He looked at her. 'It is pretty sordid. She lost everything because of me, her student place and all possibilities of a job.' He remembered her retching and asked. 'You were more careful?'

'Yes.' She did not want this conversation and turned it again. 'What about later, when Ishmael came to you?'

'He took me by surprise. When I had first come back, I had tried to offer Narina help. By then of course she was so hurt by my absence that she refused.'

'How long were you in Leyden?'

'A year.'

'And in that time you did not contact her once?'

'No, I couldn't . . . I didn't know how . . . how to find an address in an African township. Our worlds were so separate,' he tried to explain.

'But you loved her.'

'Yes.'

'Not enough.'

After a moment. 'No. Not enough.'

They drove on in silence for a while.

'What happened that night with Ishmael?' They had spoken simultaneously.

Wilhelm went first. 'He came to my, to our house. He knocked on the door and told me who he was. I was shocked, too shocked to think really, otherwise I would never have asked him in, would have found somewhere else to meet. But I took him into my study and we spoke for a while.

'Then Nancy, my wife, came in and saw him. Somehow – women's intuition I suppose – she instantly knew who he was. And she screamed. She threw him out. Our daughter, Sara was in the kitchen. She came to the door to see what the commotion was. She had had no idea all this time and I wanted to protect her, I wanted to keep things together for her. So Nancy got her way.'

'What about Ishmael? He needed protection too.'

'Yes, he did. I failed.' Then a little defiantly, 'I think he told me that himself! My wife and daughter were very frightened by the fire and the mangled dog.'

But Marta was uncompromising and told him what happened the rest of that long night. And what followed; how Ishmael needed to hurt to live.

'What a horrible mess,' Wilhelm said finally. 'What will we make of it in the end?'

'Isn't it a bit late to ask that question?'

'No – it's early still to know what it might mean.'

'If you wait to know what something means before you act, will you not forever be inactive?'

'I see you're back on form.'

She ignored the gentle jibe. 'Where is your family now? How come you were able to do this for me?'

'They are on holiday in Italy, they're doing a tour. Sara, like you, has nearly finished her studies.'

Silence followed. They were both uncertain of themselves now, having revealed so much. Finally he asked, 'Your friend Avril, have you known her long?'

And she told him all about Avril, her optimism and her determination to help her family to a better future. 'She might not be able to do that now.'

'Why?'

'She'll probably lose her bursary over this. All these years she's worried about it, kept out of politics and now one French play has done it.'

'Are you sure it will be that bad?' he asked. 'Are the authorities really still that severe?'

'We're in a state of emergency! Not all the world is Bracken Hills.'

'Yes, I know, Tau's father was taken in the last week of term.'

They were home just before midnight.

Ben had waited up and let them in softly. The guest room had been prepared for Wilhelm. Marta worried about the morning, when Narina would come, as she drank the Milo Ben had made for her.

'What have I done now?' she worried.

Ben looked blankly at her. She explained briefly.

'Oh,' he said and then, 'Narina made up the bed for him. She knows he's coming and he knows that she works for us. They are adults, Marta.'

And suddenly Marta grinned, 'So am I and look at the mess I am in.'

'You're no adult.'

'Am too.'

'Yes, I can tell. Come on, let's get some sleep. Do you need anything? There's arnica in the bathroom cabinet and some aspirin.'

'I'll be all right; I'll find what I need. Goodnight.' But in the corridor, she suddenly stopped, 'Ben – thanks!'

He hugged her briefly, gently. 'Sure.'

Marta resolved to rise early. She wanted to speak to Narina before Wilhelm awoke. She wanted to know that all was well.

But it was nearly mid morning before she came into the kitchen. Ruth was there alone.

'Where's Narina?'

'Marta, how are you?'

'I'm fine,' she said. 'I just need some coffee. Where's everyone?'

'It's Monday morning – they're out.'

'And our guest?'

'Has gone home, now,' Ruth said evenly.

'I am sorry; I wanted to be up – to explain.'

'It doesn't matter now. He did a good thing. He helped you all.'

'And Narina? Did he even speak to her?'

'Kind of . . .'

'What do you mean?'

'She's gone, Marta. Narina's gone. She left just after he did.'

'Has anyone looked for her?'

'Don't you think she might want to be alone?'

Marta subsided but by evening there was still no Narina.

Ben had gone to her home in the forest but there too had been no sign of her at all.

All day Tuesday they searched, notified the police and searched the forest again. Father went to Karatara to hear if Boesman had seen her and then went on to Fingo village. It was Wednesday afternoon when the police finally arrived. They had serious faces and disappeared into Father's study.

Marta heard voices but could make out no words at all. Then the door was open and she was looking up into her father's face, which was drawn and grey.

'What is it?'

'Call everyone together.'

When they were all assembled, Father spoke briefly and quietly.

'The police have found Narina.'

But Marta could not conjure relief from those words.

'They want me to identify her body.'

There was a stunned silence.

'What happened?' Ben whispered.

'Just a bunch of Tsotsis.' A policeman had stepped out from behind their father. 'They robbed her. And then stabbed her – they always do and there are never any witnesses.'

They stood in silence. Marta felt growing on her the horror of what she had done. She bit her knuckles, trying to suppress her moan but Ruth turned to her all the same.

'Marta, what is it?'

'It's my fault. It's all my fault.'

'Marta,' her father began.

'It is. It is. If I had not brought Wilhelm into the house–'

'No, lady,' the policeman interrupted her, 'No, lady, these Tsotsis, they take anyone – anytime.'

The other man asked quietly, 'Did she have any family you could notify?'

'Ishmael,' Marta breathed, realizing how long it had been since that name had been said in this house.

Her father restrained her, 'No one knows whether he is alive still, Marta.'

'Bomani knows,' she reminded him.

'We cannot wait until a relative is found.'

'I will go with you to identify the body.'

'I'll come, too.'

'You'll do nothing of the sort. Ruth, keep an eye on her. I will be back as soon as I can.'

Father and the policemen left. The afternoon waned slowly. Marta, Ben and Ruth sat in shocked silence.

'We should let Simon and Jacob know.' Ben went to the telephone.

'We should let Ishmael know,' Marta thought and crept away. She found her way to Narina's house, found the key under the disa flowerpot at the side and let herself in.

She had never been beyond the kitchen but now she tiptoed quickly to the bedroom. There were only the three rooms, bed, kitchen and living. It was neat and bare, so it did not take long to look for something in that house.

In the bedroom she found a box under the bed. Marta sat back on her heels after she had drawn the box out. She hesitated now before opening it – half afraid of what she might find and still expecting Narina to walk in behind her and ask what she was doing.

The thought that there was no Narina now finally made her open the box. It was full of letters, neatly folded back into their envelopes. Each one was addressed to Narina – care of the Reben's address. How had she not known about them? She opened the top one, feeling like a thief.

Dear Mother,

I hope this letter finds you well.
I have been on tour with the Theatre Company. A Midsummer Night's Dream was a complicated set but I am getting better at building them. It is good when we are on tour. I am not so restless then. I have begun carving in my spare time. Animals. I am not much good yet but it keeps me busy. I am getting better. Soon I will send you one you can recognize. It will be a loerie, I think.

Your son,
Ishmael

They were nearly all like that. Neat and correctly written, shy and full of news. Marta took the box and hurried back home, before her absence should be noticed. She went to her room and tried to write a letter to Ishmael, to tell him that his mother was dead.

Her father found her slumped over her desk in the evening.

'What are you doing, Marta?' She tried too late to hide the letter.

'I see you found Ishmael's letters.'

'You knew about them? You knew where Ishmael was, after Tokai?'

'I knew about the letters. I brought them for Narina.'

'All the time?'

'Yes.'

'Why did you never tell me?'

'We thought it best. You seemed to have forgotten

him, you never asked.'

'Forgotten? I have never . . . never . . .' She could not breathe. Her chest tightened, her mouth she knew was a gaping hole but no sound would come out and no air got in. Her father lifted her arms and was telling her something – she did not know what. But she found herself sitting then with her head between her knees and the world had come back.

'Ishmael' she whispered, 'Ishmael.' And then as memory came back, 'Narina.'

She turned her back on her father and heard him shuffle things on her desk.

'Don't you touch them!' She flew at him, grabbing the papers away. He left her standing in the room clutching Ishmael's letters to his mother without another word.

And in those weeks, before and after Narina's and Uncle Simon's funerals, Marta watched her father struggle to find words for her. She did not help him. She knew that Ishmael's world and hers were too different, too far apart and the people who had crossed the divide between them were dead. And no one spoke of the reasons for their deaths, no one.

She did not know how to forgive the silence. In that silence too, her own humiliation and bewilderment about Pierre found no words.

And no one asked her about it.

They were packing, because time was running out and the forestry commission needed Farleigh as a station. The last bits of the contract had been finalized now.

It was sad to watch. Her father seemed defeated and the tension between him and Jacob, who was working for the forest conservation department, was palpable and constant and silent and unbearable. No pretence of normality would cover this.

Finally Marta asked to spend some of her holiday

with Avril and her family. Her puzzled father let her, though she saw the fear rise in his eyes again as she asked.

Avril was the eldest in a family as loud and cheerful as Marta's own used to be. Her mother kept an iron control over them all while apparently letting chaos rule. The house was bright yellow. In the overrun garden it glowed like a small star in the dusty bleakness of the Cape Pleins.

Avril did not let Marta rest much when they arrived.

'Come and meet my grandmother – she is a history book all by herself.'

They made their way along the dark corridor to the back of the house where there was a dim room in which sat a grand old lady, dressed in lilac and resting her feet on a plush red stool as she knitted a jumper for some grandchild.

'Come in, child,' she said. 'So this is Marta?'

'Yes, Granny.'

'You two get into a lot of trouble together?'

'Oh, Granny, don't start.'

'Ag, child,' her grandmother said, 'it is nothing compared to the troubles I have seen.'

'Troubles?' Marta dutifully asked. 'What troubles?'

The old woman launched into the first of many stories of when she had lived in District 6 and they had all walked all the way to the Pleins. 'All day, it took,' she relished it now, 'all day in the dust walking away from our home.' Then she had an idea: 'You must take Marta. Show her where the house was.'

'I will.'

And the next day the two girls set out and they walked in shocked silence about the ghostly emptiness. When they got back, two men were sitting at Avril's mother's table, firing questions at her, while the children all huddled in the cover of the guava tree in the back garden.

'Who is it?' Avril asked her oldest brother, Dean, who was about sixteen.

'You had better not go in,' he said.

'They're probably police.' Juanita her younger sister said, wide-eyed.

'What would the police want with us?' Avril asked. 'I am going in.'

'That might be exactly what they want,' her brother warned, 'this way, at least, Ma can say she doesn't know where you are – and what you've been up to at university.'

'Shhh,' the warning came from the top of the tree.

'They're coming out.'

The two men shook hands politely with Avril's mother and left in their white Toyota Corolla.

'Avril,' she called turning round, 'are you back?'

'Yes, Ma.'

'Come in, please I need to talk to you,' her face was ashen with worry.

Avril had lost her bursary. Marta found her later in tears on the bed.

'What will I do now?'

'I don't know. Have you tried speaking to anyone at the university? Explaining what happened, why you were detained. It was not political action … Well not direct, anyway.'

'Somehow I don't think they'll understand. Those two were from the education department.'

'But you're such a good student,' then, 'What will you do?'

'I will have to find a job.'

'No, you can't do that. Not with your results. That would be a waste – and you know it.'

'And what do you propose?'

'We must at least try the university. There must be other bursaries you could try for.'

In the morning they phoned the university to see what possibilities for funding there might be.

Avril dialed, her fingers shaking. She waited while the phone rang.

Someone answered.

'Hallo, I am Avril Ritter, an English, French and History student. My bursary has been revoked and I was wondering whether you could send me any information about available funding for the second half of year.'

She had to hold while they found files.

Marta watched. Avril sat up, 'Yes, hallo.' Then a long silence again.

'But . . . Who . . . Oh . . .'

She put the phone down, dazed.

'What is it?' Marta asked impatiently.

'My fees for the rest of the year have . . . they've been paid in full,' Avril said.

'What?'

'My fees–'

'Yes, I heard you, but what . . . Do you know who might have done such a thing?'

'No and they wish to remain unknown, the guy just told me.'

'Will you accept?'

'I don't think it is up to me. It is done.'

'Maybe it was someone who saw the play?'

'Or the festival committee – maybe they feel responsible?'

'Maybe.'

Marta had to leave the next day, the puzzle still unsolved. Ruth had more or less ordered her to return for their father's farewell from Farleigh. The preparations had begun before she was even back. Ruth, who was on holiday, had briefly moved back home to help. Simon was home too and Maia toddled happily amongst the business.

Simon and Ben were stringing up lights all around the courtyard and in the tree, in its middle. From the carpentry were brought trestle tables, which were arranged around the tree.

Little Maia helped Marta pick out paths with small candles in bowls of sand.

In the kitchen, Ruth and Mieta were baking and making salads and huge bowls of fruit punch, too. Marta kept away from the kitchen; she could not yet bear its busy emptiness.

As the day wore on, everybody retreated a bit, collected their thoughts in preparation for the evening. Ruth called the brothers and sisters together for a quick practice of the songs they were to sing and the music to play for the occasion.

Evening came and they all dressed up and gathered under the tree, which alight now, was resplendent in the twilight. This marvel called forth little cries of delight from Maia, who could barely contain herself but twirled with excitement in the spinning, dancing lights. The candles on the paths had to be put out eventually for fear that she would try and touch the dancing flames. This brought tears until Simon came up with the idea of floating lights on the fish pound, which she watched in amazement but could not touch. Soon after, Maia fell asleep on her Uncle Simon's arm. He carried her about proudly for a while and then put her down on his own bed. She slept through the speeches praising her grandfather's work at Farleigh for thirty years, and only half woke for the songs they sang.

There were many guests, and all had come to pay respects to Father and his work. Marta looked at his careworn face, which softened into a smile as he talked with Ianni Stavros. This gratitude means more to him than anything the mission failed to do for him, she realized. She did not know how to fit his work for the people of Farleigh with his silence about politics – and about Ishmael.

'Hey, Marta what's on your mind?' Simon asked, 'we have not had much chance to talk have we?'

'There is so much I do not understand.'

'Ah, the beginning of wisdom,' he joked.

'Simon – why? Why did Father give his life so much for the people of Farleigh? But he did not want me to be friends with Ishmael?'

Simon watched Ruth with Maia for a while and did not answer.

'Are we racists, too? Here on Farleigh? Is it possible?'

'No, Father's choice had nothing to do with race. I think he was just afraid of what would happen to you. He saw everyday what it did to Narina to have a child lost to crime and in the hands of the police. He did not want that for you.'

'How can you be sure it had nothing to do with Ishmael's race?'

'Father was no racist.' Simon spoke fiercely now.

'Is it possible to separate anything we feel about another human being from race in this country?'

'It has to be if we want to go on living here. Look at Father's work with the people. I just think he let his fear for his child – for you – overrule his conscience because in Uncle Simon he had seen what happened to people who crossed swords with the police.'

'Doesn't that make a lie of his mission work?'

'Perhaps.'

No answer came from Ishmael to the news about his mother. Marta read his letters and gradually pieced together what his life must have been after he was finished with Tokai. There was a photo in one of the letters. Marta examined it for hours, searching for the child she had known. Sometimes she thought she could see him. She wrote to him again, care of Bomani.

When she returned to university, Marta took the photo but was glad to immerse herself in her books. They seemed the only thing of permanence now. The only thing she could grasp with any clarity. She was glad too to have Avril still with her, working by her side. Glad to have to work to get an honors bursary, which she did. They both did.

She continued work in the language laboratory into her honors year, despite the initial twinges of memory of a melodious warm voice correcting her pronunciation at first and then reading poems to her through the speakers when she should have been working on the airport conversation.

She was also asked by Professor Waldman whether she would take on the tuition of two pupils at one of the local schools who needed teaching towards their matriculation exams in German. They did not have a German teacher, as there were only these two pupils. The parents would pay handsomely. Marta agreed, needing the money.

To her surprise she enjoyed teaching. The two pupils were very different. One was a cricket-and-rugby-playing blond boy, named Theo, who spoke German well enough but cared little for literature or accuracy in writing. He took German to please his mother and was idle but pleasant. The other was a black girl from Namibia, named Miriam, whose German father wanted her to learn his language. Marta was fascinated to watch this child – so much more between cultures than she was but who could not have cared less. She cared neither for being black nor German, only for being a girl and sixteen. 'It looks so much easier to see the world like this. Why didn't I?' she could not help wondering.

One day as she walked back down the still, April-green roads to the university from school, Avril came to meet her waving a journal.

'What is it?' They stopped on the little bridge at the bottom of Croft Street.

'It is a French Journal. Prof J. just gave it to me. It has Pierre's paper on us in it.'

'It has? On us? What does it say?'

'I haven't read it yet, I was waiting for you. It's French, academic French.'

'It will take quite a bit of reading.'

'Well, let's hope it is worth the effort.'

They headed across the field and stopped at their small digs on New Street. 'I'll make the tea,' Avril said, 'you find the French dictionary.'

Marta cleared the desk as well. Avril brought in the huge mugs of tea with some Ouma rusks and then they sat down together.

'You read,' Avril said, 'and try to piece the grammar together. I'll look up words.'

'Hey, we graduated in this language, remember.'

'Yes, no thanks to him.'

'Oh, don't start. It was ages ago.'

'Yes, as was the last bit of French I read.'

'OK, here it is. "*Berenice* in a new context".'

'Imaginative title,' Avril snorted.

'Let's just get through, shall we?'

Marta read slowly, translating as she went. '"I was fortunate to work with a multiracial group of talented young students recently in South Africa, where we put on a *theatre-of-the-imagination* version of Racine's *Berenice*. Without a set and props, without even a stage, we had only the voices and bodies of the students with which to work."'

Then there was quite a long bit of his particular interpretation of Racine's plays and biography, which they decided to skim.

'Ah, down here he comes back to us – the bit that actually matters,' the humor feeble, she knew.

> *'In increasingly difficult circumstances the students displayed a focus and commitment rare in simple class drama. I was particularly moved by the way the students used their own political circumstances and environment to influence their understanding of their characters and the play as a whole.*
>
> *'The choice between love and duty to a crumbling empire with a prejudiced and demanding populace became remarkably powerful in the South African context, despite the inexperience of the performers. So much so that the security police were alerted and attended the show. In the circumstances, they could not have been paid a greater compliment, though of course, it came at great cost.*
>
> *'The production came under threat, which attended bodily in the final week of rehearsals. It brought out the strength and courage of the performers, who refused to put a stop to their production. In fact they made the ending almost Brechtian; controlled and thoughtful, instead of the usual sentimental elegy one is subjected to in too many theatres.*
>
> *'Ironically, I have never been so moved by Berenice's final words as when they were spoken, that night, with the police closing in:*

In this grim hour, I wish
To make a crowning effort. I shall live

And shall obey your orders absolute.
Farewell. Reign. We shall never meet again.'

'And *that* is as much of an apology as you're going to get,' Avril's voice sounded cynical and harsh but she put her arm around Marta all the same.

While she was thinking about this, Marta knew Father and Ben were moving out of Farleigh for the last time. She had not seen the new house in George to which they had moved, though Ruth had said it would be beautiful with some work. She remembered her father's determination to keep doing whatever came next and went to the library. She had an essay to complete.

She looked sadly up from her reading of Blake and out of the library window at the drab, dusty winter lawns behind it. She thought about Blake's Jerusalem and how she had thought to find it here – in the City of Angels, with its many churches and tradition of learning and the arts. She thought back to her arrival here, her admiration of Callum's easy charm and then of Pierre's cool sophistication.

What was she left with now? She stared blindly out of the window amongst the long empty tables on the middle floor of the library. She wondered if she had thrown all her beliefs overboard to no purpose – to be left empty-handed. She felt stupid and lost all over again.

Two students came in and sat at the end of her table. 'I don't see what makes him so great,' one of them was saying, 'or any of the other so-called masters.'

'That's because *you* don't understand his world. You don't understand what he was painting.'

'No, it is because he does nothing new, exciting or interesting. He just copies the world. He just shows what is there. Well, fine – it looks real, but it's not interesting. Not like Picasso.'

'Oh, you arrogant philistine,' she was teased. 'Look!' And the girl in dungarees leapt to the shelves, took a volume of Rembrandt from the shelf and said. 'Look, look, and look. Look at what he does with the light, look at how he makes the people glow, or the landscape – here in this storm. Who else has shown so well the divine spark in the humblest peasant? In even the rocks on the mountains.'

Marta sat rigid, listening.

The conversation of the two students went on to other topics and they soon found the books they needed and left. They left the Rembrandt volume lying on the table.

Marta walked by and put it in her bag. She did not know why but her heart was thundering by the time she got back to her room, where she took it out gingerly, found the painting, carefully slipped in a bookmark without looking at it and then hid the book at the bottom of her cupboard. She was glad Avril was not home. Then she finished her essay on Blake.

That evening there was a phone call for her from home. It was Jacob.

'Guess what, Marta?'

'What?'

'Some woman's written a book about the Knysna elephants and now they're making a movie. They are going to film some of it here. We have been asked to help.'

'Yes?'

'Would you like to get involved, too? They need extras and help in the forest.'

'Why would you even think that I would say yes?' she asked.

'Well it is interesting work,' he faltered, 'and it is happening here, in our forest.'

'I'm done with the forest.'

And that holiday she stayed in Grahamstown despite

321

the festival. In fact she helped out at some of the musical gigs and helped a friend run a stall of candles.

But her dreams were full of mountains, forests and long hopeless searches for things she could not even name. She woke exhausted from these dreams.

She threw herself more and more into her teaching, preparing these two young strangers for their exams. They had to read Dürrenmatt's *Die Physiker* – and nothing in the rest of their education or even their lives had prepared them for that.

The insanity of the play with its many mirroring worlds was not biting social satire to them but merely insane. Marta did her best to fill in their historical gaps, to make clear to them the overwhelming reality the Cold War had been.

'At school,' she told them, 'we constantly had soldiers coming in to warn us about the rooi gevaar. It is how the government justified so much of its injustice – still does, now.'

But they could not see it. Their lives had been privileged in ways Marta could not imagine.

When parents' evening came, she was taken to task about the politics she was teaching the two.

'My daughter does not need politics, she needs grades so she can get a degree and live a civilized life,' one of the fathers stormed at her.

'But, Mr. Sonfeld', she tried to explain, '*Die Physiker* is about politics, it's about the Cold War.'

'What?'

'It's about what political illusions do to the truth and to minds which care about it.'

'Well, who put such nonsense on the syllabus?' He blustered now.

'It's not nonsense,' she said, 'they will learn compassion from it.'

'And they get graded on compassion in exams, do they?'

She had no answer to that.

The headmistress came to her afterwards. 'Stick to the exam work, will you?'

Marta was glad to slip away, feeling out of place in such comfortable privilege. But in class she felt compelled to counter the philistinism, still.

The two students, idle before their parents' visit, were now cheeky and brash.

Whenever she mentioned anything that could be remotely interpreted as political (and she wondered whether the fact that they could spot it now marked a triumph of her teaching after all) they queried, 'Will this come up in the exams?' insolently drawling with raised eyebrows.

She all but gave up but then the wall in Berlin came down and she could not keep quiet. But all the blond child of privilege – the princeling as she privately called him – could see, was the triumph of capitalism, as he called it – and business, which he determined to make his life.

It was a relief when their study leave finally started and she was off the hook with them. But the sense of failure trailed after her, especially as the question of what she would do loomed over the last of her own exams.

Even with bursaries she could not afford to keep on studying full time. Her family needed her to earn money along with the others. But she had no idea what she could do. She quite enjoyed teaching but that would require another full year to obtain her diploma. Avril seemed remarkably relaxed about finding a job.

'There will be plenty out there,' she assured Marta. 'I will find one when I am home. For now I want to concentrate on the Renaissance and the French Revolution, thank you very much.'

Marta grimaced. They had big essays due the next day and she had barely made a start, had dithered about which topic to choose and read critical texts only sparingly.

Their afternoon essay writing marathon was interrupted by the arrival of the post, in which was an invitation for both of them, to the prize giving of Bracken Hill School, from Wilhelm.

Marta was puzzled, 'Why has he invited us? I don't really want anything more to do with him. He knows that.'

Marta had told Avril the story in fury, though she had never been entirely satisfied with Avril's response. She was contrary again now.

'Well *I* want to go.'

'Why?'

'It sounds an interesting school,' she said looking up from the brochure.

'How would you know?'

'He spoke to me about it when I was in hospital – when you ran out on him. He came back to see that I was okay till my parents arrived.'

'Oh,' Marta was embarrassed, remembering that day. She looked curiously at her friend. 'You can go, I'm not stopping you.' And she meant it.

'Thank you!'

'When is it, anyway?'

'First week of the holidays.'

'Well, essays first then. Tea?'

They worked quietly and companionably. The days passed.

When they had written their last exam, they packed the small house which they had shared for that year and said a rather sad farewell. Neither of them yet had much idea of what the next year would bring, though they each had a few applications running. Avril was coming to stay with them for a bit – partly to go to the prize giving, partly because they did not know when and how they would see each other again.

They closed the door a last time, handed the key in, left crumbs for the dikkops in the back garden and drove away in Jacob's old Mazda, which he had lent them for this last term. They drove slowly out of town, past the Monument – their quick glances at each other as they passed were all they needed to know both were remembering.

'It was a good performance,' Avril said.

'Yes. It was.'

SIXTEEN

'How do I look?'

'Why do you even care?'

'Just help me.'

'You look great. You could be one of the business mums – an estate agent, perhaps.'

'Really?' Avril looked hurt.

But Marta could not take it back. She changed the subject instead.

'Who's taking you?'

'Jacob is.' Marta did feel a twinge of envy now but she did not want to go back on her publicly stated intention. Nor did she think she would know what to say to Wilhelm now. She had never seen him in his scholarly capacity and there was still Narina.

So she pretended indifference and did not even wave her brother and her friend off.

Ben looked at her. 'Don't you think this has gone on long enough?'

'I don't know.'

'Hey,' Ben changed tack, 'come and have a look at what I have been making.'

He took her out to the garage and showed her a rocking chair.

'Ben it's beautiful,' she cried. 'Is this your first one?' Marta had never seen one so intricately carved and beautifully balanced.

'It is my second. This one is on commission.'

'Oh that's great, Ben.' Then, as realization dawned, 'You're an artist.'

'No, an apprentice. Oom Jan over in Knysna has agreed to take me on. No wages yet but the pieces that I get commissioned to do are mine.'

'Are you happy with that? Is that what you want?'

'Yes, Marta. I never wanted to leave the forest.'

'It's funny isn't it – I never want to go back to the forest.'

'I never quite understood that.'

'You know, a couple of days ago, when we were driving over the Outeniquas coming towards the forest, for the first time in years, I felt I was coming home. I did not wish home were somewhere else.' She paused, searching for words, their meaning.

'But it's beautiful here.' Ben put in.

'Yes, it's just that then, when everything seemed to have gone so wrong, it all seemed to have started with the forest.'

'How do you mean?' Ben was following her only absentmindedly as he rubbed his chair carefully with a lightly oiled cloth. This made Marta venture further than she usually did in these conversations.

'It's superstitions, and full of hopes and dreams, which are all dead now.'

'You'd better not say that to Jacob.'

'I know. I do wish he would get out of the forest. It is such a no-hope place.'

'I don't think he wants to. He is fighting so hard for it – and now also for the elephants.'

'What – elephants, again?' Her back stiffened with attention now.

'He is trying to convince the government to reintroduce some elephants to breed with the remaining three. To get a herd going again.'

'And?'

'Well, so far, the government is not interested. They are still afraid of being blamed when the elephants destroy property.'

'Well – there you go. Sounds like a pipe dream to me, not even a new one at that. The government's too busy for elephants. There are all these people, you know, and a revolution and sanctions and the economy.'

But the irony was wasted on Ben. 'Jacob keeps fighting.' He was irritated with her now and closed the garage door harder than he needed to. He turned the conversation on her.

'What will you do now?'

'I'm waiting on replies to several applications.'

They left it at that.

Father came home from Paccaltsdorp and Blanco looking haggard and unhappy as he came into the kitchen. He put the kettle on and then sat at the table, with his head in his hands.

'What is it, Father? You're very late.'

'There are too many who are dying,' he answered. 'They come back from the mines, they are thin and exhausted, and they get flu when it's cold. It becomes pneumonia, and they die.'

Marta handed him a steaming mug.

'And no one is paying any attention. The young are dying and no one cares. I have three funerals this weekend. And AIDS is simply not on anyone's political agenda.'

Marta made him a sandwich too but did not know what to say. She sat quietly with him as he ate. Jacob and Avril came home and Ben opened the door for them.

'How was it?'

'Meet the new history teacher at Bracken Hills School,' Jacob said with a flourish and a bow as Avril walked in.

'What? He gave you a job?' Marta ignored the happy intimacy that seemed to have sprung between her brother and her friend for now.

'Well, yes. It is sort of a bursary obligation.' Avril looked anxiously at her friend.

'What do you mean?'

'It was Wilhelm who paid the rest of my fees when the education department pulled my bursary two years ago.'

'Did you know then?'

'No, I figured it out a bit later, made some enquiries and confirmed it.'

'Why didn't you tell me?'

'Why do you think?'

She gave up, defeated. 'Do you want something to eat?'

'Yes, please,' Jacob said and ushered Avril past her to the lounge to discuss the news with others less prickly about it.

Marta made a plate of sandwiches and a pot of tea and brought it through to the lounge. The mood was congratulatory; in fact Ben had found a bottle of champagne and even now was struggling with the cork.

'And how do you feel about working at a school like that?' Johannes Reben was asking Avril. 'It is, after all an expensive, private school. It even has boarding, doesn't it?'

'Yes, I know,' Avril was serious now, too, 'but he made it sound very inspiring – and they do offer some bursaries.'

'Yes, he did,' Jacob joined in. 'And the private schools have always led the way in liberalism – ever since the missionary schools.'

329

'Can you really compare this to a missionary school?' his father asked sternly.

'It is a descendant of a missionary school. The private schools, especially the church ones, were the first to go multi-racial in the '70s. Bracken Hills was part of that. They took in black children even when the government threatened to close them down. They are now in the forefront of developing a new curriculum for democracy.'

'He made that sound inspiring?' Ben could not resist a little teasing. Marta remembered how grumpy Wilhelm had always been, how he kept to himself and everyone at a distance.

Avril restrained him with a hand movement. 'Well, no, he talked about being a community of, of learning and the pursuit of truth.'

'And he quoted St Augustine,' Jacob put in for his father's benefit.

Marta wanted to snort but felt tears well up instead. She saw in her mind's eye again his painting on the kitchen wall.

She looked away out of the window to hide it.

Avril stood up and came over to her. 'Marta, there is a place for you, too,' she said.

'We're not even qualified,' Marta countered. 'I don't want to be a teacher.' She kept staring out into the dark.

'We could still be doing everything together. And you said you had liked teaching at St Andrew's in Grahamstown.'

'I don't know. I would have to forgive what he did.'

'I'm not sure that is up to you.' Her father had joined them at the window. 'Sometimes mercy, like vengeance, is God's alone.'

Marta turned burning eyes to her father.

Avril filled in hastily, 'He has asked you to come and see him tomorrow, to talk about it.'

'What, at his house?' she flared.

'At the cottage "up near Millwood." He said you'd know where that is.'

'Yes, I do.' Marta did not stay long after that. 'Congratulations,' she whispered to Avril, 'I am going to bed. I need to think.'

In her room, she did not go to bed but stood for a long time at her window, looking out across the garden and up into the mountain, which even here in George, far away from the forest, loomed over the scene. She did not know what she should do.

Jacob knocked on her door.

'Hey, sis.'

'Hey.'

'What will you do?'

'I don't know.'

'You have to go. You have to listen to him, at least.'

'But I don't want to go back in there. I don't want anything to do with him.'

'Even after what he did for Avril?'

Marta got up really early the next day, creeping softly out of her room so as not to wake Avril. She made herself a quick cup of tea and took it out to the garden to drink. The mountain was still covered in mist and even the suburban neat gardens were mysterious and beautiful. She stood beneath the mimosa tree, smelt its sweet scent and felt the mist gather in her hair. With a few deep breaths she sensed that the forest was there as the mountain was. Beneath the mist lifting here and there now lay the deep green mountainside and the wide blue December sky beyond it. It did not seem threatening today.

She finished her tea and drove the car out of the drive. Carefully she closed the gate again. And then made her way down the street. She had taken a map but once she was out on the N2 she knew she would not need it.

Over the sea the mist had not yet lifted but she could hear it and smell it and saw again the vivid beauty of the dark forest, the pale line of the beach and then the dark, restless sea. The forest she knew was whispering and chattering and the birds just waking, while the sea was a muted roar. And people are squashed in the space between the two, she thought. They're immense and indifferent and beautiful – we are tiny, vulnerable and foolish.

She turned off the N2 onto the old Kom Se Pad forest road. She had to drive more slowly on the gravel road but the pale yellow stones soon turned dark as she drove into the shadow of the mountains and trees. She prepared to keep her doubts and fears at bay with an ironic stream of self-talk. But it felt good to be there. She had expected to be haunted by the memories but instead they came quietly, almost shyly from the forest of her mind as her eyes lighted on the forest of her childhood.

Yes, there was Ishmael, curly dark head and green eyes flashing with mischief as he dared her to jump over the stream as he did. There was his excited shout when they found the old mines and explored inside them. His endless playing with the echo in the dark. There were the trees, ancient and silent and full of life. She stopped at Millwood stream and continued on foot. The wet earth smell and the sharp tang of the fynbos engulfed her and she walked into the past. There were birds in the treetops who, disturbed at her movement, fluttered off, heavily at first and then more gracefully. She almost raised her wrist as her mind was flying again with Lady Grey and teaching her to hunt in the forest. And then she came across her mother's death in the forest. She stopped, remembering how tired her mother had been, remembering also how she had lived, how her life now was complete, while her own was not, nor was her father's, nor Wilhelm's. Standing there leaning against an old Kalander, she saw that the world needed death, just as the mind needs language to give it shape, and order, to find purpose and end. They were one and the same.

'Mother, I had no idea,' she whispered, 'I could not see it before.'

And she thought again of Edgar's closing words in *King Lear*:

> *The weight of this sad time we must obey;*
> *Speak what we feel, not what we ought to say.*
> *The oldest hath borne most: we that are young*
> *shall never see so much, nor live so long*

She was startled from her reverie by the clucking and hissing of the loerie. Without thinking, she looked for a tree to climb and then stopped herself, made herself walk, but she could not stop herself looking swiftly about. 'How memories have a life of their own,' she thought.

She could almost believe she saw a pair of brown legs disappearing up a tree and hear a familiar voice hiss 'Quick, Marta, quick. The loerie warns.' Despite herself, she stood very still and scanned the forest about her carefully, unable to deny the hope deep within of seeing a grey shadow, of hearing the rumbling of a huge stomach.

She did not but she did, she did see the loerie. Marta caught her breath. She sat green and glowing in the morning light in the witels opposite Marta and bent her head to one side as she eyed Marta from her black-rimmed eyes. She clucked again and hissed, looking straight at Marta.

'What is it?' the old Marta asked, 'What is it, loerie?'

The bird launched herself from the branch and made off, skimming just above the treetops towards Millwood village. The witels shook a long time with her leaving.

The older, wiser Marta shook off the moment and walked past the museum, still half building site, and Susie the steam engine they had found and brought back to the museum. She stood back and shook her head at the place. What a strange and brief time that had been, another of the unfulfilled promises of the forest. She wondered anxiously how soon Farleigh would be like that – part of the history, a museum, commemorating something brief and hopeful in the immensity of the forest. She did not want to think of that.

Then she heard music. She could smell bacon frying and coffee. She walked towards it. The music became recognizable. Monteverdi's *Christmas Vespers* were ringing out through the forest.

Marta hesitated; shy now, unable to think of what to say. They had parted so poorly and she had left no room for explanation.

'How do I bridge that gap?' She lifted her hand but the door opened before she could knock.

'Marta.' He stood before her, beaming, a large dark blue and white striped kitchen apron covering his bulk. Underneath he wore a white shirt and a blue tie.

'You're dressed up,' was all she could think to say.

'Well, I am hoping it'll be an occasion to dress up for.' And then one arm took her into a hug that told her they need not speak of the past right now.

'Come in before the mushrooms spoil.'

They went again to the kitchen, which was brighter today, despite the mist outside, because the light was on.

'Would you set the table? Everything you need is on the side, there just inside the door.' He paused looking at the table. 'Perhaps give it a wipe first.'

Marta looked around the kitchen and saw the old

painting. Tucked into its corner was a picture of Ishmael.

'Could we move the table outside?' she asked abruptly.

'That's a good idea.' He looked briefly at the mushrooms and bacon frying and then they maneuvered the table outside beneath the big Milkwood tree outside. Marta brought two chairs, while Wilhelm opened the window so that they could hear the music.

Then she spread the blue tablecloth and set the two places, irritated at his formality but too nervous to say anything now.

Soon he brought out the food. They sat down together and the years went away.

Almost he asked 'What did you do at school today?'

Then the loerie hissed and clucked again, persistently.

'What is that?'

'I don't know.' She did not want to think about what the loerie might want, did not want to think again that she might have news for them.

But Wilhelm went on, 'She's been clucking all morning. Something has upset her.'

The other birds fell silent as if listening but then high overhead a hawk cried and all was normal again.

All the same, Marta stayed alert.

Finally Wilhelm pushed his plate towards the centre of the table, leaned back in his wicker chair and said, 'What about this job then?'

'Tell me about it,' she hedged.

'I have a job description here, if you want to have a look. I brought it along, just in case.'

'Sure.' Looking could do no harm.

'I'll get some more coffee while you look.'

She looked through the pages of the syllabus, of the previous teacher's notes. The loerie above was now just hissing softly; it was not a warning this time but simply announcing its presence. Marta did not look up, only sat still listening.

Then she stood up and went to find Wilhelm. He was in the kitchen looking at the Rembrandt. Marta stopped in the doorway. He did not turn but began speaking.

'That school is as close as I will get to it.'

'The school?'

'It is a kind of atonement.' He turned towards her now. The photo of Ishmael was in his hand.

'Where did you get that?'

'You father gave it to me.'

He looked old and frail for the first time but she suddenly sensed conspiracy in it all, felt the old folds of silence settling around the things that mattered.

'I can't,' she said and left.

She drove, not home but to the beach out near Wilderness and stood staring out at the sea for a long time. Had she been stupid? What would she do for a living? She could not go on living with her family in this way, and she wanted to get away. But how would that be possible?

Finally she turned for home. She needed petrol and stopped at the garage. *The Herald* was lying on the counter. She picked it up, hoping to find something, anything in the job section.

There was an advert – they were looking for a journalist – an English-medium journalist. She drove into George and found the Herald office. She glanced briefly in the mirror, tidied her hair and then walked through the door. There was a heavily made up woman behind a counter.

'Yes, can I help you?' she asked.

'I would like to pick up an application form for the position you advertised.'

'Can you wait a moment?'

'Yes.'

She waited a long moment. Then the woman came back. 'The editor will see you now.'

'But I just–'

'Right through this door.' And she was ushered into a large office where a central desk was brightly lit by horizontal blind stripes filtering and reflecting the afternoon sun through the window.

A silhouette was sitting at the desk but stood up as she came in.

'Hi,' the silhouette said, 'it's good of you to speak to me at such short notice. Have a seat.' And she turned and adjusted the blinds so that they were less blinding. 'Good afternoon. I am Melissa Vinkel. But everyone calls me Kiewiet.'

'Marta Reben.'

'What made you come for this job?'

'I like writing.'

'Qualifications?'

The editor looked at her thoughtfully as Marta told her.

'Here is a piece of paper and a pencil. What do you know about the riots in Uitenhage? Tell me about them in one hundred words – no more, no less.' Marta took the sheet of paper.

'I'll be back in half an hour or so. Do you have the time to do this now?'

Marta did not see how she could not.

In forty-five minutes Kiewiet was back. Marta silently handed her the page with exactly one hundred words on it. She waited while Kiewiet read.

'When can you start?'

'Tomorrow?'

'Well, shall we say Monday? Excellent! Here – my secretary will give you everything you need and show you what to do.'

337

Kiewiet's secretary was called Susan and was wonderfully kind and helpful, seeing immediately that after her flurry of courage Marta was now feeling anxious and overwhelmed. Finally she took her down a small corridor at the back of the offices.

'And here is Abel', she said. 'Our darkroom wizard.'

They stood at a green door with an enormous sign on it – Knock and wait.

Susan knocked and the door opened a fraction.

'Yes?'

'Abel, here is our new English reporter. Could you organize a camera for her?'

The door opened a tiny bit further and a slim black man with hair greying at his temples slipped out, closing the door carefully behind him.

'Yes,' he said to Susan, who, clearly dismissed, walked back to her office.

Abel took Marta to a set of cupboards at the back of Kiewiet's office and took out a bag. He showed her how the enormous Nikon camera worked, gave her several reels of film and told her to practice.

'Will I learn how to develop the pictures?'

'No,' Abel said morosely, 'no one in the darkroom but me.'

'OK, I'm sorry.' Marta thought she might apologize to him a lot in the future.

Finally he let her go with the camera in its bag and the film, which she was to have filled by Monday, so that he could see whether she was any good with it.

She stopped briefly at Susan's desk again.

'I wonder if you could help me with one more thing,' she asked shyly.

'Yes,' Susan smiled her warm smile,' what is it?'

'Do you know of any single flats going in town?'

'The front desk will know,' she said and took Marta back to the counter, where Petra searched through her tightly clipped pieces of paper and finally gave her some numbers and addresses.

'Thank you. See you Monday.'

'You can phone from here if you like – we can organize some viewings for you,' Petra offered.

Marta gave in, though she felt painfully shy about this.

But the women were clearly vicariously enjoying her new start and helped with jocular enthusiasm. Susan drove her to the flats and talked through them all with her. She settled for one very near the library in the end. She took the papers to sign and drove home to pack.

Only once in the car did she have time to think about how her father would feel about her job, her moving out – and she kept avoiding the thought of Avril, who had been so happy and hopeful last night.

Gradually her mood sobered and she began to wonder whether she was even capable of doing the job.

Jacob opened the gate for her, stopping his weeding in the vegetable patch. She got out of the car.

'Well,' he said, 'how did it go?'

In answer she shook her new key at him and swung the camera bag onto her shoulder.

'What did you do?'

'I've got a job.'

'But not teaching?'

She only grimaced at him. They walked round the house in silence and sat in the shade of the verandah. There she explained what had happened as best she could.

'And you got your own place?'

'Yes. I can't live like you, Jacob. I cannot slip back into this world as if nothing outside had happened.'

She saw from his face that she had hurt him. 'I'm sorry.'

'It's fine,' he brushed her apology aside. 'We each find our own way.'

'Yes. I'll go and pack now.'

Both Father and Avril accepted the news quietly. Everyone helped her pack and 'settle in' – the old familiar, uneasy peace reigned over everything. It made Marta squirm but she said nothing, unsure of this new old ground.

The weekend was spent then in unpacking her boxes, finding the right places for all her things in her sunny new flat and taking photographs. The knack came back quickly, she thought.

On Sunday a phone call from her father asked whether she was coming to church. She declined, feeling bad and rebellious all at once.

She went for a stroll through town with the camera – a weight that was becoming familiar. She took photos of the flower stand and the other informal vendors along the main street and fell into conversation with one. When she got home, she wrote it up as an interview, thinking she would show to Kiewiet.

Monday morning passed in breathless anxiety, waiting for Kiewiet to read her story and waiting for Abel to process her photos.

They were finally both pronounced passable – there were enough of her pictures that were not blurred and would be usable. She was allowed to keep the camera.

Then she was assigned her 'beat' as Dan ironically called it. Dan was responsible for the Afrikaans copy, Kiewiet explained and she for the English. So her beat consisted of the English businesses, schools, clubs and churches and Dan for the Afrikaans ones. They would take turns 'on the front page' he said. She was given a list of contacts and Dan suggested she phone each one and introduce herself. She couldn't at the schools as they were still closed for the holidays but she did her best. Then she had to follow up two stories her predecessor had left incomplete and take a new photo of a family in

Heather Park, which had blurred. All this took quite a lot of organizing and rushing but Marta liked the sense of urgency. Deadline for copy was Wednesday morning, when it would be taken to the printers. Wednesday afternoon she and Dan would proof it all at the printers' office. That might take quite a long time and she could come in late on Thursday in recompense. Flexi-time, Dan said, grinning.

When she came into the office on Thursday, Marta was amazed at the change in mood. It was virtually empty.

'Where is everyone?' she asked Petra who was in the kitchenette.

'Out on the roof.'

'Where?'

'Come, I'll show you.' And out beyond Abel's kingdom was a glass door, which led onto the roof where the girls and Dan were. Dan lifted his glass of wine as she approached and toasted her. It was a good one, he said, waving his other hand at the newspaper lying on the small round glass table in the centre. She went over and saw again her words, her photos in print. She glowed with pride, despite the fact that they were about a flower show and tombola. Dan handed her a glass and then asked her.

'If you stop at an accident – what would you do? Help or take a picture?'

She paused before she answered, considering.

Kiewiet came out. 'Has anyone ordered pizza?'

Susan said she had.

'What's the matter, Marta?'

'Dan has just asked her his test of the true journalist question,' Petra explained.

'Ah,' Kiewiet took a glass of wine and then turned expectantly to Marta, 'well?'

'I honestly don't know. Wouldn't it depend on the seriousness of the accident?'

Dan patted her on her arm in mock patronizing style, 'We'll make a journalist of you yet.'

Marta wondered about that but could not help enjoying the uncomplicated friendliness of the collegial party, which took such pleasure in its own success.

'Do we ever get to write really exciting stories?' she asked

'What do you mean by exciting?'

'The big stories – the demonstrations, the big funerals, the speeches.'

'Our readers don't want to be upset – they read *The Herald* to know the world is as it should be,' Kiewiet answered.

'Don't they need to know the truth?'

'They get enough truth, don't worry.'

Marta did not know what to make of that. But it would not be long before she felt the frustration of writing only the white world of George – the beach parties, Housewives' League meetings, long service awards at Mosgas, new openings in shopping malls and Church bazaars. For now, the salary spelled a kind of freedom and she liked the gentle buzz of small town living.

After Christmas she and Jacob had helped Avril move into the flat at Bracken Hills School but she had taken care to avoid Wilhelm. She could not do that indefinitely, as she was soon called to take photos of students who had won the local inter-school debate and spelling bee competitions.

At these times Wilhelm was painfully courteous and she responded with a brisk and brittle professionalism. She never saw Avril at these events – though they saw each other on weekends and often went out together. There was a pulling away from each other that both girls found hard to explain or hinder.

She would periodically write stories about Paccaltsdorp or Blanco residents – about the many deaths and Kiewiet always took them and smiled and said she would fit them in if there was space. Sometimes there was space – not big enough and not often enough but she took what she got.

'One small voice not entirely silenced,' Marta told herself.

Then one evening, they were all at Kiewiet's celebrating Susan's birthday. The TV was on the in the lounge, where Kiewiet's husband, who worked at Mosgas in Mosselbaai, was listening to the news. Suddenly he called them all in from the pool. Everyone crowded into the room and listened in stunned silence as F.W. de Klerk spoke at the opening of parliament. He was in midsentence:

'Universal franchise, equality before an independent judiciary, freedom of religion, a sound economy, and dynamic programs directed at better education, health services, housing and social conditions for all.

I wish to put it plainly that the Government has taken a firm decision to release Mr. Mandela unconditionally . . . the government wishes to talk to all leaders who seek peace. The unconditional lifting of the prohibition on the said organizations places everybody in a position to pursue politics freely. The time for talking has arrived.'

They listened in stunned silence till the news clip finished. Gradually they turned to one another.

'Did he just say –?' Dan asked.

'Yes.'

'Did he just end apartheid?' Kiewiet completed the question.

'Do you think it's for real?'

'I think so, let's listen.' But the TV gave little more information. Then the room erupted into a flurry of activity. Petra and her husband began gathering up their things at once.

Petra was tearful. 'We have to pack at once. We have to leave.'

'Why?'

'They will murder us in our beds,' she wailed. 'Will we bring my parents into town – off the farm?' she asked her young blushing husband.

'Yes, Petra. Come on let's go.'

They left one by one.

When Marta got back to her flat, she phoned Avril. Did you hear – can you believe it?

'Just listen,' Avril held the receiver so that Marta could hear the noise from the corridor.

'The kids are beside themselves', she said. 'Tau's parents are coming home. He spoke to them just a few minutes ago. He has not been allowed to speak to them in years.'

'Who is Tau?'

'One of our standard 10s.'

'Oh. I wish I was there with you.'

Finally it had been said.

'I know you do. Why don't you come and interview these boys tomorrow? Tau is not the only one whose parents have been in exile.'

'I will.'

It took several days for Marta to get herself free to interview the boys, though. But finally she was able to drive up into the forest.

The classes were assembled in the common room when she arrived. Normal classes had been suspended, the receptionist told her with shining eyes. Some classes were sitting in the audio-visual rooms of the school. Those who could had stayed home to watch there. They watched with the crowd outside the high white walls on the TV. Avril briefly told Marta the names of her charges and then they settled down with them to watch.

'You know,' said Thandi 'I'm not even sure what he looks like.'

'Look, look, that's Winnie going in, his wife,' Neo interrupted her.

Tau sat absolutely still. 'It's hard to believe, Ma'am, isn't it?'

Avril touched his tense shoulder briefly. His father had been banned and was returning from London next week. He had been living with his grandparents for three years now.

The crowd on TV seemed to think something was about to happen but nothing did. Time was growing long. Some of the younger classes grew restless and went out into the playground. But the older ones were too afraid of missing something, though their legs were restless too and they shifted in their seats and crossed and re-crossed their legs.

Then the man on TV said, 'There is movement at the door, let's get closer to the gate.' The cameraman struggled through the crowds.

'Yes, here they come.'

But the camera was struggling in the crowd still and the class began to murmur and hiss.

The commentator continued, 'Mr. de Klerk has come out of the door. He is waiting, the security guards are worried, they scan the crowd again and again. What can we still be waiting for? No here they are, coming through the door, hand in hand . . .'

The class and the crowd alike were going wild with frustration and Marta could not hear what else he said. The camera did not get past the gate and was panning across the empty path repeatedly. Then it hovered, shifted up. Footsteps could be heard and there they were. De Klerk looked small and bald next to the tall slim and straight black man, who walked so calmly and quietly into freedom, holding his wife's hand. The camera kept on them now. They were speaking and smiling but no one else could hear what they said.

At the gate, while de Klerk already got into the waiting car, Mandela and Winnie raised their clasped hands once into the air, high above their heads.

The crowd and the class erupted.

'Viva', they called, 'viva, viva!'

All the fists in the class shot up too and then they could no longer be contained; the Mandelas got into a car too and drove away and that was the only glimpse they were allowed for now. But they surged out, many of them crying and allowed their feelings free rein outside. Class after class came out; there was hugging and crying as well as just silent dazed sitting looking up at the sky.

Avril and Marta said nothing as they looked at each other over the excited children. But they hugged fiercely when Marta got up to leave.

Marta drove slowly along the forest road, her windows down. She thought she heard the call of a loerie as she drove past Millwood. She stopped her car, telling herself that she wanted time to think, before she would go back into the noise of the office. But she was aware as she walked that she was listening for that call. And then a movement caught her eye. Something pale and large swung softly amongst the dark branches of a candlewood. She stepped closer, warily and saw that it was a bird, carved from yellow wood. An owl; huge. But otherwise magnificently lifelike as it swung its wide wings and the body bobbed up and down with graceful swoops.

Tears stung Marta's eyes as she watched the bird fly and her mind filled with memories she had believed buried and lost.

Back at the office, she phoned the conservation office. Jacob was not in but she left a message for him to phone her back. It was late that evening before he did.

'Is there a sculptor working at the museum at the

moment?' she asked without any preliminaries.

'I don't think so – funding is pretty low. Why?'

'I saw a carving in the forest today – an owl. Huge, yellow wood.' It was hard to speak about it.

'You know, Bomani has said the same thing. Perhaps you should speak to him?'

In the morning she told Kiewiet that she had heard stories about a mystery sculptor hiding in the forest, carving life-sized animals.

'It might be a story,' she said casually, 'I'd like to check it out.'

'Of course,' Kiewiet said, 'it will make a nice change from all the politics.'

Marta escaped before Dan came in and wanted to come.

Bomani was at the bush school, which was in their old home, Farleigh.

It felt strange to be driving along that familiar road again but also good. It felt like coming home and she had expected to be an outsider now.

In the slanting morning light Farleigh lay radiant on the mountainside. It felt like Sunday, it was so quiet. Bomani had heard the car drive up, for he came out to the gate to greet her.

'Marta!'

'Bomani, you're still here?'

'Yes, I came back after all. Turfloop was not for me in the end.'

They smiled a little awkwardly at one another.

'It is lovely,' Marta said. 'So peaceful away from town – like Sunday mornings.'

'Yes,' Bomani said, 'the grace of God lies on Sundays.'

Marta laughed, 'Father used to say that.'

'You don't believe it?'

'Tell me about these sculptures that you've found.'

'They appear suddenly.'

'Where?'

'Millwood, out at Dolphin's Peak is one, also at Gouna there is one at the river, where the swing used to be.'

'Our swing? Ishmael's and mine.' It was still strange to say his name aloud.

'Yes. I am sure it is someone who knows the forest very well. They are always perfectly placed.'

'Placed?'

'To catch the wind and yet be protected. To look to the sea as well.'

Marta felt rising in her a painful hope.

'Bomani, can you show me where each of the sculptures is?'

'Yes – come into the office, we have a map on the wall.' He swung his hands to dry them and led the way across the hall to what had been her father's study.

Against the wall hung a big map. It had pins stuck in at various points and dates written next to the pins. On the desk were piles of papers and she glanced down at them. There were sketches of elephants and trees and pages of closely written notes. Bomani was standing at the map, pointing out the sites.

'What are all these, Bomani?' she asked, her eyes scanning the piles.

'Jacob's notes about the elephant sightings.'

Marta remembered Jacob's elephant dreams.

'There are three left, we try to keep track of them.'

'Yes.' She picked up one of the pages of notes and read. '"Went out today, knew that I would see her. Followed the loerie. The forest coming into summer nicely, the disa blooming and Gouna recovered well from the fire, Millwood Sunday – still. The loerie took me to Marta's tree – and there she was, her ears flapping

348

softly at me, like they did when she had good news."'

Marta stopped reading, went back. 'Marta's tree?'

'Bomani,' she asked, struggling to keep her voice level as she stepped round the desk towards the map with him. 'Where is Marta's tree?'

'Don't you know?' But then he saw her face.

'Here,' he said, 'it is here, the big Kalander in Millwood.'

'Thanks.' Marta leaned against the wall.

'You OK?' Bomani asked awkwardly.

'Yes, yes. I am fine.'

'Would you like a bit of time here?'

'Yes, thank you!'

'Just shout if you need anything. Or . . .' he paused.

'What is it Bomani?'

'We had a break-in a few days ago.'

'Really? What got taken?'

'That's just it – nothing. It's very strange.'

'Yes.' She was impatient for him to be gone.

She sat down and stared unseeing out of the window a while. Then she got up and went back to the map, looking closely at the place marked with a small neat capital M.

She found Farleigh on the map and then traced the path from Farleigh, across the Homtini to the M with her finger.

Marta's tree was just inside the margin of where the two sheets of the map were aligned together against the wall. As her finger traced towards it, she felt something under the map. Carefully she lifted the edge and saw beneath the map, pinned into the place where Marta's tree stood was a feather.

She recognized it at once.

Softly she prised the feather loose, remembering how it had passed between them in her mother's dark blue watch case so many times. She slipped it delicately into her pocket between two sheets of tissue paper she found

on her brother's desk. And, calling to Bomani that she
was going for a walk she hurried out of the house, across
the orchard and out of the back gate.

The path to the Homtini was only a little overgrown –
clearly still used occasionally. At the river, she saw that
the swing had been repaired and hung as it had always
hung, waiting for them to swing across.

She took it in her hand, tested it and wondered
whether she would still be able to swing over the river.
Then she took a deep breath, grabbed the rope as high up
as she could reach, took two steps back and swung over.
She bit her lip and held her breath in lieu of the whoop.

Marta almost made it to the other side. She only
got a little wet. How familiar it all felt and smelt as she
splashed to the other side.

From a witels there hung a carved bird. Marta caught
her breath at its beauty. Carefully she stretched her hand
out, touched a wing. The great creature began to move,
the wings sweeping up and down, the bird rising and
falling like waves.

She walked on, half afraid that she would lose her
way, half sure that she would step right. And as she
walked she felt in her pocket occasionally for the feather.
It was still there. It had been there all these years – and
she had not known.

By the time she got to the old Kalander she wished
she had brought some water. It was nearly midday and
very hot. But she only took the feather from her pocket
and looked at it. Suddenly she felt foolish – what had she
done?

Why had she taken it and come here? She did not
know. Something old inside her, something she had
not listened to in years had taken her here and now she
did not know what to do next. The tree was a beautiful
old tree; it stood a giant amongst the others still. But
it remained a tree. She did not know what she had
expected.

Exhausted, she sat down at the roots and waited, without knowing why.

She sat leaning against the tree, looking up into the green-blue light and shade of the forest and felt the tree against her back. Something caught her eye. There was another bird, more beautiful than the last, swinging in these branches. She did nothing, just watched as it swooped silently up and down, up and down. This one was a loerie.

She did not hear him come but something awakened her as he stood over her, seeing the feather in her hand.

'You kept it.'

'Yes.'

'All these years? And then you left it for me to find again.'

'It was stupid.'

'Perhaps. Stupid to take it, too?'

'No, I am glad you did.'

'Yes.'

'Now we are both here.'

'Again.' They looked at one another for a moment. 'You make these birds?'

He picked up a rock, fidgety. 'Yes.'

'Still making things fly?' It was only partly a question.

He grinned, turned and threw the rock he had been playing with up through the trees. It arced across their tops into the bright light and then it slipped back into the foliage and landed on the ground with a soft thud.

Book Group Questions

1.   A strong underlying force of the novel is the relationship between Ishmael and Marta. Discuss this friendship. What stands in its way, what supports it?

2.   Early in their friendship, Ishmael brings Marta a feather – what is the significance of this feather for the two children? What do you think is the significance of the title?

3.   This novel has a great deal to say about race relations in South Africa. How did the black and white communities interact in this story both within and beyond the borders of Farleigh?

4.   What view does the novel offer of education – its personal and social roles? Its abuses?

5.   Discuss the role of families in the novel.

6.   What is Wilhelm Stander's secret? What do you make of his role in the novel?

7.   How important is the setting to the novel? What is the role of the forest and of the elephants?

8.   How does the novel present loss? What is the effect of juxtaposing personal loss and the wider political suffering?

9.   The novel repeatedly quotes other texts – what is it suggesting about reading, about literature and art in growing up/in society?

10.   Is this a colonial or a post-colonial novel?

Born in Northern Cape of South Africa, Gisela Hoyle grew up on a mission farm there, which, she says, 'is as glorious a childhood as you can get in terms of landscape and freedom' but also made her aware even as a child of the problems of Apartheid South Africa. Since then her interest in the relationship between people and the place they inhabit has informed her writing. She now lives, teaches and writes in England and has found in a long and varied teaching career, that getting to know people invariably means getting to know their stories, and that's really what it's all about.